Walden
of Bermondsey

PETER MURPHY

First published in 2017 by No Exit Press,
an imprint of Oldcastle Books Ltd,
PO Box 394,
Harpenden, Herts,
AL5 1XJ
noexit.co.uk

ISBN

978-0-85730-122-2 (print)
978-0-85730-123-9 (epub)
978-0-85730-124-6 (kindle)
978-0-85730-125-3 (pdf)

2 4 6 8 10 9 7 5 3 1

Typeset in 11.5pt Minion
by Avocet Typeset, Somerton, Somerset, TA11 6RT
Printed in Denmark by Nørhaven

For further information please visit crimetime.co.uk/@noexitpress

CONTENTS

FOREWORD

By HH Judge Nicholas Hilliard QC
The Recorder of London

I remember speaking to Peter Murphy when I first learned that he was writing novels which would draw on his many years of experience in the criminal courts. I asked him to be merciful in his portrayal of the Resident Judge. I had an interest of my own because I was at the time the Resident Judge ('RJ') at Woolwich Crown Court and Peter was one of the judges there. I had no idea that he was in fact contemplating a whole book written from the RJ's perspective.

Peter is of course perfectly placed to write these stories because he moved on from Woolwich to become the RJ at Peterborough. The job title is rather misleading. As readers will discover, the fictional Judge Charlie Walden no more lives at Bermondsey Crown Court than any other RJ lives at their court centre. But the RJ is a permanent presence and runs the operation, and all this combines to provide some rich seams, over and above the particular drama of the courtroom, which Peter has artfully mined. We place a high value on judicial independence, and running anything which involves judges as participants provides plentiful opportunities for individuals to come into conflict with 'group think'.

Peter has recorded it all with an accurate eye and an authentic ear. In doing so, he has created a series of interesting characters and highly entertaining narratives. And Charlie Walden, hard-pressed but invariably well-meaning in the face of conflict and dilemma, deserves a place in the pantheon of fictional legal figures. Of course, I have no doubt that, as always, any resemblance to actual people and events is at least meant to be entirely coincidental.

So I am glad that Peter has been kind to the RJ. I very much hope that Charlie Walden agrees and may perhaps be persuaded to share some more of his experiences in the future. I am only sorry that the Old Bailey where I am now the Resident Judge sometimes manages to irk him just a little. I shall see what I can do in case there is a further instalment.

Nicholas Hilliard
Recorder of London
Central Criminal Court

WHERE THERE'S SMOKE

WHERE THERE'S SMOKE

Monday morning

At about eight o'clock on a brisk, clear October evening, Father Osbert Stringer, parish priest of the Anglican church of St Giles, Tottenham, and a confirmed bachelor, was in the kitchen in his vicarage enjoying his supper: a cheese omelette and home fries, washed down with a bottle of Old Peculier. The vicarage is next to the church, on its south side. According to his witness statement, Father Stringer happened to look out of his kitchen window and thought he noticed flashes of light coming from the direction of the church. Moments later he thought he saw smoke, and moments after that, he thought he heard a loud noise, as in heavy objects falling to the ground. Leaving the remains of his omelette, he rushed out of his back door, only to see, to his horror, flames inside the church. He immediately called 999. By the time the fire brigade brought the fire under control, the interior of the church was gutted, with the loss of all the furniture and effects inside. There were serious questions about the stability of the whole structure and it was clear that it would not be usable again for a very long time, if ever.

Fortunately, no one was using the church at the time. It was a Wednesday, and usually there would have been choir practice, but it had been cancelled. The church was generally considered an architectural monstrosity both inside and out, and was not greatly mourned. It was also fully insured. The charitably-inclined nearby Methodist church offered accommodation to

Father Stringer's congregation. So it could have been worse.

But in his witness statement, Father Stringer also said that as he ran out of the vicarage he distinctly saw a young male running from the church into the street, throwing away some kind of metal can as he did so. The police later recovered the can, which contained white spirit, a highly flammable substance often used as an accelerant. The spectre of arson raised its head. Arson investigators turned their attention to the church, and quickly found evidence of the use of an accelerant at three different sites within the church. These sites appeared to be the points from which the fire had spread.

The police were, naturally, anxious to know whether Father Stringer had recognised the young male he saw running away. He had. He told the police that the culprit was Tony Devonald, nineteen years of age, a local lad. Tony's family were members of Father Stringer's congregation, and he knew the young man well. Tony was arrested later the same evening, and when interviewed under caution, admitted that he had been in the vicinity of the church at about eight o'clock. He told the police he was there because he had received a call at home from a man whose voice he did not recognise, telling him that Father Stringer needed his help with something at the church. When he arrived at the church, he immediately saw the fire. He ran to the south door, the door nearest to the vicarage, which he found unlocked. He called out, but no one replied. He saw a metal can standing by the door. He picked the can up, and noticed that it smelled strongly of white spirit. Seeing no lights in the vicarage, he ran from the church with the intention of summoning help, and took the can with him to ensure that it was out of reach of the flames. He dropped it by the side of the road. He was unable to call for help because he did not have his mobile with him, but he heard the sirens of the approaching fire engines, and went home. He gave no explanation for failing to remain on the scene to talk to the police or the fire brigade about what he had seen. But he insisted that he had nothing to do with starting the fire.

A forensic examination of Tony's clothing revealed evidence of contact with the same accelerant as used to start the fire in the church, and his fingerprints were found on the can, though not on any item inside what was left of the church. No scorch marks or soot were found on any of his clothes, and there was no smell connected with the fire other than the white spirit. A few days later Father Stringer formally identified him at a properly conducted identification procedure at the police station. He was charged with arson, being reckless as to whether life would be endangered, a very serious offence carrying a maximum sentence of life imprisonment. The magistrates sent the case to the Crown Court for trial. Its natural home would have been the local Wood Green Crown Court, but someone at Wood Green thought that there might be too much local feeling around Tottenham for there to be a fair trial, on which rather pathetic pretext – way over the top, if you ask me – they passed it on to us; which is when it started to get interesting.

But before I go any further, I ought to introduce myself. Charles Walden is the name, Charlie to my family and closest associates. I admit to having passed sixty a couple of years ago. I have been a circuit judge for about twelve years, the last four of which I have spent at the Bermondsey Crown Court as the RJ – Resident Judge. According to the job description, an RJ is a judge who takes on the overall administrative responsibility for the work of all the judges at a court, in addition to his or her own work. In fact, the RJ's main role is to be the person to blame whenever something goes wrong. When I say 'something goes wrong', I mean that the Grey Smoothies think we could be doing whatever it is more efficiently than we do.

The 'Grey Smoothies' is the name we have adopted at Bermondsey to refer to the civil servants who oversee the working of the courts. The name derives from the standard grey office suits they wear, and from their infuriatingly self-assured belief in their own infallibility, which continues undiminished despite their tenuous grip on reality when it comes to what is actually going on in the courts. The Grey Smoothies think, speak and write in a language of their own, which bears a passing resemblance to English, but not to any form of English used by normal people. For example: they refer to anyone to whom they write as 'stakeholders' in whatever it is they are writing about. Instead of 'doing' something, they 'action' it. Instead of communicating information to others, they cause it to 'cascade down' on them. Instead of starting a project, they 'roll it out', or 'deliver it'. Any project not to be rolled out immediately – for example because 'the jury is still out on it' – is 'parked'. And then, of course, there are the two most important expressions in Grey Smoothie vocabulary: 'business case' and 'value for money'. Most Grey Smoothies find it difficult to compose a sentence without using one or both of those expressions.

Their charge that we could be doing things more efficiently than we do is, of course, perfectly true; and if they gave us the staff and equipment we need, we would do better. But questions of staff and equipment are prime business case territory, in which the Grey Smoothies reign supreme. They govern this territory using a form of magical thinking, according to which the courts should be able to function just as well, regardless of how little they give us in the way of money and resources, if only we would all just get on with it and work hard enough. So, the sad truth is that the necessary staff and equipment will not be forthcoming at any time before the ravens leave the Tower of London, or the apes leave the Rock of Gibraltar, whichever is the later.

When confronted with this reality, the Grey Smoothies get very defensive, and retaliate by demanding endless statistics: how many cases have been disposed of? Were any of them trials which collapsed at the last moment? What is the average time for every kind of case to be heard? How many hours a day did each court sit? What was the reason for any short days? How many jurors did we summon, and how many attended? How long did they wait to be assigned to a trial? And there is a statistical survey form for every sentence we pass. About the only thing they haven't asked yet is how much time we spend in the loo. We expect that request at any moment.

The court staff and I could easily spend almost every hour of our days buggering about with this nonsense, in which case, of course, there would only be one statistic, namely that the court has no time to do anything except compile the bloody statistics. So in cahoots with our list officer, Stella, I devised Bermondsey's defence against attacks of the Grey Smoothies soon after I took up residence. The defence is that we basically ignore them. This obviously annoys the Grey Smoothies, and eventually I get an irate email from a presiding High Court judge for the Circuit telling us to pull our fingers out; at which point Stella and I fabricate a few reasonable-looking numbers for them, which seems to keep them happy for a while. We are particularly proud of having the third worst record in the country for returning the sentencing survey forms; we have managed to get it down below twenty per cent. At least, this way, I have time to be a judge.

In mitigation I wish to point out that, in return for shouldering the administrative burden of the court, the RJ receives no extra remuneration, no extra recognition, and no administrative assistance whatsoever. It's a miracle that anyone ever agrees to do it. Some get bullied into it by the presiding judges. Others do so in the hope that it will give them an eventual leg up to the High Court or even the Old Bailey; and yet others out of a sense of duty. In my case, the reason is simpler. I wanted to sit at Bermondsey because it's an easy commute to and from work, and the only vacancy at the time was for an RJ; so being RJ was the price I had to pay.

You see, my good lady wife, the Reverend Mrs Walden, is priest-in-charge of the parish of St Aethelburgh and All Angels in the Diocese of Southwark. Being priest-in-charge is just like being an RJ, really, but with different robes. Her living carries with it the privilege of residing in a huge Victorian vicarage which has many fine architectural features; a large weed sanctuary, euphemistically referred to as a garden, at the rear; and no modern amenities whatsoever. It is hot in summer and freezing in winter, and generally looks as though it has not been decorated since the First Boer War. And with both our daughters having long since flown the nest to make their way in the world as single career women, it is a fair bit bigger than we need. But it is close to work for us both, and I enjoy my short stroll to court in the morning.

Along the way I stop at a coffee and sandwich bar run by two ladies called Elsie and Jeanie. The bar is secreted in an archway under the railway bridge, not far from London Bridge station, and it gets crowded if they have more than two customers at a time. But they do a wonderful latte, and a nice ham and cheese on a bap – a temptation if, as is often the case, I'm not relishing the thought of the dish of the day in the judicial mess. The only downside is that I have to listen to their various woes while the process of latte-making is going on. Elsie has a couple of grandchildren who get themselves into occasional scrapes with the law, about which I have to be non-committal because I may well see them at Bermondsey one of these days. Jeanie has a husband who seems to spend most of his time, and most of his benefits, at the pub and the betting shop. So, one way or another, they are rarely short of things to grumble about, and they usually take full advantage. Next door to Elsie and Jeanie is George, the newsagent and tobacconist, from whom I collect my daily copy of the *Times*. George has never quite forgiven me for giving up smoking two years ago, since when he has been unable to sell me cigarettes as well, but he is usually prepared with my newspaper, a cheerful greeting, and a penetrating insight into the shortcomings of the Labour Party.

Sitting in my chambers waiting for the trial of Tony Devonald to begin, I am reminded of why I decided to write down some of my experiences and reminiscences as RJ. As much as anything, it is to keep my mind occupied during the long periods of each day when I am sitting around waiting for something to happen. Why would a judge be sitting around waiting for something to happen? I hear you ask. The Grey Smoothies ask the same question. Let me count the ways.

The prison van breaks down, so they can't bring the defendant to court. The prison officers haven't bothered to read the daily court list, so they don't know that the defendant's attendance is required. The court's recording equipment, essential for making a record of the proceedings, isn't working. The video equipment, essential for playing CCTV footage to the jury, isn't working. Alternatively, the video equipment, essential for playing CCTV footage to the jury, is working but is not compatible with the DVD. The defendant is on bail and hasn't turned up. The interpreter hasn't turned up. Counsel is stuck on a train somewhere, or is double-booked. We don't have enough jurors, and can't begin a trial until a jury returns with a verdict in another court. I could go on. There are times when it is a bloody wonder we get anything done at all. How is that for a statistic? So rather than just sit here feeling my blood pressure rise, I have decided to tell a few tales about life at Bermondsey Crown Court, in the hope that we can all happily while away the hours together.

This morning, I am told that the prosecution have forgotten to warn Father Stringer that he would be required as a witness today, and he is not available until two o'clock. I grab a jury panel before anyone else can snatch them all away. We quickly select a jury at random from a panel of the good citizens of Bermondsey, and I explain to them that they are not allowed to conduct any inquiries of their own into the case, such as doing internet searches about the events or the people involved; or discussing the case with anyone outside their number; or doing anything else any rational person would naturally be inclined to do in this electronic age. There is no way to tell whether juries obey these directions, except in the rare case where a juror is stupid enough to talk about his or her research and gets done for contempt. But we have to try. The evidence in most criminal trials is dicey enough as it is, without contamination from internet sources that can't be checked. But reaching for the nearest laptop or tablet is as much an instinctive human reaction these days as raising a spear to a sabre-toothed tiger, and I suspect that once you tell a jury not to take to the internet, it is a hard temptation for them to resist.

I then release the jury until after lunch. Fortunately, the morning is not entirely wasted. Stella has found me a sentence to do. Stella is in her early forties and what we call, in the judicial mess, MFX – married but whatever you do, don't bring up the subject of family. She favours blouses and slacks in autumnal colours regardless of the season, and has short-cropped straw-coloured hair. And she is absolutely bloody brilliant. The job of list officer is an extraordinarily difficult one, calling for a high degree of organisation and planning. She has to list trials, sentences, and other hearings for four judges. This means looking months ahead in the diary, predicting which trials will fold and go short; negotiating with the CPS – the Crown Prosecution Service; fending off pushy solicitors and counsel's clerks; factoring in the absence of judges and staff who are away on leave; and generally keeping the court's workload moving forward. There are many days when a crystal ball would be just as useful as the administrative skills. Stella excels at the job, almost as if she had been born to it. But she does have an air of perpetual anxiety, as if she is always anticipating disaster around the next corner. For a list officer, this may simply be a realistic approach to life, because there is a lot that can go horribly wrong, but it tends to make me nervous whenever she appears in my chambers. Under Stella's influence, I have become accustomed to expecting the worst.

My colleague Marjorie Jenkins was supposed to do the sentence, but another matter she has in her list has turned out to be more complicated than thought, and she is anxious to start a trial. It doesn't take long. The defendant, a native of a foreign country in his late thirties, turned up at a bank with a false passport, which he tried to use for identification purposes to open an account. These days, banks and cash converters and the like can spot false passports a hundred yards down the street on a foggy day. They seem to have some kind of homing device for them. It is almost uncanny. Without the benefit of ultra-violet light and all the rest of it, they do just as good a job of weeding them out as the Border Agency. The bank called the police. Chummy made an immediate confession and pleaded guilty as soon as he had the chance. He entered the UK on a student visa three years ago, and is an overstayer. He is of previous good character, and has been working hard at various cash-in-hand jobs to make ends meet for himself, his partner (also an overstayer) and their four-year-old daughter. He was offered a much better job recently, but it was one for which he needed a bank account to receive his salary. An acquaintance offered him the false passport, with an endorsement for indefinite leave to remain in the UK, for twelve hundred pounds. Foolishly, he accepted it. Now, it's not to be. Regardless of what I do, Chummy will be deported. I give him the usual four months, allowing him a third off for his early plea. It's a standard result. We do several of these a month. I disdainfully deposit the sentencing survey form, unsullied by my pen, in the waste paper basket.

And so to lunch, an oasis of calm in a desert of chaos.

The judicial mess – what normal people would call the judges' dining room – is a rather small space, almost all of which is taken up by a huge circular table and correspondingly huge chairs. If you were planning this room from scratch, you would opt for a much smaller table. But it was free, surplus to requirements from the Ministry of Work and Pensions some years ago, so our court manager, Bob, took possession of it without worrying about details such as the size of the room. Free is a big thing with Bob, whose previous career had something to do with fund-raising for a theatre company, and much of our court management seems to depend on largesse and cheap solutions, including the recording and video equipment I referred to earlier. We have just about managed to squeeze in a small sideboard in the corner, on which there is just about room for the coffee machine.

The mess leads directly into the kitchen. As for the food, the less said the better. The official line is that the caterers do their best with a limited budget. Perhaps they do, but the thought of the jury, advocates, and court staff – not to mention the judges – putting their lives on the line each day in the court canteen or the mess is disquieting. The main area of risk is the dreaded dish of the day, which may be advertised as anything from lasagne to curry to fish and chips. Slightly safer are the omelettes, salads, and baked potatoes, which we judges tend to prefer on the assumption that there is less potential for things to go wrong. But there are many days when Elsie and Jeanie's ham and cheese seems the best option to me. Regardless of the food, lunch is important. It is usually the only chance we get to talk and pick each other's brains during the day.

As I am the last to arrive today, I take the seat just inside the door. There is just about room for the door to close behind the rear legs of my chair.

To my left is Judge Rory Dunblane, early fifties, tall with

sandy hair, a proud Scotsman, still plays a good game of squash and still enjoys his nights out with 'the boys' (whoever they may be). Divorced for almost a decade, he has a bewildering succession of girlfriends, none of whom seem to last very long. No one calls him Rory. He has been known to all as 'Legless' for as long as I have known him, and that is quite a while now. The nickname dates back to an incident during his younger days while he was at the Bar, something to do with the fountains in Trafalgar Square after a chambers dinner. No one, including Legless himself, seems to remember the details of the incident, but the name has stuck. Legless is what you would call a robust judge, who likes to get through his workload without any nonsense.

Opposite me is Judge Marjorie Jenkins, slim, medium height, dark hair and blue eyes. In her mid-forties, she has been on the bench for five years already. When she was appointed, Marjorie was an up-and-coming Silk doing commercial work, representing City banks and financial institutions, and everyone was surprised that she took what, in her world, would be seen as a menial job. Marjorie is what they used to call a super-mum, a perpetual motion machine who balances a high-powered career with her family and various voluntary works. Her husband Nigel speaks six languages fluently and does something very important for an international bank. They spend holidays in Provence, where they have a house, or in Lausanne or Rome or Cape Town, as the muse leads them. Their two children, Simon and Samantha, are away at boarding school. It seems to be generally assumed that becoming a circuit judge is a kind of career break for Marjorie, and that she will resume her upwardly mobile path once the children are older. She does tend to disappear without much warning if anything goes wrong at school. But she is a great asset, particularly for fraud cases, in which she effortlessly assimilates tons of material which would take the rest of us weeks even to read, let alone digest.

To my right sits Judge Hubert Drake. Hubert is a bit of a problem, mainly because no one is sure exactly how old he is. Apparently, the official records have him down as sixty-six, but I would bet good money that the train left that station some time ago. As far as I can tell, he is still all right in court. The Bar complain about him as being too right-wing and reactionary – which he accepts, and regards as an accolade – but I am not yet hearing that he is losing the plot. Nonetheless, I have a nasty suspicion that it is only a matter of time. As to judicial style, Hubert would have made a first rate colonial magistrate in India in the days of the Raj. He has been widowed for some years. He has a nice flat in Chelsea, and divides his time more or less equally between the flat and the Garrick Club. My main worry is that he is determined never to retire, and he says they can't make him. When he reaches retiring age they can in fact make him, and I have nightmares about the scenes we will have when that happens.

'Thanks for taking my sentence, Charlie,' Marjorie says. 'Any problems?'

'No,' I reply. 'Bog standard false passport to open a bank account. I gave him the usual four months on a plea, and he will be departing our shores before too long. Keep the Home Secretary happy.'

'Should have been two years,' Hubert mutters, looking up briefly from his lamb jalfrezi, the guise in which today's dish of the day presents itself.

'That's a bit over the top, isn't it, Hubert?' Legless asks.

'Certainly not,' Hubert replies. 'Too much of that kind of thing going on, by far. It's about time we did something about it.'

We allow the subject to drop. We have tried to take Hubert on about his attitude to sentencing in the past, and it's usually not very successful.

'Can I get some advice on something?' Marjorie asks. 'I've

got an actual bodily harm. Chummy says it was self-defence. It all happened at a rugby match. Apparently, Chummy and the complainant were on opposing teams, one of them a loose head and one a tight head, whatever the hell that means. Counsel did try to explain it to me, but it didn't make much impression. Anyway, the two of them got into a fight towards the end of the match, and the complainant ended up with a broken nose, a broken tooth, and some cuts and bruises. The question is whether –'

'Chummy was charged with ABH just for that?' Legless interrupts, aghast. Legless played a bit at outside centre for Rosslyn Park during the amateur era, and still takes himself off faithfully to Murrayfield for internationals during the Six Nations.

'The referee was an off-duty police officer,' Marjorie explains. 'It happened right in front of him and he didn't think he could ignore it.'

'You see, this is the kind of nonsense that's killing the game,' Legless protests. 'You can't have a bloody rugby match without the odd fight. It's part of the game. You shake hands in the bar afterwards and buy each other a pint, and that's the end of it.'

'Not when there is a serious injury, surely?'

'It doesn't sound very serious. In any case, you said he was only charged with ABH.'

'Be that as it may,' Marjorie insists, 'he was charged and I have to try it. The question is, whether the prosecution are allowed to tell the jury that Chummy had already received two yellow cards during the same season.'

'You mean, as evidence of bad character?' I ask, 'evidence of propensity to be violent?'

'Exactly.'

We all ponder this jurisprudential conundrum for some time.

'Well, yes, I should have thought so,' I offer.

'No, not necessarily,' Legless counters. 'It all depends on why he got the yellow cards.'

'Presumably for beating up someone else,' Marjorie says, 'a hooker, or whatever you call them.'

'You can't assume that,' Legless replies. 'You can get yellow cards for all kinds of reasons.'

'Such as what?'

'Well, almost anything, if it prevents the other side from scoring a try. If you fail to release the ball near your own line, or tackle a man without the ball, and the other side would have scored, you will get a yellow card.'

'So, I should ask for evidence about what the cards were for?'

'Absolutely. They may not be relevant at all.'

Marjorie nods. 'Right, thank you.'

But Legless is still shaking his head.

'I wouldn't let it go to trial,' he insists.

Marjorie laughs. 'How can I stop it?'

'It's a question of consent,' he replies. 'When you agree to play in a rugby match, you consent to a certain amount of violence. You can't then complain about it afterwards.'

'But only in accordance with the rules of the game, surely?' I ask.

'The rules of the game make the odd fight inevitable,' Legless replies. 'It's what rugby is all about. That's why people go to watch it. If it's nothing worse than a broken nose, it's a case for a pint, and perhaps a suspension for a game or two. But that's it.'

'But according to the House of Lords in *Brown*,' Marjorie says, 'you can't consent to injury at the level of ABH or more serious.'

That's the kind of thing Marjorie would know, without even looking in *Archbold*.

'Well, tell the prosecution to reduce the charge to common assault, and give him a conditional discharge,' Legless pleads.

'Thanks for the help,' she replies. 'Must rush.'

'Why didn't Stella give that case to me?' Legless asks plaintively after Marjorie has departed. 'I know all about the kind of things that happen in rugby matches. I would have sorted it in no time.'

I know the answer to that question, but I'm not about to tell him. There are few people more dangerous in this world than a judge who thinks he has some personal insight into the subject-matter of the case. They tend to ignore the evidence and substitute what they think they know. Far better to have a judge who is totally ignorant of subject-matter, and has no choice but to rely on the evidence. Stella and I decided long ago that Marjorie was getting this one.

'I can't imagine,' I reply.

* * *

Monday afternoon

When I said that the case of Tony Devonald had become interesting, what I meant was this. With any case of arson, you are going to need a psychiatric report at some point. Arson is a very strange offence, almost always committed by very strange people. I have always found it helps to have a report sooner rather than later. Legless ordered one when the case first came to us from Wood Green, and it is in my file. It was prepared, as usual at Bermondsey, by our local shrink, Dr Mohammed Rashid. Like all psych reports, it goes on at great length about the defendant's history from conception onwards, his relationship with his parents, his history at school, his employment record, any personal relationships, any involvement with drink or drugs, and so on and so forth. Even for someone of Tony Devonald's tender years, it runs to some thirty-five pages. Following my usual practice, I turn first to the conclusions at the end of the report, intending to skim the rest later to the extent necessary, if I have time. The conclusions are contained in paragraph 52, which states, intriguingly:

> *Despite the incidents referred to in paragraph 34, I have found no evidence that Tony is suffering from any psychiatric illness or personality disorder. He is fit to stand trial, and if convicted, to be sentenced as the court may think appropriate.*

Naturally, I turn back with some interest to paragraph 34, in which Dr Rashid has recorded the following.

> *Both Tony and his father described an occasion on which the father consulted their parish priest, Father Stringer, because of a concern that Tony might have been the subject of some form of demonic possession. Apparently, the family was concerned that some objects, such as knives and forks, appeared to move along the dining table of their own accord while Tony was seated at the table. This concern appeared to rest mainly on the observation of Tony's six-year-old sister Martha. Also, there was an occasion when a small fire began mysteriously in the garage one morning shortly after Tony had stormed out of breakfast following an argument with his mother, though the mother spotted the fire and it was extinguished without difficulty, no damage being caused. Tony told me that Martha must have been mistaken, and that he has no supernatural power to move objects without touching them. He also denied setting a fire in the garage. He said that, on Father Stringer's insistence, he permitted the priest to pray with him in St Giles's church, a process he considers to have had no effect at all. He told me that he has no particular feelings about Father Stringer or the church one way or the other, and he vehemently denies setting fire to the church.*

I sit and ponder this for some time while waiting to go into court. I thumb through the file. I don't expect the prosecution to mention it. The prosecution hasn't made an application to allow evidence that Tony had set other fires, and the evidence linking Tony to the garage fire seems a bit vague, to say the least. Quite apart from that, demonic possession is something we try to avoid at Bermondsey whenever possible. My court clerk, Carol, comes to tell me that court is assembled. Carol is in her fifties. She is amazingly good at her job, has a frightening grasp of detail, and she seems to love every moment she spends in court. Her other passion in life is football. She and her husband Ray never miss a home game at Millwall and I usually hear all about it on Mondays. They lost at home to Blackburn Rovers on Saturday, so her mood today is a bit low.

As I enter court I see Tony Devonald directly in front of me in the dock. He is a thin, frail-looking lad. He is wearing a suit which doesn't fit him terribly well, and a crumpled shirt and tie. I wonder why his parents haven't done a better job of getting him turned out properly for court. He looks very nervous.

I look down towards counsel. Roderick Lofthouse is prosecuting. He might be just what the case needs if we are going to get into demonic possession. I don't mean that the way it sounds. Roderick is generally regarded as the doyen of the Bermondsey Crown Court Bar, which is a polite way of saying that he may have been around for just a little too long. He takes advantage of his seniority to wear a two-piece grey suit which is rather too light in colour for court and about half a size too small, the jacket remaining closed rather precariously, relying on a single overworked button. He is not always as well prepared as he should be these days, relying on his instinct for a case, rather than on reading the papers, as his main method of preparation. But he is always calm and has sound judgment. He won't get flummoxed or carried away, whatever happens. Defending is Cathy Writtle, small and energetic, with disorganised hair and large brown tortoise-shell spectacle frames, who will have read every shred of paper and will know the case inside out. That also is good. Cathy's only failing is that her default setting is all-out attack, which works better in some cases than others. I'm not sure it is quite the right approach in this case.

Roderick rises ponderously, looking every inch the doyen he is, to begin his opening speech. He is as smooth as ever. He begins by showing the jury the indictment and telling them that the prosecution has the burden of proving the defendant's guilt so that they are sure, failing which they must find young Tony Devonald not guilty. That's the way we do things in England, always have, no matter what goes on in other parts of the world. Fine, heart-warming stuff. Next he explains what arson is, intentionally starting a fire, keep it simple. So far, so good. But then, he accounts for the element of recklessness about endangering life by claiming that, for all the defendant knew, the members of the choir might have been in church that evening, as they usually would on a Wednesday. Now, as the fire was set inside the church, and it would take a rather careless arsonist not to notice an entire choir belting out 'O God, Our Help in Ages Past' to the accompaniment of a pipe organ, this strikes me as not the most persuasive of arguments. Cathy Writtle apparently agrees. She ostentatiously raises her eyebrows, not quite directly at the jury, but in such a way that they could hardly miss the gesture. We haven't heard the last of that.

The consequences of the fire, Roderick continues, were very serious even as things were, but at least it was only property damage; no one was killed or injured. He describes the extent of the fire, and the forensic findings about how and where it started and spread. He describes Father Stringer running from his cheese omelette, home fries and Old Peculier to summon help. He relates Father Stringer's identification of Tony Devonald as the young man running away from the church and discarding a can later found to have contained an accelerant. He concludes by giving the jury details of the defendant's arrest and interview and announces that he will call Father Osbert Stringer.

It's an odd case in a way, I reflect. The issue is not really one of identification. Tony Devonald admits to having been in the vicinity of the church, and claims to have been running to get help. No one saw any other potential culprit. Roderick hasn't mentioned any inquiry into the phone call Tony claims to have received summoning him to the church, even though the police seized his mobile when he was arrested.

'Father Stringer, how long have you been in holy orders?'

'For more than thirty years.'

Stringer is a small, wiry man. It's hard to guess his age, except that for some reason he looks closer to sixty than forty. He has thinning white hair, a white moustache, and a neatly trimmed white beard. Everything else about him, the full-length cassock, belt – and the eyes – are solid black. There is a definite touch of the Rasputin about him. Instead of looking at Roderick Lofthouse, he fixes the jury with a stare which has one or two of them shifting uncomfortably in their seats.

'And for how long have you been vicar of St Giles?'

'For about four years.'

'Let me take you to the evening in question, the evening when your church was burned. Do you remember that evening?'

Oh, come on, Roderick, I think, no prizes for the answer to that one. But it is interesting: I look at Stringer, and I can't detect any emotion in the reply at all.

'I remember it very well.'

'Where were you at about eight o'clock on that evening?'

'I was in the kitchen at the vicarage, having dinner, an omelette and chips.'

'Was anyone else in the vicarage at that time?'

'No. I live alone.'

'And, to your knowledge, was anyone in the church?'

'No. The choir should have been there practising, but the practice had been cancelled.'

'For what reason, do you remember?'

Hesitation.

'No. Offhand, I can't remember.'

'Did anything come to your attention at about eight o'clock?'

'Yes. I happened to look out of the kitchen window, and I saw what at first seemed to be a bright light coming from inside the church, close to the altar. Almost immediately, I saw smoke drifting towards the vicarage, and then flames inside the church. I knew then that the church was on fire.'

'What did you do?'

'I ran outside at once, taking my phone with me, and called the fire brigade.'

'As you were running outside, were you aware of anyone else?'

'Yes. I saw a figure running away from the church towards Vicarage Road.'

'Can you describe this figure?'

'Male, young, late teens to early twenties, wearing a dark jacket and jeans, dark short hair, about five-seven, five-eight.'

'Father Stringer, I think that a few days later you made a formal identification of the person you saw, by identifying his image as number six in an array of nine you were shown at the police station, is that right?'

'That is correct.'

'Was this person also known to you before that occasion?'

'He was very well known to me. It was the defendant, Tony Devonald. He and his parents are my parishioners.'

'How sure are you of your identification?'

'One hundred per cent.'

'Thank you, Father. Did you notice whether the figure you saw had anything with him?'

'Yes, he was carrying what I later saw was a metal can.'

'Later saw?'

'He threw the can away on the ground as he was running

away. Once I had called the fire brigade, I went to look at it.'

'Can you describe it for us?'

'It was a large metal can, silver in colour.'

'Did you notice anything else about it?'

'It smelled strongly of white spirit.'

Roderick turns around to the officer in the case, who hands him an object contained in a large, heavy-duty plastic evidence sack, bearing various labels.

'With the usher's assistance...'

The usher today is Dawn, a thirty-something brunette who always wears bright colours under her black usher's robe. She is the court's resident expert on home remedies, and is our trained emergency first aid person. Dawn takes every verdict of not guilty as a personal affront. 'Oh, Judge, after all that work,' she sometimes says sadly once we are alone in chambers, reflecting on the loss of some defendant I have just discharged, for no better reason than that the jury were not sure of his guilt. Dawn walks brightly over to Roderick, relieves him of the package and, needing no further bidding, makes her way to the witness box to show it to the vicar.

'That appears to be the can I saw,' he confirms.

'May that be exhibit one?' Roderick asks. I assent. Dawn passes the exhibit around the jury, so that they can see the tool of the dastardly act at close quarters and be suitably horrified. They don't look too impressed.

'How long did it take the fire brigade to arrive on the scene?'

'They were there very quickly. No more than ten minutes at most.'

'Did they succeed in extinguishing the fire?'

'Eventually. But by the time it was brought under control there was virtually nothing left inside the church.'

'So the church lost...?'

'All the furniture, the paintings, statues, the silverware on the altar, my vestments, prayer books, hymnals. There was nothing left, really. I didn't discover the extent of the loss until two days after the fire. They wouldn't let me back inside until they were sure the structure was safe.'

Once more there is no display of emotion at all. Just the facts.

'Finally, Father, have you been able to use the church since then?'

'No. The church has received funds from our insurers, but the work will occupy a considerable time. We are enjoying the hospitality of our Methodist friends for the foreseeable future.'

Roderick invites Father Stringer to stay where he is, in case there are further questions. There will be further questions; you can bet your pension on that. Cathy Writtle is already on her feet.

'You were having dinner, when you noticed the fire, were you, Father?'

'I was.'

'A cheese omelette and chips?'

'I don't see what that has to do with it.'

'Neither do I. But you gave the jury the menu when my learned friend asked you what you were doing.'

'Did I? Well, perhaps I did.'

'What you didn't mention was the bottle of Old Peculier you had with it. Does that have nothing to do with it as well?'

'I can't see how that would be relevant.'

Neither can I, at present. Cathy's defence statement says nothing about Rasputin burning the church down accidentally while trying to light a candle under the influence of Old Peculier; and in any case, that scenario wouldn't entirely account for the presence of white spirit. It may be that Cathy is just engaging in a bit of gratuitous violence against the witness to soften him up. Roderick doesn't seem concerned enough to object, so I'm not going to stop her unless it gets out of hand.

'Well, let's think about that for a moment. Was it just the one bottle you had?'

'Yes, I think so. Well, it might have been two.'

'Might it have been more than two?'

'No. I don't think so.'

'You don't think so?'

'No. I am sure it was just the two.'

'Any advance on two? Going once …'

'Miss Writtle…' I say.

'Sorry, your Honour,' she replies, insincerely.

'It was just two,' Father Stringer says.

'All right,' Cathy says. 'Let's move on to something else. Was it your practice to keep the church locked at night?'

'It was locked most of the time,' Stringer replies wistfully. 'We would have liked to keep it open all the time for prayer and meditation. But in Tottenham, you know… that would just be inviting vandalism. So we kept it locked unless there was a service or a church activity going on.'

'On this evening, there should have been a choir practice going on, yes?'

'That is correct.'

'But for some reason you cannot now remember, it had been cancelled?'

'Yes.'

'How many entrances are there to the church?'

'There are two. The main entrance is by the west door. But there is a smaller door on the south side. Actually, there is also a third door leading, not from the church, but from the vestry directly out into the graveyard on the north side. But it is hardly ever used.'

'Were these doors locked or unlocked at the time of the fire?'

'They should have been locked. Perhaps it might be more accurate to say that there would have been no reason for them to be unlocked.'

'When was the last time you were in the church before the fire?'

'At about four-thirty that same afternoon. I had left some papers I needed in the vestry, and I went in to get them.'

'How did you enter the church?'

'Through the south door, as always.'

'Did you have to unlock the door in order to enter at that time?'

'Yes, I am sure I did. If it had been unlocked I would have noticed.'

'Did you lock the door when you left?'

'Yes, I am sure I would have locked it.'

'How many people have keys, apart from yourself?'

Stringer thinks for some time.

'A number of people have keys. My church wardens, our organist and choir master, the ladies who do the flowers, the cleaners. People need access to the church for various purposes throughout the day.'

'Did Tony Devonald, or any member of his family, have a key?'

'No.'

Cathy pauses to allow this to sink in, seeming to consult her notes.

'Now, you say you saw Tony Devonald when you came out of the vicarage, having seen the fire?'

'That is correct.'

'Tony does not dispute that you saw him.'

'He could not dispute it. I saw him running away.'

'You saw him running, Father. But you don't know whether or not he was running *away*, do you? He could have been running for some other reason, could he not?'

Stringer scoffs.

'Not when I saw him throwing that metal can away.'

Cathy nods and pulls herself up to her full height.

'What was Tony wearing?'

'A dark jacket and jeans.'

'Gloves?'

'No, I don't think so… well, I'm not sure. I didn't really see his hands.'

'Well, you did see his hands, Father, didn't you, if what you say is correct – that he threw down a metal can?'

'I don't know.'

'Father Stringer, what you saw was quite consistent with Tony removing the can to a safe distance and then running to get help, isn't that right?'

'That is not what happened.'

'That will be for the jury to say, Father. My question is, whether what you saw was consistent with what I suggested to you?'

'Not in my opinion.'

'Very well. Did you phone Tony Devonald that evening to ask him to come to the church for any reason?'

'Why would I do that?'

'I don't know. I'm asking.'

'No. Certainly not.'

'Did you ask anyone to make such a call on your behalf?'

Stringer suddenly becomes agitated.

'Don't play games with me, young lady…'

We are all a bit taken aback. Cathy looks at me. I prepare to lecture the witness about how to behave in court and tell him to answer the question, when he adds, quite gratuitously –

'In any case, he's done it before, hasn't he? What more do you need?'

There is a long silence. Roderick sighs audibly and looks away. The message he is sending me is: this is down to the witness, nothing to do with me. That is undoubtedly true.

'Your Honour,' Cathy says, 'may I mention a matter of law in the absence of the jury?'

I send the jury and the witness out of court. As far as I am concerned, this has put an end to the trial. The business of the fire in the garage is not admissible evidence, and it is horribly prejudicial. It should not have been mentioned. Tony Devonald is entitled to a fair trial before another jury, and once Cathy makes the request, I am bound to discharge this jury and adjourn the case to another day. The only consolation is that, once Roderick confirms to me that he instructed Father Stringer not to refer to the previous incident, which I am quite sure he did, I can threaten Stringer with proceedings for contempt for deliberately sabotaging the trial. But to my surprise –

'Your Honour,' Cathy says, 'I am not sure how I wish to proceed. I would like to take instructions from my client. I see the hour. Might I ask your Honour to allow me until tomorrow morning to decide whether or not to apply to discharge the jury?'

I agree immediately. It is the least I can do.

On my way out of the building I pass Marjorie's chambers, and poke my head around the door.

'Did you get the yellow cards sorted?' I ask.

'Partly,' she replies. 'One of them was for head-butting a blind-side flanker. So that was easy enough. But the other one was for something called side entry.'

We grimace at the same time.

'That doesn't sound very nice,' I comment. 'Do you know what it means? Is it anything to do with loose and tight heads?'

'I'm not sure I want to know.'

'It sounds like something that deserves an immediate red card, if you ask me. But I am sure Legless would say it's just part of the game. Haven't you asked him about it?'

'He seems to have gone home. I'll ask him tomorrow.'

'Try not to think about it too much this evening,' I advise. 'It might put you off your dinner.'

* * *

Tuesday morning

Fortified by a large latte, lovingly prepared by Jeanie to the accompaniment of a lament about her husband having invested the rent money in the outcome of the three o'clock at Chepstow, I make my way to chambers. Stella appears moments afterwards, to give me a date for the re-trial of Tony Devonald, and to discuss what she has available to keep me off the streets for the rest of the week. There is a two-day ABH, your typical fight outside a night-club at chucking-out time, which would otherwise go to Hubert. I can scarcely contain my excitement. But when I go into court –

'Your Honour,' Cathy says, 'having considered the matter overnight, and having taken instructions from my client, I do not ask for the jury to be discharged. We would like the trial to continue.'

I nod. 'Do you want me to tell the jury to disregard the witness's last answer?'

'No, your Honour. But I would ask that you instruct the witness to confine himself to answering my questions.'

That will be my pleasure. The jury comes into court. Father Stringer makes his way slowly back to the witness box. He looks rather sheepish. I get the impression that Roderick has already advised him about the error of his ways. To make sure, in the presence of the jury, I remind him that he is still under oath, and, as Cathy has requested, I give him a thorough bollocking and a lecture about behaving himself, on pain of having to show cause why he should not be held in contempt. This appears to have the desired effect.

'Father Stringer,' Cathy begins, 'yesterday afternoon, you told the jury that my client, Tony Devonald, had, quote, done it before, unquote. The jury may be surprised to hear that, given that Tony is a young man of previous good character. Would you care to explain to them what you meant by it?'

The witness is on the defensive now. He senses that no good is going to come of this.

'Well,' he begins slowly, 'there was a time a couple of years ago…'

'Let me help you,' Cathy volunteers. 'Tony's father came to you and told you a story about knives and forks moving on their own in the Devonald household?'

'Yes.'

'And he suggested to you that Tony might have had something to do with that, yes?'

'Yes.'

'And he told you that a fire had started in the garage?'

'Yes.'

'And he suggested that Tony might have had something to do with that, too?'

'Yes.'

'Just a couple of pieces of paper set on fire?'

'I don't remember all the details.'

'No damage was done, and no accelerant was used, is that right?'

'I…'

'I am sure my learned friend Mr Lofthouse will correct me if I am wrong.'

'I have no reason to doubt what my learned friend says,' Roderick confirms disinterestedly. It is quite obvious that Father Stringer can expect no more sympathy from that side of the court.

'I will take your word for it,' Stringer replies sullenly.

'Thank you. Were you also made aware that the stories about automotive cutlery at the Devonald house came from a six-year old girl?'

'Yes, I believe so.'

'A six-year old girl who was also in the house when this rather small fire started? Tony's sister, Martha?'

'That may be so.'

'It was so, wasn't it?'

'Yes.'

'Thank you. Did you interview Martha?'

'No.'

'No. Instead, you prayed with Tony, didn't you? In the church?'

'I did.'

'Did he seem to you to be possessed by any demons?'

Father Stringer looks down. He really doesn't want to get into this.

'Well, did you notice any demons leave him when you were praying?'

'No,' he concedes eventually.

'No. What did Tony tell you about the fire in the garage?'

'He said he didn't know how it started.'

Cathy studies her notes and pretends to sit down, but then pushes herself up again abruptly, giving the impression of having carelessly forgotten her final question. It is an old trick for drawing attention to a question, and she carries it off well.

'Oh, just one last thing, Father. You told the jury that you could not remember why choir practice had been cancelled. Do you remember telling the choir master, Mr Summers, on that very same afternoon at about one o'clock that it would be inconvenient for choir practice to be held on that evening?'

If Cathy intended to throw Father Stringer off balance, my impression is that she has succeeded.

'Inconvenient?'

'Yes. Is that what you told Mr Summers?'

Hesitation.

'I can't think of any reason why it would have been inconvenient.'

'My question was: is that what you told him?'

'No. Not as far as I remember.'

'And no reason comes to mind why choir practice should have been cancelled on that evening?'

'None that I can think of. You could ask John Summers.'

Cathy smiles.

'Oh, we will. Thank you, Father.'

She sits down definitively. She really has finished now. It was a gutsy call to carry on with this jury and try to turn the demonic possession-based fire-raising into something of a joke; to try to turn it back on the prosecution. What's more, I think she may have pulled it off. I give her a quick nod of appreciation, and she gives me a sly grin in return. Roderick asks a couple of completely pointless questions in re-examination, for the sole purpose of not allowing Cathy to have the last word. But he fails to dispel the aura her cross-examination has induced, of something not being quite right.

Roderick is now ready to proceed with his forensic evidence. Most of this is undisputed, so following the usual practice, most of the investigators' reports and the fire fighters' witness statements will be read to the jury instead of calling the witnesses to give evidence live from the witness box. But copies of the reports must be made for the jury, and as usual, no one has thought of doing that in advance of the trial, and the CPS's photocopier is broken. In fairness, this is its normal state. There is no money to replace it, though there is apparently endless money to waste on the courts not sitting for hours on end while we wait for copies. Bloody Grey Smoothies again. There is nothing for it but to adjourn.

And so to lunch, an oasis of calm in a desert of chaos.

I enter the mess to find a bit of an atmosphere. Marjorie and Legless are both picking distractedly at sandwiches, and looking rather flushed.

'I hope I'm not interrupting anything,' I say.

'They are talking about having a bit on the side,' Hubert

replies. His dish of the day is billed as tagliatelle ai funghi. It looks revolting.

'*Going in* at the side,' Legless snarls.

'Well, something to do with the side,' Hubert says.

'What, at the lunch table?' I reply, hoping to lighten the mood a bit. 'That's not very good manners.'

'Legless is still trying to get me to stop the case,' Marjorie complains. 'All I asked for was some help about some technical aspects of this insane apology for a sport, and I'm being made to feel like a fascist for allowing a perfectly proper case of mindless violence to be prosecuted in my court.'

'It's a one-match suspension at worst,' Legless fumes. 'Well, perhaps two. If he is convicted – which he shouldn't be.'

'And as if that isn't bad enough,' Marjorie continues, 'the bloody jury sent a note this morning asking whether the referee had referred the incident to the television match official, and whether they were allowed to see the replay.'

'What's wrong with that?' I ask innocently.

'It's an amateur game, Charlie,' Legless replies in exasperation. 'They don't have bloody television coverage. This isn't the Premiership, or the Six Nations, for God's sake. It's a bunch of lads having fun on Saturday afternoon, and now one of them is being persecuted because things got a bit out of hand. If the referee had exercised a little common sense, it would have been dealt with in the club house.'

'Well, perhaps that's what separates us from our Saxon and Celtic forbears,' Marjorie suggests icily, 'that we settle criminal matters in court rather than the club house.'

Hubert looks up again from the tagliatelle ai funghi.

'The Celts had well-organised courts from quite early times,' he says. 'The Welsh, particularly. The Welsh had a code of laws, and courts to enforce them, when Birmingham was still a swamp.'

Recalling that Marjorie has family connections near

Birmingham somewhere, I choke back the obvious witticism. This is no time to risk stirring things up any further.

'Has anyone seen the new Turner exhibit at the National Gallery?' I ask.

* * *

Tuesday afternoon

The story revealed by the arson investigators seems simple enough. The fire was set inside the church at three different sites. The sites were linked by chains of papers, books, and wooden chairs, all carefully positioned and liberally doused with white spirit. The arsonist had done enough to ensure that the sites would link up and merge into one fire hot enough to consume anything in its path, which would burn out only when there was nothing left to consume. The heat and smoke would have been intense. Even the fabric of the building was scorched, and its metal structural supports had buckled. Its stability could not be assured without tests. The building was essentially a shell. It was unquestionably a case of deliberate, pre-meditated arson.

The investigators have produced an extensive album of photographs showing the damage throughout the church. It wasn't quite Brighton Pier, but it was pretty bad. One of them, George Kenworthy, is called live to take the jury through the album and explain the detail of the evidence, one photograph at a time. It is a slow process, which takes up much of the afternoon. The jury are fascinated. Now, they have no doubt about how serious the fire was – or about what would have happened if anyone had been trapped inside the church. Eventually, Roderick is satisfied with the impression his evidence has made and sits down.

Cathy stands quietly.

'Mr Kenworthy, are you familiar with the evidence of the

fire brigade officers who first arrived on the scene? Were you present in court earlier when it was read to the jury?'

'Yes, I was.'

'Are you aware that there was evidence that, while the west door and the vestry door were locked, the south door appeared to have been unlocked?'

'Yes.'

'It is clear, isn't it, that the fire was set inside the church?'

'Yes.'

'And the arsonist deliberately chose to set fires at three different sites within the church?'

'Yes.'

'Not only that, but the arsonist constructed trails of debris – chairs, paper, and so on – which virtually guaranteed that the three sites would merge?'

'It certainly appears so.'

Cathy pauses for a moment and nods.

'That is a fairly sophisticated technique, wouldn't you agree?'

Roderick rises to his feet. He has seen where this is leading, as have I, and he would like to head it off.

'Your Honour, I'm not sure why the sophistication of the technique, if such it be, is relevant. I don't even know whether the witness is able to express a view on that, one way or the other.'

'Why don't we ask him?' I suggest. 'Mr Kenworthy, with your experience of such matters, are you able to venture an opinion?'

'Yes, your Honour,' he replies. 'I would agree with that. It is a sign of someone who knows something about fires. Of course, it is also something one could read about, or find on the internet without too much difficulty.'

I nod, and hand back to Cathy.

'In fact, even the use of white spirit as an accelerant is evidence of careful planning, isn't it?' she asks.

'It is evidence of planning, certainly. That does not make it sophisticated. The use of accelerants is a common feature of arson offences.'

'Of course. But do the circumstances, taken together, indicate that this fire is likely to have been the work of an experienced arsonist?'

Roderick is up on his feet again.

'I can't say that,' the witness replies, before Roderick can object. Satisfied, he resumes his seat.

'Can you at least say that it is unlikely to be the work of a teenager with no experience of arson, still living at home with his parents?'

'Oh, really, your Honour,' Roderick complains, hardly bothering to rise.

'Aren't you asking him to speculate, Miss Writtle?'

'He is an expert, your Honour. If he is unable to form an opinion, he can say so.'

'All right,' I agree. 'Can you say one way or the other, Mr Kenworthy?'

Kenworthy smiles.

'Let me put it this way. Such a teenager would not be at the top of a list of suspects.'

'Thank you,' Cathy says.

'But, of course, that is on the assumption that one has enough suspects to compile a list.'

Roderick grins happily.

'Does it strike you as at all odd,' Cathy continues, apparently undaunted, 'that there was no sign of soot or fire damage on Tony's clothing, and no smell of smoke?'

Kenworthy considers this for some time.

'Yes. In the circumstances, that is a bit unexpected.'

'Would you tell the jury why?'

'Given that fires were set at three different sites, and given that the arsonist had to move between them, there was a good chance that something would have stuck to his clothing at some point.'

'The south door and its lock were not badly affected by the fire, were they?'

'No. The south door was left ajar. Of course, that tended to assist the spread of the fire, but it probably protected the door itself to some extent.'

'So you had surfaces there which were capable of bearing latent prints?'

'Yes.'

'Tony's fingerprints were not found on the door or the lock, were they?'

'No. They were not.'

'Even though they were on the silver metal can which had contained the white spirit?'

'That is correct.'

'Yes, thank you, Mr Kenworthy.'

And that is it for the day. Photocopier permitting, Roderick will call the officer in the case tomorrow to deal with the police investigation, including the defendant's interview under caution. We are making good progress, and despite Cathy's limited successes in chiselling away at the prosecution's evidence, it seems to me that young Tony is probably bang to rights for this. I am beginning to consider what I am going to do by way of sentence.

* * *

Tuesday evening

On evenings when the Reverend Mrs Walden and I have nothing very much to do – a circumstance far more common in my case than in hers – we sometimes adjourn to the Delights of the Raj, a dimly lit, secluded Indian in Kennington, where we partake of poppadoms, samosas, a chicken Madras, a sag aloo, and a couple of Cobras. The Reverend Mrs Walden likes to cook, and is rather good at it, but with all she has going on in the evenings

– with the Parochial Church Council, the women's group, the youth group, and all the rest of it – she is often quite happy to delegate dinner to me. As my own culinary repertoire is limited, my signature dish being a passable spaghetti Bolognese, this usually means either the Raj or our local Italian/pizza place, La Bella Napoli.

Before my marriage to the Reverend Mrs Walden, I had no idea what went on in the average Anglican parish. There are times when it makes your hair stand on end, and the Reverend has encountered it all during our time together. Parish councillors who have their hands in the collection plate, or around a bottle of communion wine; organists with an unusually close interest in choir boys; lay preachers having a bit on the side; and earnest evangelicals telling her she shouldn't be doing her job because Jesus didn't recruit women as disciples. Any suggestion that women are not qualified to do something gets the Reverend Mrs Walden very stirred up. And you should hear her on the subject of Jesus and Mary Magdalene some time. She has a few things to say about the two of them that you didn't learn about in Sunday school, I can assure you.

But this week we are dealing with her efforts to prevent her church from being ripped off by a firm of dubious builders, who somehow managed to gain the approval of the Diocese sufficiently to be awarded a contract to refurbish the interior of the building. Since they started, two weeks ago, it has been a saga of late arrivals, shoddy workmanship and extravagant claims for extras. It has been a full-time job just fending off the builders, while trying to persuade the Diocese to do something about the situation, other than make snide insinuations that she could have managed the project better. Her feelings towards some of the diocesan staff are, shall we say, less than charitable. Her venting about this has used up our two Cobras.

'Get me another Cobra, Charlie,' she says, 'and tell me about your day. Perhaps I can stop obsessing about all this for a while.'

'You're going to find my day quite interesting,' I promise.

We enter the unusual territory of a third Cobra, and I tell her all about Tony Devonald, and the fire at St Giles, Tottenham, and the white spirit, and the unexplained cancellation of choir practice.

'Yes, I remember reading about that in the *Standard*,' she replies. 'Apparently it really gutted the church, reduced it almost to a shell. Well, you've seen the photographs. I expect you know that already.'

'It virtually destroyed the place,' I confirm. We drink in silence for a few moments.

'It doesn't sound too good for the young man, does it? Are you expecting a conviction?'

'Barring a minor miracle,' I say.

She smiles. 'Never discount the possibility of a miracle.'

'I never do,' I reply, thinking of my job at Bermondsey generally. 'But I haven't told you the best bit yet.'

She leans forward expectantly. I tell her all about Martha Devonald, and her tales of auto-kinesis at the dinner table, and the parents' theory of demonic possession, and the small fire in the garage, and about the priest praying with young Tony in the church and finding no demons, and how Cathy Writtle turned the whole thing back on the prosecution. I am doing my best to relate this part of the story with a certain humorous touch, but I see that the smile is gradually fading from her face, to be replaced by a look of concern. She does not respond immediately.

'Is that all the man did?' she asks eventually. 'Take the boy to the church on his own and pray with him?'

'Apparently.'

'Good God.'

I look at her for some time.

'I take it you think he should have done more?' I ask.

She shakes her head. 'Charlie, you know me,' she begins.

'You know that I don't have any truck with all that mediaeval claptrap about demonic possession. But if your parishioners come to you with a story like that, you can't just blow it off. You have to do something.'

'What would you have done?' I ask.

She thinks for some time.

'Well, first, I would have spoken to the little girl – Martha, was it? – with her parents.'

'And said what?'

'I would want to know whether she understands the importance of speaking the truth, and how wrong it is to tell lies to get someone else into trouble.'

I smiled. 'We are not allowed to cross-examine children any more, however many lies they tell.'

'I'm not talking about cross-examining her, Charlie. I'm talking about making clear to her how serious the situation is. I would have reassured her that she wasn't going to get into trouble, provided she told me the truth. So then, we have two possibilities. First possibility, she admits she was telling porkies, and Tony is off the hook. Second possibility, she sticks to her guns, in which case I then have to speak to Tony again, with the parents.'

'You have something of a problem, either way,' I point out.

'Agreed. But at least we have somewhere to start. Frankly, whichever way it goes, I am going to recommend that the parents think about consulting a child psychologist. Whatever is going on has to stop before some real damage is caused.'

I sip my Cobra thoughtfully.

'All right, I see that. But what if the vicar is one of those who *does* subscribe to demonic possession? He might not be thinking in terms of child psychologists.'

She scoffs.

'If he really does believe in demonic possession, his conduct is even worse – in fact, it is inexcusable.'

'Why so?'

'If you really think you are dealing with a case of demonic possession, you don't just take the boy into church and start some random prayer session with no one else involved.'

'What should you do, then?'

'First, you get all the advice and support you can. You contact your bishop and get him involved.' She pauses. 'Look, we don't really go in for that kind of thing in the Anglican Church. But the Roman Catholics do, and they have a whole protocol, with specially trained priests and counsellors. Whether or not there are demons, you are probably dealing with a mental illness of some kind, which needs proper handling. They don't just let the parish priest dive in without any preparation at all. It's just asking for trouble. He had no idea what he was letting himself in for, and he should have known that.'

She takes a long drink.

'What did you say his name was, again?'

'I'm not sure I did say,' I reply. 'But it's Stringer. Father Osbert Stringer.'

She puts down her beer glass and seems to focus on a statue of the elephant god Ganesh in the small alcove opposite our table.

'What?' I ask.

'I'm sure I have heard that name before,' she replies.

'Well, it would have been in the press reports of the fire, I'm sure.'

She shakes her head.

'No. I know it from somewhere else. But I can't think where.'

Back at home, I get ready for bed, and retire with a cup of hot camomile tea. After three Cobras I want to make sure that I sleep soundly, and camomile tea usually does the trick. I am about to turn off my bedside light when I notice that the Reverend Mrs Walden is not with me. She does sometimes sit up late reading, particularly if she wants to check something for her forthcoming Sunday sermon, but tonight she has seemed more in the mood to fall into bed and drift off. I put on my dressing gown and slippers and make my way to her study, from which emanates the sound of a computer keyboard being punched with deliberation. I enter to find the Reverend, still fully dressed, in the middle of what looks like a complicated search. She turns and looks at me.

'I knew it, Charlie. I knew I had heard the name before.'

I glance at the computer screen.

'You mean Father Osbert Stringer?'

'Yes. I couldn't for the life of me remember how I knew it, so I googled him.'

'I am glad you are not on my jury,' I say. 'I would have to do you for contempt.'

'Contempt or not, I think your jury should see this,' she counters.

'Oh?'

She clicks a couple of buttons, types in a command, and invites me to come closer to the screen. It is an article in the *Toronto Star*, from about eight years ago. The article has two photographs; one of a slightly younger Father Osbert Stringer wearing his trademark full-length black cassock; the other showing the burnt-out ruins of the former Church of St Anthony of Padua in the parish of East York, just outside Toronto. The article goes on to record that a mentally disturbed young man of the parish had been arrested and was about to appear in court for a preliminary hearing. I am fully awake again now. The Reverend Mrs Walden and I exchange a meaningful look.

'It gets better,' she says.

'Better?'

'Or worse; depending on how you look at it.'

She clicks and types quickly again. Up comes a second article, rather difficult to read on the screen.

'I can tell you what it says,' she offers. 'This was four years before the Toronto fire. It's from a newspaper called the *Weekly*.'

I look more closely. 'South Africa?'

'Father Stringer was serving in South Africa at the time, in Bloemfontein, to be precise. The first article I came across was in something called the *Volksblad*, but that was in Afrikaans, so it wasn't much help. But then I came across this.'

'My word, he gets around, doesn't he?'

'Yes, he does. And guess what?'

I look at her blankly.

'You're joking.'

'No, I'm not. This time the church was called St Peter and St Paul, and again a young man was arrested. The difference is that by the time this article was written, the young man had been tried and convicted.'

We exchange the look again.

'Remember Lady Bracknell?' she asks.

I remember Lady Bracknell well. We had seen a good production in the West End a few months earlier.

'To have one church gutted by fire may be regarded as a misfortune; to have two churches gutted by fire looks like carelessness,' I reply.

'And to have three churches gutted by fire,' she adds, 'looks bloody suspicious, if you ask me.'

We are silent for some time.

'What made you think to do this search?' I ask.

'I suddenly remembered why the name seemed familiar. There was an article I read some time ago in the *Church Times* about priests who had served in different countries. Stringer was mentioned. I was trying to track that article down, but I couldn't find it. So I widened the search. I had no idea about all this until I found the Toronto article. Charlie, I'm not sure anyone else will have joined up these dots.'

'No, they probably haven't, not with him changing country

on a regular basis. You probably wouldn't find the connection unless you were looking for it.'

'What are you going to do?' she asks.

'What do you mean?'

'Well, you can't ignore this. It may be highly relevant to your trial.'

'I'm not sure there is anything I can do about it,' I reply.

She is indignant.

'What? Charlie, this young man you have on trial may be innocent. Stringer may be a serial arsonist who knows how to shift the blame to vulnerable young men. You can't just stand by and watch your young man get convicted, knowing what you know. You have to tell the defence lawyer.'

'I can't.'

'What? Why on earth not?'

'Clara, I'm not allowed to contact the defence and suggest that they look for evidence. That would be the end of my career on the Bench, such as it is. In any case, what would I tell them? That my wife and I found some old press reports which we think may be suspicious?'

'May be? Charlie, there is no "may be" about it.'

'Perhaps so. I still can't do it. It wouldn't be proper.'

'Spoken like a true lawyer,' she says accusingly.

'I *am* a lawyer,' I point out.

'That's no excuse.'

She thinks for some moments.

'Well, look, if you can't just tell the defence counsel, tell both sides. Then the prosecution can't claim to be taken by surprise.'

I think about this. I could, of course, call both counsel into chambers privately and suggest that further inquiries be made. Cathy Writtle would ask for an adjournment. Having brought the subject up myself, I could hardly refuse her that. We might even have to start the trial again at some future date. Perhaps by then Father Stringer will have moved on to Australia in search of new churches to burn down. But it still looks awfully like judicial interference on one side of the case, doing the defence's job for them. Why haven't Cathy and her solicitors been here before us? Perhaps they have. Perhaps it didn't check out. I don't know what the evidence was in those cases. In particular, I don't know what the evidence was against the two young men involved. Perhaps there was compelling scientific evidence. The articles are very brief. It may be that they are not terribly accurate. If newspaper reports of what goes on at Bermondsey Crown Court are anything to go by, they may be largely fictitious. Eventually I decide to do what I always do in case of doubt – procrastinate and hope it will all go away. I decide to wait until the close of the prosecution case and see how the land lies then. I have no reason to think it will lie much differently, but hope springs eternal.

The Reverend Mrs Walden is not pleased when I communicate this decision to her. She stalks off, muttering to herself, stage right. I'm not sure how late it was when she finally came to bed.

* * *

Wednesday morning
The CPS photocopying machine being miraculously restored to health, there are now copies of the transcript of Tony's police interview for myself and the jury, and Roderick now calls the officer in the case, DS Major, to give evidence. He outlines for the jury the course of the investigation and the arrest of Tony Devonald. He summarises the results of the forensic testing of Tony's clothing, before turning to the interview.

Advised by the duty solicitor, Tony answered every question put to him, without a single 'no comment' – these days, a creditable thing in itself. He told the police repeatedly that he had nothing to do with the fire, often volunteering it without being asked. Then there was the matter of the mysterious phone call, about which the prosecution has so far said nothing. He was at home at the time, he said. He did not recognise the voice. But he was sure that the man told him that Father Stringer needed his help with something at the church. He slipped out of the house without telling anyone, thinking that he would not be away long. When he arrived at the church, he saw the fire, and immediately ran to the south door because it was the door nearest to the vicarage. The door was unlocked. It was impossible to enter the church because of the searing heat, but he called out to find out whether anyone was inside. There was no reply. The vicarage seemed dark. It was then that he noticed the metal can standing by the door. It smelled strongly of white spirit. He ran from the church with the intention of summoning help, and took the can with him to ensure that it was out of reach of the flames. He dropped it by the side of the road. He was unable to call for help because he had left his mobile at home, but soon afterwards he heard the sirens of the approaching fire engines, and went home. Roderick asks DS Major to await further questions.

'Just to clarify, then, Detective Sergeant,' Cathy begins, 'apart from the traces and smell of white spirit on Tony's clothing and his fingerprints on the metal can, there was no scientific evidence linking him to this offence at all, was there?'

'Apart from those things, no,' the Sergeant replies. His manner suggests that he thinks that really ought to be enough.

'Well, there was no such evidence inside the church, was there?'

'No, Miss. But there again, the church was burned quite thoroughly.'

'Yes, but not entirely, was it? The south door and its lock survived, didn't they?'

'They did.'

'And it is a reasonable inference that whoever started the fire entered through the south door, isn't it?'

'Is it, Miss?'

'The south door was unlocked, and the metal can containing the white spirit was found at the south door.'

'With respect, Miss, we only have your client's word for that.'

'That's not entirely true, Sergeant, is it? The south door was unlocked when the police arrived.'

'Yes, but we don't how when, or by whom it was unlocked.'

Cathy smiles. 'That's exactly right, Sergeant. We don't know that, do we?'

'No, we don't.'

'Could it have been the same person who cancelled choir practice so suddenly?'

Roderick is half way to his feet. She raises a hand.

'Sorry, your Honour.'

She pauses for effect.

'Now, let me move on to something else. Tony told you, didn't he, that he had received a phone call asking him to go to the church at about the time of the fire, to help Father Stringer with something?'

'That is what he said, yes.'

'Did the officers seize his mobile phone when he was arrested?'

'They did.'

'And was the phone interrogated to see whether there was any evidence to support what Tony had said?'

'Yes.'

'And was the result of that investigation that a call was received at about seven-forty with a duration of about forty-five seconds?'

'That is correct.'

'Long enough for some conversation to take place?'

'I suppose so, yes.'

'Well, it's not a missed call, is it?'

'No, I would presume not.'

'Were you able to establish the number from which the call originated?'

'Yes, Miss, it was made from the public call box on Vicarage Road.'

'Not far from the church?'

'Less than two hundred yards.'

'And no doubt the phone box was checked for fingerprints or other scientific evidence?'

The Sergeant makes a pretence of checking the record of the investigation, and feigns a look of resignation.

'I know an officer went to take a look. But you wouldn't expect to find anything usable in a phone box with members of the public going in and out all the time. There was no way to preserve it as a scene by the time we were aware of it.'

'That's a "no", is it?'

'No check for fingerprints was made.'

'Very well. But there is no doubt, is there, that a call was made to Tony's phone from the call box at about the time he claimed in his interview?'

'That would appear to be correct, Miss, yes.'

'Thank you, Sergeant. Lastly, can you confirm please that Tony Devonald is nineteen years of age, and that he has never been convicted of any offence, and that he has never received any caution, reprimand, or warning?'

'That is correct, Miss.'

Cathy sits down, and the Detective Sergeant leaves the witness box.

'Your Honour,' Roderick announces grandly, 'that concludes the prosecution's case, subject only to preparing a few agreed facts for the jury. If I might have a few minutes to inquire into the continuing health of the CPS photocopier, I would be most grateful.'

'Your Honour, I would appreciate a few minutes also, to confer with the defendant before we go any further,' Cathy adds.

I turn to the jury.

'Short break, members of the jury. You will have time for coffee, I expect.'

They don't seem in any way distressed by the news. In fact, as it turns out, they have more than enough time for coffee. I soon get a message suggesting that I release the jury until two o'clock. Nothing to do with the CPS photocopier, for once. Something has come up, and Cathy needs more time to confer with her client. Fair enough, I think. He is probably nervous about giving evidence. He will have to, whether he wants to or not, if he is to stand a chance of getting off. But she may have to persuade him of that, and I don't want to rush her.

And so to lunch, an oasis of calm in a desert of chaos.

I enter the mess with some trepidation, fully expecting to find the rugby wars still in full flow, but to my relief, calm seems to have descended.

'How is your case going?' I ask Legless.

'Fine,' he replies. 'Should finish the prosecution case tomorrow. No problems.'

Nothing amiss that I can detect.

Marjorie likewise, when I ask her the same question. 'Yes, fine. We are making good progress. I may get the jury out late this afternoon, but more likely tomorrow morning.'

'Hubert?'

Hubert looks up from the dish of the day, described on the menu as pasta puttanesca.

'Oh, it's all nonsense,' he complains, 'two foreigners attacking each other in a pub. Deport both of them if it was up to me. Waste of public money.'

'Is there a bad injury?' I ask.

'Couple of broken ribs, cuts to the head, that kind of thing. Nothing serious.'

'How is your case going?' Marjorie asks.

I decide to tell them about my dinner at the Delights of the Raj with the Reverend Mrs Walden, and about her subsequent computer-based research.

'I'm not sure what, if anything, I should do about it,' I confess. 'What do you think?'

'I wouldn't say anything,' Legless advises. 'You can't jump into the arena on behalf of one party. Besides, as you say yourself, you can't be sure what the previous matters were about, whether they have any relevance. There would have to be a complete investigation, which would derail the trial.'

'I agree that it would derail the trial,' Marjorie says, 'but I think you have to say something, Charlie. There is a real risk of injustice. You don't have to jump into the arena. I would just have counsel into chambers, tell them you stumbled over some information; you are worried about the possibility of a miscarriage of justice; and give them time to reflect about what to do. If I know Cathy Writtle, she will invite you to discharge the jury and order a retrial once they have had time to investigate properly. The officer in the case might well want to look into it, too.'

I nod, still undecided.

'I did that once,' Hubert says.

'Did what?'

'Told counsel about some information I had which might have been relevant.'

'Really?'

'Oh, yes. It was while I was sitting at Southwark for a week or two, years ago. Fraud case. John Sugden prosecuting, and that awful woman – God, what was her name? Fulton, Fulberry, something like that, dreadful woman – defending. The defendant was giving evidence and Sugden was cross-examining, and he asked the defendant where some transaction had taken place. Can't remember what the transaction was, but obviously fraudulent, because he eventually went down like a lead balloon, and I gave him –'

'What was the information, Hubert?' I ask.

'The information? Oh, yes. Well, he tells Sugden that the transaction was consummated at the Garrick Club. I couldn't believe my ears. "Did you say the Garrick?" I asked. "Yes, your Honour," he says, bold as brass. I was horrified. "What were you doing at the Garrick Club?" I ask him myself. He turns to me, looking a bit surprised. "I am a member, your Honour," he replies. "What?" I say. "You can't be a member of my Club. You're an undischarged bankrupt!" Counsel are trying to interrupt, of course, but I was furious. I rose immediately and telephoned the Secretary of the Club, and do you know what he told me?'

'I have no idea,' I reply.

'The bounder wasn't a member at all. Never had been. It was a complete lie. What do you think of that?'

'Shocking.'

Hubert returns to his pasta puttanesca.

'Hubert, how does that relate to the problem I have?' I ask.

He looks up again.

'What? Oh, yes. Well, I told counsel what I had found out, of course.'

'So you saw both counsel in chambers?'

'Good God, no. In open court. The man had told the jury a lie in open court which reflected very badly on the Garrick, and I saw to it that it was corrected in open court. I took judicial notice that he wasn't a member and told the jury that was the end of it. Well, I couldn't drag the Secretary away from his work just to give evidence about it when it was such an obvious lie, could I? It would have been a complete waste of his time.'

* * *

Wednesday afternoon
I am still mulling it all over, two minutes before I am due back
in court. But it seems I am to get a reprieve. Carol comes in to
tell me that counsel are going to request an adjournment until
tomorrow morning. I am not sure whether having more time to
think about it is going to help, but at least it gives me an excuse
for not doing anything just yet. I go into court to hear what they
have to say.

'Your Honour,' Cathy begins. 'I have received some
information during the lunch hour which may be highly
relevant to the case. I have not had the opportunity to look
into it in any detail, but it may well be that in due course I will
be asking your Honour to allow Father Stringer to be recalled
for further questions to be put in cross-examination. My
learned friend has been kind enough to make some inquiries,
and it seems that Father Stringer would not be available until
tomorrow morning, but could attend then.'

For some reason I cannot immediately define, I feel taken
aback. The shadow of a suspicion crosses my mind. I must have
been sitting staring vacantly at Cathy for some time, because
she has to get my attention again.

'Your Honour?'

'Yes. Yes,' I reply. I am really not sure how to continue. 'Well,
of course, if it should be necessary... but, well, perhaps you
could tell me what the information is?'

'Your Honour, I would prefer not to say anything about it in
open court, certainly until I have had the chance to look into it
in more depth.'

Roderick rises to his feet.

'If I may, your Honour, my learned friend has been good
enough to tell me in outline what is involved, and on behalf
of the prosecution, I agree that it is a matter which should

be inquired into further. I also agree that, depending on the result of those further inquiries, it may be right to recall Father Stringer.'

I have no choice. Cathy is entitled to the chance to look into whatever it is. I will have to be patient until tomorrow.

* * *

Wednesday evening

This evening, I come very close to asking the Reverend Mrs Walden a direct question. Over dinner – ironically a cheese omelette and chips, a dish to be known in future in the Walden household as an Omelette à la Stringer – I tell her about the surprising developments in the case of Tony Devonald. She listens attentively, but does not seem quite as surprised as I would have expected. Part of me thinks that perhaps this is not coming as news to her. Another part of me dismisses that idea as absurd and tells me to get a grip. But still, it seems to me that she is acting rather suspiciously, being quite evasive.

'I'm sure defence counsel must have gone down the same road we did,' she says as if butter wouldn't melt in her mouth. 'The only surprise is that no one thought to do it before now.'

She then changes the subject, rather abruptly, to my way of thinking. But I can't quite bring myself to say anything. After all, I am still not sure what awaits me on the morrow.

* * *

Thursday morning

Jeanie is in a much better mood this morning. Her husband made a rather more successful investment in a race at Chester yesterday afternoon, she tells me, and the rent is safe for another month. George is up in arms over the Chancellor's latest economic proposals, which he sees as the latest instalment of the personal vendetta being carried out against him by the Government. But all in all it is a cheerful enough stroll to court, with an exceptionally good latte to look forward to. Naturally, by now, I am very curious indeed to see what is going to happen in court.

As it is Thursday, Stella is getting anxious about the list for tomorrow, and the list for next week, both of which are apparently fraught with the potential for disaster.

'I've got that appeal against conviction from the Magistrates Court,' she complains. 'It's down for between two and three hours, and I've got two magistrates lined up. But I need a judge to preside, and I don't know who I've got.'

'Which appeal is that?'

'Bushell. That chap who was convicted of driving without due care and attention and claims he was suffering from automatic something or other.'

'Automatism?' I suggest.

'Yes, that's the one. He's calling a neurological specialist, who can only come tomorrow before leaving to start a year at Harvard. So we've got to get it on.'

'I think Judge Jenkins and Judge Drake are both likely to get their juries out today,' I reply as soothingly as I can. 'I'll ask them at lunch. I wouldn't worry about it.'

I pause.

'Don't tell anyone, but I think there's even a chance I may be free myself.'

She raises her eyebrows.

'I thought Devonald had at least another couple of days to go.'

'Something's come up. We may have a witness recalled this morning, and if we do, it may be that the prosecution case will take something of a hit. I'll make sure Carol lets you know.'

'That would be great, Judge.' Stella almost manages a smile.

'In that case, you can do the appeal, and I can give you Raven next week.'

'What's that about?'

'Sexual assault. Groping a sixteen-year-old on the tube during the rush hour.'

I close my eyes.

'Nothing is certain yet, Stella, of course,' I reply. 'I may be quite wrong. Devonald may still have a day or two to go.'

'I'll come and see you just before two o'clock,' she says.

As I enter court, I see Father Osbert Stringer sitting in the back row next to DS Major. It may be my imagination, but it seems to me that the Detective Sergeant is keeping something of a close eye on him. As soon as the jury has been brought in, Cathy is on her feet.

'Your Honour,' she begins, 'thank you for the time you have given us. I'm pleased to say that it has been used productively. Further information has come to light which I anticipate may be highly relevant to the questions the jury have to decide, and I now ask that Father Stringer be recalled to answer further questions in cross-examination.'

'By all means.'

Father Stringer proceeds slowly from his seat at the back of the court to the witness box, with what looks to me like a dead-man-walking attitude.

'You are still under oath, Father,' I say as neutrally as I can, before nodding to Cathy.

'Thank you, your Honour. Father Stringer, you told the jury on Tuesday that you had been in the ministry for some thirty years, is that right?'

'That is correct.'

'And you have been vicar of St Giles, Tottenham, for the past four years?'

'Yes.'

'Before coming to St Giles, you spent a good many years working abroad, did you not?'

'I did.'

'You were featured in an article in the *Church Times* about priests who had worked in a number of different countries?'

'Yes. The Anglican Communion is a world-wide church, and there are some, such as myself, who feel called to serve different parts of the Anglican family.'

Cathy nods.

'I don't intend to ask you about all the churches you have served in, Father, but there are one or two the jury might find to be of interest. For example, some eight years ago, you were ministering in Canada, were you not?'

'I was in Canada for more than five years.'

'During which time you were priest in charge of the church of St Anthony of Padua in a suburb of Toronto called East York, yes?'

'Yes.'

'Father Stringer, please tell the jury what happened to the church of St Anthony of Padua?'

'What happened to it?'

'Yes, what happened to it. In other words, if I were to travel to East York tomorrow, would I be able to see the church of St Anthony of Padua for myself?'

Father Stringer seems a bit reluctant to answer.

'I believe it has been rebuilt,' he replies quietly, 'though not on its former scale, of course.'

'Rebuilt?' Cathy says, feigning surprise, with a quick look in the direction of the jury. 'Why was it necessary to rebuild it?'

The witness looks down.

'There was a fire.'

'Indeed. In fact, the church burned to the ground, did it not?'

'Yes.'

I glance over at the jury. They are sitting up and taking notes now.

'And was this while you were priest in charge?'

'Sadly, yes.'

'Sadly, yes. Father Stringer, what was the cause of the fire?'

'The police determined that it was a case of arson.'

'Indeed? Did they discover who was responsible?'

'They arrested a young man. I believe the court later made a hospital order in his case. I am not sure whether he was ever tried.'

'Was the young man in question known to you?'

'Yes. He was a member of the congregation. But he was seriously disturbed. Very seriously disturbed indeed.'

'Did this seriously disturbed young man use an accelerant to set the fire?'

'As I recall, yes.'

'He used white spirit, didn't he?' she asks. 'In a metal can?'

'He may well have done... it was some years ago. I don't remember all the details.'

'Well, let's see how well you do if I go back a little farther in time. Before Canada, you spent a number of years in South Africa?'

'Yes.'

'Were you one of the ministers at the Church of St Peter and St Paul in Bloemfontein?'

'Yes.'

'This, of course, is even longer ago, but by any chance, do you happen to remember anything happening to that church?'

'There was a fire.'

This time, there is an audible gasp from the jury. Roderick is studying some papers, probably in preparation for his next case. He appears to have lost interest in this one.

'Yes. To take matters shortly, Father, the Church of St Peter and St Paul also burned to the ground, and once again, a young man of your congregation was charged with the offence of arson.'

'And he was convicted,' Stringer protests.

'Yes, indeed he was,' Cathy replies quietly. 'And I am sure you are hoping that Tony Devonald will follow in his footsteps.'

'I have no idea what you mean,' the witness splutters.

'You know exactly what I mean,' Cathy says.

She pauses for some time. Until now, she has been pressing full speed ahead. The pause is abrupt. At first I think it is solely for effect, but as it goes on, I am not so sure. Every eye in the courtroom is fixed on her. I am not going to rush her.

'Before I go on, Father Stringer, I want to give you the opportunity to correct the evidence you gave on Tuesday. I ask you to admit to this jury that you phoned Tony Devonald and asked him to come to the church shortly before eight o'clock on the evening of the fire at St Giles; and that the fire was already blazing when Tony arrived. If you make that admission, I will conclude my cross-examination.'

'That is completely untrue,' Stringer replies. He is almost shouting.

Cathy nods.

'All right. Father, I am sorry I have to raise this, but you leave me no choice. I believe your parents, sadly, are both dead. Is that right?'

Now I sit up and take notice, as well as the jury. This is something new. Of course. I should have known there would be more. So far, Cathy has been following the path the Reverend Mrs Walden uncovered in about fifteen minutes. Since then, she would have had every pupil in her chambers pulling an all-nighter. If there was more to find, of course they would have found it.

Father Stringer has turned a whiter shade of pale, as they say. He turns to me in desperation.

'Is this really relevant, your Honour?'

'I don't know,' I reply. 'Please answer the question and we shall see.'

'My parents both died when I was very young,' he replies.

'Yes. They died on the same occasion, didn't they?'

'Yes.'

'In a fire at the family home?'

'Yes.'

'You were the only child?'

'Yes.'

'And you were not inside the house when the fire started, were you?'

'No. I was playing in the shed in the garden.'

'Where your father kept his tools and various materials used in home decoration?'

'Yes.'

'Including white spirit?'

'That was a complete misunderstanding.' He is almost shouting again.

'The police found you with it, didn't they? There was evidence of white spirit on your clothes.'

'I was nowhere near the house. I was in the shed.'

'By the time the police and the fire brigade arrived, yes, I'm sure you were.'

'I was not prosecuted.'

'No,' Cathy agrees. 'You were too young. You were only nine, weren't you?'

There is no reply. She does not press for one.

'Lastly, Father Stringer, I would like you to look at something.'

Cathy gestures towards DS Major, who is sitting behind Roderick. The Sergeant hands her a small clear plastic evidence bag with an exhibit label attached. She proffers it to Dawn, who takes it from her and cheerfully sets out for the witness box.

'What is this, Miss Writtle?' I ask.

'Your Honour, DS Major told the jury yesterday, quite correctly, that no forensic evidence in the form of fingerprints and so on was found in the phone box in Vicarage Road. But the officer who went to search did remove a number of items found there, and she inventoried them. Her inventory is in the unused materials. It occurred to me yesterday to have a look at one item, described as a small black button. DS Major helpfully found it for me.'

Stringer is staring through the plastic like a stricken man.

'Father Stringer, I am showing you the small black button found in the phone box. The jury will see in a moment or two that it is a quite unusual button, covered with black cloth, with no button holes showing on top. I am going to ask you whether you recognise it, but before I do, I think it only fair to tell you that I was able to have the button examined yesterday by a gentleman who works for J Wippell and Co, and who is prepared to give evidence, if necessary. So that the jury will understand, Father, J Wippell and Co is an old-established firm which supplies clerical garments to clergymen of the Church of England. Is that right?'

'Yes.'

'Now, can you tell the jury what kind of button that is?'

'It is the kind of button used on cassocks,' he replies, barely audibly.

'The cassock being the garment that you are wearing in court today?'

'Yes.'

'Is it yours?'

'No. I have no reason to think it is. There are no buttons missing from my cassock.'

'I'm sure that is true. But then, you have had plenty of time to replace it, haven't you?'

Roderick can't even be bothered to object. I give Cathy a look, pro forma.

'Sorry, your Honour. So, we must assume, must we, that it is simply a coincidence that this button was found in the phone box in Vicarage Road not long after someone phoned Tony Devonald from that very box and asked him to come to the church?'

'The button doesn't prove that I was there.'

'No,' Cathy replies, 'it doesn't. But I think it is enough for my purposes. I have no further questions, your Honour.'

She pauses only for a moment.

'Your Honour, I believe that my learned friend Mr Lofthouse is now about to close his case once more. If so, there is a matter of law I wish to mention in the absence of the jury.'

I look across the court at Roderick who climbs wearily to his feet.

'Your Honour, I do now formally close my case again. To save time, I do not resist the application my learned friend is about to make. I ask only that your Honour not release Father Stringer. I understand that DS Major would like a word with him.'

'In that case, Miss Writtle,' I say, 'I don't think there is any need to send the jury out.'

I turn to the jury and address the thin, angular gentleman sitting nearest to me in the front row, juror number one, who is about to become the foreman of the jury without being elected in the usual way.

'Members of the jury, you have been put in charge of the case, and it is for you to return a verdict on the indictment. But I have the power to withdraw the case from you if I take the view that the defendant could not safely be convicted, based on the evidence which has been presented.'

I scan the jury. There is no problem. They know, and they agree.

'In the light of the evidence we have heard this morning, I

have formed the view that it would not be safe to allow the case to proceed any further. Would the gentleman in the front row on my side please act as foreman? Please stand and answer the questions the clerk is about to ask you.'

Carol takes over.

'Mr Foreman, on his Honour's direction, have you reached a verdict on which you are all agreed? On his Honour's direction, do you find the defendant Anthony Devonald not guilty of arson being reckless as to whether human life would be endangered?'

'We find the defendant not guilty,' the foreman confirms.

'You find the defendant not guilty, and that is the verdict of you all?'

The foreman looks around. Most of the jurors are nodding, which is sufficient in the circumstances, and he confirms that it is indeed the verdict of them all. The jurors are looking a bit confused, as juries always do in this situation. Obviously, the foreman doesn't really know whether it is the verdict of them all or not. It's a nervous moment for me too. It is a bloody strange procedure. We don't allow the clerk to ask the other jurors what they think, just in case some bright spark disagrees with the judge and insists on continuing with the case. I've never had that happen, and if it did, I would simply discharge the jury and have my own way in the end. But it's still very strange to tell a jury that they are responsible for returning the verdict and then tell them what the verdict has to be. I'm not sure it reflects much credit on the law for consistency.

Be that as it may, Tony Devonald is a free man. I order him to be discharged from the dock. Thinking that the happy moment deserves a judicial witticism, I add, 'You are free to go. But don't go moving the knives and forks around again without using your hands.'

He looks at me almost sadly.

'I can't do that anymore,' he replies. 'The power deserted me about a year ago.'

I allow a suitable amount of time for Cathy Writtle to receive well-earned praise from her client and his family, before asking Carol to invite both counsel into chambers for a cup of tea. She is walking on air, as she should be. She will be flavour of the month with her instructing solicitors after this. I congratulate her on the victory.

'Did you ever get to the bottom of the mysterious cancellation of choir practice?' I ask.

'Not entirely,' she replies. 'The choir master is pretty sure it was Stringer who phoned to cancel, but whoever it was left a message with one of his children. He would have said that he knew of no reason why choir practice should have been cancelled.'

I hesitate.

'That was an extraordinary history you brought up about Stringer.'

She grins. 'Yes, not bad, Judge, was it?'

'Where did you find all that information about him? On the internet, was it?'

I swear she is working very hard to suppress a smile. She does not reply immediately. Roderick is looking away into space somewhere.

'It was brought to the attention of my instructing solicitors,' she replies eventually. 'Quite unexpectedly.'

'Really?' I say. 'That's a bit odd, isn't it? I would have thought your instructing solicitors might have found it on their own. They are supposed to investigate the case, aren't they?'

Cathy nods and finishes her tea.

'Yes, but you know how that goes nowadays,' she replies. 'Apparently, someone came forward with it yesterday morning.'

'But who...?'

She stands rather quickly and replaces her wig.

'Judge, do excuse me. I'm sorry to rush, but my clerk left

a message for me to get back to chambers as soon as I could. Thanks for the tea.'

They are gone. Stella has left the file for Raven on my desk. Having no excuse to avoid it, I begin to read about the delights of contemporary life on the tube.

And so to lunch, an oasis of calm in a desert of chaos.

I relate the events of the morning to a spellbound audience. To my surprise, Marjorie and Legless now seem to be getting on like a church on fire, their disagreement about rugby apparently forgotten. Gingerly, I ask about the case.

'Jury's out,' Marjorie says. 'I'm betting they will be back soon after lunch.'

'Which way do you think it will go?'

'Oh, he's going down,' she replies cheerfully. 'The referee had a perfect view, and Chummy was a disaster in the witness box.'

'What are you going to give him?' Hubert asks. 'Two years sounds about right to me.'

'That would be a tiny bit over the top, Hubert,' Marjorie suggests.

'Haven't you heard, Hubert?' Legless asks. 'We have things called sentencing guidelines these days.'

'Complete bloody waste of time,' Hubert replies. 'We know how to sentence people without that kind of nonsense. Bloody government has to interfere with everything these days.'

'I've talked the sentence over with Legless,' Marjorie says. 'I'll give him a community order for twelve months, with a load of unpaid work, and I will order him to pay compensation to the victim.'

'And?' Legless says, with a mischievous smile.

'And I will indicate from the bench, even though I have no power to order it, that his club should suspend him for two games, and that he owes the victim a pint in the bar next time their clubs meet.'

Legless nods with satisfaction.

'And thus is justice done,' he says.

* * *

Thursday evening

'You'll never guess what happened today,' I say. I am pouring a glass of Chianti for the Reverend Mrs Walden in the kitchen as she cuts up vegetables for her fettuccine primavera.

'Oh?' she replies. 'What was that?'

'Well, it turns out that the defence solicitors for Tony Devonald –'

'That's the young man in the arson case, isn't it?' she asks innocently without looking up.

'Yes. It turns out that they received a visit yesterday morning from a mysterious person who told them about the two previous fires associated with Father Osbert Stringer.'

'Really?'

'Yes. And, as it turned out, there is a bit more to the story than we thought.'

'Oh?'

'Yes. When he was nine, he burned down his house with both his parents in it. They were both killed, but he was too young to be taken to court.'

This time she does look up, and suspends the downward stroke of her kitchen knife, which stops, frozen in her hand, in mid air. Then she shakes her head, and suddenly brings the knife down with a vengeance on a head of broccoli.

'What happened in court?'

'The defence recalled Father Stringer for further cross-examination. Cathy Writtle – Tony's barrister – buried him, six feet under. The police are interviewing him. I wouldn't be surprised if they charge him.'

'What about Tony?'

'I stopped the case, of course. He is safely back in the bosom of his family.'

She smiles.

'Well then, it really is just as well that the solicitors found out, isn't it?'

She applies the knife to a green pepper.

'When you say it was a mysterious person who told them, do you mean that whoever it was didn't leave their name?'

'Either that, or asked that their name be kept secret.'

'Well I never,' she says. 'Still, it's a good thing whoever it was went to the solicitors, isn't it? Otherwise, they might never have known about it. You didn't say anything, did you?'

I taste my glass of Chianti. I savour it for a moment.

'As it turned out, it was unnecessary. I'm sure I would have,' I reply, sounding unconvincing even to myself. 'I was in chambers, on the point of decision, when they asked for an adjournment yesterday, and again this morning. If they hadn't known about it by this morning, I would have…'

'Yes, I'm sure,' she replies. 'All the same, Charlie, I'm glad someone tipped them off. Aren't you? It would have been quite wrong for that young man to be convicted.'

'It would,' I agree. 'Still, wouldn't you love to know who it was? It's a bit of a coincidence that someone came forward just after –'

The Reverend Mrs Walden puts the knife down and sips her Chianti.

'Charlie, there are certain things we are not destined to know.'

'Are you suggesting that it was an angelic visitation?'

'Perhaps,' she replies. 'In any case, it is something of a miracle, isn't it? And we all need the odd miracle now and then, don't we?'

Well, with my job, I can't disagree with that, can I?

FIRST PAST THE POST

FIRST PAST THE POST

About two months ago

'If you ask me, guv,' George says as he rifles through a stack of newspapers in a search for my copy of the *Times*, 'the last real leader the Labour Party had was Hugh Gaitskell, and that's going back a few years, that is. Bit before my time, obviously, but I remember my old man going on and on about Hugh Gaitskell; he thought the world of Hugh Gaitskell, he did. He was what a real politician should be, my old man reckoned, a real touch of class. The sort of bloke you would have been proud to have as prime minister, the sort of bloke who wouldn't have embarrassed you when he was talking to foreigners. They broke the mould with him, my old man reckoned, and I reckon he was right. They don't make them like that anymore, guv, do they? I mean, who have they had since? Harold Wilson? Blimey, you must be joking. And as for Tony Blair – well, don't even get me started on Tony Blair...'

This was about a week before polling day. I don't know what it is about elections, but for a few weeks every few years, the whole country seems to be obsessed by politics for a short, frantic time, only to forget about it all minutes after the last results have been announced and the lucky winner is having his photograph taken outside number 10 Downing Street. You can't avoid talking about the election anywhere you go. In the final few weeks of saturation-level news reports, we become a nation of political pundits. The check-out girl at Sainsbury's can quote you the latest polls. People you run into down the pub, who usually struggle to talk about anything except football, suddenly know how often Oldham West has changed hands since the War, and what swing there would have to be for it to change hands again, and what it would mean for the outcome in the rest of the country if it did. Now, I expect it from George. In all the years I have been buying the *Times* from him during my daily morning stroll from the vicarage of St Aethelburgh and All Angels to the Bermondsey Crown Court, I have rarely found him wanting for some pithy piece of political wit – usually at the expense of the Labour Party, on whom he is particularly hard, even though he would never vote for anyone else if his life depended on it. But in the last week or two of the campaign, even Elsie and Jeanie are up in arms.

'You can't trust any of them, can you?' Jeanie says on the morning before polling day, as she puts the finishing touches to my ham and cheese bap. 'They're all the same, aren't they? They will promise you anything to get your vote, but once they get in, they either do the exact opposite, or they never do anything at all. I don't know why we waste our time voting for any of them, personally.'

'I think they ought to be tougher on crime,' Elsie joins in, as she hands me my latte and takes my money. 'Well, you'd know all about that, in your job, sir, wouldn't you? But if you ask me, there's too many criminals walking around on the streets instead of doing their time inside, where they belong.'

As Elsie's grandchildren regularly come to the attention of the local police and youth court, I am not quite sure why she would want a government over-keen on law and order, but if I get into that with her I would be there for the rest of the morning. In any case, judges are not meant to express political opinions. We are not supposed to divulge our political views, attend fundraisers, or do anything else which might suggest a party allegiance. We are not even allowed to comment publicly on the government's generally miserable performance in the field of criminal justice, even though we know more about it than anyone else, and could tell them exactly what they are doing wrong. If any of us were to breathe a word of criticism in the hearing of the press, even accidentally, the Grey Smoothies would have a meltdown and declare the judge in question to be a clear and present danger.

That doesn't mean we don't have political opinions, of course. We are just as entitled to vote as anyone else, and like anyone else we have to make up our minds who to vote for. My preference is no secret to those who know me well, and I don't think I hide it very well if I get drawn into talking politics. 'A conservative judge?' some may scoff. 'Surely not. Who would have guessed that?' But that's just a cliché. We are not all alike. Even within our small community at Bermondsey we have a wide range of opinions. Marjorie has had her flirtations with liberalism. Legless would vote for the Scottish nationalists if he could. And as for Hubert – well, I'm not sure there is a party to represent Hubert's views. He rather disapproves of democracy as an institution and, if I understand him correctly, would prefer a benevolent oligarchy of the right kind of chaps, who would mostly be members of the Garrick Club.

I do adhere to the Conservative path. But don't get me wrong. I'm not an extremist. I don't read the *Telegraph*, or anything like that. I do my bit at election time to keep the blue flag flying high, but to be honest it's a bit of a lost cause; my vote doesn't have much impact in Bermondsey usually, and in any case the Reverend Mrs Walden and I tend to cancel each other out, she being more of the Liberal/Green persuasion. Sometimes you have to wonder how much it all matters at the end of the day. That's the problem with the first past the post system, they say. But you have to try, don't you?

'And if you ask me,' George says on the morning of polling day as I try to wrest the *Times* from his grasp in the interests of making it to court on time, 'Michael Foot could have been a great leader in different circumstances. I mean, they always say he was a natural backbencher, don't they, and he should never have become a minister. But I think he was a bit unlucky, coming at the time he did. I mean, let's be fair about it. The odds were stacked against him, weren't they? And then, of course, there was Jim Callaghan. Now, there was an interesting man, but his problem was...' Eventually I manage to pull away and leave Jim Callaghan to the next customer.

* * *

Monday morning

As I stroll to court this morning, I wonder what George would have to say about the case I have today. He's going to have quite a bit to say tomorrow morning, I reflect, by which time it will have been all over the media, including the evening news on TV. The Reverend Mrs Walden has been deputed to record the news for posterity, since her understanding of such technical matters is far superior to mine. Between us we will collect a copy of each of the day's newspapers. Because I am about to do what the Grey Smoothies call a high profile case. I am going to have my fifteen minutes of fame. I have some reservations about it, of course.

All judges are a bit camera-shy, because we know that encounters with the press rarely end well for us. They tell you that when you are sworn in. You do a series of photographs for various official purposes, and they make it clear that there is one particular photograph they will send to the *Sun* or the *Mail* if you do something really stupid. And if you do something really stupid, you automatically become a 'Top Judge'. You may be the lowliest Recorder or a circuit judge sitting in the smallest court in the land, but screw a case up spectacularly and overnight you experience a mystical ascent to the highest echelons of the judicial hierarchy. You've all seen the headlines: 'Top Judge grants bail to Homicidal Maniac'; 'Top Judge lets Armed Robber off with Suspended Sentence'; 'Rape Victim asked for it – Top Judge.' Top Judges, believe me, never come out of it well. But today, it is a risk I am willing to take.

I could have got rid of it. We did have a tentative inquiry from the Old Bailey about whether we might like to transfer it over there, and from one or two senior Grey Smoothies about whether we might like a High Court judge to sit with us to try it. We declined both offers politely, and we had the perfect excuse. Waste the time of the Central Criminal Court or a High Court judge on two counts of racially aggravated ABH? Not going to happen. In addition, it is a first for Bermondsey, being asked to take a case from off circuit which is too hot to handle locally, and we are not going to give it up.

Usually, it is the Bailey or more upmarket courts such as Southwark, Manchester, and the like, that get cases which have to be moved away from their home court. But for some reason, the circuit concerned asked us. Hopefully it will set a precedent. Why that decision was taken is anyone's guess. It is possible that someone thought there might be less press presence, as if the press were incapable of tracking the case down to Bermondsey and then finding their way to the court. I'm willing to bet they won't have any trouble at all. By the time I get to court there will be reporters and TV vans with those huge aerials parked outside and the whole apparatus of modern-day media coverage of a major event.

Before I go in through the judges' entrance, unobserved by what I hope will be a multitude of ravenous paparazzi, I sneak a look around the corner at the front of the court. So far, there is only one TV van, and a couple of people standing around who look as though they might be reporters. The only other sign of unusual activity is a couple of elderly gentlemen carrying a sign which reads: 'Government Hands off our Pensions'. It's probably a bit early. I'm sure the crowds will build as the day unfolds.

'Will the defendants please stand,' Carol, the clerk, begins once court is assembled. The two gentlemen in the dock stand slowly. They look harmless enough, each dressed in a suit and the appropriate tie, blue for one, red for the other. But the prison officers are taking no chances with this one. There are three officers in the dock, one of them stationed between the defendants to maintain a safe distance between them. I have to smile. I've seen less security for heavy grievous bodily harm cases bordering on attempted murder. Someone on high obviously thinks it would be a political hot potato if anything kicks off in this case, and has passed the message down the line to the officers on duty. I find myself wondering whether the decision to place red tie on the left and blue tie on the right was conscious or subconscious. Either way, it is a pleasing touch.

'Are you Liam Voss?'

'I am,' the defendant on the left with the red tie replies. He is in his mid-twenties, and has an angry shock of black hair and dark, brooding eyes. He gives the impression that he might be more at home in a black leather jacket and jeans.

'Are you Richard William Mayfield?'

'I am.' This time it is the turn of the defendant on the right with the blue tie. Mayfield is in his fifties, with a well-groomed appearance, dark hair turning to grey immaculately combed back, silver cufflinks protruding beneath the sleeves of his jacket. A greater contrast to Voss could hardly be imagined.

'May it please your Honour,' Roderick Lofthouse begins, 'I appear to prosecute in this matter. My learned friend Miss Writtle appears for Mr Voss, and my learned friend Mr Blanquette for Mr Mayfield.'

I am pleased to see all three. I am very glad to have counsel I know. Even if he no longer has quite the same detailed grasp of his cases as he did when younger, Roderick still has a formidable instinct for finding the jugular vein, and even more importantly, with his seniority, he undoubtedly has the gravitas for the big occasion. As for the defence, no casting director in Hollywood could have improved on it. Cathy Writtle is a human attack drone, perfect to represent red-tie Voss in a cut-throat ABH case. Julian Blanquette is the perfect foil for Cathy, dapper and understated, relying on subterfuge and innuendo where Cathy relies on aggression. It should be a good show.

The public gallery and press seats are filling up nicely now. The seats we call the press seats, by the way, are simply seats in the public gallery. A press presence is something of a rarity at Bermondsey, so we don't normally make the distinction, and any passing reporter who happens to grace the court has a free choice of seat. But today, Carol has placed a few sheets of paper bearing the legend 'reserved for press' on the front row of the public gallery in honour of the occasion.

'Your Honour,' Roderick continues, 'my learned friends have indicated that there is a point of law which your Honour should decide before the jury is sworn. It is simply whether there is any basis for the prosecution's allegation of racial aggravation. Does your Honour have the indictment?'

I certainly do have the indictment, and I have spent some considerable time meditating on it in my chambers during the past week. Though not intended as such, the indictment is a mantrap waiting to clasp its jaws over a helpless judicial limb and drag an unwary judge into the nightmarish world of the Top Judge. The legal argument the defence want me to decide is the spring which will activate the trap's fiendish mechanism, and Roderick is about to wind it up.

'Your Honour,' he begins, 'the indictment contains two counts, which are identical: except for the fact that in count one Mr Voss is charged as the defendant and Mr Mayfield is alleged to be the victim; whereas in count two, Mr Mayfield is charged and Mr Voss is alleged to be the victim. The Crown's case is that both defendants were guilty of simultaneous, unprovoked attacks on each other, and are both guilty of assault accordingly. I understand that the defence in the case of each defendant will be one of self-defence. The issue for the jury will be: who was the aggressor and who struck the first blow?

'If I may read the particulars of count one by way of illustration, it is alleged that on or about the ninth day of May of this year: "*Liam Voss assaulted Richard William Mayfield, thereby causing him actual bodily harm, and at the time of doing so, or immediately before or after doing so, demonstrated towards Richard William Mayfield hostility based on his membership (or presumed membership) of a racial or religious group, namely the British upper class.*"

'Your Honour, the events in question began on the late evening of the eighth of May, which as I am sure your Honour will recall, was polling day. Both defendants were candidates in the general election in the constituency of Clavering West with Baddiefield, which, in case your Honour is not familiar with the area…'

'Not at all, I'm afraid,' I admit.

'Neither was I, your Honour, until I looked at a map in the course of preparing the case. But it appears that it is a small, mainly rural constituency in Warwickshire, no great distance from Coventry. Because of the small size of the Clavering West constituency, the count did not take long, and the result of the election was announced between twelve-thirty and one o'clock on the morning of the ninth. I should perhaps add that the constituency of Clavering West with Baddiefield has traditionally been a marginal one. The retiring MP, Mr Marcus Stoddie, had held it for the Conservatives at the previous two elections, but with a very small majority. It was widely believed that his successor, the defendant Mr Mayfield, might have difficulty in holding on to it, and that the defendant Mr Voss, the Labour candidate, had a good chance of winning it.

'The events which led to this indictment are shown with admirable clarity on the DVD which we will show to the jury, and it may be convenient if I show it to your Honour now.'

'Ah,' I say, 'so it was caught on CCTV?'

Roderick beams. 'Oh, no, far better than that, your Honour. It was captured by a visiting camera crew from the BBC, which was filming the announcement of the result for the live coverage of the election on BBC One.'

This exchange between Roderick and myself, with its insinuation of surprise and revelation is, of course, completely *faux*. There is no one in Great Britain who has been awake and paying attention for the last few weeks who has not seen this piece of film over and over again. It was an instant hit. The BBC had intended it solely as part of its election coverage, but the drama made it a news item in its own right, and of course, it went viral on the internet within minutes of being broadcast. Since then, it has been replayed endlessly on various TV channels, and has been the butt of jokes on every comedy, quiz, and talk show imaginable. This is one problem we are going to have with the jury panel shortly, when we try to find twelve jurors who can try this case with some pretence of neutrality. It is also the reason why the Midland Circuit got rid of the case to Bermondsey as soon as it decently could. There would be absolutely no chance of jurors within striking distance of Clavering West with Baddiefield doing, or being seen to do, justice to this case.

It is also the reason why the case has been fast-tracked. Mr Mayfield is anxious to take his seat in the House of Commons, and Mr Voss is anxious to start looking for a new constituency, and both are anxious to know what the future holds. The answer to these questions may be provided by the jury. Someone may have to stay after school if convicted on this indictment, and that would not look so good on future election leaflets.

Roderick picks up the remote and pushes the button. The large screens around the courtroom burst into life, as does the far smaller screen I have on my bench. The familiar logo of BBC One news appears, and we hear a male voice pontificating about exit polls. A female voice chimes in from somewhere off camera.

'I'm sorry to interrupt you, but we are getting reports that the Clavering West with Baddiefield constituency in Warwickshire is about to declare, and we are going there live now for the announcement. It is worth reminding you that Clavering West with Baddiefield is something of a bellwether constituency, a highly marginal Tory seat, and we may well learn a great deal about the way things are going when we find out whether or not the Tories' Richard Mayfield has managed to hold off a strong challenge from Labour's Liam Voss.'

The scene shifts from the studio to what looks like a rather run-down church hall. We see two rows of trestle tables, with folding chairs for the vote counters, occupying most of the floor space. Most of the counters seem to be still sitting around the tables. On the stage at the far end of the hall there is a small podium, and the Returning Officer, a short, officious-looking man in a dark grey pin-striped suit, a formal white shirt and a red tie, is taking his place in front of it. The candidates have positioned themselves around him, and one can clearly see the defendants, wearing their appropriately-coloured rosettes, one on either side of the Returning Officer. To Voss's left there is an earnest looking man who looks to be in his thirties, wearing a brown suit and a Liberal Democrat orange-yellow rosette. To Mayfield's right is an equally earnest young woman in a long green cotton dress, a whole armful of brightly-coloured bracelets and a huge Navajo silver necklace, whose rosette proclaims her to be the candidate of the Green Party. Behind them are one or two other people whose affiliation I can't quite place. The Returning Officer has the results in his hand, and is putting on his reading glasses. The hall, which until now has been resounding with nervous chatter, suddenly falls deathly quiet.

'I, *Matthew Charles Malone, being the Returning Officer for the Constituency of Clavering West with Baddiefield in this United Kingdom Parliamentary General Election, do hereby give notice that the number of votes recorded for each Candidate in the said election is as follows:*

Marie Cuthbertson, Green Party, 1546

Derek Hamilton, Liberal Democrat, 781

Richard William Mayfield, Conservative Party Candidate, 14896

Liam Voss, Labour Party Candidate, 14444

Celia Wingate, Monster Raving Loony Party, 42

Henry Yates, Warwickshire Independence Party, 11

'The number of ballot papers rejected was as follows: want of an official mark, none; voting for more candidates than voter was entitled to, 37; writing or mark by which voter could be identified, 3; being unmarked or wholly void for uncertainty, 72; total 112.

'And I declare that Richard William Mayfield is duly elected as the Member of Parliament for the Clavering West with Baddiefield Constituency'.

There is an outbreak of reasonably good-natured applause, cheering, and booing from those assembled. Richard Mayfield raises a victorious arm towards the heavens, then turns to shake the hands of the other candidates, all of whom, with the notable exception of Liam Voss, take his hand with as much goodwill as they can muster. Voss remains motionless, his arms folded across his chest. Mr Malone is giving those assembled further information about the size of the eligible electorate and the percentage turn-out in the constituency. The BBC's female voice-over is to be heard making the rather superfluous observation that the Conservatives have held the seat, albeit with a small majority, and is preparing to hand us back to the pundits in the studio.

But for whatever reason, her producer has decided that we shall linger in the church hall in Clavering West with Baddiefield long enough to hear the beginning of Richard Mayfield's victory speech. It proves to be a historic decision, and thankfully there is a transcript to enable us to follow what happens in the subsequent confusion. After thanking his agent and his tireless party workers, Mayfield is gearing up to emphasise that he intends to represent all the electors of Clavering West with Baddiefield, regardless of party affiliation, and to work with his colleagues in government for the good of the country in general and his constituency in particular, when he is rudely interrupted by a loud bellow.

'This must be stopped. There has been a fraud. I demand a recount!'

The interruption emanates from Liam Voss. There is no doubt about that. At first, Mayfield ignores him and proceeds to describe some of the many improvements in their lives the voters may expect as a result of his election. But Voss is not to be silenced. The following is recorded in the transcript.

> Voss: *'This is ridiculous. There has been a fraud. Recount, recount, recount!'*
>
> Mayfield: *'Oh, for goodness sake, shut up! The voters don't want you; they have made it clear that they want me. Just let it go. They don't want sour grapes. They've heard enough of you during the past few weeks as it is.'*
>
> Voss: *'It's not sour grapes. There has been a fraud. It's obvious. I mean, how could they prefer a prat like you, for God's sake? The numbers are too close to call. I demand a recount!'*
>
> Mayfield: *'You were offered a recount. It's too late now. The result has been declared.'*

Malone: 'That's correct, Mr Voss. You were offered a recount and your agent turned it down. I'm afraid it's too late to change anything now. In any case, I supervised the count personally, and I can assure you that there is no question of any error.'

Voss: 'My agent is an idiot. There is no way the voters preferred this toffee-nosed git to me. I have evidence of a fraud. I demand a thorough investigation.'

Malone: 'Now, just a minute…'

Mayfield: 'What did you call me, Voss?'

Voss: 'I called you a toffee-nosed git. What are you going to do about it?'

Malone: 'Gentlemen, please. I must ask you to remember where you are…'

Mayfield: 'How dare you talk to me like that. I will thank you to remember that I am now your Member of Parliament.'

Voss: 'You toffee-nosed, upper class git!'

Mayfield: 'You moronic, working class lout!'

The only contribution the transcript can make after this point, until the scene ends with the swift arrival of the police, is that there was 'general confusion, with various blows being exchanged' – a description which is accurate as far as it goes, but not particularly helpful to anyone trying to reconstruct the events in an orderly sequence. What is plain to see is that Voss and Mayfield lunge at each other at virtually the same moment. Both punches seem to connect. They spring at each other and lock arms, and before you know it they have wrestled each other to the ground, and have rolled together off the stage on to the floor of the hall some three feet below, where they land with a jarring thud. Even then, they continue wrestling, trading blows and insults. Various supporters wade in at this point, and you have to think that a wholesale riot is about to ensue. But mercifully, the supporters behave rather more sensibly than their candidates, doing their best to prise them apart, while

Malone helplessly calls for order from the podium. Not long after that, the police arrive and the footage ends.

The result of the fracas, as I know from the file, is that the newly elected Member of Parliament for Clavering West with Baddiefield is carted off to the local A and E, where he is treated for numerous cuts and bruises and a fractured right wrist. His unsuccessful challenger is treated at the same facility, albeit at a safe distance, for numerous cuts and bruises and two broken ribs. We are now definitely in ABH territory. In law, actual bodily harm means any bodily injury, however slight. On being released from hospital in the early hours of the following morning with analgesics and head injury advice, both are bailed to attend the police station a few days later for interview.

Needless to say, the whole scene has its funny side, and during the many showings it has had, it has spawned a new genre of 'Clavering West jokes', such as: the count featured a big swing towards Labour, followed immediately by a big swing towards the Tories. Those of us who are called on to deal with the legal aftermath of the Clavering West count must ignore such trivia and concentrate on the cold, hard facts, which of course we will make every effort to do.

'I am not sure I can add very much to that,' Roderick says, pausing the DVD. 'It may be best if I defer to my learned friends for the defence at this point, and your Honour can hear me in reply after hearing from them.'

Cathy Writtle has been elected to present the point of law on behalf of the defence.

'Your Honour, this is a joint submission on behalf of both defendants. My learned friend Mr Blanquette is content for me to begin,' she says. 'He will add anything he considers necessary on behalf of his client after I have addressed your Honour on behalf of Mr Voss.'

'Yes, Miss Writtle,' I reply. I have a feeling that this is the only thing in the case about which the two defendants will have any measure of agreement at all.

'Your Honour, the prosecution say it is a racial or religious aggravation for Mr Voss to call Mr Mayfield an "upper class git"; and for Mr Mayfield to call Mr Voss a "working class lout". It is our submission that a British class, whether upper, middle, or working, does not constitute a racial or religious group. The prosecution must amend the indictment to delete the element of racial or religious aggravation, and proceed on the basis of simple ABH without any aggravation.'

She looks towards Roderick.

'For clarification, may we take it that the Crown say this is a case of racial rather than religious aggravation? I assume that not even the CPS contends that the British upper class is a branch of the Church of England.'

Roderick rises slowly to his feet with a smile.

'Your Honour, I have heard the Church of England described as the Conservative Party at prayer, so I am not sure it is beyond argument, but I am content to rest my case solely on the basis of racial aggravation.'

'I am much obliged to my learned friend,' Cathy replies without conceding even the ghost of a smile, although personally, I rather enjoyed Roderick's response. 'Racial aggravation is defined by section 28 of the Crime and Disorder Act 1998. It defines a racial group as: *a group of persons defined by reference to race, colour, nationality (including citizenship) or ethnic or national origins*". By no stretch of the imagination is the upper or working class a racial group as defined by the section.'

'Why do you say that?' I ask. 'After all, as much as we might prefer to think we have put all that behind us in this day and age, people are born into one class or another, aren't they?'

'Your Honour, class is in the mind of the beholder,' Cathy insists. 'It is not a legally recognised category. We recognise racial and ethnic groups as part of the British community; we define them, we keep statistics on them. But there is no legal definition of upper class, middle class, or working class. Those are simply terms used by certain people who, for one reason or another, would like to see themselves as being socially different from others, and create that image of themselves in their mind.'

'But if people think of class as belonging to separate groups,' I reply, 'might it not be argued that groups based on class are just as deserving of legal protection as other groups in society, and that Parliament must be taken to have extended that protection to them?'

'That is not what Parliament has done, your Honour. Parliament has accorded protection to people who are readily recognisable as members of racial groups based on race, colour, ethnicity or nationality. If someone demonstrates hostility to a member of that kind of group, it is easy for a court to decide whether he knew, or must have presumed, that the other person belonged to that group. It's usually obvious. But you can't know, or presume, someone to be upper class or working class by looking at them. Applied to members of a political party, it is pure speculation, a cliché at best.'

Cathy and I continue in this vein for some time. I am not really sure how far we are getting in probing the tricky question of what, if anything, Parliament intended to do about class when enacting section 28 of the Crime and Disorder 1998, but both of us are keenly aware of the growing number of reporters in the courtroom taking copious notes. The Top Judge menace is not far from my mind. Julian Blanquette has nothing much to add on behalf of Richard Mayfield. Finally, I turn to Roderick.

'Miss Writtle has a point, doesn't she?' I ask him. 'One can be identified quite easily as belonging to a group identified by colour or national origin or ethnicity, and so on, but how can you say that someone belongs to the upper or working class when there is no way to tell from his appearance, and there is no legal definition of what upper class or working class means?'

'That's where the word "presumed" comes in, your Honour,' Roderick replies. 'Actually, I agree with my learned friend Miss Writtle about one thing. It is simply a cliché to call someone an upper class git just because he is a member of the Conservative Party; just as it is to call someone a working class moron just because he belongs to the Labour Party. Of course it is. But that is exactly what the legislation is about. Parliament intended to criminalise demeaning language, even if the defendant is mistaken about the actual group to which the victim belongs, as long as it is proved that the defendant presumed the victim to belong to that group.'

'But today, people are free to become socially mobile, aren't they? You've had your champagne socialists joining New Labour, and you've had your East End barrow boys-made-good joining the Tories.'

'Yes, your Honour. You also have high-born individuals like Tony Benn becoming socialists. But that doesn't mean that the old stereotypes don't still exist.'

'No. But can't people change class nowadays, if they make enough money, for example? And what about people from ordinary backgrounds who are elevated to the House of Lords?'

Roderick has to think about that one.

'Your Honour, I am not sure that being socially mobile is the same thing as changing class. In America, I suspect it probably is. Of course, the Americans pretend that they don't have a class structure, although they obviously do, and it is obviously very much based on money, power, influence and the like. But not in this country. Money has never been a portal into the upper class, particularly if earned in trade. Neither has marriage, or even a life peerage. There are some echelons of our society, your Honour, into which one has to be born.'

After further exchanges, I decide to take some time to consider the matter. By now one thing has become abundantly clear. The question of law I have been asked to decide is the Top Judge's hospital pass. I need to think about it, and I need to get some advice, before I open my mouth. I adjourn until two o'clock.

And so to lunch, an oasis of calm in a desert of chaos.

'Who is the Conservative candidate?' Hubert asks after I have tried to explain the problem to my assembled colleagues.

'What has that got to do with it?' I ask.

'Well, if it's anyone I know, I can tell you immediately whether he's upper class or not.'

'That's hardly the point, Hubert,' I reply. 'But if you must know, his name is Richard William Mayfield.'

Hubert looks up from his dish of the day – moussaka according to the weekly menu – and appears to be searching through his memory banks.

'Mayfield… Mayfield… no, doesn't ring a bell. I am fairly sure he's not a member of the Garrick. I would remember if he was. Some new chap, probably – the Edward Heath wing of the party, by the sound of him.'

'Thank you, Hubert,' I reply.

'But in any case, it must have been the other chap's fault, mustn't it?' he says.

'Excuse me? What?'

'The other chap, left-winger, Labour party fellow. It was obviously his fault. Mayfield was doing no more than defending himself.'

'How do you know that?' I ask. 'You haven't even seen the TV footage.'

'Stands to reason,' Hubert replies. 'No Conservative is going to pick a fight with another candidate at the count, especially with a socialist. No, it's obvious. The Labour fellow must have started it. That's how they work. Violence is a part of their political creed. You only have to read Marx.'

Mercifully, Legless weighs in before this exchange can go any further.

'The prosecution's argument is a complete load of cobblers, Charlie,' he insists. 'Cathy Writtle is exactly right. A person's class, assuming that means anything in law, doesn't make him a member of a racial group, not in any normal use of the language.'

'Yes, but we are not talking about normal use of the language, are we?' Marjorie points out. 'We are talking about Parliament's use of the language. That's the problem when you give something such a wide definition. You end up catching people in a net who were never meant to be caught. It wouldn't be the first time Parliament didn't think something through before rushing it on to the statute book.'

'Are you saying that a defendant can be convicted of a racially aggravated offence just for calling someone upper class?' I ask.

'I don't think that *should* be the law,' Marjorie replies, 'but the way the Act is written, it's definitely arguable.'

'It's all gone too far,' Hubert says.

'What has?' Legless asks.

'All this nonsense about racial aggravation. That's why children can't have the Robertson's Golly any more when their mothers buy marmalade, isn't it? We all had them as children, and it never did us any harm.'

'We can't have racial abuse, Hubert,' Marjorie replies. 'Parliament was right to do something about that.'

'I couldn't agree more,' Hubert says, 'if it *is* a case of racial abuse. But look at the kind of nonsense we have to deal with all the time. A group of lads go out on Saturday night, and they are all getting on perfectly well. But at the end of the night, they've all had a few drinks, and there's a bit of an argument over a girl or over the football, and someone calls someone else a "white bastard" or a "black bastard". Usually, nothing comes of it. It's just a bit of banter. If blows are exchanged, it's because the chap doesn't like being called a bastard, not because he's been called white or black, which is no more than a statement of the obvious. And in the old days, if anyone got arrested, the police would keep him in the cells until Monday morning and the magistrates would deal with him. Now, it has to come up to us because it's racially aggravated and we have to get a jury to deal with it. And Charlie's case is just another example. Stuff and nonsense. It's all gone too far.'

'That's all very interesting, Hubert,' I say, 'but it doesn't help me very much. I've got the world's press in court, listening to the case and hanging on my every word. Which way should I go on this? The way it looks to me, I'm damned if I do, and damned if I don't.'

'Absolutely,' Legless agrees. 'If you chuck out the racial aggravation, they will say you are soft on racially motivated crime. If you leave it to the jury, they will say you are pandering to political correctness and stifling freedom of expression.'

'So, what I should I do?'

'I have no idea,' Legless replies.

I turn to Marjorie. She shakes her head.

'It's a tricky one,' she says.

'Well, thank you both,' I reply.

'Don't do anything,' Hubert suggests.

'What?'

'Don't do anything,' he repeats, 'at least not for now.'

'But…'

'Charlie,' he continues, 'it's not necessary to decide it now, is it? Let it go until the end of the prosecution's case. That's when it should be decided, in any case. That will give you some time to think. You can always withdraw the racial aggravation from the jury at that stage.'

I find myself nodding in agreement.

'That's not a bad idea,' I reply.

'In addition,' Hubert continues, 'if you wait, there's every chance that you might get some movement during the trial.'

'Movement?'

'Yes. One assumes that both these chaps want to live to fight another day.'

'I'm not sure…'

'I don't mean literally fighting, Charlie,' Hubert points out. 'I mean fighting an election next time round. They may be a bit worried about what their party's head office thinks about it all. As the trial goes on, it will probably occur to them that it's not doing them any good to have their antics paraded before a jury under the gaze of the press. I wouldn't be surprised if someone comes forward with a creative solution. In which case, you are off the hook. Worst comes to worst, you have a day or two to think about the law. But I still think it was all the Labour fellow's fault.'

There are times when Hubert produces some genuine wisdom. I congratulate him on it. He looks pleased, but feigns an offhand wave of the hand.

'Think nothing of it, Charlie. Just a matter of having cantered round the paddock a few times.'

'Talking of which,' Marjorie says, 'and forgive the horrible segue, but I have a case about a racehorse and I need some advice about it. The defendant is a woman in her seventies. She's called Gertie.'

We all look at her.

'What is she charged with?' Legless asks.

'Fraud,' Marjorie replies. 'Her husband Jimmy trained racehorses in stables at Newmarket. She acted as secretary for the stables.'

'Newmarket?' I say. 'Is this another example of Bermondsey attracting work from afar? We must be establishing a bit of a reputation.'

'Either that, or we are a convenient place to dump cases no one wants,' Marjorie smiles. 'Anyway, they had a horse called

Major Stanley, two-year-old, very promising, already attracting serious attention. Sadly, he broke a leg in training one morning and they had to put him down. Nobody's fault, just one of those things. In fact, it wasn't even obvious at the time. He pulled up lame, but it wasn't until they got him back to the stable that they realised how bad it was. Unfortunately, there had been an administrative error. Jimmy hadn't renewed the owner's insurance policy and Major Stanley wasn't covered – or at least, not for anything like what he was worth.'

'Oh, dear,' Legless says.

'Yes. Unfortunately, they tried to solve the problem by getting a binder later that same morning without disclosing what had happened, and only reported the death two days later. The only other people involved were the horse's work rider, who was riding him when he fell, and the vet who issued the death certificate. The police don't think the work rider was in on the fraud, and he is going to be called as a prosecution witness. The vet, on the other hand, almost certainly was in on it. Not many insurance companies cover racehorses, and they are extremely vigilant, especially when a horse dies within a short time of being insured. They would have insisted on a certificate from the vet, so the prosecution say it couldn't have been done without his connivance. But the vet seems to have gone walkabout a year or two ago, and nobody knows where he is. Unfortunately, while Jimmy dealt with the insurance policy, Gertie was the one who called to report the death.'

'Sounds like fraud to me,' Legless says.

'Well, what about the husband, Jimmy?' Hubert asks. 'Hasn't he been charged?'

'Deceased,' Marjorie replies. 'This all happened almost ten years ago, and it only came to light because the insurance company ceased trading and they brought in auditors to pore through the books from the dawn of time. By that time, Jimmy had died.'

'What on earth is her defence?' I ask.

Marjorie shrugs. 'In interview she told the police that she didn't understand what was going on. She just kept the books and did what her husband told her to do, she didn't really know what was going on, and there was no dishonesty.'

The reaction around the room does not bode well for this line of defence.

'I know, I know,' Marjorie says. 'I did try to nudge her and her counsel towards a plea, but she wouldn't budge. I am sure she is afraid I will send her inside, and then of course there will be confiscation proceedings. She will lose everything. I would like to give her a suspended sentence. Do you think I can?'

'What was the loss to the insurance company?' I ask.

'A little over a quarter of a million.'

We are all silent for some time. Legless shakes his head.

'I think you could,' I say. 'Just. She is unlucky that she is the only one left to prosecute. Given her age, and I assume she is of previous good character?'

'Yes.'

'Then, I would say you could suspend it,' I say, looking for support. 'Just.'

'It ought to be about two years,' Hubert says, 'straight inside. You can't have people doing that kind of thing when it affects racing. People invest a lot of money in good horses. I know several chaps at the Garrick who have a share in a racehorse. There's a lot of money at stake. You might knock a bit off for her age, bring it down to eighteen months, perhaps.'

Marjorie sighs in frustration.

'Give her a suspended, Marjorie,' Legless says. 'You probably shouldn't. But I suspect that no one except Hubert will criticise you.'

* * *

Monday afternoon

The lunchtime discussion has clarified the options for me. Hubert is right. I can buy myself some time, and perhaps avoid making a decision at all. If that doesn't work, of course, I will eventually have to decide what to do, and I am being pulled in two directions.

Part of me is leaning towards Cathy Writtle's side, because I know exactly what has happened here. The investigating police officers would have charged both men with ABH in the interests of fair play, and bunged it up to the CPS to decide what to do next. Some bright spark in the CPS has seen the political dimension – two public figures misbehaving so spectacularly in public, calls for strong action. Not to mention a bit of positive publicity for the CPS. It's a bit like the parliamentary expenses scandals, in a way. It becomes more serious because it is Members of Parliament fiddling the books rather than your average member of the public. They ought to know better. They must be made an example of. The same bright spark has found just the way to do that.

Once he or she committed the words 'racial aggravation' to paper, the fate of Richard Mayfield and Liam Voss was sealed. They are words which, once written down, cannot be unwritten. In the world of the CPS, if you suggest that a possible case of racial aggravation, however tenuous and improbable, might be ignored for reasons as politically unacceptable as common sense, you might as well start thinking about your next career move. You have committed one of the few unpardonable sins. Once the bright spark proposed an indictment for racially aggravated ABH, the case moved past the point of no return. Part of me wants to stand up for common sense.

But another part of me is seeing the Top Judge headline: 'Race laws don't apply to MPs – Top Judge'. And it won't only be the tabloids. I could write the leader in the *Guardian* myself.

When court assembles, I thank counsel profusely for their clear and well-presented submissions on a most difficult and troubling point of law, and announce that, in my view, the proper time to deal with the matter is not now, but at the close of the prosecution's case. No one seems unduly distressed by this, so I immediately ask for the jury panel to be brought down to court.

In this country, there is usually nothing particularly complicated about selecting a jury. The jury manager typically sends us a panel of fourteen to sixteen, from which we select twelve at random. Thank God we don't do what they do in America, where they cross-examine the prospective jurors for any hint of possible bias, and where it sometimes takes days or even weeks to put a jury in place. We do ask a few questions, to weed out any jurors who may happen to know someone involved in the case, and sometimes we mention a venue such as a pub, just in case any of the panel may be a regular there. Subject to that, we take the first twelve, their names drawn by Carol after shuffling the name cards. But this case is a bit more tricky than usual.

Hubert is not the only one who might be inclined to make assumptions about who was to blame based on tribal loyalty, and justice has to be seen to be done. We must do our best to ensure that we have a fair-minded, impartial jury. The problem is that we can't take the obvious step of asking them how they voted. It would be against the law. Everyone is entitled to keep their vote a secret; and if we ask them whether they support, or are members of, any given political party, we are effectively violating that rule. So some time ago, at a trial readiness hearing, counsel and I came up with the following solution.

This morning, when they reported for jury service, each juror was given a form to fill in. The form gives a short statement of the facts of the case, and asks them to answer five questions. The first is whether they have been following the story of the

Clavering West with Baddiefield election in the press, on TV shows, or on the internet.

The next is whether they have seen the TV footage of the fight in the church hall.

The next is whether they strongly support, or are members of a political party. In bold, capital letters, underlined, the juror is instructed to answer this question simply yes or no, without naming the party.

The next is whether they voted in the recent election. A similarly emphasised instruction directs them to answer simply yes or no, and not to say for whom their vote was cast.

The final question, the crucial one, is whether they can put aside any sympathies or prejudices they may have and decide the case solely on the basis of the evidence, which is what they will have to promise if they become members of the jury. We have not, of course, asked them whether they regard themselves as upper, middle or working class, though you can almost make an argument for asking that question in the circumstances – which is a further indication, it seems to me, of how out of hand this case has been allowed to get. While the panel makes its way down from the jury assembly room to court, counsel and I read through the results. It seems promising.

There is always one, of course. One juror cannot resist telling us that he has served as secretary of his local Conservative party. Another has served as a local councillor, but mercifully does not disclose her party affiliation. Everyone is fully aware of the story, and only one claims never to have seen the TV footage. Everyone thinks they can be fair and impartial and put everything aside except the evidence. It is not going to get any better than this, and fortunately the prospect of a Bermondsey juror knowing anyone involved in a case from the Midlands is fairly remote. It does not take us long to empanel the jury: six men, six women, one of the men Sikh, one of the women Muslim, two other men sounding Eastern European but with perfect English; altogether a rather typical Bermondsey jury. I give them the standard warnings about not discussing the case with anyone else, and staying away from the inevitable press and TV news coverage, and away we go.

Roderick opens the case briefly, provides the jury with copies of the indictment, takes them through it, and shows them the TV footage. There are a few sniggers as they watch, only to be expected. He then announces that he will call his first witness, the Returning Officer, Matthew Malone. Mr Malone appears to be wearing the same dark suit and red tie he was wearing at the count.

'Mr Malone,' Roderick begins, 'the jury may not be familiar with what it is a returning officer does. Can you briefly describe for us what your duties are?'

'I can indeed,' Malone replies, rather self-importantly. 'As returning officer, I am wholly responsible for the conduct of the election in the constituency. On polling day itself, I am responsible for making sure that the polling stations are properly manned, and are open for the prescribed periods of time, and that voting is conducted in an orderly manner. I am also responsible for ensuring that all the ballots are brought safely to the hall to be counted, that the count is conducted properly, and that all the postal ballots are mixed in with the other ballots to be counted. If there are disputed ballots which may have to be discounted, I must discuss them with the candidates' agents and then make a decision.'

'You mean, if a ballot is unclear?'

'Yes, or if someone votes for two candidates, or signs the ballot and discloses his identity.'

'And I think there were some examples of such ballots in this election?'

'Yes, there were one hundred and twelve in all, if I remember rightly. Then, once the count is complete, if the result is close, I ask the candidates whether anyone wants a recount, and if so, a recount is conducted. Finally, I must announce the result. I do this verbally at the end of the count, and I must then prepare a written report. In the following few days, there are various administrative duties, such as returning the deposits to all the candidates who received at least five per cent of the vote.'

Roderick nods and consults his notes.

'I want to return to the question of recounts for a moment,' he says. 'This was a close election, wasn't it?'

'Relatively close; the Conservative majority over Labour was four hundred and fifty-two.'

'In those circumstances, should a recount take place?'

'Not unless one of the candidates, or his agent, requests one.'

'And how do you manage that?'

'When the votes have been counted, and all the bundles of ballots have been checked, we have what we call the provisional result, which is the final count unless anybody objects. I notify the candidates and their agents of the provisional result, and give them time to consider. If anyone asks for a recount, we conduct a recount as quickly as possible. If no one requests a recount, the provisional result becomes the final result, and I declare it.'

'Did you follow that procedure in this instance?'

'I did.'

'Did anyone ask for a recount?'

'No. The only person who could really have asked for a recount was Mr Voss's agent, Sam Friend. His candidate was the only one who could have been affected. But Sam didn't ask.'

'In the TV footage the jury have seen, Mr Voss is heard to describe Mr Friend as an "idiot" for not demanding a recount. Do you agree with Mr Voss?'

'No, not at all. Sam has been the Labour agent for years, and he knows that Clavering West is a marginal constituency. The Clavering part of the constituency is mainly rural, which tends to vote Conservative, but there is a sizeable urban area around Baddiefield, which tends to go for Labour. The margin of victory has often been a matter of a few hundred votes, usually in favour of the Tories, but not always. In 1992, it went Labour with a majority of less than a hundred. In some other constituencies, a majority of four hundred and fifty-two might well trigger a recount, but not in Clavering West with Baddiefield.'

'Are you aware of any evidence which suggests that there was any fraud involved in the election?'

Mr Malone takes a deep breath and exhales slowly.

'I was not aware of any such evidence at the time when the result was declared. I and my staff are always on the lookout for any irregularities. We look carefully at the postal ballots, and we keep a check on all the polling stations as voting proceeds. Nothing untoward was brought to my attention. If anything like that had been reported, I would have delayed the declaration and investigated the matter.'

'Are you aware of any fraud, as you stand here today?'

'Fraud? No,' Malone replies. 'But there was a suspicious circumstance, which was brought to my attention later in the evening, after Mr Mayfield and Mr Voss had been taken to hospital.'

'Please tell the jury what that circumstance was.'

'Two boxes containing ballots were found in a storage room at one of the polling stations. One of Mr Voss's supporters, who had considerable experience in that part of the constituency, thought the number of boxes taken to the count was too low and raised the alarm. I was told later that he was signalling to Mr Voss while I was declaring the result. Unfortunately, neither Liam nor Sam knew anything about it until it was too late.'

'Did you cause an investigation to be made?'

'I did. I'm afraid the results were inconclusive. We are not able to determine with any certainty how it happened. There were reports of Conservative supporters hanging around outside the polling station when they shouldn't have been, while the boxes were being removed, but there was no evidence of actual wrongdoing. It was a bit sensitive, because the polling station was in a district which traditionally leans towards Labour.'

'I see. Were the votes in those two boxes counted?'

'Yes, of course. Thankfully, they did not alter the outcome of the election. It turned out that there had been something of a swing back to the Conservatives in that district, so their majority remained more or less the same.'

'Thank you, Mr Malone. Finally, did you see how the altercation between Mr Voss and Mr Mayfield started?'

'Not really. To be honest, you have a better view from the TV footage than I had. I had one standing each side of me. Just after I declared, I remember the various candidates shaking hands, then I remember Richard beginning his speech, and some words were exchanged, and suddenly there was a flurry of arms, and the next thing I knew, they had rolled off the stage. As to who moved first, I couldn't say.'

'Too close to call?' Roderick smiles.

'Exactly,' Malone replies. 'We would definitely need a recount on that.'

'How long have you served as a returning officer?'

'Oh, it's been more than twenty years now. I've returned for local and national elections, everything.'

'Have you ever seen anything like this before?'

'No. I've seen groups of supporters have a go at each other once in a while, which usually doesn't last long because the police are never far away. You will occasionally get two candidates exchanging a few words, but I've never seen it go further than that – not between candidates. It was quite a shock, I don't mind telling you.'

'I'm sure it must have been,' Roderick says. 'Please wait there, Mr Malone. There may be some further questions.'

'Mr Malone,' Cathy begins, 'may I ask you to look at part of the TV footage with me?'

The DVD has been paused at the critical moment, just after Mayfield has called Voss a 'working class lout'. I suspect the jury is going to see the record of these few seconds quite a lot as the trial proceeds. Cathy rewinds, plays the scene to the same point, and stops.

'Now, Mr Malone, you are standing behind the podium and slightly to the right, as seen from the body of the hall, when the first punches are thrown, yes?'

'Yes.'

'The first punches are thrown just in front of you, over the top of the podium?'

'That's correct.'

'And Mr Mayfield turns to his left, doesn't he, turns his whole body towards Mr Voss?'

'Yes.'

'And brings his right arm around to punch at Mr Voss with his right hand?'

'So it appears, yes.'

'And he connects before Mr Voss, doesn't he?'

'I couldn't say who struck or landed first. It all happened so fast.'

'But looking at the TV footage now, would you not agree that Mr Mayfield struck and landed first?'

'To my mind they seem to strike at the same time.'

'Would you like to see it again?'

'Not really. I've seen it lots of times, and it doesn't improve my memory of the events.'

'Mr Malone, Mr Voss made a clear suggestion that some fraud had occurred, didn't he?'

'I don't know about clear. He did say there must have been fraud, but he didn't say what he was referring to.'

'He asked for a recount, didn't he?'

'He did, yes.'

'On the ground of fraud?'

'Partly on the ground of fraud. He also said that the voters of Clavering West with Baddiefield couldn't possibly have preferred a toffee-nosed git like Richard to his good self.'

General laughter, including from the jury. Cathy walked into that one. She joins in the laughter, taking it with good grace.

'It's normal banter,' Malone adds, rather sheepishly.

'But you wouldn't agree to a recount, would you?'

'I have no power to conduct a recount once the result has been declared,' Malone replies. 'Once the result is declared, it can be set aside only by an election court, and even then, only in the most exceptional circumstances. If Liam or Sam had come to me with any concerns before I declared the result, I would have looked into it.'

'Lastly, as we have all heard, Mr Voss called Mr Mayfield a "toffee-nosed, upper class git". Did you understand any of those words to be a racial slur of any kind?'

'No, of course not,' Malone replies. 'You hear that kind of thing all the time between candidates and their supporters – well, except for the Green Party, of course. It's just a bit of banter. Usually people have a laugh about it, but that night, for some reason, it got out of hand. But it's got nothing to do with race, if you ask me.'

Cathy nods.

'Yes. Thank you, Mr Malone.'

She resumes her seat and Julian springs lightly to his feet.

'Mr Malone, would you say the same about Mr Mayfield calling Mr Voss a "moronic working class lout"?'

'I would.'

'Thank you. Did you see Mr Mayfield offer to shake hands with Mr Voss immediately after the declaration?'

'Yes, I did.'

'What was Mr Voss's response to the offer?'

'He refused to shake hands with Mr Mayfield, and folded his arms across his chest.'

'Yes. Was Mr Voss the only candidate to make any complaint about the count?'

'Yes, he was.'

'And, as you have said, you have a considerable responsibility as returning officer for the proper conduct of the election. How seriously did you take that responsibility?'

'I took it with the utmost seriousness.'

'Thank you, Mr Malone. I imagine that if I put to you that Mr Voss was the one who struck first, you would give me the same answer as you gave to my learned friend. You would say that you really didn't see, and the footage has not assisted you in remembering. Is that right?'

'It is,' Malone replies.

'In that case, I won't take up your time unnecessarily,' Julian says with a smile, resuming his seat.

On that note, we adjourn for the day. The case will not proceed any further this afternoon because I have to sentence two elderly gentlemen who were caught operating a small-time cannabis factory in a modest house not all that far from the court. The police found thirty-five mature female plants under cultivation, with high intensity lights, watering system, extractor fans, and all mod cons, plus a number of wraps, digital scales and plastic bags – the drug dealer's tool kit – plus about five hundred pounds in cash. For personal use, they explained to the police, medicinal, since both of them have arthritis and God knows what other ailments of approaching old age and they can't seem to persuade the NHS to give them a serious remedy. And, yes, perhaps when friends come round they might offer them a smoke – in much the same way as one might offer a guest a glass of wine, as one defendant told the police in interview – but they don't sell the stuff. The only money changing hands would be a voluntary contribution to expenses.

Complete nonsense, obviously, but all the same I dislike these cannabis cases. What a bloody waste of time – our time, the police's time, everybody's time. It is legal in so many places now, especially for medicinal purposes, that as a judge I'm buggered if I'm going to send anyone to prison if there's any way to avoid it. If I can give a defendant a discharge or a community order – and I almost always can – then that's what I am going to do. The Reverend Mrs Walden is in favour of legalising cannabis completely, so much so that the other day she actually took a few like-minded parishioners to their first 4/20 rally. Her bishop didn't bat an eyelid. The Reverend Mrs Walden thinks it's only because people like Mayfield and Voss don't have the courage to stand up to the puritans in their parties and act on the evidence of their own scientific advisers that we have this problem. I feel myself agreeing with her more and more. These gentlemen are of previous good character except for a couple of cautions for simple possession, and they are not going anywhere near prison. I find myself resenting making the inevitable order for forfeiture and destruction of the plants and growing equipment.

* * *

Monday evening

I hurry home, and I am in good time to settle myself down in front of the TV with a bottle of Old Speckled Hen for the start of the BBC news. The Reverend Mrs Walden has set the ITV news to record, and joins me with her glass of amontillado. The news begins with stories from the Middle East and one about the economy. Well, that's fair enough, I think. I can't expect top billing. There are other important things going on in the world. But when we get to a story devoted to the question of whether badgers constitute a serious danger to other wildlife in Wiltshire, I find myself getting anxious. Surely one of the great political stories of the day should take precedence over a few predatory badgers in Wiltshire? Where is the BBC's sense of priorities? What can the producer be thinking about? And then the unthinkable – what if they don't think it's newsworthy at all? Absurd, I tell myself. After all, I didn't imagine the TV van outside court. And then, finally, my patience is rewarded.

'The trial began today of two candidates in the recent election in the Warwickshire constituency of Clavering West with Baddiefield. Conservative, Richard Mayfield, fifty-six, who won the seat for the Tories and is now the Member of Parliament for the constituency, and Liam Voss, twenty-nine, the Labour candidate, traded insults and became involved in a fight at the count, just after the returning officer, Matthew Malone, had declared the result. Both are charged with racially aggravated assault, and both deny the charges. Roy Jones is at Bermondsey Crown Court.'

Inevitably, to my delight, the infamous BBC footage begins to roll, though without the sound. No doubt the BBC doesn't want to be caught broadcasting terrible racial epithets like 'upper class' and 'working class' before the watershed, when there may be children listening; regardless of the fact that adults and children alike must have heard them hundreds of times before the bright spark at the CPS educated us all about what they really mean. As it is finishing, Roy Jones is shown standing outside the main entrance to the court. The Reverend Mrs Walden beams and punches me gently two or three times in the arm. I feign indifference, but I know she is not fooled for a moment. Jones begins to speak.

'There was some laughter in court this afternoon, when this now celebrated footage shot by the BBC was played for the jury hearing the charges against the two warring politicians. The jury was told that neither defendant denies striking blows, but both claim to have been acting in self-defence. The returning officer, Matthew

Malone, gave evidence for the prosecution, and told the jury that
although Liam Voss demanded a recount just before the fight
began, he had no power to conduct a recount once the declaration
had been made. He added that Mr Voss's agent, Sam Field, had
declined the offer of a recount, suggesting that the majority of
four hundred and fifty-two votes, though thin, was not unusual
for this notoriously marginal Tory seat. Mr Malone declined to
say who had struck the first blow, saying that he had been in no
position to see. The trial continues tomorrow, and although there
was laughter in court today, it will not be a laughing matter for
either man, should they be convicted. Roy Jones, BBC News, at
Bermondsey Crown Court, London'.

We return to the news anchor and the subject turns to
football.

'Is that it?' I ask peevishly. 'They didn't even mention me.'

'I'm sure they will, later in the week,' the Reverend Mrs
Walden assures me.

Too bloody right, I concur silently, and it will probably
be the day I step into my Top Judge role. The Reverend Mrs
Walden prevails on me to take her to the Delights of the Raj for
a chicken Madras and a couple of Cobras by way of celebration.
When we return we watch the recording of the ITV news. They
don't mention me either.

* * *

Tuesday morning

'May it please your Honour,' Roderick begins, 'I call Derek
Hamilton.'

We are all beginning to feel we know the main characters
by now, so often have we seen them on the stage in the church
hall. Hamilton is no exception. We have seen him a number of
times, standing there rather helplessly and looking as bemused
as everyone else when the fisticuffs begin.

'Mr Hamilton, I believe you were the Liberal Democrat candidate in the Clavering West with Baddiefield constituency, is that right?' Roderick asks.

'Yes.'

'And we see you on the stage, standing to the left of Mr Voss and slightly behind him, during the declaration?'

'Yes, that's correct.'

'Did you hear the exchanges of words between Mr Mayfield and Mr Voss before any punches were thrown?'

'Yes, I did.'

'There is no dispute about it. Mr Voss called Mr Mayfield a "toffee-nosed, upper class git", and Mr Mayfield called Mr Voss a "moronic, working class lout." Is that what you heard?'

'Yes.'

'Did that lead you to look in their direction?'

'Yes, it did.'

'What was the next thing that happened?'

Hamilton shakes his head.

'It all happened so quickly. It was all a blur, really. But they started trying to punch each other, and it certainly seemed to me that they were both successful in landing blows on each other. I don't remember how many times, probably two or three each. Then they had their arms around each other, there was a bit of a wrestling match, and they fell over together just in front of the podium, but they lost their balance and rolled off the stage, still grappling and trying to punch each other.'

'I see,' Roderick says. 'What did you do at that point, Mr Hamilton?'

'Nothing, at least for several seconds. I was in shock, to be honest. I looked around at the other candidates, and they seemed to be having the same reaction. Eventually, after a few seconds, we all reacted at the same time and ran to the front of the stage to see what was happening.'

'And what *was* happening?'

'My Mayfield and Mr Voss were still wrestling on the floor, down below us. Then I saw a number of party supporters and vote counters wade in and try to get them off each other. It took a while. They both seemed determined to continue fighting. But eventually, the supporters pulled them apart and got them away from each other, and took them to opposite sides of the hall.'

'Then what happened?'

'I heard some of the supporters shouting that they had suffered some injuries and needed to go to A and E. Someone called an ambulance. But the police arrived first. They had officers stationed outside the hall, I believe, so they were on the scene almost straight away. They calmed things down. We waited for the ambulance. Mr Mayfield and Mr Voss were taken away. And that was it, really.'

Roderick pauses.

'Now, Mr Hamilton, please think very carefully about the question I am about to ask you. Casting your mind back to when the fight started, you told his Honour and the jury that they started to punch each other. If you can say, who struck the first blow?'

Hamilton appears to ponder the question carefully. He shakes his head.

'It all seemed to happen at once,' he says ruefully. 'I'm sorry.'

'That's quite all right, Mr Hamilton,' Roderick smiles. 'Please wait there. There may be further questions.'

Inevitably, Cathy invites Hamilton to watch the TV footage yet again.

'Looking at that footage again, Mr Hamilton, do you not think that you may be mistaken? Would you not say that Mr Mayfield struck the first blow?'

'No. I would not,' Hamilton replies.

'Very well. Mr Voss called Mr Mayfield a "toffee-nosed,

upper class git". Did you understand any of those words to be a racial slur of any kind?'

Hamilton laughs. 'No, not at all.'

Cathy sits down and gives way to Julian.

'Mr Mayfield called Mr Voss a "moronic, working class lout." Did you understand any of *that* to be a racial slur?'

'No. Certainly not.'

'I am sorry to ask you this, Mr Hamilton. But look at the footage just once more, please.'

At which point the trial suddenly takes a surprising turn. This happens sometimes. It is difficult to define how it happens, but there are sometimes moments when the chemistry of a trial, as the Reverend Mrs Walden would say, shifts. There is no mistaking the shift when it happens, and it often affects the outcome. What prompts the shift in the chemistry of this trial, who can say, but it certainly begins with Julian, who, apparently believing that the gods of advocacy are on his side, decides to push his luck. His question is a very dangerous one. If it goes wrong, he is going to be stuck with a very damaging answer. The footage is played yet again. Hamilton stares at it like a man possessed. I am sure he is feeling guilty about not seeing what he is supposed to. But all of a sudden, his eyes move back to alight on Julian and you sense that he has seen something new.

'Seeing that again, Mr Hamilton, although things do move quickly, do you not see that Mr Voss strikes first?'

'Now that I see it again,' Hamilton replies, 'I would have to agree with you. It's very close, but yes, Mr Voss does appear to strike just before Mr Mayfield.'

A veritable ripple goes round the courtroom and I see the reporters scribbling and tweeting furiously. Cathy looks aghast, but there is nothing she can do about it. I must admit that, dangerous or not, Julian's question reflects my own sense of it. I had a vague impression that, although the first blows look more or less simultaneous, Voss is quicker off the mark by a whisper. Mayfield definitely reacts by striking out himself before Voss lands his blow, but that would not deprive him of his claim of self-defence – you don't have to wait to be hit before defending yourself. There is no way to tell what the jury see, or think they see, but that's my impression.

'Thank you, Mr Hamilton,' Julian says, with the air of a man who cannot understand why it has taken so long for the obvious to be acknowledged for what it is. He is so excited that he almost forgets to ask about the offer of a handshake, and has to stand up again abruptly after having sat down.

Next, Roderick calls Marie Cuthbertson, the Green Party candidate, and to the amazement of all in court, there is almost a replay of Derek Hamilton's evidence. The only real difference is an amusing interlude when Ms Cuthbertson confesses to watching Voss and Mayfield wrestling and swearing at each other on the floor below the stage, and has a momentary fantasy that they could both be disqualified for grave misconduct during the count, resulting in an unlikely electoral gain for the Green Party with its 1546 votes. She admits that she was soon disabused of that idea by Mr Malone. Ms Cuthbertson, too, was taken by surprise when the fight broke out, ran over to the stage after Voss and Mayfield had plummeted to the floor below, and had no clear impression of who, if anyone, struck first.

But when invited by Julian to watch the footage just once more, she concedes that Voss does appear to move just a fraction before Mayfield. More ripples around the courtroom, and one can sense the bookies narrowing the odds on a Conservative win. Cathy is looking a bit pale and is understandably chagrined that the gods of advocacy have deserted her so completely. Julian, of course, is looking very pleased with himself, and with the reward he has reaped for asking not one, but two very dangerous questions.

But the gods of advocacy are fickle. It is rare for them to stay entirely loyal to one side throughout a trial, and when Roderick calls Celia Wingate (Monster Raving Loony Party) and Henry Yates (Warwickshire Independence Party) the chemistry shifts yet again. When it comes to bottle, Cathy Writtle is second to no one, including Julian Blanquette. Emboldened by his success, or perhaps becoming a little desperate, seeing defeat staring her in the face, Cathy poses the same dangerous question to both witnesses, and to universal astonishment, both agree that Mayfield could just have beaten Voss to the punch.

Julian makes a strenuous effort to change their minds, but without success. Obviously rather bemused, Roderick tells us that the only remaining witness is the officer in the case, who will tell the jury about the course of the investigation and deal with the police interviews of the two defendants. After this, the prosecution will be ready to close its case. He asks for a little time to finalise and copy the interviews for the jury, and I suggest that we resume after lunch. We could all do with some time to re-group, and in any case Marjorie has asked whether I could sentence a burglar for her, as she does not want to interrupt the trial of her seventy-year old defendant, Gertie. It is a welcome diversion.

After the sentence, I find that I still have about half an hour before lunch, and my mind returns to the conundrum of racial aggravation. Not one of the other four candidates understood 'upper class git' or 'working class lout' to have any racial connotations, and I must say I am having a lot of trouble with the idea myself. On the other hand, I can't entirely exclude Roderick Lofthouse's reading of the Act, and if I withdraw the issue from the jury, the bright spark at the CPS is likely to tell him to interrupt the trial and take the matter to the Court of Appeal. If that happens, we would have to adjourn the trial for a day or two to allow the Court time to hear his appeal. If they agree with him, we would then have to continue the trial. On the other hand, if I leave it to the jury and they convict, it will go up to the Court of Appeal anyway. It's a dilemma I have faced before, though not with so many eyes on me, and I know that there is only one hope of avoiding the Court of Appeal altogether: let the jury work it out. I've been watching them, and they seem to be paying close attention. I conclude it may be my best bet.

In the meanwhile, I ask myself: what is the case the jury have to decide? It suddenly occurs to me that we have ended up with two coalitions: one between the Conservatives, the Liberal Democrats and the Green Party; the other between Labour, the Monster Raving Loony Party and the Warwickshire Independence Party. The jury will have the casting vote. They have to decide which one they prefer or, to echo Jeanie, whether they are prepared to vote for any of them. In a moment of whimsy, I pen my report of the election as a judicial returning officer.

I, Charles Walden, being the Judge in the trial resulting from certain events occurring during the United Kingdom Parliamentary General Election in the Constituency of Clavering West with Baddiefield, do hereby give notice that the number of votes recorded for each Candidate in the said trial as being the aggressor, the person who struck the first blow, is as follows –

Richard William Mayfield, Conservative Party Candidate: 2
Liam Voss: Labour Party Candidate: 2

The number of ballot papers rejected was as follows: unable or unwilling to make up his bloody mind and claiming he was unable to see what happened: 1; others present at the time, but not called by the prosecution for whatever reason: God knows how many; total 1+ God knows how many.

And I declare that the result of the election is a tie.

The only trouble with this is that in a general election, if the number of votes is tied after a recount, the election is decided by the drawing of lots. You can't decide trials like that. There are times when juries are totally deadlocked when I think it might not be a bad idea, but we can't. All we can do is press on and invite the jury to give the casting vote.

And so to lunch, an oasis of calm in a desert of chaos.

'How is the great electoral violence case going?' Legless asks with a smirk.

'You may well laugh,' I say. 'So far, the Lib Dems and the Greens are supporting the Tories, and the Monster Raving Loony Party and the Warwickshire Independence Party are supporting Labour.'

'Well, that just proves my point,' Hubert says, looking up from his chicken Kiev, the kitchen's offering as dish of the day.

'In what sense?' I ask.

'It stands to reason,' he replies. 'If the only people who agree with the Labour chappie are barking mad, what can you expect? I told you he would be convicted.'

'As a matter of fact, they were perfectly good witnesses,' I say, 'and I'm not sure which way it's going to go. I won't be particularly surprised if the jury fail to reach a verdict.'

'Have you decided which way you're going on the racial aggravation question?' Marjorie asks.

'I'm going to leave it to the jury,' I reply.

'Oh, come on, Charlie,' Legless protests.

'I'm serious,' I reply. 'I think the wording of the Act supports the prosecution as a matter of law. As Marjorie said yesterday, Parliament didn't think this through, and someone needs to tell them to bugger off and stop being so stupid. But with the nation's press looking on, I'd prefer to let the jury tell them, rather than doing it myself. "Top Judge" red alert, and all that kind of thing.'

'Quite right,' Hubert says. 'That's why we have juries, to bring a bit of bloody common sense to bear on this sort of nonsense. Perhaps someone in Parliament will sit up and take notice for a change.'

'I'm not sure how much confidence I have in that, Hubert,' I reply. 'But at least I can try to salvage this case.'

'Old Bertie Simmons got the Top Judge treatment once,' Hubert says.

'Who?' I ask.

'Bertie Simmons. Used to sit in Wales, somewhere, Carmarthen, I think – or was it Mold? Can't remember. This was years and years ago, now. It wasn't the *Sun*, though. It was the *Times*, no less.'

'What did he do?' Legless asks.

'He gave some chap a conditional discharge for interfering with a sheep,' Hubert says. 'But it wasn't the sentence that got him into trouble.'

We wait expectantly, looking at each other, but Hubert seems on the point of returning to his chicken Kiev.

'I have a feeling I'm going to regret asking this, Hubert,' Marjorie says, 'but if it wasn't the sentence, what was it?'

'What? Oh, the Top Judge thing? Oh, yes,' Hubert continues. 'No, it wasn't the sentence. Chummy was of previous good character, so no one was too bothered about that. No, what got Bertie the Top Judge treatment was, he said he didn't think interfering with a sheep was an offence known to the law of Wales, and the case should never have been brought. He ordered the prosecution to pay the defendant's costs, and ordered them not to bring any more cases about sheep in his court in future.'

'What happened to him?' Marjorie asks.

'Nothing, as far as I know. He sat on quite happily until he retired. The Lord Chancellor probably had a quiet word with him in private, but nothing more than that. Quite right. Nothing to make a fuss about. Johnny Makin brought him to the Garrick for dinner one evening. That's how I heard about it.'

'How are you doing with Gertie, Marjorie?' I ask.

'Ah, well, interesting you should ask,' she replies. 'For most of the morning, she seemed to be going straight down the tubes, as we predicted yesterday. The prosecution called the work rider, and he was very solid on the date when the horse died and so on. But then, they called the financial investigator who looked into the insurance company's records after it went belly up, and guess what?'

'I have no idea,' I reply. 'Did he wobble on the dates?'

'Not yet,' Marjorie says. 'But the prosecution served a further witness statement the investigator made only this morning. It seems that, originally, the auditors thought the company went under just because of financial mismanagement. Now, they think it may have been a case of fraud.'

'That's all very interesting,' I reply. 'But how does that help Gertie? If she concealed the horse's death until after an insurance policy was issued, she would still be guilty wouldn't she?'

'I agree,' Marjorie said. 'But when he went through the documents again just before trial, the investigator found an indication that the fraud may have been the work of one particular executive, and that this executive may have falsified many of the records to cover his tracks – including dates. I have Piers Drayford prosecuting. You know Piers. He's a stickler for doing the right thing. He's not sure he can rely on the documents if this turns out to be true. The investigator asked for some more time to look into it, so I have adjourned until tomorrow morning.'

'Well, well,' I said. 'That would be a turn-up for the book, as they say in the racing world.'

'Yes,' Marjorie smiles. 'Who knows? Gertie may be first past the post yet.'

* * *

Tuesday afternoon

The afternoon is a dull affair, and some of the journalists start to wander off in search of a more entertaining way to pass the time. For a moment, I even think I see the Top Judge menace receding a little, though I quickly realise that it will return with a vengeance if I depart from my planned script.

Most of the afternoon is consumed by the reading of the defendants' police interviews. It is difficult to stay awake during this process at the best of times, and ninety minutes of poring over the transcripts of two interviews, with Roderick reading the role of the defendant and the officer in the case, DI Bridge, reading the questions, does nothing to stave off the post-prandial instinct to snooze. I give the jury – and everyone else – a break in between interviews, which helps a bit, but all in all it is a dreary afternoon.

The interviews, in any case, shed little light on the case. Both defendants answered all the questions put to them, and stoutly maintained that they were acting in self-defence, striking only to ward off a blow struck against them. Mercifully, it eventually comes to an end. All that remains in the prosecution's case now is to present a few agreed facts, which are read to the jury. These include the fact that both defendants are men of previous good character. This done, Roderick closes his case. It is just after four o'clock by now, and we will not begin the defence case today. But the moment has now arrived. I must rule on the racial aggravation question. The hour of the Top Judge is at hand, and there is no way to avoid it.

There is nothing I can do but follow the script I have written out – and written it out I have, word for word. I wouldn't normally do that for a ruling of this kind. If I can't give an off-the-cuff ruling on your average application to withdraw a case from the jury by now, it's time I retired. But this isn't your average application, and I am aware of pens and pencils at the ready in the press seats to record my every word. So not only am I going to read it verbatim, but as soon as I have finished, I am going to provide the journalists with copies, so that no one has any excuse at all for misquoting me.

I won't bore you with it all. What it comes to is this. I am personally doubtful that a British class, whether upper, middle or working, should be regarded as a racial group. But I have been persuaded by the prosecution that section 28 of the Crime and Disorder Act 1998 can be read in this way, and it is for Parliament to make the law, not me. I will, therefore, leave the issue of racial aggravation to the good sense of the jury in the confidence that they will do the right thing. I end by suggesting that Parliament might give further consideration to what its intention was in enacting the section, and whether they intended to include classes as racial groups. This is always a good way to end a ruling. It shows you have thought about it, that you know that Parliament has the last word, and are doing no more than offering your guidance in the spirit of cooperation between the branches of government. All in all, I am quite happy about it.

* * *

Tuesday evening
Not a bloody word on the news. All right, fair enough, there is some serious stuff going on in the Middle East, and there have been two murders in Northampton, but still, you would think that the definition of racial aggravation would rate a mention. But not a word. At least we got some coverage in the papers. The Reverend Mrs Walden has been through the day's newspapers

and marked the relevant passages with paper clips. No one mentions me by name except the *Times* and the *Mail*. The *Mail* pours scorn on the idea that a class can be a racial group, and opines that it just shows how far we have gone down the road of political correctness, so much so that we have become a laughing stock in the eyes of the world – which I had no idea we had. Nothing to do except monitor the papers again tomorrow. Surely there will be something about my ruling, even if it is only a thorough bollocking by the *Mail* for being the High Priest of political correctness.

Still, at least no one has called me a Top Judge. Yet.

* * *

Wednesday morning
Cathy calls her client to give evidence. He looks rather downtrodden, as if he is not entirely happy with the way the case has gone thus far. Well, I don't suppose he is. The prosecution's case has ended exactly as Roderick had predicted in his opening speech. The evidence is consistent with both defendants striking out at more or less the same time, in which case the jury would be entitled to convict both, and as things stand, the odds are very much in favour of Roderick potting both of them. One or both defendants are going to have to come up with something different if one of them is going to be first past the post in this contest.

'Mr Voss, you were the Labour candidate in the Clavering West with Baddiefield constituency, is that right?' Cathy begins.
'Yes.'
'Was it your first time to fight the seat?'
'It was my first time to fight any seat.'
'Tell the jury why you want to go into politics.'
This isn't strictly relevant, but no one is going to object. He is a man of previous good character, and the jury is going to

have to decide whether or not to believe him. Roderick will give him a lot of leeway. Julian is certainly not going to intervene, as he will be planning to take Richard Mayfield down exactly the same road when his turn comes.

'I want to make a difference,' Voss replies, 'and for me, that means the Labour Party. I've been a member of the Party for several years, and while I was at university I spent my summers working for local parties in different constituencies, mainly Conservative-held seats. Finally, it was time for me to find a seat for myself.'

'I don't want to take the time of the jury re-living the whole campaign,' Cathy says, to universal relief, 'but generally, were you happy with the way it was run?'

'Yes,' Voss replies. 'I had no complaints. We always knew it was going to be a hard fight. Clavering West may be a marginal seat, but the Conservatives have almost always managed to hold on. My team worked very hard, as did I. We thought we might have done just enough to take it, but Richard also fought a good campaign, and we knew it would be close.'

'You call him "Richard"', Cathy observed. 'Tell the jury what your relationship with Mr Mayfield was like during the campaign.'

'It was very good,' Voss says, and I see Mayfield nodding in the dock. 'I'm sure most people think we are at each other's throats the whole time. If you watch Prime Minister's Question Time, you are bound to get the impression that we never do anything except abuse each other and shout each other down. But you can't spend your whole life slagging your opponents off. Nothing would ever get done. We disagree, we debate, we present ourselves and our arguments to the public, but it's nothing personal – at least not for me. Whenever I came across Richard when we were out campaigning, we were polite to each other, and we even had a laugh together once or twice – mostly at the expense of the Warwickshire Independence Party.' Mayfield nods again.

'All right,' Cathy says. 'Now, let me come to the evening of the count. The jury has seen the Clavering church hall, where it was taking place. What time did you arrive at the count?'

'About eleven-thirty,' Voss replies. 'It had been a long day. I went home to grab a bite to eat, and change my suit, then I went to the hall to meet Sam, my agent.'

'Did Sam give you any information at that time?'

'It wasn't so much information as his impression. Sam is a very experienced agent. He sensed from the exit polls that we had come close, but probably not taken the seat, though of course, nobody really knew at that stage.'

'How did you feel about that?'

'I felt disappointed, naturally. As I say, I had hoped we might have squeezed it. But I couldn't let it show, obviously. You have to keep up appearances in front of your campaign workers, and as I say, no one actually knew anything yet.'

'Did there come a time when the Returning Officer, Mr Malone, informed you of the provisional result?'

'Yes. It must have been about half an hour before he eventually declared it. He took all the agents aside and told them that the Tories looked to be winning by a few hundred votes, and asked the agents whether anybody wanted a recount. That meant us, of course. None of the other parties was close enough to challenge.'

'Did you discuss that with Sam?'

'Yes.'

'And what did he advise?'

'He thought we had to accept the result. We both knew the constituency is a marginal, and there is never much of a majority, so by Clavering West standards, it was a clear enough win. There were no special circumstances to make us think otherwise. Sam left it up to me, of course, but I took his advice. We told Mr Malone that we didn't want a recount.'

'We heard that, after the declaration, you called Sam an

"idiot" for not demanding a recount. What do you say about that now?'

'It was totally wrong of me,' he replies. 'Sam had no reason to think that anything was wrong at that time. I have apologised to him since.'

'But after you and Sam had made that decision, did you receive any further information?'

'Yes.'

'What was that?'

'One of our campaign workers, Mike Edwards, had been at the polling station in the Vauxhall district, which usually leans towards Labour. He told me that something suspicious had gone on there.'

'Suspicious in what way?'

'There were reports of two boxes full of ballot papers being locked away in a room and not counted, and Mike said there was a heavy presence of Tory campaign workers at the polling station.'

'When exactly did Mike give you this information?'

'Literally, as I was walking up on to the stage. Mr Malone was in place, as were the other candidates, and he was about to begin the declaration. Mike was out of breath. I think he had had to run part of the way back to the count, and lost track of how late it was. He was trying to tell me what had happened, but I was pulled on to the stage by someone before he had even finished telling me.'

'So, Mr Malone was making the declaration? What happened then?'

'Mr Malone was declaring the result. Mike was standing right in front of the stage, and mouthing some words in my direction, but I only got some of what he was trying to say. Eventually, I realised that he was trying to get me to demand a recount. I looked around for Sam, but he was behind me somewhere, off stage. I was on my own.'

'By the time you came to that realisation, had the result been declared?'

'Yes. Richard was shaking hands with the other candidates and starting to make his victory speech.'

'What did you do?'

'I had no idea what to do. Mike had alerted me that there might have been a serious irregularity, and there was Richard, waffling on about how everyone was going to be entering a new golden age because the Tories had held Clavering West, and all that kind of crap,' – he looked towards the dock – 'sorry, Richard, no offence intended.'

'None taken,' I hear Mayfield reply.

'And I just didn't know what to do. Eventually, I interrupted Richard and demanded a recount.'

Cathy nodded. 'Yes. Now, the jury have seen what happened from that moment on. But I want to take you through it so that you can explain what happened from your point of view.'

She begins to play the, by now, instantly recognisable scene once more. She pauses it when the two have begun to grapple, but before they have rolled off the stage.

'We hear you demanding a recount, Mr Voss. Can I just ask you this; did you know at that time that it was too late for a recount once the result had been declared?'

'I did know, but in the confusion I had forgotten about that.'

'I see. Now, it's obvious from what we have seen that you and Mr Mayfield begin fighting. In your own words, tell the jury how it all started.'

Voss shrugs. 'It all happened so quickly. As I said, I was trying to demand a recount, Mr Malone was saying that I couldn't have one, and Richard was telling everyone what a good thing it was that he had been elected. I'm afraid I lost my temper and said some things I shouldn't have said.'

'Essentially,' Cathy reminds him, 'you said that the voters couldn't possibly have preferred Mr Mayfield to you, and you called him a "toffee-nosed upper class git". Is that right?'

'Yes,' Voss agrees after a pause. 'I would like to apologise to him today.'

'Accepted, of course,' I hear Mayfield say from the dock.

'When you used the expression "upper class git", did you intend that as any kind of racial slur?'

Voss shakes his head vigorously. 'No, of course not. I don't understand how anyone could possibly think that.'

'I quite agree,' I hear, from the dock.

'Mr Mayfield,' I say, 'please don't interrupt. You will have your turn in due course.'

'Yes, your Honour,' Mayfield replies. 'I'm sorry.'

'What happened next?' Cathy asks.

Voss takes a deep breath. 'I thought I saw Richard begin to throw a punch at me. I reacted by throwing one at him.'

'Did his punch land on you?'

'Yes, he caught me on the right cheek, close to my nose.'

'Did your punch land on him?'

'Yes, somewhere on his face. I'm not sure where.'

'And then what happened?'

'We continued trying to hit each other,' Voss replies, 'and the next thing I know we had our arms around each other, we were on the floor and we were heading towards the edge of the stage. Just before we rolled off, I remember thinking, "This can't be happening. I hope to God my mother isn't watching". She was, of course,' he adds sadly.

'And we know that you were injured and had to go to A and E, as did Mr Mayfield.'

'Yes. Again, I would like to say that I am sorry about that.'

'You learned subsequently, I think, that there had in fact been some irregularity at one of the polling stations, as Mike Edwards had told you, but that it did not affect the result of the election. Is that right?'

'Yes.'

'Do you make any criticism of Mr Malone?'

'No. Not at all. Mr Malone dealt with the election very fairly.'

Cathy pauses to consult her notes.

'And finally, Mr Voss, so that there is no doubt about what you are saying. When you struck Mr Mayfield for the first time, why did you do so?'

'I believed that he was about to punch me, and I was defending myself.'

'When you struck him again during the ensuing fight, why did you strike him?'

'To defend myself.'

'Oh, come on, Mr Voss,' Julian begins. 'You lost your temper and struck out in anger, didn't you?'

'No. I thought Richard was going to hit me, and I was right.'

'But you were angry, weren't you?'

Voss pauses. 'Yes, I was angry, but not with Richard.'

'Oh, really? You had been told that Conservative Party workers had been seen loitering in the vicinity of the polling station where these two boxes were mysteriously locked away. Isn't that right?'

'Well, yes, but I didn't associate that with Richard.'

'You didn't think the Tories were up to no good, trying to make sure they held on to their slender majority by nefarious means?'

'I didn't think for a moment that Richard was involved in anything like that. Supporters do get out of hand sometimes, and you have to calm them down, but at no time did I think that Richard had anything to do with it.'

'Looking at the TV footage again today, Mr Voss – and you are welcome to see it again if you wish – would you not agree that you made your move before Mr Mayfield? You were the one to strike first?'

There is a silence, and I sense Cathy getting a bit tense.

'Yes, I think that's probably correct.'

Cathy closes her eyes briefly, but recovers quickly, making a pretence of writing herself a note.

'You agree with that?'

'Yes,' Voss replies again, 'I may have beaten him to it by a matter of a second, but I only struck him because I was sure he was going to strike me – as indeed he did.'

'And it wasn't because you thought there might have been fraud, it was too late for a recount, and you were angry? Wasn't that the real reason?'

'No, it was not.'

Julian sits down with a brief look towards the jury. Roderick stands, but almost immediately sits down again.

'I don't think I have anything to add to that, your Honour.'

Cathy asks a couple of tentative questions, but she knows she is on dangerous ground, and has every chance of making matters worse. The evidence of Liam Voss is complete. Cathy calls three short character witnesses who tell us what a good, honest, helpful and caring man Liam Voss is, and that is the end of his case.

'Judge Jenkins would like to see you in chambers, Judge,' Carol says confidentially, standing and turning round to face me. 'She says it's urgent.'

I look at the clock. Coming up to twelve o'clock.

'Can't it wait until lunchtime?'

'Something to do with the twins at school,' Carol replies. 'She has to leave. But she was most insistent about seeing you first.'

I announce that I may have to rise for some time.

'Your Honour, in fact, I was going to ask if I could have some time before opening Mr Mayfield's case,' Julian says.

'You have until two o'clock,' I reply.

I adjourn the case accordingly and make my way to Marjorie's chambers. She is packing various items into a large handbag and shows every sign of being anxious to get away.

'I'm sorry, Charlie,' she says, 'I have to go to see the twins at school.'

'Oh, dear,' I say, 'nothing too serious, I hope.'

'Sounds like a bad cold, but the school's worried in case it's the flu. I'm sure it's nothing, but they are insisting on my being there, to take them home if needed. Nigel is in Geneva all week. Stella wanted to give me a sentence or two to do this afternoon, but Hubert says he will do them for me.'

I'm sure he will, and I'm just as sure that I will be listening to him moaning about it at some length during lunch.

'What about your trial?' I ask.

'That's what I had to see you about,' she replies. 'You remember I told you yesterday that Piers Drayford wasn't sure he could rely on the insurance company's documents?'

'Yes. You said there was a suspicion that someone may have been fiddling around with them to cover up a fraud.'

'Yes, well it's more than a suspicion now. It all unravelled once the financial investigator saw a pattern of alterations in the insurance company's documents. He is now saying that all kinds of shenanigans went on, including the wholesale alteration of the dates on which policies were issued, funds were received and paid out, and so on. It's so bad that Piers felt he couldn't rely on the records any more as evidence against Gertie –'

'But that must mean…?'

'Exactly, Charlie. The whole prosecution case was based on dates, so this morning Piers threw his hand in and offered no further evidence.'

'So Gertie is a free woman?'

'She is, indeed.'

'Well, I am very happy to hear that, Marjorie,' I say, 'but why the urgency to drag me off the bench and tell me now, when you're so anxious to be on the road?'

'The fraud involved the systematic diversion of funds by one particular executive for his own benefit, to the tune of about seven hundred and fifty thousand pounds over a period of three years. Of course, the investigator knows the identity of this man. It wasn't mentioned in open court, because needless to say, the Old Bill are now anxious to talk to him and they don't want him doing a runner. But Piers asked to see me in chambers, and gave me this note with the name written down. He thought you ought to see it.'

I take the note and read it twice before I believe it.

'Bugger me,' I say.

'Yes,' Marjorie says. 'Quite a coincidence, isn't it? Piers also gave me this, which he thought you might find interesting. Has any of his election material made its way into evidence in your case?'

'No,' I reply. 'I suppose no one thought it was very relevant.'

She hands me a bright glossy blue and white election leaflet which sings the praises of one Richard William Mayfield, Conservative candidate for the constituency of Clavering West with Baddiefield, and draws particular attention to the candidate's successful career in business before entering politics, including his stint as chief financial officer of a certain Wild Hart Insurance Company.

'Which, I take it, is the company involved in your case?' I ask.

'The very same,' Marjorie replies. 'I understand that the financial investigator would like to sit in your court and monitor your trial, if you don't mind.'

'He is as welcome as the flowers in May,' I say. 'But I don't think he will learn anything from it. My case isn't about money.'

'No. But Piers says the police and the CPS are thinking of contacting the Electoral Commission, and they want to know how your case ends before they decide what to do.'

This does get my attention.

'What? With a view to setting aside the result of the election?' I ask.

'Well, it's too early to say that,' she replies. 'But they think that someone who could commit fraud on the scale Mayfield apparently has would be quite capable of fraudulently diverting a couple of ballot boxes if he thought it might help to get him elected. At any rate, they think it is worth looking into.'

'Well I never,' I say. 'So Mr Mayfield will be having his collar fingered, will he?'

'The moment you and your jury have finished with him.'

For some inexplicable reason, this information gives me a certain satisfaction.

* * *

Wednesday afternoon

After lunch, which today was not an oasis of calm, but an endless round of complaints from Hubert, in between bites of his chicken korma dish of the day, about Marjorie taking off to see the twins again and leaving him with two sentences, we are ready for the case of the putative fraudster, Mr Richard Mayfield.

'I'm not going to ask you about the campaign or the events of polling day in general,' Julian says, after carefully establishing his client's previous impeccable character and passion for honesty and integrity in politics. 'If my learned friend Miss Writtle has any questions about any of that, of course, she will be free to do so during cross-examination.'

'No, thank you,' Cathy signals immediately.

'If you knew what I know,' I find myself thinking, 'you might not be quite so quick off the mark with that.'

'I'm much obliged,' Julian says. 'Mr Mayfield, tell the jury what you remember about what happened after Mr Malone had declared the result of the election.'

'Well, I was delighted, needless to say,' Mayfield replies. 'I shook hands with the other candidates, except for Liam, who had his arms folded and refused to take my hand.'

'Did you think anything of that?'

'No, not really. I was slightly disappointed. You shake hands after a result is declared, just to show no hard feelings. But it didn't bother me. I had my acceptance speech in the inside pocket of my jacket. I took it out, and skimmed through it while Mr Malone was giving out the rest of the information. Then I stepped up to the microphone to make my speech.'

'Then what happened?'

'When I was trying to give my speech, I heard Liam start shouting something about wanting a recount. I ignored him at first, but it soon became impossible to concentrate. We traded insults, as you know.'

'Yes. Mr Mayfield, when you called Mr Voss a "working class lout", did you intend that in any sense as a racial slur?'

'No, of course not.'

'When he called you an "upper class git", did you take that as a racial slur?'

'No. I did not.'

'I'm not going to ask you to look at the footage again, Mr Mayfield. Others may, but I think the jury have seen it often enough by now. Did there come a time when you struck out at Mr Voss?'

'Yes.'

'Tell the jury why you did that.'

'Out of the corner of my eye, I saw him reaching over the microphone to punch me. I swung back at him to defend myself.'

'And why did you continue to strike him during the time when you were scuffling on the floor.'

'For the same reason.'

'Did you have any reason to be angry with Mr Voss, or to want to hit him?'

'No. Not at all. I had won the election. All I wanted was to make my speech, and go across to the Pig and Whistle for a drink. My supporters had organised a victory party in their upstairs room, and I was anxious to get to it. It had been a long day. The last thing I needed was to get into a fight with anyone.'

'At the time, were you aware of any explanation for Liam Voss attacking you?'

Mayfield thinks for a moment or two.

'No. Of course, I didn't know about the two missing ballot boxes until much later. I just assumed it was a bit of sour grapes. He had lost and he was upset about it and wanted to take it out on me. It was a loss of temper, I would say, a momentary lapse.'

Cathy and Roderick in turn make a valiant effort to change Mayfield's mind about all of it, but with a marked lack of success. Indeed, the longer Mayfield stays in the witness box, the more confident he seems to become. He also calls three or four character witnesses to say what a good chap he is, though no one from the Wild Hart Insurance Company. We agree that we will do closing speeches and summing-up tomorrow.

* * *

Thursday morning

Nobody takes very long about it. Actually, it is a pretty simple case. The choices facing the jury are clear enough. They could convict both defendants on the basis that they each attacked the other at more or less the same time. They could convict one, but not the other, finding that one was defending himself against an attack by the other. Or they could find themselves unsure of what happened, and acquit both defendants. If they do convict either defendant, they can do it either with or without racial aggravation. All three counsel take the jury through these choices, as do I. The press, whose attendance has been flagging over the last day or so, are back in force today, so I take the opportunity to hammer home my position on the relationship between the British class system and the scourge of racial aggravation, emphasising how much the English system of jury trial owes to the common sense of juries in taking this kind of decision, and how confident I am that their common sense will prevail. I send the jury out just before lunch.

* * *

Thursday afternoon

They come back just before four o'clock. As Carol asks the defendants and the foreman of the jury to stand, I see that the financial investigator has found himself a place to lurk, in company with two youngish gentlemen in dark suits, who look very much like detective constables attached to a branch of the Met concerned with serious crime. You learn to spot them after a while.

'Members of the jury,' Carol says, 'please answer my first question either yes or no. Has the jury reached verdicts on each count on which they are all agreed?'

The foreman is a man in his thirties, casually dressed in a blue shirt without either tie or jacket.

'Yes, we have.'

'On the first count of the indictment, charging Liam Voss with racially aggravated assault occasioning actual bodily harm, do you find the defendant guilty or not guilty?'

The foreman consults his note. He has obviously recorded the jury's decisions word for word, a wise precaution with so many eyes on him.

'We find Mr Voss guilty of assault occasioning actual bodily harm, but without any racial aggravation.'

'You find Liam Voss guilty of assault occasioning actual bodily harm, but without any racial aggravation, and is that the verdict of you all?'

'It is, your Honour.'

'On the second count of the indictment,' Carol continues, 'charging Richard William Mayfield with racially aggravated assault occasioning actual bodily harm, do you find the defendant guilty or not guilty?'

'We find Mr Mayfield not guilty.'

'You find Richard William Mayfield not guilty, and is that the verdict of you all?'

'Yes, your Honour.'

'Thank you, Mr Foreman,' Carol replies. 'Please be seated.'

To my amazement, looking into the dock, I see Voss and Mayfield do something they didn't manage to do at the count. They shake hands, apparently quite cordially. What they say to each other, I can't hear, but there seems to be no animosity between them. I order Mr Mayfield to be discharged. He leaves the dock. The posse is keeping a quiet eye on him, but of course will not make its move until either he or I leave court.

Cathy stands.

'Your Honour, despite the late hour, I wonder if I might seek to persuade your Honour to deal with sentence today? If your Honour feels that a custodial sentence is called for, then of course, I would ask for an adjournment for a pre-sentence report. But if your Honour feels that this was a case of a momentary loss of temper, in circumstances which offer, certainly not an excuse, but at least an explanation, and if a non-custodial sentence is in your Honour's mind, then Mr Voss would prefer to be dealt with today. He has a number of important decisions to make about his future career.

'And if your Honour will not think it presumptuous, may I add this? My instructing solicitors have spoken to Labour Party Headquarters. If Mr Voss were to receive a community order, there would be no bar to his standing as a candidate again. Only if he were to receive a prison sentence would he be barred. As your Honour knows, he is a man of previous good character...'

Her voice trails away. It doesn't take me long to decide. I have no intention of sending Voss to prison, even if the assembled reporters are mentally egging me on in the interests of milking this case for one more good story. He has already suffered enough for his moment of widely-publicised stupidity. I agree to hear mitigation now. But before Cathy can say another word, the temporarily vindicated Honourable Member for Clavering West with Baddiefield steps boldly forward.

'Your Honour, if I may, I would like to say a word for Liam as a character witness.'

I can't help it. I have to laugh at the thought of Richard Mayfield acting as a character witness for someone. The financial investigator and his cohorts also seem to find it funny. In a few minutes from now, the humour may be apparent to everyone, but it's not quite time for that. So why not? After all, I don't *officially* know anything adverse to Richard Mayfield, do I? Of course, Cathy makes no objection; it's an unexpected offer of help.

'Yes, all right, Mr Mayfield,' I say. 'I'm only laughing because I've never had anything quite like this happen before. Come and take the oath.' He does.

'Now, what would you like to say?'

He surveys the courtroom self-importantly. Of course, with so many reporters looking on, what better opportunity could there be for some good publicity to kick off his parliamentary career? A handsome show of magnanimity in victory is one of the hallmarks of the statesman, and never does any harm. And he has beaten Liam Voss to the post twice now. Hasn't he?

'Your Honour, Liam is a good young man. We may represent different parties, we may have different political outlooks, but we have shared the camaraderie of the campaign trail, and every time I have come across him, he has been friendly and courteous. What happened on the night of the count was wholly out of character, and I am quite sure it will never happen again. He became distressed by what he thought might have been an irregularity, and he over-reacted. He just lost his temper for a moment, that's all it was. I would not like to see his career in politics ended because of this. I hope you will find it in your heart to deal with him leniently.'

'Thank you, Mr Mayfield,' I say. 'In the light of the injuries you received, that is a very generous gesture.'

I ask Cathy if she wants to add anything, while signalling to her that there is no need. I sentence Liam Voss to a community order for twelve months, and order him to perform a few hours of unpaid work for the benefit of the community. I ask if he understands the sentence.

'Yes, your Honour, thank you,' he replies. 'I would like to apologise again to Mr Mayfield, and to the people of Clavering West with Baddiefield. My only regret, and it is entirely my fault, is that I have deprived myself of the opportunity to earn their trust and represent them as their MP.'

I can't resist it.

'Oh, I wouldn't write that off just yet, Mr Voss,' I say as I rise for the day. 'They say a week is a long time in politics, don't they? I wouldn't give up hope entirely if I were you.'

* * *

Thursday evening

The Reverend Mrs Walden and I watch the evening news, which reports on the verdicts, and has a further, very satisfying, segment showing the Honourable Member for Clavering West with Baddiefield protesting vigorously as he is led by two detectives from the main entrance of the Bermondsey Crown Court to a waiting car. The news anchor explains that Mr Mayfield is helping police with their inquiries into an alleged fraud, and has denied any wrongdoing.

The Reverend waits for the news to be over, and tells me to close my eyes. This is always the harbinger of a surprise of some kind, and I obey, wondering what on earth it could be. It's not my birthday, after all. Then I feel paper being pressed between my hands, and open my eyes. At first, I think I may have a heart attack. But as I take it in, I smile. It is an editorial in the *Mail*.

PARLIAMENT MUST RETHINK RACE LAW – TOP JUDGE

One of the country's most senior judges has told Parliament that it should look again at the law of racial aggravation, following an attempt this week to convict two men of racially aggravated offences of assault, during which they called each other 'upper class' and 'working class'. Rejecting a defence application to remove the claim of aggravation from the indictment, Judge Charles Walden, Resident Judge at Bermondsey Crown Court, said that Parliament should have thought more carefully about whether it really intended to include a social class in the concept of racial abuse. The judge added that he was confident that the jury would use their common sense and do the right thing.

The Mail agrees. Thank goodness we have at least one Top Judge who is prepared to speak out against the rising tide of political correctness…

Well, it goes on for a bit, naturally. It is a well-written piece, and accurate, and you can't always take that for granted with the press these days. We may even have to have it framed. I feel my body start to unwind a little. After all the anxiety, I can't say I am unhappy with my Top Judge experience, and thank God, I didn't even have to make any comments about the treatment of sheep in Wales. The Reverend Mrs Walden suggests that this calls for a visit to La Bella Napoli, for some pasta and a bottle of decent Chianti. I agree. Well, what else should a Top Judge do after striking a blow for common sense?

UNTIL THE REAL THING
COMES ALONG

UNTIL THE REAL THING
COMES ALONG

Monday morning

I try not to complain too much about the cases I am given to try. I have to set an example as RJ. If I complain, my brother and sister judges will feel entitled to complain as well, and then where would we be? They complain enough as it is and it's not going to help to have them complaining about things I can't do anything about. I have no control over the offences people commit. It's not as though I can pop out to the George and Dragon at lunchtime and put in a request, you know: 'Look chaps, we are all getting a bit bored with burglary and possession of small amounts of cannabis up at the Crown Court. Can't you pull your fingers out and see if you can give us something more interesting? A bit of serious GBH or a decent armed robbery, or at least supplying a reasonable amount of crack cocaine? Even a modest cannabis factory would be better than the rubbish you're sending us now.'

So we are stuck with what they *do* get up to, and someone has to do the work that comes in. That's just the way it is. In any case, the only person to complain to is Stella, and it does no good to complain to Stella. Our list officer is impervious to suggestions that you might prefer to try this kind of case rather than that, or that you just don't like a certain kind of case. Any such suggestion is likely to be met with a look which, without any need for words, makes it abundantly clear that the work of the court would grind to a halt if judges only tried the kinds of case they enjoy: quite apart from the sheer moral degeneracy of avoiding work you don't like.

All the same, I feel entitled to be a bit aggrieved by my assignments over the past three months. I have done nothing but what are politely termed 'historic' sexual cases – eight of them, to be precise – utterly unrelieved by any change of subject-matter. A historic sexual case is one in which the court has to listen to tales of gropings and worse from as long ago as thirty or forty years, with a defendant aged seventy or older, and a complainant whose memory of the gropings has spontaneously returned after being repressed for many years, or who has decided to come forward thirty or forty years after the event for any one of a hundred different reasons, some good, some bad.

The historic sexual case is a species which has always been with us, but has become increasingly common since the words 'Jim fixed it for me' came to be engraved, seemingly for eternity, on the very fabric of the space/time continuum. Some such allegations are undoubtedly true; some are undoubtedly false; all of them are nightmares for everyone involved. Over the course of thirty or forty years, witnesses have died, records have been lost, and memories have faded to such an extent that the surviving witnesses often have no idea in what decade relevant events occurred, let alone what year or month. They are the most difficult of all cases to try, particularly for juries. God knows how juries ever make sense of them, but in almost all cases, somehow, they seem to feel their way through and reach verdicts. But it comes at a price. They hate every minute of those cases – you can tell by their faces – and when the verdicts have been returned I excuse them for further service for five years, as a token of empathy. Weighed against the thin odds of being called for jury service again within five years, this is not quite as substantial a reward as it may seem, and I suspect it strikes most jurors as a hollow gesture.

Still, it's a bloody sight more of a gesture than judges get, even when we do three months' worth of historical cases without pausing for breath. My wife, the Reverend Mrs Walden, thinks we should all be offered counselling. Well, as I always tell her, I could name several judges who are in need of counselling regardless of the kinds of case they are trying, but she says that's not quite what she means. She points out that people in other walks of life – teachers, social workers, ministers such as herself – are offered counselling as a matter of routine, and they would be in counselling every spare minute of their lives if they were exposed to half the stuff we deal with, day in day out, on the bench. I'm sure she is right, but it will never happen.

Almost all judges think they are immune from any emotional reaction to the cases they try. It is a badge of honour for us to declare ourselves to be entirely unaffected by the horrific scenes of sexual violence, 'indecent images' of children, and general depravity which flit through our courtrooms in the course of an average week. The Reverend Mrs Walden thinks this is either an extreme form of denial or final proof of her theory that judges belong to some alien species denied access to the panoply of emotions experienced by normal human beings. I keep telling her that exposure to this kind of stuff is just part of the job, nothing that can't be dealt with by resort to a good lasagne and a bottle of decent Chianti. The Reverend Mrs Walden calls this self-medication. Well, I suppose it is, but someone has to medicate us and who else is going to do it?

Not the Grey Smoothies, that's for sure. The Grey Smoothies would never approve the expenditure involved in such an apparently pointless gesture as making counselling available to judges. No business case can be made, they would say, for maintaining the sanity of judges, especially in these times of austerity. I suspect the only way we would ever get funding for judicial counselling is for some judge to go postal, force his way into Grey Smoothie HQ with an AK-47 and reduce the future civil service pension bill by a few claimants. I doubt that will ever happen. We are all too well behaved.

The worst thing is that there is no end in sight. There seems to be an endless supply of these historic cases. The truth is, Jim has fixed it for all of us.

Even so, when Stella comes into my chambers last Friday afternoon with the list for today, I do think, just for a fleeting moment, that my luck might have changed.

'Something a bit different for you next week, Judge,' she announces. 'A case called Dudge.'

'Thank God for that. That's a relief,' I reply. 'What is it? A bit of burglary, a spot of GBH, an affray, a good benefit fraud, perhaps?'

Stella has the grace to look slightly guilty for having raised my hopes.

'Well, no... it is a rape case, Judge.'

I am deflated.

'How is that different, then?' I ask.

'Well, it's not historic,' she replies. 'It happened four months ago. I thought that might be easier for you. It's the usual Saturday night thing.'

By 'the usual Saturday night thing' Stella means that the case follows a pattern well known to Bermondsey Crown Court, and indeed to Crown Courts throughout the land. When I read the case papers this morning, comforted by one of Jeanie's lattes, I see that she is right. It's hardly necessary to read the whole file. After reading the complainant's account of things I can guess the rest. You could write a summing-up which would work for any case like this. All you have to do is change the names.

The complainant's name in this case is Stacey. Stacey goes out with her mates on Saturday night as usual, leaving home, a flat near the Oval, at about ten-thirty. They've been knocking back some blue vodka concoctions at home before venturing forth, to get themselves in the mood. They make straight for the Blue Lagoon, a notorious Bermondsey night club where they make the acquaintance of Chummy, Mr Dudge, who has just arrived with his mates after several pints of lager in the George and Dragon. To cut a long story short, Chummy and Stacey have a few rum and cokes together, and in all probability – knowing the Blue Lagoon, as I do, from its frequent mentions in dispatches – partake of some controlled drugs in one of the loos before Chummy broaches the subject of whether Stacey might be interested in coming back to his place. As convention demands, Stacey consults her mates, who think Chummy looks all right and wish her well, making sure that she has their mobile numbers in her phone in case things go wrong. So far, no real dispute about the evidence.

But as from their arrival at Chummy's place at about three o'clock in the morning, the two stories begin to diverge. Chummy says they have a beer or two, but no illegal substances, and jump happily and perfectly consensually into bed where they do all the usual things before falling asleep. Stacey says that she has nothing more to drink except a Diet Coke, but she suddenly comes over feeling very tired, and collapses on to Chummy's bed, where she remains sound asleep until she awakes to find Chummy having sex with her, sometime around four-thirty to five o'clock. She immediately demands that he stop, jumps out of bed, dresses and rushes out into the street, calling for a taxi as she goes. Stacey says that she was far too tired to have consented to sex – suspiciously tired, in fact, and there are dark hints of the use by Chummy of Rohypnol, the notorious 'date rape' drug. Unfortunately, before going to the police, Stacey takes two or three days to consult her mates to get their opinion about whether or not she has been raped, because obviously she can't report it without asking them. By this time, it is too late for the crisis centre staff to detect Rohypnol, or to collect any scientific evidence, for that matter. So we are in all-too familiar he-said-she-said territory.

So I go into court feeling fairly sure that I know what to expect. Aubrey Brooks is prosecuting. Aubrey is in his mid-forties and sits as a Recorder – a part-time judge – sometimes at Bermondsey. He is one of those rare men who can genuinely be described as debonair, which is quite an achievement while dressed in barrister's robes. He is low-key and self-deprecating in manner, but woe betide a witness who mistakes that for any lack of interest or inattention to detail. He can attack with the speed and venom of a cobra when he needs to, and Chummy will not have an easy ride if he gives evidence. Susan Worthington is defending. She is tall and imposing, very bright, and in the cobra-stakes she can match Aubrey strike for strike. I smile with relief. It's always good to see two safe pairs of hands in a case like this.

Aubrey explains that Stacey will be giving evidence in the courtroom, screened from the defendant. Usually in this kind of case, her evidence in chief would be given by way of a pre-recorded video interview prepared by the police, after which she would be cross-examined either behind the screen or by live TV link. But something has gone wrong with the recording. You can hardly see Stacey on the video because the officer has her sitting too far away from the cameras, and the quality of the audio is not great either. Aubrey thinks it would be better for her to give evidence live, and Stacey has no objection. So we empanel a jury, and away we go.

In most he-said-she-said cases it's not long before the momentum begins to swing towards not guilty. It's a question of the burden and standard of proof, of which the jury are well aware. They can't convict unless they are sure of the defendant's guilt, and where there is no supporting evidence on either side, it can often be difficult for the jury to be sure of anything. But this case shows signs of departing from the usual pattern. Stacey has dressed quite formally for court in a smart dark blue business suit with a light blue and white scarf and modest heels. She turns out to be an excellent witness, and is convincing when she talks about the sudden crushing onset of fatigue, and about her lack of enthusiasm for having sex with Chummy on a first date. Of course, she hasn't been cross-examined by Susan Worthington yet, so it's early days, but the jury seem to be sympathetic and are paying close attention. Except, that is, for one of them.

Juror number three, a youngish man, mid-twenties, short dark hair, wearing a grey sports jacket, red tie and light green slacks, seems rather perturbed. He seems to have difficulty in sitting still in his chair. He looks distinctly pale. In fact, once or twice he almost seems to be having a panic attack of some kind. I think I see him sweating, and he keeps putting his hand over the lower part of his face. I see Susan Worthington looking at him also. If it wasn't a rape case I would ask him if he needs a break, but I don't want to interrupt Stacey if I can avoid it. I would like to make sure we finish her evidence today, so that she doesn't have to come back tomorrow, and I am sure Susan will need quite some time with her. It's not unusual for a juror to come over a bit squeamish during a sex case; they usually get over it as the trial wears on. Besides, at the start of a trial I always tell the jury to ask for a break if they need one, and the juror hasn't said anything, so we press on. At one o'clock, Stacey's evidence in chief having been concluded, I adjourn for lunch and think no more about it.

No oasis of calm in the desert of chaos today. We are in the middle of a serious dispute with the Grey Smoothies, which has progressed to the point of requiring a face-to-face meeting – something the Grey Smoothies try to avoid at all costs, and which, should it become unavoidable, they schedule at the most inconvenient time possible. Such as lunchtime, when I want to be having lunch with my colleagues, finding out what is going on at court today. But today is an occasion when a meeting is unavoidable. We have reached an impasse, and it has become clear that further emails and phone calls are not going to solve the problem.

The subject of the disharmony is the dock – or rather the lack of a dock – in court three, where Legless usually sits. Part of the reason for having a dock is that it has, or should have, a solid glass front, which inhibits defendants from trying to escape and from assaulting prison officers, barristers, court staff, members of the public, or, of course, the judge. But there is a kind of dock, known with good reason as an insecure dock, which does not have a glass front. In fact, it has no front at all, and depends entirely on the goodwill or present mood of the defendant to keep him from escaping or going on a rampage. That is what we have in court three.

The Grey Smoothies love insecure docks because they are about ten thousand pounds cheaper on average than real docks. There are some courtrooms, in which less serious work is done, in which insecure docks may be acceptable. Court three is not one of them. Legless is trying and sentencing serious offenders every day of the week. Many of them are disposed to violence, and some of them have every incentive to try to escape, and the risk that there will be a serious incident will continue until someone installs a secure dock; which, given the Grey Smoothies' preoccupation with money, may be a long time. I have every intention of changing that if I can, and I have been lobbying hard, but I am pessimistic about my chances.

Their leader is called Meredith; that's her first name. Meredith rejoices in the title of cluster manager, which sounds vaguely indecent, but actually means simply that she acts as a Smoothie for more than one Crown Court – any quantity greater than one being referred to in Grey Smoothie-speak as a 'cluster'. She is clad in the inevitable grey suit, just a little too tight in the waist if you ask me, with a yellow blouse and high black heels. Her nails are painted a bright red and she is wearing a huge bracelet of interconnecting gold loops around her right wrist. It is big enough and loose enough to collapse with an annoying series of metallic clicks on any table or desk to which her arm gets too close.

I haven't met Meredith before. For reasons I have never understood, the Grey Smoothies move their underlings around, not only between locations but also between jobs, on a regular basis, with the result that you often find yourself talking to someone about a problem which has been going on for years, only to find that they have come down from Newcastle the day before and know nothing about it. Meredith may have been in the Magistrates Court last week, or may be in the Magistrates Court next week, in which case someone else will have to learn all about court three, and then we start again.

Her sidekick is called Jack. He looks about fourteen. His grey suit seems too short in the arm and leg, as if he has suddenly put on an inch or two and outgrown it after a good night's sleep, and he is wearing a violent purple tie which does not quite reach the top of his collar.

Stella is with me. Strictly, it ought to be Bob. But as court manager, Bob's allegiance, in theory at least, is to the Grey Smoothies. In practice, he takes much the same view of them as Stella and I; but he can't be seen to oppose them, so we have arranged a meeting for him away from court, and Stella is here to hold my hand instead. Together the four of us troop off for the inevitable site inspection of court three, which we have all seen before, presumably so that the Smoothies can satisfy themselves that we have not made any sneaky changes on our own to boost our business case. I have invited Legless to join us for the site inspection, but he has declined for fear that he may say something out of place. So may I, but I have to be here.

'As you can see,' I begin, 'it is a fairly small courtroom, certainly not on the scale of court one. I think it should be obvious that any defendant determined to do so would have little trouble in jumping out of the dock, after which he would be free to try to escape, or to assault persons present in the courtroom.'

Meredith is taking notes.

'Don't you have a dock officer?' Jack asks.

'Yes, we do have a dock officer,' I reply, 'who may well be a woman, and not very large. The defendant may be a man over six feet in height and weighing fifteen stone.'

'The Ministry's view is that women are just as capable as men in the role of dock officer,' Meredith observes sourly, pausing in her note-taking.

'I'm not suggesting otherwise,' I reply, apparently a touch too pointedly, judging by the look Stella is giving me. It's not a good sign. We are less than ten minutes into the meeting and my temperature is rising already. 'All right, let's say the dock officer is a *man* and not very large. He is still not going to be able to stop the defendant if he makes a break for it.'

'Can't you call for back-up?' Jack asks. 'I thought all courts were equipped with panic buttons.'

'They are,' I confirm, 'and if there happen to be other officers free they will come to our aid – in five to ten minutes. By which time Chummy has either legged it or done in a couple of barristers or both.'

'Chummy?' Meredith inquires with a supercilious raising of her eyebrows.

'The defendant,' I reply patiently. 'It's a technical term.'

Meredith appears to make a note of this.

'Well, why can't you just have more than one dock officer in the dock if you know you have a defendant who is likely to misbehave?' Jack wants to know.

I have been hoping someone would ask that.

'Firstly,' I respond immediately, 'we don't always have the luxury of having more than one dock officer available. The contractor doesn't supply enough of them, because they are not receiving funds for more than one, you see. Something to do with the Ministry not seeing a business case for it, I believe.'

I give Meredith a smile, which she returns with a glower.

'And secondly, you never know who is going to kick off

and who isn't. It's not always the ones facing the most serious charges or the longest sentences. The worst dock-jumper we ever had was a serial shoplifter.'

'Really?' Jack asks.

'Tesco's,' I reply. 'Joints of meat mainly. The occasional bottle of vodka to wash them down with. You can't ask for a whole team of dock officers for someone like that.'

Meredith walks slowly around the well of the court, after which the site inspection concludes and we return to my chambers. Meredith flicks through her notes.

'How many times has it happened?' she asks suddenly.

'What? Someone jumping out of the dock?'

'Yes. You said the shoplifter was the worst of them. How many have there been since you became Resident?'

I sigh inwardly. This is not our best point.

'It has happened on one other occasion to my knowledge.'

'In court three?'

'No. But I don't see what that has to do with it.'

'Well, was it in a court with a secure dock?'

'Yes, as it happens.'

'So, it can happen in any court?' Meredith asks.

'A defendant who was using an interpreter got out of the dock in court one while the dock officer was letting the interpreter out of the dock. He let the interpreter out before taking the defendant down to the cells, which is not proper procedure. He should have taken the defendant down first. That wasn't the shoplifter. The shoplifter escaped, or tried to, from court three. There have been one or two other cases where a defendant tried to kick off, but he couldn't go anywhere because he was in a secure dock.'

'I see,' Meredith replies. She is scribbling furiously. 'Did any of these defendants succeed in escaping?'

'No.'

'Why not?'

'They were detained by a court security officer or a police

officer before they could leave the building.'

'Did either of them assault or injure anyone?'

'No.'

'I see.'

Meredith finishes her note.

'Well, I'm not quite sure how you make a business case for this,' she comments, apparently to Jack.

'I'm not sure you can,' Jack agrees. 'No escapes, no injuries.'

'What?' I gasp.

Jack shrugs.

'It's a matter of statistics,' Meredith explains. 'To make a business case you have to have some statistics, some evidence of occurrences significant enough to require action. With money being as tight as it is, we have to ensure that a secure dock would represent good value for money for the taxpayer.'

'There have been a few incidents of assaults at other courts,' Jack concedes.

'But nothing here,' Meredith replies.

'And they don't even have docks in civil and family courts, do they?' Jack asks.

Stella and I exchange blank stares.

'What kind of statistic would you like?' I ask.

'What do you mean?' Meredith asks.

'Well, would it be enough if an armed robber escaped from court, or a rapist perhaps? Would an escape be enough in itself? Would he have to injure someone in the course of escaping? If so, would a dock officer be enough, or would he have to injure a barrister or solicitor, or even a judge – or are we expendable?'

Meredith looks askance.

'There's no need for sarcasm,' she replies.

'I'm not being sarcastic,' I protest. 'I am trying to make you understand that court three is a serious incident waiting to happen. What if it were a member of the public? What if a member of the public were to be killed or seriously injured?'

For a moment I have her attention. Judges and lawyers can be left to take their chances, but an incident involving an innocent member of the public would be a political issue. The Minister might have to take an interest. Questions might be asked in the House.

'We would still need a statistic,' Jack ventures eventually. 'Otherwise we will have to park it for now.'

But Meredith does not reply immediately.

'We will take your case to the Circuit administrators,' she says after some thought. 'I can't guarantee anything, and it may take some time. It's a question of the money, you see.'

'Yes, I quite understand,' I reply. 'I suppose Judge Dunblane will just have to make sure he renews his life insurance policy.'

'It's not as if you don't have a dock,' Jack points out. 'I mean, there is a dock.'

'Not in any real sense of the word,' I reply.

'Well,' Jack says, 'it may have to do.'

Then for no apparent reason he laughs.

'Until the real thing comes along.'

Meredith, Stella and I stare at him blankly. He has the grace to look embarrassed.

'It's an old song, isn't it?' he stammers eventually. '"If it's not a dock it will have to do, until the real thing comes along". Except that the song wasn't about a dock. It was about love. I think.'

This effectively brings the meeting to an end. We all shake hands awkwardly and the meeting is over. It is five to two. Lunchtime is also over. I take a hurried bite of Elsie's ham and cheese bap before throwing on my robe and wig.

* * *

Monday afternoon
'Counsel would like to see you without the jury,' Dawn says as she takes me into court.

Aubrey Brooks remains standing as I take my seat on the bench.

'Your Honour, we have asked to address you before the jury returns to court because there has been a… well, a development,' he begins.

This sounds ominous.

'Yes, Mr Brooks?'

'Your Honour, at the conclusion of her evidence in chief, Stacey asked the officer in the case, DC Walker, whether she could make a further witness statement. The officer explained that she wasn't allowed to speak to anyone until she had finished giving evidence, but she was insistent. The officer came to me. I spoke to my learned friend, and we agreed that the right course was to allow her to make a further statement, as long as the officer asked her no questions except those strictly necessary to allow the statement to be taken. Your Honour should have a copy. I handed one in to your learned clerk.'

Sure enough, a handwritten witness statement is on the bench in front of me.

'Give me a moment or two to read it, Mr Brooks,' I suggest. He quietly resumes his seat.

The handwriting, presumably that of DC Walker, is perfectly legible. After the usual declaration of truth and the date, it reads as follows.

I am the complainant in this case, and this morning I gave evidence in front of the jury about the rape committed against me by Mr Dudge. As soon as I came into court, I recognised a member of the jury. He is the young man sitting in the front row of the jury, the third juror from the end of the front row on my right. His name is Brian. I will now describe the circumstances in which I am acquainted with Brian.

About three years ago, I was employed as an escort by a firm based in Central London, which I can name if required to do so. This involved me being a sex worker. I would meet clients at their hotel, or sometimes in their homes. I would have sexual relations with the clients for money. Brian was a regular client for over a year. I would meet him at a small hotel because he is married. He used to tell me that his wife spent long periods of time away on business trips. I have no doubt that the member of the jury to whom I have referred is my client, Brian. I know this because I remember certain things he would ask me to do in bed. I can elaborate on this if required to do so. He wouldn't have known it was me until I came into court. He wouldn't have known from my name. When I was working, I used the name Lola, and my hair was a different colour.

I wish to add that I am making this statement only because I am worried about Brian being on the jury. I have been told that no one is allowed to ask me about my past sexual history just because I have been raped, and I hope this is correct.

Aubrey rises to his feet as I replace the statement on the bench.

'I don't propose to ask her to elaborate unless your Honour thinks it necessary,' he says.

'I quite agree,' I reply. 'I take it that one or both of you will have an application?'

'Your Honour,' Aubrey says, 'my learned friend and I agree that your Honour has no option but to discharge the jury, and order a retrial at such time as a wholly new jury panel is available.'

'I have asked my learned friend to reassure Stacey that her sexual history will play no part in the case,' Susan adds.

About half an hour later, having discharged the jury for what I told them were administrative reasons, I invite both counsel into chambers for a cup of tea and a laugh. It's not often you can have a laugh about Crown Court cases, especially one like this. They are all so desperately serious. But that's why you have to see the funny side when there is one. You can only imagine juror number three's horror when he came into court and saw his Lola facing him from behind the screen. It would be enough to put anyone off their lunch. Fortunately, he has escaped the encounter without lasting harm, and so has Stacey, who will have her day in court without fear that anyone will reveal her past employment. So today, we can enjoy the funny side.

'Poor sod,' Aubrey says. 'Imagine him sitting there during my opening and then seeing her come into court and having to listen to her evidence.'

'All the while thinking of his wife, and how he would ever explain it to her if Stacey blew the whistle on him in court,' Susan adds.

We chat for a few minutes until Stella knocks and enters bearing a file.

'Ah, I'm glad to find you both still here,' she says to counsel. 'I've just had your clerks on the phone, and since you are now free for a couple of days, and since I have Judge Walden available, I am putting the case of Wilbraham Moffett in for tomorrow.' She beams at me while depositing a file on my desk.

'Ah yes, I remember Mr Moffett,' Aubrey says. 'I'm afraid this means I'm prosecuting you again, Susan.'

'Well, in that case, I had better go and look at my papers,' Susan replies. 'Thanks for the tea, Judge. See you tomorrow.'

They troop quickly out.

I pick up the file suspiciously.

'Don't tell me it's another historic,' I ask Stella pleadingly.

She positively beams. 'Have a look at the indictment,' she suggests.

I open the file and examine the indictment, which consists of a single count. Not only is it in no way historic; there is not the slightest hint of sex about the case at all. Chummy is charged with an offence I'm not even sure I knew existed, namely: doing an act in the purported exercise of a right of audience when he was not entitled to exercise that right, contrary to section

70 of the Courts and Legal Services Act 1990. I look at Stella quizzically.

'Impersonating a solicitor at the Bermondsey Magistrates Court,' she grins.

'Good Lord,' I say. 'I wonder what the defence is.'

'Insanity?' she suggests on her way out.

* * *

Monday evening

I arrive home to find that the Reverend Mrs Walden has invited Ian and Shelley to partake of some pasta with us. Ian and Shelley are the golden young couple of her church. They met as teenagers at the church youth fellowship, dated chastely for several years, got engaged just as chastely, and finally got married in the church. One can only hope that they have been a bit less chaste since then. The Reverend Mrs Walden inherited them when she took over as priest-in-charge, and although they are no longer quite as young a couple as in their glory days, they are still a fixture of church life. They are still the resident duo for young people's services, Shelley belting out a spiritual or a sixties 'folk' song with the lyrics adapted slightly to refer to Jesus instead of drugs, while Ian accompanies her on his guitar. ('Why should the Devil have all the good tunes?' Ian is wont to ask at the beginning of the set. It always gets a chuckle from the congregation, though I'm afraid the simple answer may be, 'Because he has better musicians'.) They are still on hand to help with the youth fellowship, Sunday school, the annual fête, or anything else the Reverend asks of them. Such as talking to people in some kind of trouble and giving them helpful advice on subjects they know little or nothing about.

Ian and Shelley wear sweaters and blue jeans, and don't drink. I see that the Reverend Mrs Walden has not put wine glasses out for me or herself to go with the pasta, itself an omen of the tone of the evening. No self-medication for yours truly, at least until the guests have departed.

Conversation is slow at first. Ian is trying to find a diplomatic way to ask me about the various horrors I have been hearing about during the last three months, not to mention many years before the last three months. But he is not very good at it, and I am not disposed to help him, so when he asks what is going on at court I give everyone what I imagine to be a humorous account of my meeting with the Grey Smoothies. But nobody seems very amused about the dock in court three. Eventually, he gets to the point and asks whether I ever feel the need to talk to anyone about the awful things I must have to listen to day after day.

'It must be really, really awful, Charlie,' Shelley adds, joining in for the first time. 'Really… well, there are no words, are there? Really dreadful.'

For just a moment, I contemplate letting them have it with both barrels. I am angry with these people. I am quite sure that neither of them, in their wildest dreams, has ever imagined some of the sexual acts people describe to juries in my court, and I am equally sure it would put them off their dinner, not to mention violating every canon of social conversation, if I were to enlighten them. But part of me wants to do it anyway. Neither Ian nor Shelley could imagine being the victims of the kind of conduct I have been hearing about for the past three months, and I am very happy for them. But there they are, sitting there as if they are about to break into a chorus of 'Kumbaya'. What right have they to patronise me like some youngster in the youth fellowship? And if they do, why shouldn't they at least be made to understand what it is I am dealing with?

And then suddenly I stop myself. Why am I having this reaction? What has happened to the reserves of good humour I have at court? My God, I really *do* need to talk to someone about this. Well, so be it. But it's not going to be Ian or Shelley, not if they were the last two human beings on the planet to survive a nuclear holocaust. I look across the table at the Reverend Mrs Walden, and see at once that she has been reading my mind – an irritating habit she has acquired as we have both got older. She has covered her mouth with a hand. She has realised what a mistake this has been, and she is wishing they would go away. I smile to tell her she needn't worry. I wish the same, and between us we will make it happen.

'I know a really splendid man, Charlie,' Ian is saying, a confidential whisper that sounds a bit creepy. 'He's a fully qualified psychologist, but also a man who walks closely with the Lord.'

'Really? A remarkable combination,' I reply, smiling. The Reverend Mrs Walden removes the hand from her mouth and relaxes visibly. She knows me well enough to sense that I am back up off the canvas now, and ready to punch back.

'Yes, indeed,' Ian is saying. 'He helped my Uncle Bill greatly. I don't know whether I have ever told you about my Uncle Bill?'

'I don't believe you have,' I reply. 'I'm sure I would have remembered.'

Ian nods. 'Now, *there* was a man who was under stress all the time, Charlie. Every day of his working life. And he got to a point where he was about to burn out, totally burn out.'

'Totally,' Shelley confirms. 'But he didn't walk with the Lord, did he, Ian? Not as far as we know.'

'Not before he went into counselling,' Ian agrees, 'as far as we know. Of course, we can't look into everyone's hearts to see the state of their relationship with the Lord, can we? So we can't judge.'

'I'm sure that's true,' I say. 'So, tell me, Ian, what kind of job did Uncle Bill have that caused him so much stress, poor fellow? I assume he was a nurse in a paediatric oncological ward or did several tours defusing improvised explosive devices in Afghanistan? Or perhaps he taught English literature at a school in Bermondsey? It must have been something really awful, really dreadful.'

'He worked for an insurance company,' Ian says, as if he is hardly able to utter the words.

'Ah, well that explains it, then,' I say.

'It was terrible for him,' Shelley joins in.

'It must have been.'

'He spent his whole life hearing about people's car crashes, their houses or businesses burning down...'

'Dying, even,' Ian reminds her.

'Dying, even. And the worst thing of all was: he sometimes had to deny their claims. So they got no money at all.'

'That was the worst thing,' Ian says. 'Because he was a sensitive man, a man who cared, and it tore him apart to have to deny a claim.'

I shake my head.

'Dear me. But why would he have to deny someone's claim?'

Ian shrugs matter-of-factly.

'Well, usually because they hadn't paid the premium,' he explains.

They leave about half an hour later, but not before Ian has pressed into my hand the business card of Dr Philip Moody, sometime saviour (in the professional sense only, naturally) of Ian's Uncle Bill, and made me promise at least to think about calling him. When I return after shutting and double-locking the front door after them, the Reverend Mrs Walden has already poured two large glasses of Chianti.

'Shall we self-medicate for a while?' she suggests.

'Splendid idea,' I reply. We take the glasses and the bottle over to the sofa and enjoy the quiet for a few moments.

'I am really sorry, Charlie,' she says. She takes my hand.

'Oh, it's all right. It was all quite amusing, really.'

'But you do have an awful time with those beastly cases, don't you? I just wanted to help.'

'Oh, I know. I will find somebody to talk to, Clara. I promise.

We will have to pay for it ourselves, though. No point in even asking the Grey Smoothies.'

'We can manage it,' she replies. 'I wonder who the Grey Smoothies talk to when they get stressed?'

'Each other probably,' I suggest. 'I'm not sure who else they could get to listen to them.'

'Have you got another one to do?' she asks. 'A sex case, I mean.'

'No,' I reply happily. 'I'm about to try someone for the heinous crime of impersonating a solicitor.'

'Good grief! Why on earth would anyone do that?' she asks.

'I can't imagine,' I reply, reaching for the wine bottle. 'I would have thought it would be bad enough actually *being* a solicitor. I am sure I will learn more tomorrow.'

* * *

Tuesday morning

'Members of the jury, my name is Aubrey Brooks, and I appear to prosecute in this case. My learned friend Miss Worthington represents this defendant, Wilbraham Moffett. No doubt most of you, when you received your summons for jury service in the post, thought that you might be trying a robbery, or a serious assault, or at least a case of drug-dealing. I am sure very few of you dreamed that you might be trying someone for impersonating a solicitor, and I am equally sure that some of you are wondering why on earth we are here in the Crown Court, at great public expense, trying somebody for an offence when no one was injured, or had any property stolen, or came to any real harm at all.'

Aubrey is right to address this point early on in the trial. Grateful as I am for the respite from historic sex cases, I can't avoid asking myself, wearing my RJ's hat, why we are going to spend two or three days of Crown Court time on this, when it could have been dealt with at the time in the Magistrates Court, to the extent it had to be dealt with at all. But having read the file in chambers earlier, I know the answer to that question, and it is not the answer the jury are about to hear from Aubrey.

The answer resides in the personality, if that's the right word, of the District Judge presiding at the Bermondsey Magistrates Court on the fateful day, Mr James Tooley, known to the judiciary and the profession as 'Jungle Jim'. The name derives from his propensity to dispense summary justice as if he were sitting in judgment on the local population of some far-flung outpost of empire in the early nineteenth century. He and Hubert would have made a fine pair. I'm surprised to learn that he hasn't retired by now. He has been around forever. I remember him from my days at the Bar, a striking sight on a hot day in summer, sitting on the bench in a white jacket and red cravat, his white broad-brimmed sun hat lying beside him on the bench on top of *Stone's Justices' Manual*, a huge fan whirring and rotating at his side, dispensing fines for motoring offences and shoplifting. The only thing missing was the chai-wallah to serve him tea. I have a feeling that Jungle Jim has had a lot to do with this case coming up to the Crown Court, and that he will have a lot to do with its outcome. But, as I say, that is not what Aubrey is about to tell the jury.

'The importance of this case, members of the jury, lies in safeguarding our system of criminal justice. No system of criminal justice can function, certainly not function fairly and efficiently, without a profession of advocates who prosecute, or represent, those accused of criminal offences – just as Miss Worthington and I do in this case. His Honour will direct you about the law later in the case, and you must take the law from him, but I think I can safely tell you this much: that only properly qualified persons, almost always either barristers or solicitors, are allowed to appear as advocates in our courts. The law does not allow unqualified persons to do so, for obvious reasons. It would be too easy for defendants to be given bad legal advice; their cases would not be competently presented to the court; and there would be a risk of serious injustice.'

The cynical part of me would love to add that these consequences sometimes occur even with some qualified barristers and solicitors I could name but, of course, I behave myself, and don't even glance at the jury.

'In this case, members of the jury, no one disputes that the defendant, Wilbraham Moffett, was not a qualified barrister or solicitor on the day in question. He worked as an outdoor clerk for a solicitor called Ellis Lamont. Despite the name, an outdoor clerk is someone who generally makes himself useful to the solicitor both in the office and running errands outside the office, for example going to court to file documents. Mr Moffett was working for Mr Lamont in that capacity while studying for a degree in law. It was his intention to become a solicitor in due course, members of the jury, but he was several years away from achieving that goal. You will also hear, members of the jury, that Mr Lamont was himself hardly a model solicitor. Indeed, he has since been struck off – in other words, he is no longer permitted to practise as a solicitor – though I hasten to add that that had nothing to do with the events with which you are concerned.'

No, that had to do, as I have discovered from a page on the Law Society's website, with some slight discrepancies in his clients' trust accounts. But it is interesting that Aubrey mentions it. The nature of the defence begins to suggest itself, if not to the jury, certainly to me. It is not going to be insanity. It's all going to be Mr Lamont's fault. Susan would have never allowed Aubrey to open this to the jury otherwise. She would have objected to the evidence of his being struck off, and I would have had to agree with her. It would have been irrelevant and prejudicial. But she obviously wants the jury to know about it as soon as possible.

'Mr Lamont, members of the jury, had a client by the name of Abdul Khan, who had been arrested on suspicion of supplying class A drugs, crack cocaine and heroin, and was due to appear at the Bermondsey Magistrates Court on the day you are concerned with. Mr Lamont had applied for legal aid on Mr Khan's behalf, so that he could be represented, but legal aid had not yet been granted. Anything to do with legal aid, in the experience of those of us who practise regularly in the courts, often takes an inordinate amount of time to be approved.'

Said with a slight overtone of bitterness, with which I fully sympathise, remembering all too well my own experience at the Bar of waiting endlessly to be paid for legal aid cases. I see Susan turn slightly towards the jury, nodding her agreement.

'It is not surprising, therefore, that Mr Lamont was not in a position to proceed with Mr Khan's case, and he needed to ask the District Judge to adjourn the case for a few days. There was nothing wrong with that, members of the jury, as long as Mr Lamont did so himself. He might well have made a bail application at the same time, because Mr Khan was in custody following his arrest. I should, perhaps, add, members of the jury, that a District Judge is a professional judge who sits in the Magistrates Court. I am sure you know that most magistrates are members of the public, such as yourselves, who have no legal training and serve without a salary. But in many courts now, there are also District Judges, who are legally qualified, and sit alone, and who have all the same powers as a bench of magistrates.'

And who do not always exercise the same degree of common sense, I add in the privacy of my own mind.

'Instead of attending court himself, members of the jury, Mr Lamont sent this defendant, his outdoor clerk Wilbraham Moffett, to the Bermondsey Magistrates Court with instructions to represent Mr Khan at his hearing, and to ask the District Judge, Mr James Tooley...'

He is dying to say 'Jungle Jim', I know, because he and Susan have exchanged a grin which neither can quite hide.

'...to grant an adjournment for seven days to allow legal aid to be granted. You will hear that the defendant complied with those instructions, even though they were quite improper, and, the Crown say, the defendant knew they were improper. You will hear that the defendant presented himself at the Magistrates Court dressed as a solicitor, wearing a smart suit and tie – as he is today; that he introduced himself to the court legal adviser and the usher; that he signed in as if he were a solicitor, so that his name appeared on the list of advocates given to the District Judge; that he took a seat in the row reserved for advocates; and that he addressed the District Judge as if he were a qualified solicitor, when Mr Khan's case was called on. That, members of the jury, is known as exercising a right of audience. With the usher's assistance I will now give you a copy of the indictment.'

Dawn eagerly takes the copies and distributes them to the jury, one between two.

'Fortunately, members of the jury, the District Judge became suspicious, for reasons you will hear in due course, and caused inquires to be made, with the result that the defendant was arrested. He was interviewed by the police under caution in the presence of a solicitor – not Mr Lamont, I hasten to add – and, as he was perfectly entitled to do, answered "no comment" to all questions put to him.'

As a judge you sometimes pick up a certain lack of detail in parts of the prosecution's opening, as if there is some uncertainty about quite how well that part of the case is going to go. Aubrey's account of the events leading to Moffett's arrest has been concise, to put it mildly. I am trying to picture the scene in court, and in Jungle Jim's chambers, and it is difficult to picture from what little the jury have been told. But a ray of light is beginning to penetrate my mind about Jungle Jim's involvement with this case, and I will await confirmation with interest.

'But I anticipate, members of the jury, that the defendant will deny that he acted in the way the prosecution alleges. Now, finally, I must make it clear that the prosecution has the burden of proof in this case, if you are to convict. The prosecution brings this case, and the prosecution must prove it by calling evidence. What I or my learned friend may say is not evidence. The evidence comes from the witnesses who will give evidence, and the documents you will see. The defendant does not have to prove his innocence; indeed, he does not have to prove anything at all. We must prove the case so that you are sure of the defendant's guilt before you can convict. If you are not sure – if, as we used to say in the old days…'

I do wish counsel would stop referring to the time during which I used to practise as the 'old days'.

'…you have a reasonable doubt – then you must find the defendant not guilty. But the Crown say that the evidence will make you quite sure in this case, and that the appropriate verdict, once you have heard the evidence, will be one of guilty.'

Aubrey turns towards me.

'With your Honour's leave, I will call my first witness, Kenneth Jessop.'

Dawn escorts Kenneth Jessop to the witness box. He is not a tall man, but when he takes the oath he does so with the firm voice and erect posture of a former non-commissioned officer, which is indeed what he is.

'Mr Jessop, please tell the jury what you do for a living.'

'I am a court usher, sir.'

'At the Bermondsey Magistrates Court?'

'Yes, sir.'

'And for how long have you been employed in that capacity?'

'For twelve years, sir,' Jessop replies proudly. 'Ever since I was discharged from the Army with the rank of full corporal.'

'Yes, I see,' Aubrey continues. 'Now, I am sure the jury will already have some idea of this, because of course we have an usher in this court too…'

Unbidden, Dawn turns to give the jury a wave and a smile.

'...but perhaps you could give the jury a brief idea of what your duties are as an usher in the Magistrates Court.'

Jessop shakes his head.

'There is quite a lot to it. Before court begins, I have to prepare the courtroom, put out water and glasses for the magistrates, the witnesses and the lawyers. Then I have to collect the list from the office and make sure it is put up outside each court, and one or two other places. Then I have to make sure all the lawyers sign in.'

'Yes, I want to ask you about that,' Aubrey says. 'When you say "sign in", what does that mean exactly?'

'We ask all the lawyers who are appearing to sign a copy of the list, sir, so that the magistrates know who is representing the prosecution and the defence in each case. It is my job to make sure that they all sign in. Of course, most of them are regulars and you get to know the regulars, so once I see them and they tell me who they are representing I add the name to the list myself. But obviously, I don't know them all, so I keep a look out for anyone acting like a lawyer – you can spot them a mile off once you get used to the job – and I ask them to sign in. Of course, some of the defendants are not represented, so it's not every case that has someone signed in.'

Aubrey nods.

'Thank you, Mr Jessop. Now I want to take you back to the morning of the seventh of May last year. Do you remember that morning?'

'I certainly do, sir.'

'Let me ask you this first. Obviously, there is more than one courtroom at Bermondsey, and am I right in thinking that you would be assigned to a particular courtroom?'

'Yes, sir. On this particular morning I was in court one.'

'And who was due to preside in that court?'

'The District Judge, sir, Mr Tooley. We had a bench of

magistrates in court two, if I remember correctly, but Mr Tooley was in court one.'

'What sort of list did you have?'

Jessop gives a little snort.

'It was a very busy morning, sir, more than fifty cases in the list, most of them quite short matters, overnight drunks and prostitution, a few bail applications, then a road traffic list. It was going to keep us busy, I can tell you.'

He turns to Dawn.

'I'm sure you have your busy days here, too.'

'Oh, we do,' Dawn replies. Carol, our court clerk, puts a finger to her lips, and Dawn looks at me and mouths 'sorry'. The jury snigger.

'Mr Jessop,' Aubrey says, 'if you would be kind enough to address yourself to the jury, rather than the usher...'

'Yes, sir. Sorry, sir.'

'And if you would kindly look at this document.'

Grateful for something to do to divert attention from her previous contribution to the proceedings, Dawn rushes to Aubrey, takes the document from his outstretched hand and scurries to the witness box. Jessop looks at it.

'Do you recognise this?'

'I do, sir. This is the list for the morning of the seventh of May last year.'

'Exhibit one, your Honour?'

I nod.

'If you would look down the list, please. Is case number thirty-two the case of a defendant called Abdul Khan?'

'Yes, sir.'

'Thank you. Another document, please.'

Dawn scurries again.

'Do you recognise this?'

'Yes, sir. This is a copy of my sign-in sheet for the same morning.'

'So, that is a copy of the list on which there are some signatures?'

'Yes, sir.'

'And some entries in your handwriting, presumably the regulars. Is that right?'

'Yes, sir.'

'Exhibit two, your Honour.'

'Yes,' I say.

'Now, would you please look on Exhibit two for case number thirty-two. Is there any name written there for that case?'

'There is, sir.'

'Is the name in your handwriting, or someone else's?'

'It is the person's handwriting, sir, not mine.'

'And what name is it?'

Jessop scrutinises it closely

'It appears to be the name Wilb-something Moff-something, sir. It's not very easy to read.'

Susan springs to her feet.

'There is no dispute about it, your Honour. It is the defendant's name, and he signed the sheet.'

'I am much obliged to my learned friend,' Aubrey says. 'Mr Jessop, was Mr Moffett one of your regulars?'

'No, sir. In fact, I had never seen him before that morning, and I have never seen him since.'

'Do you know a solicitor by the name of Ellis Lamont?'

Jessop thinks for a moment or two.

'It rings a distant bell, sir. I can't put a face to the name, but it does seem somewhat familiar.'

'But not one of your regulars?'

'Oh, no, sir. I know all my regulars by name.'

'Yes, I am sure you do. Can you tell the jury how Mr Moffett's signature came to be on your sign-in sheet?'

'As far as I remember, sir, I was standing outside court one. It was still only about nine-fifteen, nine-thirty at the latest.

I'd just put the list up a few minutes before. He came up to me, handed me a business card, and said "Abdul Khan". I remember that; just the name, "Abdul Khan". I looked down the list, pointed the case out to him, and he signed the sheet. Simple as that.'

'Did Mr Moffett say anything at all apart from "Abdul Khan"?'

'No, sir.'

'Now, you said he handed you a business card?'

'Yes, sir.'

'Look at this, please.'

Dawn has it in Jessop's hands in a flash.

'Do you recognise this?'

'Yes, sir. That is the card he gave me.'

'Exhibit three, please, your Honour. I'm sure there is no dispute about it. Does it say: "Ellis Lamont and Co, Solicitors" and does it give an address, telephone number, fax number, and email address?'

'Yes, sir.'

'Is there any other name on the card?'

'There is, sir. Just under the name of the firm it gives the name Wilbraham Moffett.'

'Yes. Just hold that up so that the jury can see, would you, Mr Jessop? You will be able to see it at closer range later, members of the jury.'

'Mr Jessop, how was Mr Moffett dressed when he approached you?'

'He was wearing a dark suit and a tie, sir.'

'Did he look like a solicitor?'

Susan is on her feet even before Aubrey has finished the question.

'Oh, really, your Honour!'

A look from me is all it takes.

'I will ask it differently,' Aubrey concedes, with a grin which acknowledges that he was trying to get away with one. 'Mr

Jessop, given the defendant's appearance, the fact that he asked you about the case of Abdul Khan, the fact that he gave you a business card for Lamont and Co, and the fact that he signed the sign-in sheet by case number thirty-two, what conclusion, if any, did you reach about Mr Moffett?'

'I assumed he must be Mr Khan's solicitor,' Jessop replies.

'Were you present in court when Mr Khan's case was called on?'

'I'm really not sure, sir. I don't think so. With such a busy list, I have to keep running in and out of court all the time, checking that I have the defendants and lawyers and witnesses ready to go when they are called on. I can't keep track of all the cases after they are called on.'

'No, of course. Do you remember seeing Mr Moffett again that morning?'

'Just once, sir. It was just before lunch, I think. I saw Mr Moffett with two police officers, apparently about to leave the building. I learned later that he had been arrested. I didn't know why at the time. I can't remember seeing him again, apart from that.'

'Do you remember whether you noticed him sitting in any particular place in the courtroom at any time during the morning?'

'I'm sorry, sir. I may have seen him. I just can't remember.'

'Yes, thank you,' Aubrey says. 'Please wait there. There may be some more questions.'

Susan gets slowly to her feet.

'You *assumed* that Mr Moffett must be Mr Khan's solicitor, did you, Mr Jessop?'

'That's correct, Miss.'

'Because you can spot a solicitor a mile off, right?'

'Well...'

'That's what you told my learned friend Mr Brooks.'

'Well, yes, I can usually tell… yes.'

'Did Mr Moffett ever *tell* you that he was a solicitor?'

Jessop thinks about this for some time.

'Well, he signed the…'

'Please listen carefully to the question, Mr Jessop. Did Mr Moffett ever *tell* you that he was a solicitor?'

'No, Miss. He just gave me his card.'

'Ah yes, the card,' Susan says. 'Do you still have the card in front of you, Mr Jessop? Exhibit three?'

'Yes.' He holds the card aloft.

'Thank you. Read it over to yourself carefully for me, if you would. Does it anywhere describe Mr Moffett as being a solicitor?'

Jessop appears to search every inch of the card with his eyes, holding it up, directly in front of his face.

'No, Miss.'

'Thank you. At any time that morning, did you hear Mr Moffett address the District Judge for any purpose at all?'

Jessop shifts uncomfortably.

'Well, as I said, Miss, I had to be in and out of court …'

'I am not criticising you, Mr Jessop. I understand that you had a busy morning. I am just asking whether you heard Mr Moffett address the District Judge.'

'No, Miss.'

'One last thing. Did Mr Moffett have a briefcase with him?'

'I believe he did, Miss, yes.'

'Thank you. I have nothing further, your Honour.'

As Jessop leaves court, Carol turns around to face me.

'I think there is a note from the jury, your Honour.'

She dispatches Dawn to collect the note from juror number seven. It is always a dramatic moment in court as the folded note is brought to the bench, even if it is only to ask for a smoking break. I open it. It reads: 'Are we going to hear evidence from the District Judge?' It is a perfectly reasonable question. I had wondered about it myself. I did not see a witness statement from Jungle Jim anywhere in the file, and Aubrey did not advertise him as a witness in his opening – both fairly clear indicators that at least at present, the answer to the jury's question is no. It seems a strange omission. But it is a question for the prosecution, not for me, so I really need to hear from Aubrey before going any further.

'Members of the jury, why don't you take a short break for coffee?' I suggest, 'and I will discuss your note with counsel.'

The jury having left court, I read the note, and Aubrey stands silent for some time, as if in meditation.

'Your Honour,' he replies eventually. 'I may need some time to consider how to respond to that question.'

'I'm not sure why, Mr Brooks,' I say. 'I am sure the prosecution must have given some thought to this. It does seem rather a basic question.'

Susan is grinning wickedly at Aubrey.

'Your Honour, I want to put this as diplomatically as I can,' Aubrey says. 'We *are* dealing with Ju… with Mr Tooley.'

The light begins to dawn. Jungle Jim is acting up, not cooperating. Perhaps he has gone off his malaria meds.

'Yes, I see,' I reply. I consult with Carol. We have a sentence to do at some point which may well take the rest of the morning. I can give Aubrey time without any real problem. I release the trial of Mr Moffett until two o'clock.

The sentence is of one Josh Gavel, a forty-year old with a shaved head wearing green combat trousers and black army boots. He has pleaded guilty to having two dogs dangerously out of control in a public place. I have photographs of both dogs, which rejoice in the names of 'Beast' and 'Mangler' and look ferocious. The veterinary expert who examined them confirms this in his report, saying that both animals tried to bite him during his examination. One is a Staff, the other some American breed, any example of which is prohibited in this country, whether individually ferocious or not. Gavel was in charge of them on a walkway on the south bank of the River, near HMS *Belfast*, where he judged it would be safe to let them off their leashes. They took advantage of this to savage someone's King Charles Spaniel within an inch of its life before being restrained.

Chummy is accompanied by an entourage of three young women with spiked hair in gothic dress, who sit sullenly in the public gallery. After listening to a long opening from the prosecution, and an impassioned plea from the defence, I give him a suspended sentence with unpaid work; order him to pay compensation to the owner of the King Charles; order Beast and Mangler to be destroyed; order Chummy to pay costs; and disqualify him from owning a dog for five years. I'm half expecting it to kick off. This is the only form of capital punishment we still have in our courts, and Chummy and friends don't look like the sort to take the death sentence without some form of protest. I'm grateful we are not in court three. But in fact, Chummy collapses in the dock in floods of tears, and has to be comforted by the matronly dock officer. His entourage seem embarrassed to witness this, and stalk quickly out of court, as if disowning him publicly as the pathetic loser he obviously is.

And so to lunch, an oasis of calm in a desert of chaos.

There is a conservative culinary mood in the mess today. Apparently, yesterday's dish of the day, described as paella, was almost too terrible to describe. Because paella is, to say the least, exotic by the standards of the Bermondsey judicial mess, everyone voted to try it. It was unanimously condemned. Marjorie says she felt sick for the rest of the day, and even Hubert, who alone among us is generally tolerant of the dish of the day, found it too much. I, of course, was spared because of my meeting with the Grey Smoothies, and the general feeling is that I have dodged a bullet. The kitchen have officially blamed the paella on a Spanish assistant cook, who made it to celebrate her last day at court before returning to Madrid, presumably to poison her own countrymen rather than ours. Legless has opted for the cheese salad, which he is eying suspiciously. Marjorie has a dish from home, which looks like bean sprouts in soy sauce in a Tupperware container. Hubert is starting on a baked potato with baked beans. I have brought in a ham and cheese bap from Jeanie and Elsie.

'So, what happened with the Grey Smoothies?' Legless asks. Of course, I haven't had the chance to tell him about it.

'I'm afraid it was the usual nonsense,' I reply. 'They don't see a business case.'

Marjorie is outraged.

'What's it got to do with a business case?' she demands. 'Court three is downright dangerous.'

'We don't have any statistics to back up our position,' I reply.

'But Legless had that shoplifter chap who was always trying to escape,' she insists.

'Yes I know, but he didn't succeed in escaping, and more importantly, he didn't kill or maim anyone. That's the kind of statistic they say they need.'

'Perhaps we could offer some defendant a reduced sentence to fake an escape,' Legless suggests bitterly. 'We could get some fake blood and ask one of the ushers to feign an injury.'

'If we had supplies of yesterday's paella,' Marjorie says, 'we could fake an environmental disaster. Every defendant in the building could escape. Can you have someone extradited from Spain for ABH?'

'I'm sorry,' I say. 'It's not completely hopeless. They did say they would look at it again.'

'Is that like the cheque being in the post?' Legless asks sadly.

'Something like that,' I reply.

There is a depressed silence for some time. Then Hubert brightens up.

'I hear you're trying a chap for impersonating a solicitor,' he says.

'Yes,' I reply, glad to change the subject. 'It seems a strong case, but the jury has sent a note asking whether the prosecution is going to call the District Judge.'

'Who is it?' Legless asks.

'Jungle Jim.'

There is loud laughter, good to hear.

'Well, of course, they wouldn't call Jungle Jim, would they?' Legless asks. 'I wouldn't if I were prosecuting. Not unless I was desperate. God only knows what he might come out with.'

'I know,' I say, 'but I'm not sure what else they have. The actual charge is exercising the right of audience, but the only witness they've called so far, the usher, didn't know whether Chummy had opened his mouth in court or not. The legal adviser suggests in her statement that he gave his name, but she's not very clear about anything else.'

'Was it just the one occasion?' Hubert asks.

'Yes.'

'Well, that's not very serious, is it?'

'Not particularly, but to hear Aubrey Brooks open it to the jury, you would think the whole system of criminal justice was under attack.'

'Aubrey is such a *poseur*,' Legless says.

'He's got a point, though,' Marjorie responds. 'You can't just have every Tom, Dick and Harry traipsing around the courts pretending to be lawyers, can you?'

'Why not?' Legless grins. 'It happens here all the time.'

'There was a chap at the old Marlborough Street Magistrates Court who got away with it for two years,' Hubert says.

'What?' I say.

'Oh, yes,' Hubert replies. 'I forget the chap's name, but he used to appear in front of the regular Stipendiary Magistrate – that was in the days when they were still called "Stipes" instead of all this modern nonsense about District Judges. Roddy Coverdale was the Stipe. Marvellous chap. It was a real treat to see him with all the drunks and ladies of the night at Christmas. They had an arrangement with him, the ones who were down on their luck and had nowhere to go. They would put a brick through the window of some shop or other, they would come before him on Christmas Eve, and Roddy would put them inside for fourteen days, so they got a warm bed and a bit of Christmas dinner to tide them over. You wouldn't get one of these new-fangled District Judges doing that, would you? He knew them all by their first names, did Roddy. Did your heart good to see him at work. I used to go down to Marlborough Street on Christmas Eve if I was free, just to watch him.'

'But what about the solicitor?' Marjorie asks.

'What? Oh, yes. Well, I heard about that from Roddy at dinner at the Garrick one evening. This chap got away with it for two years or more. He used to turn up beautifully dressed, immaculate dark suit and tie, perfect manners. He seemed to know the law, and Roddy says he was always very persuasive. Roddy thought he was better than most of the real solicitors who appeared before him.'

'So how was he found out?' Marjorie asks.

'If I remember rightly,' Hubert replies, 'he didn't turn up one day for an adjourned hearing for one of his clients. It turned out later that he intended to be there, but he wasn't feeling very well. So Roddy asked the defendant who his solicitor was, and wanted a phone number, and the man didn't have one, of course, so the whole thing came to light. The strange thing was that, as far as Roddy could discover, he never charged his clients a penny. Apparently, he just enjoyed being in court.'

'How long did he get?' Legless asks.

Hubert seems surprised.

'Oh, Roddy didn't have him prosecuted,' he replies as if it

were the most obvious proposition in the world.

'What?'

'No, of course not. Well, he didn't do any harm to anyone, did he? He probably saved the legal aid fund a small fortune over a year or two. No, Roddy gave him a fiver out of the poor box and sent him on his way, told him he was going to check with all the other courts in the area to make sure he wasn't trying it on somewhere else. He did confiscate his tie, of course.'

We are gazing at Hubert in wonder.

'The chap used to wear an Army and Navy Club tie,' Hubert explains. 'The Army and Navy wasn't Roddy's club, of course. He was a Garrick man through and through. But he was a stickler for protocol; he couldn't have Chummy running round in a club tie when he wasn't a member, even if it wasn't Roddy's club.'

To my surprise, I find myself feeling some sympathy with Roddy Coverdale.

'I suppose one could take the view that if a defendant doesn't have a solicitor, an impersonator will have to do,' Marjorie laughs.

'I suppose so,' I say. 'At least, until the real thing comes along.'

* * *

Tuesday afternoon

Aubrey is not ready yet to reveal whether Jungle Jim will be going into the witness box, and at my invitation he tells the jury this when we resume at two o'clock. The jury look, not annoyed exactly, but exasperated. In his absence, at least for now, Aubrey calls the legal adviser to the magistrates, Nadia Hepple, a precise, competent woman in her late thirties, dressed in black as she would appear in her own court.

'Mrs Hepple, could you just help the jury to understand what your function is as a legal adviser?'

'Yes, of course. As the title suggests, my main job is to ensure that the magistrates understand the law, and to answer any questions they may have about the law, court procedure, evidence, and so on.'

'Would I be right in thinking that your job is somewhat easier when you are sitting with a legally qualified District Judge rather than a bench of lay magistrates?'

'Usually,' she smiles, 'though not invariably.'

This produces a chuckle around the courtroom. Mrs Hepple is charming as well as competent, and I see the jury warming to her.

'Now, is it right,' Aubrey continues, 'there is no dispute, that on the morning of the seventh of May last year you were sitting in court one with District Judge Tooley?'

'That is correct.'

'What kind of list did you have that morning?'

'As I recall, it was a long list of bits and pieces, overnight charges like drunk and disorderly, a few bail applications, then a list, road traffic mostly if I remember rightly. On mornings like that my job is really court management, to assist the District Judge in getting through everything as efficiently as he can.'

'And how would you do that?'

'I talk to the usher all the time, find out which cases are ready and which require more time, advise on the order in which cases should be called, and so on. And, as always, I take a note of the proceedings. That's the most important part, really, to make sure there is an accurate note of the proceedings.'

'Is that because the magistrates must keep an official record for future reference, for example if a higher court, or someone involved in the proceedings, needs to know?'

'Yes, we have to be able to produce a certificate whenever necessary. As is the case in this court, I'm sure.'

'Indeed. Can I ask you to look at this document, please?'

Mrs Hepple puts on her reading glasses.

'This is a copy of the note I made regarding one particular case on that morning.'

'On the seventh of May?'

'Yes.'

'Which case was that?'

'That was case number thirty-two in my list, Abdul Khan.'

'When did you make that note?'

'As the proceedings were going on.'

'Exhibit four, please, your Honour. Now, Mrs Hepple, refreshing your memory from your note as far as you need to – I take it there is no objection…'

'None, your Honour,' Susan confirms.

'…I am obliged. Referring to your note, can you tell the jury what transpired in the case of Abdul Khan on that morning?'

'Yes. The case was called on at about ten past twelve. Mr Khan was in custody and was brought up from the cells with an interpreter. I confirmed his identity, and he immediately asked why his solicitor had not been down to the cells to see him.'

'How did you react to that?'

'I think both Mr Tooley and I immediately looked at the sign-in sheet to see whether he was represented.'

'May the witness please see Exhibit two? Do you recognise Exhibit two, Mrs Hepple?'

'Yes, that is the sign-in sheet.'

'The jury had heard from Mr Jessop that he does his best to make sure that representatives sign in before court begins, is that right?'

'Yes, Ken updates the list from time to time and gives me the most recent edition, and I provide the District Judge with the information. In this case, there is a signature against case thirty-two, but it is very difficult to read.'

'Then what happened?'

'There were a number of solicitors in court at the time, and I think one barrister. The District Judge asked if anyone was representing Mr Khan.'

'Did anyone respond to that?'

'Yes, the defendant, Mr Moffett.'

'Whereabouts was Mr Moffett at that moment?'

'He was sitting in the advocates' row with the defence solicitors.'

'And how was he dressed?'

'He was dressed properly for court, wearing a suit and tie.'

'How did Mr Moffett respond?'

'In a very strange way indeed. Instead of getting up and speaking to the District Judge, he simply raised his right hand.'

'Let me ask you this, Mrs Hepple. Is it the practice in the Magistrates Court, as it is in this court, for an advocate to stand when addressing the bench?'

'Yes, always.'

'What did Mr Tooley say or do, if anything?'

'He asked Mr Moffett his name.'

'Did Mr Moffett reply?'

'He did. He said, "Wilbraham Moffett, but people call me Wilbur."'

There is some laughter, in which Susan joins with a glance towards the jury.

'I see you looking at your note. Did you make a note of his exact words at the time?'

'I did.'

'Did Mr Moffett stand while giving that reply?'

'No. He did not.'

'Then what happened?'

'Mr Tooley leaned down and said to me...'

Mrs Hepple is a professional and knows better than to answer that question without allowing Susan the opportunity to object. She pauses. Susan duly objects to the hearsay, taking full advantage of the occasion to remind the jury of the absence of Jungle Jim.

'Without telling us what was said,' Aubrey continues, 'what did the District Judge do, and what did you do?'

'Mr Tooley stood Mr Khan's case out for a short time. Mr Khan was taken back down to the cells. Mr Tooley then rose, and at his request I brought him a telephone number for someone at the Law Society. I then heard Mr Tooley speak to someone on the telephone for several minutes.'

'Then what happened?'

'Mr Tooley and I went back into court. Mr Khan's case was called on again, and he was brought back up. Mr Tooley asked Mr Moffett whether he was a solicitor representing Mr Khan, and Mr Moffett replied that he was, again without standing. Mr Tooley then said, "I don't believe you. The Law Society has never heard of you. I'm going to do something about this."'

'What did the District Judge in fact do about it?'

'There were two uniformed police officers in court waiting for their cases to be called on. Mr Tooley asked them to arrest Mr Moffett on a charge of exercising the right of audience when he wasn't entitled to.'

'Did they arrest him?'

'They did. I heard the officers give Mr Moffett the proper caution and he was taken away. We adjourned Mr Khan's case. One of the other solicitors in court volunteered to go to see Mr Khan and find out what was going on. I believe that solicitor's firm ended up representing Mr Khan from that point on.'

'Did Mr Moffett say anything when he was arrested?'

'Yes. He said, "All I wanted was an adjournment for seven days."'

'Did you make a note of that answer at the time?'

'Yes.'

'Thank you, Mrs Hepple. Nothing further, your Honour.'

'Mrs Hepple, there is nothing unusual about a man wearing a suit and tie to court is there?' Susan begins. 'It doesn't necessarily mean that someone is a solicitor, does it?'

'No, of course not.'

'A man *employed by a solicitor* might dress in that way, isn't that fair to say?'

'I would hope he would.'

'Quite. A person employed by a solicitor might also carry a briefcase, wouldn't you agree?'

'Of course.'

'When Mr Moffett was arrested, what steps, if any, were taken to establish whether he might have privileged papers relating to Mr Khan's case in his briefcase, and to safeguard those papers properly?'

Mrs Hepple is visibly taken aback.

'I wasn't aware that Mr Moffett had a briefcase.'

'So, for all you know, if he had a briefcase and if that briefcase contained privileged papers, they might have been seized by the police with no intervention by your court, is that right?'

'I suppose so, yes.'

'Can we agree, from the description you have given of the proceedings, that Mr Moffett obviously didn't have the first idea about how to behave in court?'

She smiles. 'I would have to agree. Yes.'

'Not the first idea of how to act as an advocate in court?'

'I would agree.'

'Not only that – he hadn't even been down to the cells to see Mr Khan before court began, had he?'

'Apparently not.'

'Again, he seemed to have no idea of what he was doing?'

'None at all, as far as I could see.'

Susan pauses.

'Mrs Hepple, the only point on which I challenge your evidence at all is this. You said that Mr Tooley asked Mr Moffett whether he was a *solicitor* representing Mr Khan, and that Mr Moffett said he was?'

'That is correct.'

'Might it be that Mr Tooley asked *whether his firm represented Mr Khan*, not whether Mr Moffett himself was a solicitor?'

'That is not the note I made.'

'I appreciate that, Mrs Hepple. I am asking you whether there is any possibility that your recollection and your note may be mistaken.'

'I don't think so. I am always careful about my notes.'

'No doubt Mr Tooley could clear it up for us, if he were to be called to give evidence about what was said?'

Aubrey struggles to his feet to object, but does not quite make it in time.

'I'm sure he could,' Mrs Hepple replies brightly.

'Thank you, Mrs Hepple, nothing further.'

Next, the prosecution calls Mr Abdul Khan, who is celebrating his recent release from prison after serving the prescribed half of a sentence imposed on him by Hubert following his plea of guilty to two counts of supplying crack cocaine and heroin. Mr Khan gives evidence with the assistance of an Urdu interpreter, because although his command of English is adequate for normal social and business conversation – such as that involved in selling wraps of class A drugs on the street – it is apparently not quite up to the more intricate language of the courtroom. Mr Khan tells us that he wanted Ellis Lamont to represent him in connection with the charges he faced last year, as he had in the past in connection with other matters, and that Mr Lamont had applied for legal aid. Mr Khan had understood that there might be some slight delay and an application for a short adjournment, but he expected Mr Lamont at least to come to see him in the cells. But no one came to see him on the seventh of May before he was taken to court. He was surprised when Mr Moffett claimed to be representing him, because he had no idea who Mr Moffett was. He had no recollection of what was said between the District

Judge and Mr Moffett, and was very surprised to see Mr Moffett being arrested, an event which he claimed not to understand at all. He subsequently asked another firm of solicitors to represent him, and pronounced himself very satisfied with their work on his behalf. Susan has no questions in cross-examination.

Aubrey calls evidence of Ellis Lamont's being struck off, followed by the evidence of the police witnesses dealing with the defendant's arrest and interview, all of which passes quickly and without challenge. He then asks for the jury to be sent home for the day, so that he can have one last chance to reflect on the District Judge before formally closing his case. The jury seem none too impressed by this, and as an additional irritant, Aubrey's clerk has called to say that he has a case in the morning list in the Court of Appeal tomorrow morning, which takes precedence over the Crown Court, so we will be unable to resume the trial until after lunch. I send the jury away. He then asks if he and Susan might see me in chambers. He seems unusually diffident.

'Jungle Jim is playing up, is he?' I ask.

'That's one way of putting it,' Aubrey replies. 'I have already told Susan this, so there is no reason why I shouldn't tell you as well, Judge. The CPS have made repeated approaches to District Judge Tooley to make a witness statement and give evidence, but he refuses point blank.'

'For what reason, for God's sake?'

Aubrey exhales heavily.

'He says it's beneath his dignity, Judge.'

I am truly taken aback.

'Beneath *what*? Oh, for God's sake. Leaving aside the fanciful concept of Jungle Jim having such a thing as dignity…' I pause. 'We are in chambers, you understand?'

'Of course, Judge,' they both reply at once.

'Leaving that ridiculous notion aside, has anybody explained to him that I have power to order him to attend this court to give evidence? Would you like a witness summons? All you have to do is ask.'

Aubrey nods.

'I've been giving some thought to that, Judge. It's one of the reasons it's taking so long. If it had been a more serious offence, I would be pushing more. But in this case I thought it would be prudent to consult at the highest level of the CPS before asking for a witness summons for a sitting judge. It may have reached the desk of the Director of Public Prosecutions himself, I'm not sure. I have given them a deadline of four o'clock this afternoon, so hopefully we will know soon.'

'Yes, well, I see the wisdom of that,' I agree. 'If it is of any help to you to mention to the Director that the court is growing impatient, please don't hesitate.'

'Thank you,' Aubrey says, 'though I am actually more worried about the jury.'

'You should be,' I observe. 'I sense they really want to hear from Jungle Jim, and I think they are likely to hold it against the prosecution if they don't.'

'As they should,' Susan says. 'In any case, I don't think it's got anything to do with his dignity.'

'Oh?'

'He's embarrassed,' she continues simply, 'because he could have prevented this whole piece of nonsense, and he knows it.'

'How could he have done that?' I ask. 'The defendant is entitled to come to the Crown Court for trial for this offence.'

'It should never have got as far as that. We are only here because Jungle Jim had him arrested. Surely, all he had to do was to threaten him with contempt, or say, "Look here, young man, you're getting yourself into trouble. Call your boss now and tell him to get down here within the next hour, or he's the one who's going to be in hot water." There was no need to have him arrested. In addition to the waste of public funds involved in trying this nonsense, it caused all sorts of problems for Mr

Khan and his new solicitors. It took them weeks to recover the privileged papers in Moffett's briefcase, and I am sure the police took a good look at them before handing them back.'

I nod. She has a point. It was a typical Jungle Jim piece of palm tree justice. Make ruling first, engage brain later. But there is nothing we can do about that now, except to conclude this 'nonsense' as quickly and as fairly as possible.

* * *

Wednesday afternoon
It has been a light morning. Stella unloaded on me the few bail applications and plea and case management hearings we had listed, so I have at least freed up the other judges to get on with their trials, even if I can't resume mine until Aubrey returns from whatever savaging he may be getting in the Court of Appeal. Lunchtime is likewise uneventful. Legless has been told to expect a verdict in his trial, a domestic burglary, immediately after lunch. Marjorie and Hubert are making progress with their street robberies. All seems in order.

When we resume, Aubrey tells me and the jury, without any elaboration at all, that the prosecution does not intend to call the District Judge as a witness, and that he is now closing the prosecution's case. Susan is on her feet in a flash.

'Your Honour, there is a matter of law I wish to raise in the absence of the jury.'

The jury trail wearily out of court, looking quite forlorn.

'Your Honour,' she begins as soon as the jury have gone, 'I'm going to ask that you withdraw the case from the jury. There is no evidence on which the jury, properly directed by your Honour, could safely convict Mr Moffett of this offence.'

I stare at her for a few moments. Aubrey is hovering, but I signal to him to leave it to me.

'Miss Worthington,' I reply, 'the defendant is charged with impersonating a solicitor. He attended the Magistrates Court dressed like a solicitor, signed in as a solicitor, gave the usher his card, seated himself in the solicitor's row, and when questioned, told the District Judge that he was a solicitor.'

'Yes, your Honour. That's my learned friend's, "if it walks like a duck and quacks like a duck…" argument. But it doesn't work.'

'I'm afraid I don't follow.'

'Your Honour, my learned friend thinks he is prosecuting Mr Moffett for impersonating a solicitor. But that's not what Mr Moffett is charged with. He's charged with "*doing an act in the purported exercise of a right of audience.*"'

I take a moment to digest this.

'It's not an offence to attend the Magistrates Court wearing a suit and tie,' she continues, 'even if carrying a briefcase. It's not an offence to look like a solicitor. It's not even an offence to sit in the row reserved for solicitors, though admittedly it's not the most intelligent thing to do.'

'So, what does that mean?' I ask eventually. 'What amounts to exercising a right of audience?'

'Ah, well, there your Honour has, if I may say so, hit the nail right on the head.'

'I'm glad to hear it,' I reply, disingenuously.

'Because in fact, your Honour, this case seems to raise that very question.'

For the first time, I am beginning to feel slightly uneasy. When counsel says that a case 'seems to raise' a question, the implication is that there is going to be a point of law which may not have been decided before, and that I am going to be called upon to decide it myself. That's just a short step from finding myself being mauled in the Court of Appeal one of these days, as may well have happened to some poor sod in Aubrey's case this morning.

Susan pauses to consult a note.

'Your Honour, at the Bar, we're not allowed to exercise a right of audience before completing the first six months of our pupillage training. According to our rules of conduct, exercising a right of audience means "conducting any part of a case in court". The natural meaning of "conducting part of a case" is that you advance the client's case in some way: either by addressing the court about the law or the facts of the case or by asking the court to take action of some kind.'

'Well, he did say something in court about wanting an adjournment for seven days,' I reply weakly.

'That was in reply to the caution when he was being arrested,' Susan points out. 'It hardly qualifies as advancing the client's case.'

I recover slightly.

'But he did address the court twice when Mr Khan's case was called on, didn't he? In fact, according to Mrs Hepple, he said he was Mr Khan's solicitor. Isn't that enough?'

'I would submit not, your Honour. That doesn't advance the client's case at all. If he had addressed the court about the case, even if only to ask for an adjournment, I concede that would be enough. But he didn't.'

A memory comes to me, and I decide without any real reflection to offer it as a possibly relevant argument. In two minutes or less, I will regret having done so.

'I remember when I was a pupil in my first six months,' I say. 'My pupil-master, who practised mainly in the Family Division, was very able but had a very active social life. It was not at all unusual, when we were in the High Court, for him to have a luncheon appointment, and arrive back at court a few minutes late for the afternoon.'

This is all perfectly true, by the way. Basil was a delightful man, and could be quite brilliant in court, but he was a man of independent means and had a clear sense of his priorities. In particular, he never allowed his practice to stand in the way of his social life. That is one reason why it was such a brilliant pupillage. I did most of the work of preparing our cases, and as a result I learned an incredible amount – even if my overriding memory of my first six months is of a long period of unending panic. Counsel are looking at me rather strangely.

'The point is,' I explain, 'that whenever he was late back, I had to stand up in front of a High Court judge, not to mention opposing counsel, and ask the judge to rise for a few minutes to accommodate him. Fortunately, they were always very nice about it. But in six months, I must have made that application to every judge of the Division. Was I conducting part of the client's case in court?'

'I think that supports my argument, your Honour,' Susan smiles, 'and I would say, no, of course not.'

She looks at Aubrey, who is also smiling, albeit for a different reason.

'Your Honour, I'm afraid I can't agree with my learned friend there. As my learned friend herself conceded a moment or two ago, asking for an adjournment is enough. That is conducting a part of the case.'

'All I did was ask the judge to rise for a few minutes,' I protest. 'That hardly amounts to asking for an adjournment.'

No one responds to this plea, and I feel myself going hot and cold.

'I'm sure no possible harm could have come of it, your Honour,' Aubrey continues soothingly after an awkward silence, 'and there must be a statute of limitations of some kind after so many years. I see no need for us to remind your Honour of the caution.'

'What it comes to, your Honour,' Susan says, quickly changing the subject, 'is that there is no evidence that the defendant conducted any part of Mr Khan's case. At worst, he may have intended to do so, and taken certain preparatory steps towards doing so, but the quick thinking of the District Judge' (she gives me a sly grin as she says this) 'prevented him from carrying out his intention. He has acted stupidly, of course, but he has not committed this offence.'

She sits down.

'Your Honour,' Aubrey begins, 'even accepting my learned friend's definition of "exercising a right of audience", your Honour himself made the point earlier. Where a defendant dresses like a solicitor, acts like a solicitor, signs in as a solicitor, positions himself in the solicitors' row, and tells the court that he is a solicitor when the case is called on, he conducts a part of the case…'

He is interrupted by the quiet but noticeable ringing of the phone on the clerk's desk. Carol picks up and answers. Aubrey is continuing to speak, but I am somewhat distracted. Replacing the receiver, she calls quietly to Dawn, who quickly walks the short distance between her chair and Carol. They whisper furiously for some seconds before Dawn throws off her gown, makes a very half-hearted bow in my direction and hurries from court. Aubrey stops now. The phone rings again and Carol confers with someone briefly. She turns to me.

'I'm sorry, judge, but I need you to rise. Now. Stella will meet you in the corridor.'

'Why? What's happening?' I ask. 'I'm in the middle of…'

'Please, Judge. It's important. I will take care of things here.'

I have no idea what is going on. I can't see or hear anything untoward. If there were a fire or a bomb threat, surely Security would have activated the alarms? But Carol is obviously deadly serious. I stand.

'I'm sorry,' I say, 'but it appears that I am needed urgently elsewhere. I will be back as soon as I can.'

As I leave, I hear Carol ordering everyone not to leave court, to stay where they are.

Stella leads me quickly along the corridor to the judge's entrance to court three. She holds the door open for me and we enter. It is the most astonishing sight I have ever seen. The judicial chair has been pushed back to the far end of the bench. In the place where the chair should be, two security guards are holding down a man whose arms are handcuffed behind his back. In the well of the court, a dock officer is sitting in a chair, holding a blood-stained handkerchief to his head. Clare, the court clerk working court three today, is doing her best to comfort him. Two barristers are sitting in their places, looking rather shell-shocked. To my immediate right, I see Legless sprawled full length on the floor, fully robed except for his wig, which is lying against the wall at his feet. He seems to be trying to get up, but Dawn, our designated first-aider, is trying to keep him down.

'Bit of bother, Charlie, nothing to worry about,' he says. 'All under control now. Police are on the way. They will be here any moment.'

This announcement seems to irritate the man in handcuffs, who lets loose with a barrage of abuse. There is then a flurry of movement from the security officers, and what looks like a punch or two in the direction of the solar plexus, whereupon the man suddenly quietens down again.

'Would someone please tell me what is going on?' I ask.

Clare leaves the dock officer and comes to stand next to me.

'The jury came back with a verdict of guilty a few minutes ago,' she explains. 'We excused them and Judge Dunblane started hearing argument about sentence. He said he would order a pre-sentence report, but as custody was virtually inevitable, he would remand the defendant in custody for the report to be prepared.'

She looks questioningly at Legless.

'My very words,' he confirms.

'Then, all of a sudden,' Clare says, 'the defendant kicks off. He throws poor Bert to the ground in the dock and kicks him in the face. I push the panic button, and so does Judge Dunblane. It doesn't take Security very long to respond, but before they can get here, the defendant has charged the bench. There were some people blocking the public entrance to the court, you see, Judge. Anyway...'

I have already guessed the rest. If the public entrance was blocked, Chummy must have been heading for the judge's entrance, hoping to get out of the building from the judicial corridor. He is probably reasonably fast, but he is not very big, and to get to the judge's entrance he would have to attempt an inside break against a former centre for Rosslyn Park. Not a chance. Legless would have felled him with a textbook tackle.

'He picked the wrong judge, Clare, didn't he?'

'He certainly did, Judge,' Clare replies, eyeing Legless with unmistakable pride and admiration. 'Judge Dunblane is a real hero. He will probably be in all the papers tomorrow morning, perhaps even the six o'clock news on the BBC tonight.'

'I can see the headline in the *Sun* now,' I say. '"Have-a-Go Judge nabs Runaway Crook."'

Legless moans. He is not a big fan of the *Sun*. But the groan makes me look at him more closely. He seems a bit pale.

'Are you all right, Legless?' I ask.

'I've sent for an ambulance, Judge,' Dawn says. 'They are on the way.'

Legless is trying to fight Dawn off and lift himself up.

'I don't need a bloody ambulance,' he insists. 'I am perfectly all right. All in the course of a day's work. Where's Clare? Ask her to call on the next case.'

'I think he's concussed,' Dawn says to me. 'Will you speak to him, Judge? He is not going to listen to me, but he needs to stay down until the paramedics can look at him.'

'Dawn is right, Legless,' I begin. But before I can say any more, Legless makes a massive effort to push himself up using his right hand. This is followed by a blood-curdling scream, after which he collapses in a heap back down to the floor, holding his right arm with his left.

'I think he may have broken his right arm as well,' Dawn observes.

'He was thrown against the wall with quite a jolt when he made his tackle,' Clare adds. 'The defendant hit his head and went out like a light until after Security arrived, but I think Judge Dunblane banged his arm just as hard.'

'I think court three is adjourned for the afternoon, Legless,' I say. 'Just stay there until the ambulance arrives. Then you can take all the time you need off to recover. Stella will get us a Recorder to sit for as long as you need to take off.'

'No need for that,' Legless insists, rather breathlessly. 'You can list me at ten o'clock tomorrow morning.'

But he makes no further effort to get up. Two police officers have arrived and are now carting Chummy away to custody. I see Hubert and Marjorie standing at the judge's entrance. Apparently, all courts have been adjourned for the afternoon. No matter, I think. Thank God it isn't any worse.

'This happened at Winchester, years ago,' Hubert says. 'Or was it Aylesbury?'

Mercifully, before he can get any further with this reminiscence, an ambulance crew arrives and starts seeing to Legless and the dock officer. I get out of their way and return to the judicial corridor. Stella is waiting for me. She has already noted the need for a Recorder. As we are about to go our separate ways, she stops me.

'You do realise what this means, Judge, don't you?'

I must have looked blank. In all the excitement, and my concern for Legless, I can honestly say it had not crossed my mind. It crosses it now with the speed of a Japanese high-velocity express train.

'We have our statistic,' I reply. 'Don't we?'

'We certainly do,' she says. 'I've already alerted the media. Would it be appropriate for me to contact the Grey Smoothies and inform them of the afternoon's events – as a matter of courtesy, so they don't have to read about it for the first time in tomorrow's *Mail*?'

'I think that would be entirely appropriate,' I beam, before returning contentedly to my chambers.

* * *

Thursday morning

Elsie and Jeanie have been reading about Legless in the *Sun* and the *Mail*, and they have all kinds of questions about him, most of which I'm not about to answer. I have asked for an extra shot of espresso in my latte, which I may need to keep me awake and alert in court this morning, and while it is prepared I release a few anodyne biographical details about Legless, without disclosing any of the more colourful aspects of his history, such as the origins of his nickname, which I'm hoping the papers won't dig into.

'We need a few more people like him, don't we, sir?' Jeanie asks, 'people who will stand up to criminals and have a go. Do you think they will give him a reward?'

'I really couldn't say...'

'Well, they should.'

'He'll get a commendation, more likely, won't he?' Elsie says. 'That's what they did with my Uncle Albert during the War when he burned down the NCOs' mess at Kettering.'

Jeanie and I look at her for a few seconds.

'Why would they give him a commendation for doing that?' Jeanie asks.

'He didn't intend to burn it down, did he?' Elsie explains. 'Someone had locked the doors, leaving the lights on one night, hadn't they? This was during the Blitz, and there was an air raid warning. Someone had to get in there and put the lights out before the bombers came, which Uncle Albert did. Unfortunately, he had to climb in through a window, and he threw his cigarette on the ground before he went in, and they'd spilled petrol outside when they were refuelling the big lorries earlier in the day, hadn't they? So it all went up. The bombers were heading straight for them, but when the pilots saw the fire, they thought they must have hit that target already, and they went home. So they gave Uncle Albert a commendation for his quick thinking and his bravery in climbing into a burning building.'

George thinks Legless should get the OBE, if not a knighthood. I give him a bigger order than usual. I think it may be prudent to have a copy of the *Sun* and the *Mail*, in addition to the *Times*, just to check on what's being said. I am amused to see that my prediction of the *Sun's* headline has come true, almost word for word. I feel somehow encouraged. And there is good news even before I go into court.

'Message from the Grey Smoothies,' Stella says, 'from someone very highly placed. Statistic delivered, business case made. The Ministry prides itself in taking prompt action whenever a situation of danger comes to its attention, and will be taking immediate steps to install a secure dock in court three at Bermondsey Crown Court. This to be confirmed by the Minister himself at a press conference later this morning.'

'How splendid,' I reply. 'I hope you've told Judge Dunblane. He really took one for the team, didn't he?'

'You can tell him yourself,' she replies. 'He's in his chambers with his arm in a sling and a huge bottle of aspirin. He insisted on being listed at ten o'clock.'

I shake my head.

'What if something kicks off today? He can't make a tackle with only one arm.'

'In that case, they will probably close court three to start construction this afternoon,' Stella smiles.

'Has he seen the *Sun*?' I ask.

'We thought we would keep that from him until after court this afternoon,' Stella replies.

Once in court, I tell counsel that I agree with Aubrey, and that I'm going to leave the case to the jury. It's not a decision I have taken lightly. In fact, I lay awake a good deal of the night thinking about it, which isn't like me at all. Usually, I make a decision and move on without worrying about it unduly. And it's not that I'm unsure about the law. Even without hearing what Aubrey would have said if he hadn't been interrupted by events in court three, I feel I have no alternative but to agree with him. As she always does, Susan made a forceful and attractive argument, but it flies in the face of the daily reality of the courtroom. On any common sense view of the matter, Wilbraham Moffett exercised a right of audience at least once on the fateful day.

But there's something about this case that disturbs me. I can't help feeling some sympathy for Moffett. All right, obviously, he's a complete idiot, and he was the architect of his own downfall; but I derive little comfort from that. Even if he is an idiot, he is nothing worse than an idiot, and he doesn't deserve to be hauled before the Crown Court. He was abused and taken advantage of by a dishonest solicitor, and then abused further by a mindless District Judge who could have solved the problem, if there ever was a real problem, with a few words of warning. If Moffett goes down for this offence, his hopes of a career in the law will be gone, and all he will have to remember them by will be the large debt he has already acquired in the course of two years of study towards a law degree. Unfortunately, I can't see what I can do about it, other than hope that the jury will take a charitable view.

Once I've decided to leave the case to the jury, it moves forward with truly astonishing speed. Susan announces that Wilbraham Moffett will not be giving evidence, thereby opening and closing the defence case in a single breath. It's probably a good call. In law, no defendant is under any obligation to give evidence. In practice, though, juries like to hear the defendant say he didn't do it and regardless of the law, it's usually a good idea for the defendant to humour them. But in this case, there's nothing useful Moffett can tell the jury that they haven't already heard from the prosecution witnesses; and based on my view of the law, none of that offers him much chance of an acquittal. I will have to direct the jury that, even on the facts as Susan presented them, he seems to have exercised a right of audience. In the circumstances, calling him to give evidence and allowing Aubrey to savage him in cross-examination isn't an attractive prospect. Susan has calculated that her best chance is to let the jury convict if they must, and go up to the Court of Appeal to argue that I've got the law wrong. If the Court of Appeal agrees with her, they will reverse the conviction. Almost certainly, it's her best shot.

So we're ready to move to closing speeches. Both Aubrey and Susan are short and to the point, and in almost no time at all it's my turn. I sum up as sympathetically as I can. I have to be firm about the law, of course, but I certainly don't suggest that the jury have no alternative but to convict. In fact, I travel some distance down the other road, as far as I decently can while trying to remain neutral as between prosecution and defence. I try my best to paint Moffett in a positive light, and I remind them more than once of what Susan has said about the various shortcomings of Ellis Lamont and about the prosecution's failure to call Jungle Jim. I'm not sure whether any of this has made an impression. They're not giving anything away. I get them out just before lunch.

* * *

Thursday afternoon
Stella has transferred a sentence to me from Hubert's court, a dangerous driving, but it doesn't take long, and the rest of the time I'm reduced to sitting in chambers waiting for the seemingly inevitable disaster in the life of Wilbraham Moffett to materialise. Despite Ellis Lamont and Jungle Jim, I can't see

what would detain the jury for long. Even if they have some sympathy for the defendant, I've left them little choice; their verdict ought to be a foregone conclusion. But, as I ought to know by now, it doesn't always work that way with juries.

Jurors start their first week of service as a collection of individuals who have never met each other before, and who often resent being dragged away from home or work into a new and strange environment to meet each other now. But once they are engaged in a case, something remarkable happens. This random collection of individuals somehow becomes a jury – a unique creature with its own identity and its own values, a creature that won't be told what to do, and stubbornly does what it thinks is right. This isn't always convenient, as every judge knows to his or her cost. If you try too hard to nudge a jury in one direction, they're likely to go in the other, and we've all had cases where we've subtly suggested an acquittal only to find ourselves staring at a conviction delivered in record time – and *vice versa*. It's frustrating, but at the same time comforting, because stubborn juries are one of the great protectors of our liberties; and besides, no judge I know would want the responsibility of finding defendants guilty or not guilty. We are only too glad to leave it to juries, because at the end of the day there is safety in numbers and in collective common sense. Apparently, this jury is no exception, because after deliberating until three-thirty about the foregone conclusion we are all expecting, they send me a note, signed by the foreman.

Your Honour, we regret to advise you that the jury is hopelessly deadlocked. Six of us think the defendant is guilty. Six of us think we should find him not guilty, because without evidence from the District Judge we can't be sure we really know what happened. Nobody is moving and it seems that we won't be able to reach a verdict. Sorry.

I sit and ponder the note for some time. I can't help smiling, but it's not a happy smile. Jungle Jim's 'dignity' has played its part in the case after all. Now, thanks to him, we're looking at a retrial, involving not only three or four more days of Crown Court time but also weeks, if not months, of anxiety about his future for Wilbraham Moffett. But that's down the road. For now, I have to manage the situation, and it's not quite as straightforward as the note might suggest.

The foreman, I'm sure, thinks that's the end of it; that I'm about to discharge them and send them home, their work on this case having come to an end. But it's not quite as simple as that. I can't just accept the deadlock and discharge them. In the old days, verdicts had to be unanimous, but for many years now, once the jury has been out for a little over two hours, the court can accept a majority verdict of ten to two or eleven to one. But first, I have to give them what's called the majority direction. I have to tell them what majorities are acceptable, and I have to ask them to keep on discussing the case and do their best to reach a unanimous verdict. The note makes it pretty clear that that's not about to happen in this case, but I have to ask them to try. There's no point in giving them the majority direction today. By the time I give it, we would be within half an hour of sending the jury home for the day. I decide to explain all this to the jury, after which I send them away until tomorrow morning.

* * *

Friday morning

Arriving in chambers armed with my latte from Jeanie and Elsie, I find a message from Marjorie, asking to see me before court to ask me about a sentence she has listed this morning. I remember the case well. It's a horrific GBH involving a nasty permanent injury to the victim, and she's contemplating sending Chummy down for a very long time. That's something that gives all of us the jitters, even when we are convinced that there's no alternative, and a friendly ear is always welcome. There's no doubt at all that Marjorie has got it right, and after I've reassured her, she asks about my case. A friendly ear sounds good to me, too, at this juncture, so I sit down in front of her desk with my latte and unburden myself to her about my impending hung jury and my frustrations with Jungle Jim, and indeed the case in general.

'The worst part of it,' I say, 'is that this young man is going to be kept hanging on until we can fit the retrial in, wondering whether he's ever going to become a solicitor.'

She thinks for some time. Then, without replying, she reaches for *Archbold*, flicks through the index and alights on the page she needs. She walks around to me and points me to the passage she has found.

'What about this?' she asks. 'If you have a hung jury, why don't you give this a try?'

I read the passage she's found and suddenly I feel a weight fall from my shoulders.

'Thank you, Marjorie,' I say. 'You always seem to find answers like this. How on earth do you do it?'

She shakes her head. 'It's bloody Jungle Jim who should have found this, not me,' she replies.

As soon as I take my seat in court, I give the jury the majority direction and send them back out. It only takes about five minutes. I have other matters to deal with during the morning, of course, but I'm not going to leave the jury out for long. I have no illusions that further time is going to make any difference, and in any case, I'm now very keen to see if Marjorie's suggestion will work. I can't rush them too much, but if they don't send another note within an hour or so, I'll bring them back and discharge them. Which, just over an hour later, the foreman having assured me that no amount of time would enable them to reach a verdict, unanimous or otherwise, I duly do.

'Your Honour,' Aubrey says, 'my learned friend and I will consult the list officer about a date for the retrial. May we interrupt and mention the matter once we're ready?'

'Well, just before you do that, Mr Brooks,' I reply, 'can we just consider whether a retrial is really necessary?'

Both Aubrey and Susan are looking blank.

'Your Honour,' Aubrey says hesitantly, 'the prosecution intends to proceed against Mr Moffett, so there must be...'

'Let me explain,' I interrupt. 'I've listened to the evidence in this case for two days, which is two days longer than the District Judge was prepared to devote to it. I have also considered further the provisions of section 70 of the Courts and Legal Services Act 1990. It provides that anyone guilty of the offence of exercising a right of audience when not entitled to do so is also guilty of contempt of court – an offence which could and should have been dealt with in the Magistrates Court.'

'Yes, your Honour. But...'

'Having reflected on this provision,' I continue, 'I have reached three conclusions.

'The first is: that if the District Judge had paid half as much attention to section 70 as I have, he might well have dealt with this case as a contempt, instead of having the defendant arrested and tried in the Crown Court.

'The second is: that Mr Moffett is undoubtedly guilty of contempt of the Magistrates Court.'

I see Susan begin to twitch.

'Give me a moment, Miss Worthington. I haven't quite finished. My third conclusion is: that his contempt was a matter of stupidity rather than criminality, and that he was badly treated and let down by a solicitor who was supposed to be training him for the profession. From this I conclude that it would be out of all proportion for his legal career to be brought to an abrupt end by a conviction for this offence.'

I see I now have their undivided attention.

'So, what I propose to do now is to rise for, shall we say, twenty minutes. At the end of that time, if Mr Moffett is disposed to plead guilty to contempt of court, I would propose to give him an absolute discharge. The result of that would be that the Law Society would take no action against him and he would be able to continue his studies to become a solicitor.' I pause, just for a moment. 'Of course, if he doesn't want to plead, we will have to set a date for a retrial. I'm hoping that won't be necessary but we shall have to see. Let me know.'

'I will take instructions,' Susan says.

'Your Honour,' Aubrey says, 'I would have to consult with the CPS as to whether that plea would be acceptable to the Crown.'

'Yes, of course, Mr Brooks,' I reply. 'And when you do so, please explain to them that I take a very dim view of the prosecution's failure to compel the District Judge to give evidence. In fact, I think it might fairly be described as a failure of prosecutorial discretion on the part of the Director of Public Prosecutions; and it may well have made it impossible for Mr Moffett to receive a fair trial. No possible criticism of you, Mr Brooks, of course; you did your best. But if we have to try this case again, I would be obliged to consider the implications...'

Aubrey looks at me for some time.

'In the circumstances, your Honour, I feel confident that the Director would leave the matter in my hands.'

I smile contentedly.

'Good. Well, let me know. If you need longer than twenty minutes, you can have it, of course.'

* * *

Friday evening

There are some weeks when things just go right. This week has been one. Legless is going to get his secure dock in court three and Wilbraham Moffett is free to continue his quest to become a solicitor. I only hope that he finds the real thing this time to help him reach his goal, rather than Ellis Lamont. But all things considered, it has been one of those weeks when the job seems really worthwhile. I have taken the Reverend Mrs Walden out to La Bella Napoli to celebrate with some excellent steamed sea bass, a fresh salad, and a fine Valpolicella.

Stella has given me another historic for Monday, but oddly, the thought doesn't bother me. I do need to talk to someone about it all, and I really think I will. But it is true that a change is as good as a cure, and the nonsensical case of Wilbraham Moffett has been a breath of fresh air. It is also true that a drop of something nice and some great music can pour balm on the evils of the world.

When we return home, the Reverend Mrs Walden has a few things to do before retiring for the night, so I decide to relax in my favourite armchair with a nice glass of Armagnac, and I find myself in the mood for some music. I investigate the Reverend's impressive jazz collection, acquired during her student days, which contains some great classics. Not normally my first choice in music, if I'm honest about it, but tonight for some reason it seems right. I select a Billie Holliday album, lie back, and allow her beautiful, sad, haunting voice to wash over me.

'Oh, that's lovely,' the Reverend calls out from somewhere in the distance. 'Turn it up a bit. I haven't heard that for such a long time.'

When Billie approaches the end of the song, I sing softly to myself alongside her, and we reach for the high final notes together.

I'd lie for you,
I'd cry for you,
I'd lay my body down and die for you.
If that isn't love, it will have to do,
Until the real thing comes along.

ARTISTIC DIFFERENCES

ARTISTIC DIFFERENCES

Last Friday afternoon

I daresay most Crown Courts have some kind of memorial to Resident Judges past, but I think it is fair to say that not many go to quite the same lengths to remember them as we do at Bermondsey. Let it never be said that we don't do things in the grand style. There is a tradition we have kept going from the court's earliest days that, on retiring, each Bermondsey RJ has his portrait painted and hung with due ceremony in the judicial mess. The portraits are the work of a Dutch artist called Jan van Planck. On Friday it was the turn of my immediate predecessor, Terry McVeigh. Terry retired when I took over, and is now living an apparently blissful life in Herefordshire somewhere, where he breeds some special kind of rabbit, serves on the Parish Council, haunts one or two good local hostelries, and generally blends in with the natives. But on Friday he sportingly returned to the court to play his part in the great tradition, his part consisting of joining us for lunch and a glass or two of wine before the portrait was officially hung.

It all seemed to go well. We enjoyed lunch (catered in, you understand, from Basta Pasta, a nearby Italian deli, not the usual stuff from our court kitchen). I made a short speech. Terry made a short speech. We congratulated Jan van Planck, who is always invited to lunch on these occasions, on his work. And finally we hung the painting alongside the others already in place. With Terry's, we now have five. Rather dreamily, after a glass or two of an acceptable white Burgundy selected for the occasion by Marjorie, I found myself envying Terry; anticipating my own time in this happy situation; seeing in my mind's eye my own portrait enshrined in the mess for posterity – which, the way things are working out, will be my only and modest claim to making a mark on history – and then returning to some idyllic life of leisure shared with the Reverend Mrs Walden. After lunch, we bade Terry farewell and sent him home to his rabbits with our blessing and an open invitation to visit us whenever he wishes, an invitation which has to be made, but which neither he nor anyone else expects to be taken up.

Everyone seemed to enjoy the occasion, but I could not quite bring myself to relax and have a good time like everyone else. This, I admit, was entirely my own fault. I had a guilty conscience, you see. Stella and I had practised a subterfuge on my fellow-judges by concealing a rather awkward circumstance from them. In mitigation, I honestly believed at the time that it was a necessary evil, but for some reason that reflection did not salve my conscience very much. The only good news was that it worked. No one knew of the awkward circumstance during the unveiling, although inevitably, that is now about to change. The subterfuge and the awkward circumstance concerned Jan van Planck's presence at lunch. By way of explanation –

The relationship between Jan van Planck and the Bermondsey Crown Court has always been a slightly delicate one. It dates back to the earliest days of the court, which became operational in the mid 1990s. The RJ at that time, the first of the lineage, was Freddie Prideaux, a strange, taciturn man who I remember from my time at the Bar as someone lacking a sense of humour and having a rather inflated idea of his own importance. Hubert had just been appointed when the court opened. He is the only one of the current Bermondsey judges who was here in Freddie's day, and it is from Hubert that I derive my knowledge of the Jan van Planck history. The story Hubert tells is that when Freddie was drawing close to retirement, about four or five years after taking the helm as RJ, he decided to initiate the tradition of the portraits. The tradition would begin immediately with a portrait of Freddie himself. One might have thought that a suitable photograph, nicely framed, would have sufficed for this purpose, but Freddie had grander ideas. Freddie's vision was for a portrait in oil executed by a distinguished artist. The artist he selected for his portrait was Jan van Planck. Don't ask me where Freddie found the funding for this project. It is a secret handed down on a strictly need-to-know basis, that is to say, from RJ to RJ, and that's all I'm going to tell you. If the Grey Smoothies got wind of it, Terry McVeigh's portrait would be the last in the series, and I have a personal interest in ensuring that it continues – at least to the extent of one more.

Jan was undoubtedly qualified for the task in terms of ability. He was about thirty years old at the time, with a number of portraits and other works, landscapes and still life studies in the Dutch tradition, to his credit. He had his studio and shop above an Indian restaurant in London Bridge Road, and was attracting some attention on the London art scene. The only slight problem was that he had also attracted the attention of the Bermondsey Crown Court. A year or so earlier, Hubert had presided at Jan's trial on a charge of handling stolen goods. I had heard the story before, but Marjorie and Legless had not, so when I happened to announce that the van Planck portrait of Terry McVeigh was complete and ready to be delivered, Hubert took it upon himself to tell the story again in the judicial mess over lunch.

'Freddie knew all about it,' Hubert points out, 'but it didn't seem to concern him at all. He didn't seem to have any problem with commissioning van Planck to paint his portrait, despite everything.'

'What was the case about?' Marjorie asks.

'Jan has three very nice watercolours for sale in his

studio,' Hubert recalls. 'Very nice, actually. Unfortunately, it transpires that they were all stolen from a private collection in Hertfordshire, a country house, forget exactly where, not too far from St Albans, I think. Unfortunately for Jan, the police get a hot tip as to where they might find some of the loot, they get a search warrant, they turn his place over, and lo and behold, abracadabra, what should they stumble across but three of the best pieces from the burglary. So Jan is nicked, the police interview him, and he gives them a complete cock-and-bull story about some man turning up unannounced out of the blue at his studio with the paintings. "Morning, Jan, my name's Joe Bloggs, and I'm liquidating my dear old deceased grandmother's estate, and would you be interested in acquiring these fine watercolours at a reasonable price amounting to about a fifth of their real value?" Poor old Jan, being a trusting fellow, doesn't suspect for a moment that there might be anything dodgy about it, perish the thought, so he stumps up the money and the deal is done. Unfortunately for Jan, the police don't believe a word of it. They suggest that, as a professional, he must have known that he was getting the watercolours at a ridiculous price. So he is charged with handling stolen goods, and it comes before me. Open and shut case if I ever saw one.'

'But he was found not guilty, wasn't he?' I ask rather nervously, recalling that Jan van Planck has received the court's commission and been entertained to lunch five times since then.

'Freddie knew all about it,' Hubert insists. 'But he still commissioned van Planck and invited him to the court.'

'Well, yes,' Marjorie says, 'but if he got off –'

'Well, yes, he got off,' Hubert replies. 'Of course he did. We had Harvey Steel prosecuting, didn't we? Absolutely bloody useless. It's a wonder anyone was ever convicted of anything in those days. Harvey Steel couldn't get Fagin convicted of handling stolen goods, never mind Jan van Planck. And he's prosecuting serious frauds now, so I hear. No wonder the banking system is falling apart. And Jan van Planck remains a man of previous good character. Absolute bloody travesty.'

Hubert returns rather disconsolately to his penne arrabbiata, the dish of the day, which today is an especially aggressive shade of deep red. At which point, to my considerable relief, the conversation dies a natural death, and the subject does not come up again. So I do not have to reveal the guilty secret Stella and I have concealed, along with Monday's list, namely: that on Monday, Jan van Planck will be visiting Bermondsey Crown Court again; and not for lunch or a glass of wine.

Monday morning

Armed with Elsie's strongest coffee and Jeanie's bacon, lettuce and tomato sandwich for lunch, I make my way to court. I find myself creeping furtively along the corridor to my chambers, almost as if I am afraid someone may confront me – which I am. It's not my fault, I argue to myself. It's not my bloody fault that Jan van Planck got himself charged with fraud just as he was finishing Terry McVeigh's portrait, and we were already on the hook for his fee. It's not my bloody fault that his trial is listed to begin on the Monday following the Friday on which he was our honoured guest – if not in a sense the Court's artist in residence – drinking our wine and eating our canapés to his heart's content. But it might as well be, for all the comfort I draw from my own argument. It is equally arguable, I have to concede, that I should have withdrawn his invitation for Friday, a course urged on me repeatedly by the Reverend Mrs Walden, who always has a good common sense approach to these matters. But protocol is protocol; we have invited him to all the other unveilings, and given the presumption of innocence, it seemed to me that it would have been a bit uncharitable to cast him out for Friday. Now, I'm thinking that, uncharitable or not, it might have been the wiser course. But in any case, it's too late now; the die is cast. It is going to be awkward in court, to put it mildly. And all my colleagues are going to know as soon as they glance at the list which Stella and I have so carefully concealed until now. 'VAN PLANCK, Jan, for trial', it proclaims, all too loudly. Let the games begin.

'May it please your Honour, members of the jury,' she begins, 'my name is Susan Worthington, and I appear for the Crown in this case. My learned friend Mr Julian Blanquette appears for the defendant, Jan van Planck, who, as you know, is the gentleman sitting in the dock at the back of the court.'

Jan is in his fifties now, and like many Dutch people, is remarkably tall and thin. He smiles engagingly in the direction of the jury until a brief glance from Susan hits him like a blast of icy air from Siberia, and causes him to shift his look hurriedly down to the floor. Mercifully, he hasn't tried to make eye contact with me, and I have studiously avoided looking at him. You would almost think we had some kind of guilty secret between us.

Susan Worthington is an imposing figure, tall and composed, and today she has about her an air of severity she seems to reserve for cases in which she is prosecuting. On the defence side, she can sometimes come across as a bit fussy, and sometimes even sounds like a librarian telling someone to keep their voice down in non-fiction because people are trying to work. But not when she is prosecuting. When she is prosecuting, she can put you in your place with a single glance, as she just has with Jan van Planck, in a way which might take most barristers a couple of minutes of speech. She exudes an atmosphere of strictness and discipline. Legless thinks she would make a wonderful dominatrix, though quite how he is qualified to make such a judgment he has never revealed. Julian Blanquette could not possibly be mistaken either for a librarian or a dominatrix, but he is lively and energetic, and never lost for the *bon mot*. He sometimes goes a bit too far with the humorous asides, though always in such a way that it is difficult to be annoyed with him. When it suits him, he is also very good at appearing to be thoroughly confused. With some barristers, this is a genuine condition, but with Julian it is a carefully rehearsed ruse to catch opponents and witnesses off guard. He does not resort to it often, but when he does, it is surprising how well it works.

'With the assistance of the usher,' Susan continues, 'I will distribute copies of the indictment, one between two.'

Dawn stands with a smile, and hands the copies to me and to the jury in turn.

'As you will see, it consists of a single count of fraud. The prosecution alleges that Mr van Planck, "*dishonestly made to Elmer G Pratfall a false representation, namely that a painting offered by the defendant for sale was 'Woman drinking Wine with a Drunken Soldier' by Gerrit ter Borch, circa 1658–1659, intending thereby to make a gain for himself or to cause loss to Elmer G Pratfall, or to expose Elmer G Pratfall to the risk of loss*".

'Members of the jury, in due course, His Honour will explain the law to you and you must take the law from him, not from me. But I can safely tell you that a representation is false if it is untrue or misleading, and the person making it knows that it is, or might be, untrue or misleading. In this case, the prosecution will prove that the representation made by this defendant was indeed untrue, and that he knew perfectly well that it was untrue.'

Susan reaches down to her right. Immediately, the short gentleman in the dark suit and tie sitting behind her, a CPS factotum of some kind, leaps out of his seat and assists her in holding up a framed canvas covered by a large piece of grey cloth. The factotum then picks up a thin, rickety-looking wooden easel, which he unfolds and stands up on its legs, and between them they proudly display to the jury the work allegedly claimed by Jan van Planck to be 'Woman drinking

Wine with a Drunken Soldier', by Gerrit ter Borch, circa 1658–1659.

I freely confess to a complete lack of knowledge of Dutch painting circa 1658–1659, and of the work of Gerrit ter Borch in particular, and I assume that the same applies to the jury; though you never know with juries. They come from all walks of life, and I recall more than one case in which counsel had barely finished apologising for the case being rather technical when a member of the jury raised his or her hand, and cheerfully said not to worry, he or she had been dealing with that kind of thing at work for years and could explain it all to the rest of them. In this case, someone will produce an expert to explain it to us, I feel sure. Genuine or not, it looks a nice enough piece. I would be happy to have it on the wall at home. Apparently, Susan has had the same thought.

'It looks pretty enough, members of the jury, doesn't it? I'm sure we would all be happy to hang it in our living room. As would Mr Elmer G Pratfall, an American gentleman, an attorney from Sacramento, California, the victim in this case; or at least, Mr Pratfall was happy to hang it in his living room until he realised that he had purchased not the genuine "Woman drinking Wine" painting, but a quite ordinary copy of it, of unknown provenance, and certainly not painted by Gerrit ter Borch. You may ask, members of the jury, why that should matter if Mr Pratfall liked the painting? The answer is quite simple. It matters because of the price the defendant Jan van Planck demanded for this ordinary copy – which was no less than fifty thousand pounds. The prosecution will call an expert on Dutch art of the period, a Dr Smalling, who will tell you that while that price would not have been unreasonable if the painting were what Mr van Planck claimed it to be, a price of closer to five hundred pounds would have been more appropriate for this ordinary copy.'

Despite this apparently damning statement, Jan van Planck

is looking quite content and Julian Blanquette is scribbling furiously, and I have an odd feeling, for which I cannot account at all, that something Susan is saying is going to come back to haunt her later in the trial.

'How do we know that this painting is not the genuine "Woman drinking Wine"?' she is asking rhetorically. 'Quite simple, members of the jury. The genuine painting is in a private collection. We know exactly where it is, and it is certainly not here in the Bermondsey Crown Court. What you see before you is a grossly over-priced copy.'

She turns to eye it with a suggestion of distaste.

'And that, of course, members of the jury, is the basis of this charge of fraud. The defendant Jan van Planck is a professional art dealer, as well as being Dutch himself...'

Julian raises his eyebrows at this apparent non-sequitur.

'...and the Crown say he knew perfectly well that this was not the genuine painting he told Mr Pratfall it was, and he knew perfectly well that it was not worth the price of fifty thousand pounds he demanded for it. That is the Crown's case in a nutshell. The only other thing I want to say is that the Crown brings the charge and the Crown must prove the charge so that you are sure of the defendant's guilt, if you are to convict. Mr van Planck is not called on to prove his innocence. Indeed, he doesn't have to prove anything to you at all. You must be sure of his guilt in the light of all the evidence. What I and my learned friend may say is not evidence. The evidence comes from the witnesses. And with his Honour's leave, I will begin by calling Elmer G Pratfall.'

Elmer G Pratfall is a large, rotund man dressed in a light brown three-piece suit. He walks slowly and not quite in a straight line, as though his weight is beginning to become a bit of a problem. His dark brown hair is thinning, and it is difficult to guess his age, though I imagine he is somewhere between forty and fifty.

On entering the witness box, he gives me a nod and examines the book Dawn hands him, apparently to make sure that it is a genuine bible before committing to tell the truth while holding it.

'Mr Pratfall, I think your name is Elmer G Pratfall, is that right?' Susan begins.

'Yes, Ma'am.'

'And I believe you are an American citizen; you are an attorney by profession, that is to say, a lawyer; and you reside in Sacramento, California?'

'That is correct, Ma'am.'

'Do you practise alone, or in a law firm?'

'In a law firm. I am the senior partner of the firm of Pratfall, Wallace, O'Malley, Bailey, Sanderson and McHugh. We have just over a hundred lawyers in the firm, partners and associates.'

'I see,' Susan says. 'Can I clear one matter up, just so that the jury will understand. Is your interest in art connected with your law practice in any way, or is it a purely private interest?'

'Purely private,' Pratfall replies. 'My law practice is in the field of corporate defence, representing banks and other corporations in civil lawsuits brought against them in the state and federal courts in California. So I am concerned with commercial litigation in cases involving large amounts of money. We don't do any of this kind of stuff.'

Pratfall waves an arm in front of him magisterially.

'What kind of stuff would that be?' Susan asks, before she can stop herself. It's not really relevant to anything, but since he has started off along that road, she can't just let it go. I have every sympathy with her; if she doesn't ask, Julian will have a field day with it when his turn comes.

Rather belatedly, Pratfall realises that he may have been a tad undiplomatic.

'Criminal work,' he replies. 'Not that I have anything against criminal work, you understand.' He turns to me. 'I'm sure you understand, your Honour. This stuff has to be done. And those who do it are doing a fine job, especially here in England with all the barristers and such. All I was saying is…' His voice trails away, but he continues to look at me, almost imploringly.

'It is a good rule of thumb, Mr Pratfall,' I say, 'that when you find yourself in a hole, you should stop digging.'

He nods.

'Yes, your Honour.'

Susan has recovered her composure. Julian is chuckling away to himself, and several of the jurors are joining in.

'Let's turn, then, to your interest in art,' Susan suggests. 'How long have you been collecting works of art?'

'Going on twenty years.'

'And what got you started as a collector?'

Pratfall looks up at the ceiling as if the question calls for considerable thought.

'I guess it was my wife, Julie Mae,' he replies eventually. 'She always likes to have nice things on the wall. When we were just starting out, we had all kinds of nonsense, even movie posters and the like, and stuff from concerts we went to in Sacramento, you know, when big acts come to town, Elvis impersonators and such, because we really loved the King…'

He offers a smile to the court, but no one is returning it, and he resumes his attorney demeanour.

'But then, when my practice took off and I made partner, I started to earn more, and Julie Mae had minored in art history at Sacramento State, and she started to look at some work by local artists, and we bought a few, and I guess we just got hooked on owning genuine original paintings, and it all went from there.'

'I see,' Susan says.

'And then, in addition to that,' Pratfall continues unbidden, 'it was a good deal from a tax point of view to buy some works of art, as long as they were genuine. My tax attorney said it would be a good thing to do, and I guess that was another reason.'

Susan closes her eyes briefly. Julian is staring at Pratfall like a hawk eyeing a rabbit, and I find myself looking forward to his cross-examination.

'How did you first come to contact Jan van Planck?' Susan asks.

'Well, I was spending time over here in London each year, because we have some clients here, including syndicates at Lloyds of London, and some others, and this is a great city to buy art if you have the money. I would bring Julie Mae with me, and while I was working earning the money, she would be going round the dealers trying to spend it.'

'And Jan van Planck?' Susan asks patiently.

'Jan, yes. OK. A client mentioned his name, someone at Lloyds if I recall correctly, and said they had commissioned Jan to do some work or other, and had been pleased with the results, and that he had some interesting stuff in his studio. So one afternoon, I thought, "What the hell? Might as well check it out," and I went along to look him up.'

'Did you go to his studio on London Bridge Road?'

'Yes, Ma'am.'

'And when you went to the studio, did anything in particular catch your eye?'

'Yes, it surely did. I saw this really neat painting he had for sale.'

The CPS factotum and Dawn gently pick up the work in question, one at each side rather like a couple of assistant auctioneers at Sotheby's, and carry it to the witness box for Pratfall to inspect.

'Is that the painting you were referring to?'

Pratfall purses his lips, trying to suggest that it is all a painful memory.

'Yes, Ma'am,' he replies in a quieter, suitably forlorn voice.

'Exhibit one, please, your Honour,' Susan says. I nod my agreement.

'I may regret asking this, Mr Pratfall,' she continues, 'but would you please tell the jury what it was that drew you to this particular painting?'

Pratfall gazes at it fondly.

'It sure is pretty,' he replies, 'and you just know it has to be old.'

'Quite so,' Susan agrees. 'Did you have any conversation about this painting with the defendant, Mr van Planck?'

'I did.'

'Please tell the jury what the conversation was. Please speak slowly because people are taking a note, and please be sure to tell the jury word for word what was said, as far as you remember it.'

It is an important moment. Pratfall makes a show of remembering, half closing his eyes to create an impression of intense concentration. After almost a minute of this, he begins as we all sit with our pens poised.

'I told Mr van Planck that I liked the painting. I asked him if it was for sale. He said it was. I asked him what it was, exactly. He said that it was the "Woman drinking Wine with a Drunken Soldier", by Gerrit ter Borch, circa 1658–1659.'

We all pause to make a note and take this in.

'Were those Mr van Planck's exact words, Mr Pratfall, or…?'

'Those were his exact words,' Pratfall insists, interrupting her.

'Very well. And how did the conversation continue?'

'I asked him how much he wanted for it. He said fifty thousand pounds. I said OK, and that was it.'

I see several members of the jury raise their eyebrows. Julian is smiling to himself. Susan takes a deep breath.

'When you say that was it, Mr Pratfall, I assume you mean that you agreed to buy this painting, Exhibit one?'

'Yes, I did.'

'And when you agreed to buy it, what did you understand Mr van Planck to be selling?'

Pratfall stares at her blankly. She tries her best to come to his rescue.

'Well, when you were asked to pay fifty thousand pounds, why did you think this painting was worth such a large sum?'

Finally, he sees the light.

'Oh, right. Yes. Well, obviously, because it was the real McCoy, the genuine article. Not a copy and such like.'

'Did you make any inquiries about it, yourself, before agreeing to buy it?'

'No, Ma'am. Mr van Planck is an art dealer. He's the expert. I'm not. He had been recommended to me. I trusted him, and I relied to my detriment on the false representation he made to me.'

Susan nods. 'Did you pay Mr van Planck fifty thousand pounds?'

'I did. I returned to his studio on the following day with a banker's draft, and took possession of the painting.'

'Still believing it to be genuine?'

'Absolutely.'

'And is it in fact genuine?'

Before Pratfall can reply to this question, Julian leaps to his feet.

'Your Honour,' he interjects quickly, 'a point of law arises. May the jury retire?'

The jury know by now that this is part of the routine. I warn every jury at the beginning of a case that counsel will probably have legal issues to raise, which are my job to deal with, not theirs. If you don't warn them they are bound to get a bit suspicious at being thrown out of the courtroom from time to time for no apparent reason, and they may suspect that counsel are trying to keep evidence from them – which, of course, they often are. So I invite the jury to grab a quick cup of coffee for a few minutes, and they file dutifully out of court.

'Your Honour,' Julian continues, 'my learned friend cannot ask this witness for an opinion as to whether the painting the jury have seen is genuine. He is not qualified as an expert in the authentication of art, let alone seventeenth-century Dutch art. If my learned friend wishes to go down that road, she will have to call an expert who is qualified in that field.'

Susan seems a bit irritated by the objection.

'If my learned friend had studied his brief more closely,' she replies pointedly, 'including the witness statements, he would have seen that the Crown does propose to call Dr Edgar Smalling, an acknowledged expert in the field of Dutch art. I would also like to point out that there can hardly be any dispute that the painting in question is not genuine.'

I look at her quizzically. I half expect Julian to be upset at the rather personal nature of her comment, but instead he is grinning, which only serves to irritate Susan even more.

'Your Honour,' Susan continues, 'as I told the jury in my opening speech, the original "Woman drinking Wine with a Drunken Soldier" is in a private collection. It is certainly not standing on an easel in the Bermondsey Crown Court. The jury will be shown a catalogue photograph of it in due course, and Dr Smalling will explain the situation when he gives evidence.'

I look at Julian.

'Mr Blanquette, if that's right, I can't quite understand why you should object to Mr Pratfall being asked about it. It may well be that he is not technically qualified, but if there is no dispute –'

'Oh, there is very much a dispute,' he replies. 'The problem is with the use of the word "genuine", which, as your Honour no doubt knows, is something of a loaded word in connection with works of art.'

'I'm afraid I didn't know that at all, Mr Blanquette,' I admit. 'I must confess I have always thought that something is either genuine or not. It's a bit like being pregnant, isn't it? You either are, or you're not.'

'I'm afraid not, your Honour. Now, if my learned friend had used the word "original" instead of "genuine", I would have no objection. When Dr Smalling – whose witness statement' (he turns towards Susan) 'I have in fact read with some care – gives evidence, I hope to make the distinction between the two words quite clear to your Honour, the jury, and even to my learned friend.'

Susan has now assumed a look of thunder.

'I look forward to my learned friend enlightening us all in due course,' she comments icily.

'So do I,' I say. 'But for the moment, so that the jury are not unduly delayed, would you have any objection to re-phrasing the question?'

'I will do so, your Honour,' she replies, 'pending my enlightenment.'

Julian is positively beaming. 'I am much obliged to my learned friend.'

I ask Dawn to bring the jury back and sit back in my chair to wait, when there is an unexpected interruption from the witness box.

'Excuse me, your Honour,' Pratfall says, 'but aren't you supposed to say "sustained" or "overruled"?'

'I beg your pardon, Mr Pratfall?'

'In California, the judge has to say "sustained" or "overruled" whenever there is an objection. Otherwise he doesn't make a record, and the parties have to insist on that, because if the judge doesn't say one or the other, he hasn't ruled, and the parties can't appeal if he gets it wrong.'

I see Susan looking at Pratfall in dismay.

'How interesting,' I reply. 'That's not the practice here, I'm afraid.'

'I am surprised to hear that,' Pratfall adds.

'But if it will make you feel more at home,' I say, 'I will ask if counsel would like me to say "sustained" or "overruled".'

I smile blandly at both.

'That won't be necessary, your Honour,' Susan positively growls.

'Actually, I can't believe you people still argue points like that,' Pratfall says, apparently under the impression that he has stumbled into a symposium on comparative law. His tone sounds mildly disapproving.

'I beg your pardon?' I ask.

'Points of evidence like that. Even sending the jury out, instead of just approaching the bench. I mean, it is really archaic. I thought rules of evidence pretty much went out with the Ark.'

Susan now looks incandescent, and is trying her best to get Pratfall's attention to tell him to shut up, but he is staring straight at me and can't see her.

'You don't have technicalities like rules of evidence in California, do you, Mr Pratfall?' I ask. 'Jurisprudence hasn't quite reached that level of sophistication in California, has it?'

Pratfall waves the question away with a hand across his face.

'Reached that level? No, sir. We are way past that level. That stuff was OK during the Gold Rush, I guess, but today, we have the Truth in Evidence Act. Witnesses can say whatever they have to say.'

'Really?' I say. 'The Truth in Evidence Act? Does that mean that all witnesses in California tell the truth?'

Pratfall ponders this for a while.

'No, your Honour, I don't guess it does.'

'Well then, it's not really much of a Truth in Evidence Act, is it?'

'It's just that we don't have many rules of evidence anymore.'

Julian Blanquette and Jan van Planck are thoroughly enjoying the show, but I decide it is time to bring it to an end.

'Do you still have contempt of court in California?' I ask.

Pratfall is saved from the consequences of any further injudicious remarks when Dawn puts her head around the door to tell me that the jury are ready to come back. But at that exact moment, the phone purrs quietly. My clerk, Carol, answers, then stands and turns around to speak to me.

'I'm sorry, Judge,' she whispers. 'Stella says could you rise, please, and meet her in chambers? Apparently, something urgent has come up.'

'Did she say what it is about?'

'No, Judge. Just that you were to rise immediately, if you would.'

I signal to Dawn to stand the jury down, and announce that I am adjourning for a time, as yet unspecified, to deal with an administrative matter. Pratfall looks put out. Perhaps they don't have adjournments in California since the Gold Rush, either.

When I get back to my chambers, to my consternation, I find Stella and our building manager, Bob, standing together in front of my desk, hands folded in front of them like naughty children summoned to the headmaster's study. They both look a bit white around the gills and are conveying the distinct impression that something dreadful has occurred. This is nothing unusual for Stella, who always exudes the aura of impending disaster, but Bob is generally a calm enough fellow, and his obviously troubled demeanour does cause me some concern. For a terrible moment, I speculate that Hubert must have snuffed it. He looked perfectly all right when I last saw him on Friday, but you never know at his age, and the way he tucks into the kitchen's dish of the day so recklessly every lunch hour, you have to think it is only a matter of time.

'Would you mind coming with us, Judge?' Bob asks.

I extend an arm to invite them to lead the way, which they do at a good pace, and we arrive at the judicial mess, where Bob throws the door wide open. For a moment I see nothing. But then, my gaze alights on the series of portraits of RJs past, and my eyes open wide in horror. The portrait of Terry McVeigh has been grotesquely defaced. Someone has added to his face what is quite unmistakably a handlebar moustache executed in black paint, a moustache which is rather too large to be strictly realistic and indeed extends along almost the entire width of the canvas.

'I found it this morning, Judge,' Bob says, 'when I came in to check they had cleared everything away after Friday.'

'I don't believe my eyes!' I exclaim involuntarily. 'How in God's name has this happened?'

'Someone must have been in and done it,' Bob replies, stating the obvious with a shrug.

'Whoever it was,' Stella adds, 'they weren't very tidy about it, were they?' She points to a number of spots of black paint on the sideboard and carpet close to the portrait.

'I will start an inquiry immediately, Judge, of course,' Bob volunteers.

'An inquiry?' I ask, momentarily taken aback. But I realise at once that he is quite right. This is not an accident or an act of God. Someone has deliberately given Terry a huge moustache in black paint, and given that it must have been someone with access to this part of the building, the list of suspects must be quite limited.

'Yes,' I reply. 'Yes, I suppose you should. How will you go about it?'

'I suppose I will have to question the staff, one by one.'

'We could call the police,' Stella suggests.

Bob and I shake our heads in unison as we share a vision of how this is going to look on the front page of the *Sun*. It is surprising how often visions like that creep into one's head in the course of judicial business.

'I think we ought to look into the matter ourselves at this

stage,' I reply. 'You had better take the picture down for now and put it somewhere safe before the culprit can strike again.'

'Right you are, Judge,' Bob says.

There is an awkward silence.

'I don't suppose you have any suspects in mind?' I ask.

Bob and Stella exchange furtive glances.

'I don't want to say anything before I have the chance to question everyone, Judge,' Bob says. 'It wouldn't be fair.'

'No, quite,' I agree.

'On the other hand,' he continues, 'and I don't intend any disrespect, Judge, but you probably know yourself that Judge McVeigh wasn't, how shall I put it, universally popular with the court staff.'

That is something of an understatement. 'Remote', 'unfriendly' and 'abrasive' were among some of the more favourable judgments about Terry that filtered out to other courts from Bermondsey during his tenure as RJ. It suddenly occurs to me that Bob's inquiry may not be an easy one, despite the apparently limited number of possible suspects.

'And we will have to find someone to advise us about whether the picture can be restored, won't we, Judge?' Stella asks. 'We can't just throw it away, can we? Not after the amount of money it cost.'

No, we can't. Neither, on the other hand, can we mount a twenty-four-hour watch over it. And the one person I need to consult about restoration is the one person I can't talk to at the moment, and quite possibly, depending on the outcome of the case, for a considerable time to come. I look at my watch. It is by now well after twelve o'clock. I need to think.

'You had better tell everyone in the van Planck case they are released until two o'clock,' I say to Stella.

And so to lunch, an oasis of calm in a desert of chaos. I hope.

When I take my seat in the judicial mess, there is an awkward atmosphere. Marjorie and Legless are tucking into lunches they have brought from home. Marjorie's looks like a dreadfully healthy bean-shoot and pepper concoction in a brand new plastic container. Legless has a far more prosaic hearty bacon and egg sandwich in front of him. I have the distinct impression that they are grinning at each other between bites, and resisting an urge to laugh. Hubert has ignored my arrival completely. He is tucking into the dish of the day, billed as chicken and wild mushroom risotto, with a vengeance, a copy of the *Times* by his side, and he is giving every impression of being absorbed in an article about something going on in Malaysia. But as I am making a start on my sandwich, he finally deigns to acknowledge my presence.

'Oh, there you are, Charlie,' he says. 'Good of you to join us. What have you got in your list today?'

The question proves too much for Legless, who almost chokes on a piece of bacon. I take a deep breath.

'You know perfectly well what I have in my list, Hubert,' I reply. 'I am trying Jan van Planck on a count of fraud.'

He looks up as if astounded.

'By Jove, that's quite a coincidence. That's not the same van Planck we had to lunch on Friday, is it, the one who painted Terry's portrait? How remarkable. I didn't see his name in the list on Friday, you see, so of course I had no idea.'

Legless and Marjorie are by now sniggering openly. I pause in the act of bringing my sandwich up to my mouth and replace it on my plate.

'There is no call for sarcasm, Hubert,' I say as calmly as I can. 'You know perfectly well it is the same Jan van Planck. And yes, I invited him to lunch for the unveiling of Terry's portrait, which is, after all, his work. And yes, I did ask myself whether it was the right thing to do. On balance, I thought it was. Applying the presumption of innocence to which Jan van Planck is just as entitled as any other defendant who comes before this court, I thought it would be wrong to tell him that he was not allowed to attend the unveiling of his own work.' I pause. 'I do understand that you may not all agree with that decision, but that was the view I took.'

'How does the case look for him?' Legless asks.

'Not too good,' I reply.

Marjorie makes a face and shakes her head.

'I think that might have been the wrong call, Charlie,' she says.

'Very likely,' I admit, finally.

Hubert shrugs. 'Well, no point in arguing about it now,' he says, returning his attention to the *Times*. 'Water under the bridge. If we had lunch last Friday with a shady art dealer who is about to be convicted of fraud, it wasn't our finest hour. But there it is. We will just have to get on with it and ignore everyone at other courts laughing at us. I hope you've asked Bob to walk round the building and make sure all our other art work is still on the walls. It would be even more embarrassing if we were to find any of our pieces for sale on London Bridge Road for the knock-down price of fifty quid, wouldn't it?'

I raise my eyebrows. I wasn't aware we had anything other than the van Planck collection which could fetch anything close to fifty quid, especially on special offer.

'It's interesting you should say that, Hubert,' I reply. 'Because, as I am sure you have all noticed, a piece is in fact missing from this very room.'

All three pretend not to have noticed, and look up at the wall far too obviously to be credible.

'Well, I never,' Marjorie says with feigned surprise. 'Terry's portrait is missing.'

'So it is,' Legless agrees. 'What's happened to it, Charlie?'

'Van Planck probably nicked it,' Hubert says. 'It's probably hanging in his studio as we speak, waiting to be sold on as a Dutch masterpiece. Well, the Dutch part would be true, wouldn't it?'

I wait patiently for the laughter to die away.

'Thank you all for your concern,' I reply. 'Since you ask, Terry's portrait has been removed and taken into protective custody.'

'Come again?' Legless says.

'Someone has committed an act of artistic vandalism,' I say, 'or to use the legal term, an act of serious criminal damage. Bob is conducting an inquiry to find out who it was, and when he does so, I have every intention of calling in the police.'

Actually, I have no such intention whatsoever, since that would mean getting the Grey Smoothies involved and risking some awkward questions about the portrait fund, but I'm getting a bit irritated with the air of levity, and I want to get their attention. Apparently I have succeeded. Legless and Marjorie look concerned, and even Hubert looks up from the *Times*.

'Vandalism?' Marjorie asks. 'What kind of vandalism?'

'I'm not sure I should tell you,' I reply. 'I understand the police like to withhold some details of crimes in case a suspect makes a mistake and comes out with something he should have no way of knowing.'

'Oh, come on, Charlie,' Marjorie insists.

'Oh, all right,' I reply with a show of reluctance. 'Someone has painted a large black moustache over his face. God only knows how much it's going to cost to restore it. Bob thinks it's probably a disgruntled member of staff – someone who wasn't particularly fond of Terry – and yes, I am aware that that doesn't narrow down the field very much. I will keep you up to date, of course.'

'Well, I think you might have to call in the police, if it's a staff member,' Legless says, reasonably enough. 'There are security issues if we have someone who is prepared to go to lengths like that and who has access to the building. I don't think we can just let it slide.'

'No, we can't,' I agree. 'Anyway, at least it's safe from further depredations for now. I don't know what the world's coming to when we have to lock the art work away inside a court to keep it safe from the staff.'

'Perhaps it wasn't the staff,' Hubert says. 'Perhaps it was van Planck himself.'

'Really?' I reply. 'First you think he might have nicked it, now you think he might have defaced his own work. And how do you suggest he gained access to the judicial mess to do the wicked deed?'

'Clever people, the Dutch,' Hubert says. 'It doesn't do to underestimate them.'

I shake my head and, after a last desultory bite of my sandwich, I return to chambers.

* * *

Monday afternoon

After a few more questions, Susan abandons Elmer G Pratfall to cross-examination.

'Let's see if I have this right, Mr Pratfall,' Julian begins. 'When you go looking for works of art to collect, the first thing you look for is something that would look nice hanging on your wall? Is that correct?'

'Doesn't everybody?' Pratfall counters.

'No doubt,' Julian continues. 'Do you also look for pieces that match the curtains?'

'Oh, really, your Honour,' Susan protests. But she sounds a bit half-hearted. Julian's question is a bit cruel, but there is no one in court who doesn't enjoy it.

'I think the quality of the work is the most significant factor in my purchases,' Pratfall replies defiantly.

'And by "quality", you mean that the painting is pretty and looks old?'

'If it's an old painting, sure. But I don't buy only old paintings.'

'So, your taste is more eclectic?'

'How's that now? Ec… what?'

'It doesn't matter. Let's talk about this painting in particular.'

'All right.'

'You thought this painting looked pretty, did you?'

'I did.'

'And it looked old?'

'It sure did.'

'And, when my learned friend asked you what Mr van Planck had said about this painting, you said this, did you not? "I asked him if it was for sale. He said it was. I asked him what it was, exactly. He said that it was the 'Woman drinking Wine with a Drunken Soldier', by Gerrit ter Borch, circa 1658–1659." Do you remember saying that?'

'I do. Those were his exact words.'

'Were they indeed?'

'They were, sir.'

'All right. I will come back to that in a moment. There was something else you said to my learned friend. I hope I wrote it down word for word,' Julian makes a show of finding the exact place in his notebook. "Mr van Planck is an art dealer. He's the expert. I'm not. He had been recommended to me. I trusted him, and I relied to my detriment on the false representation he made to me." Have I got that right? Is that what you said?'

'That is correct, sir.'

'"I relied to my detriment on the false representation he made to me." As a lawyer, Mr Pratfall, do those words have any particular significance for you?'

'Significance?'

'Have you come across them anywhere before?'

Pratfall appears to be thinking again, his eyes raised towards the ceiling.

'It is possible.'

Julian nods and turns to look briefly at the jury. 'You see, Mr Pratfall, I suspected that the law in California is not all that different from our law here, so I took the liberty of doing a little research. I found that in California, as in England, two things are required for fraud: there must be a false representation and the victim must rely on it to his detriment. Does that refresh your memory at all?'

'That may well be so. As I said before, Mr Blanquette, I don't really –'

In a dramatic gesture, Julian holds up a hand, which has the effect of cutting Pratfall off in mid-sentence.

'Oh, no, please, Mr Pratfall, don't remind us that you don't do "this kind of stuff".'

'He didn't say that,' Susan almost shouts.

'He was about to,' Julian insists.

'Sustained,' I say.

'Yes, your Honour. My point, Mr Pratfall, is that fraud doesn't occur only in criminal cases, does it? I'm sure you have encountered fraud in the commercial cases you do?'

'I'm sure I have.'

'I'm sure you have. And the reason you chose those words – very carefully, I suggest – is to make the jury believe that you have been the victim of fraud.'

'I *have* been the victim of fraud,' Pratfall insists.

'Well, let me ask you about that. Mr van Planck did not tell you that this painting was "Woman drinking Wine with a Drunken Soldier," did he?'

'He certainly did, sir.'

'What he explained to you was that this was an *original painting of the School* of Gerrit ter Borch, based on the "Woman drinking Wine". Isn't that right?'

'The School…?'

There is a lengthy silence, and it seems unlikely that Pratfall is going to respond any time soon.

'You really don't understand what I mean, do you, Mr Pratfall?' Julian asks.

'He told me the painting was genuine,' Pratfall insists.

'"Genuine" or "original"?'

Pratfall shrugs. 'One or the other. "Genuine", I think.'

'You were happy to buy the painting because it was pretty and it was old, Mr Pratfall, isn't that the case? There was no fraud here.'

'As long as it was genuine,' Pratfall replies.

Julian nods. 'Just one more thing, Mr Pratfall. Are the paintings you keep at home insured?'

'Yes, of course.'

'For their full value?'

'Certainly. Why wouldn't I insure them for the full value?'

'No reason at all,' Julian reassures the witness. 'I am not suggesting otherwise. But when you do that, you have to tell the insurance company exactly what you have, don't you?'

'You have to make a full disclosure, of course.'

'Of course. And in the case of something particularly valuable, the insurance company might send someone to inspect the piece in question, might they not, to verify what you have told them?'

'Sure. I've had that happen once or twice.'

'Thank you, Mr Pratfall,' Julian says, smiling as he resumes his seat.

Susan re-examines briefly, and Elmer G Pratfall leaves the witness box to sit in the public gallery.

The prosecution's expert, Dr Smalling, is not available this afternoon, because he has been speaking at a conference of some kind in Florence, but I am told there will be no difficulty in starting on time tomorrow morning. We adjourn. I retire to chambers, hoping to hear something about Bob's investigation, but nothing is forthcoming, and I wend my way home.

* * *

Tuesday morning

Dr Edgar Smalling is a short, elegant man clad in a dark grey, three-piece pin-stripe suit, white shirt and red tie. Susan is anxious to impress the jury with his credentials, and he gives them a comprehensive history of his academic prowess, his experience and his publications, at the end of which no one could reasonably doubt his qualifications to speak about art in general and Dutch art of the seventeenth century in particular.

'With the usher's assistance,' she continues once we are all duly impressed, 'may the witness please be shown Exhibit one?'

Dawn and the CPS factotum have got their Sotheby's routine down by now, and they whisk Elmer G Pratfall's purchase across the courtroom to the witness box before you can say Gerrit ter Borch.

'Have you had the opportunity to examine Exhibit one before coming to court today?'

'Indeed I have,' Dr Smalling replies. 'I have examined it on a number of occasions.'

'Is Exhibit one the painting known as "Woman drinking Wine with a Drunken Soldier", by Gerrit ter Borch, circa 1658–1659?'

Dr Smalling smiles. 'No, it most certainly is not.'

'What is it?'

'It is a rather indifferent copy of ter Borch's painting of that name.'

'Done by whom?'

'I don't know.'

'And when you use the word "copy" do you mean to imply that this is a more modern production?'

'No, not necessarily. It could be more or less contemporary.'

'In other words, it could be mid- to late seventeenth century?'

'Yes.'

'Now, Dr Smalling, would you explain to the jury, please, why this painting is not "Woman drinking Wine with a Drunken Soldier", by Gerrit ter Borch, circa 1658–1659?'

Julian is on his feet.

'Your Honour, I have no objection to Dr Smalling being asked to explain that to the jury, but can I just make it clear that there is no dispute about it at all. The defence is prepared to agree it. Our position is that Mr van Planck has never claimed Exhibit one to be "Woman drinking Wine with a Drunken Soldier", by Gerrit ter Borch, circa 1658–1659.'

'I am obliged to my learned friend,' Susan replies. 'But it is relevant for the jury to hear why Dr Smalling holds that opinion so that the jury will understand the full extent of the fraud.'

'*Alleged* fraud,' Julian insists.

'My learned friend will have the chance to cross-examine,' Susan replies.

'Yes, all right,' I say, 'let's not squabble. You're perfectly entitled to ask him about it if you wish.'

'Thank you, your Honour. Dr Smalling?'

Dr Smalling puts on his reading glasses, bends forward and peers at Exhibit one on the easel at his side.

'Firstly, and most obviously, it is well-known that "Woman drinking Wine with a Drunken Soldier", by Gerrit ter Borch, circa 1658–1659, is in a private collection. With a work of such importance, if it were to be sold at auction, or even stolen, it would become generally known immediately. In addition, I checked on the original when I was asked to give an opinion in this case, and the original is exactly where it should be.'

'Thank you,' Susan says. 'And have you brought with you a glossy print of the "Woman drinking Wine", taken from a book you yourself wrote on the Dutch art of the period?'

'I have.'

'Exhibit two, please, your Honour,' Susan says. 'There are copies for your Honour and the jury.'

In no time at all, Dawn has distributed the prints. Their quality is very good. Even from a print, the contrast with Exhibit one is all too obvious.

'In addition,' Dr Smalling continues, 'the quality of this painting, Exhibit one, is not good at all. It is certainly not by ter Borch. You can tell just by the brushwork. That is obvious to anyone familiar with the work of the period, even on a casual inspection.'

'So it follows from what you say, does it not, Dr Smalling, that if anyone knowingly represented this painting to be "Woman drinking Wine with a Drunken Soldier", by Gerrit ter Borch, circa 1658–1659, such a representation would be false?'

'Yes, it would.'

'Are you in a position to say what this copy would be worth, if sold on the open market?

Dr Smalling thinks for a moment or two. 'Well, of course, at the end of the day all art is worth whatever someone is prepared to pay for it. If you like a painting and very much want to acquire it, you may even be prepared to pay more for it than a dealer would ask for. That, of course, explains the inflated prices one often hears about when works are sold at auction. In my opinion, a dealer might offer this for a thousand pounds, perhaps even two thousand if he was feeling lucky. Personally, if I were to buy it – which I would not – I would think that five hundred pounds would be more than adequate.'

'What about fifty thousand pounds?'

'Ridiculous. Out of the question.'

'Thank you, Dr Smalling. Please wait there. I am sure there will be further questions for you.'

Before the further questions, we take a short break at the request of the jury, who no doubt feel the need for some strong coffee to fortify them before they listen to any more about the merits and shortcomings of Exhibit one. Julian knows that he is dealing with a dangerous witness, and seems to have an air of unusual gravity about him.

'Dr Smalling, the seventeenth century is considered to be the Golden Age of Dutch painting, would you agree?'

'I would agree with that, yes.'

'In addition to the large number of talented artists, there was a huge demand for art in the Netherlands, wasn't there?'

'There was indeed.'

'It was a time of national prosperity?'

'Yes. The Dutch were very successful in trade at the time. Their economy was flourishing.'

'Yes, and one way for prominent citizens of the time to display their wealth was to buy original works of art to hang on their walls at home. Is that right?'

'Yes.'

'Rather as many Americans do today?' Julian adds with a mischievous glance towards the jury. Elmer G Pratfall sniffs audibly from his seat in the public gallery.

'Rather as people do everywhere, in my experience,' Dr Smalling counters, 'if they have the money.'

'Yes. So there was a huge market for art, wasn't there? I believe I read somewhere that between five and ten million works are estimated to have been produced during the period.'

'I wouldn't doubt that at all,' Dr Smalling replies, 'but very few of those have survived, relatively speaking.'

'Well, we will come to that in a moment,' Julian says. 'But first, let's look at this through the eyes of the artist. Assume with me, Dr Smalling, that you are a talented artist working in Amsterdam in – let's say – 1659. You create a work of art. It doesn't matter what it is, but let's say it depicts a woman drinking wine. With me so far?'

'I'm with you.'

'Good. You show the work, everyone loves it, and a wealthy burgher buys it to hang on his wall. He invites all his friends and neighbours round for drinks so that they can admire it too. And what do you think happens next?'

Dr Smalling smiles. 'I can tell you exactly what happens next. Some of the friends and neighbours call on the artist to commission him to paint something for them.'

'Exactly,' Julian exclaims with a flourish.

'But the only original work is the one the artist sold to the wealthy burgher.'

Julian holds up a hand.

'Don't get ahead of me, Dr Smalling,' he smiles. 'We will get there, I promise you.'

Dr Smalling raises his hands. 'All right.'

'In many cases,' Julian continues, 'the neighbours wouldn't be satisfied with just commissioning work from the same artist, would they? They would want to have the same painting as their neighbour, so that they could show off to everybody that they had just as much money, and just as much good taste.'

'Absolutely,' Dr Smalling agrees, 'and the artist would create a work for them, but he would make slight differences and he would give it a different title, and everyone would be happy.'

'Yes. The neighbours would be happy because they had essentially the same painting as their wealthy friend. The artist would be happy because he was maximising the commercial value of his work, and making more money than if he had only produced the one work?'

Dr Smalling seems unsettled by this. 'Well, I suppose you could put it like that if you wanted to be crude about it.'

'How would you put it?'

'I would say that, in that day and age, it was a way, perhaps the only way, for the artist to spread the word about his work and widen his sphere of influence.'

'Fair enough,' Julian agrees with a smile. 'But let's be honest. He would also make more money. Nothing wrong with that, is there? We don't want all artists to starve to death in garrets, do we?'

'Of course not.'

'All right,' Julian looks down at his notes for several seconds. 'Now, let's talk about Gerrit ter Borch. He was a very talented artist, who flourished in the mid-seventeenth century, is that right?'

'Yes, that is correct. To give him his full name, he was Gerrit, or Gerard, ter Borch the Younger.'

'Yes. And in the period around 1658 to 1659, he painted "Woman drinking Wine with a Drunken Soldier," yes?'

'Yes.'

'And to make it clear again, whatever Exhibit one is, it is not "Woman drinking Wine with a Drunken Soldier", and we know that because "Woman drinking Wine with a Drunken Soldier" is in a private collection.'

'Among other reasons, yes.'

'Yes. But that leaves us with the question of what exactly Exhibit one is. I think we are agreed that it may well be roughly contemporaneous with "Woman drinking Wine with a Drunken Soldier"?'

'I certainly could not dispute that.'

'Would you also agree that, if it is roughly contemporaneous, whoever did this painting was aware of "Woman drinking Wine with a Drunken Soldier"?'

'Yes, I would agree. The influence is obvious.'

'I want you to look at another print, Dr Smalling, if you would. Exhibit three, your Honour, please. Again, there are copies for the court and the jury.'

He waits for Dawn to make her rounds.

'This is taken from a catalogue published by the Sinebrychoff Art Museum in Helsinki, a part of the Finnish National Gallery. Are you familiar with that Museum?'

'Yes, of course. I have given lectures there several times. I am also familiar with the painting shown in the print.'

'Would you tell the jury what it is?'

'It is a piece by Gerrit ter Borch entitled "Young Woman with a Glass of Wine holding a Letter in her Hand". It is dated around 1665.'

'Is that an original painting, in your opinion?'

'Yes, of course it is.'

'Thank you, Dr Smalling. Now, the jury will see, if they compare Exhibits two and three, that there some very obvious differences – notably the absence of the drunken soldier – but nonetheless, it is very much the same painting, isn't it?'

'It is obviously based closely on the earlier work, of course. The other obvious difference is that the woman is on the right of the picture rather than the left.'

'Yes, and in fact, what we are looking at here is an example of the artist making the most of his work, both artistically and financially. Would you not agree?'

'Yes, I think the painting's provenance confirms that.'

Julian takes a deep breath.

'Now, Dr Smalling, let me come to the core of what I want to ask you. There were some artists who had schools, weren't there?'

'There were.'

'Please explain to the jury what is meant by a "school" in this context.'

'A "school" simply means that the artist had one or more students working with him. These would be young men who had the ambition to become artists, and wished to study with a master, to learn from him and to develop their own skills.'

'Essentially, they were apprentices?'

'Yes.'

'And like all apprentices, they would work, doing various

tasks in the studio, mixing paint, carrying canvases around, and what have you, in addition to learning to paint?'

'Yes.'

'And if they had enough ability, there would come a time when the master might allow them to work on certain details of a painting?'

Dr Smalling considers.

'Yes, but usually on the working model rather than the finished product. The student would have to be very gifted to be allowed to work on the canvas.'

'But there were cases where that happened, weren't there?'

'There were.'

'And if the master had a real hit on his hands, a painting that everybody wanted, he might have to delegate some of the work, simply because he didn't have the time to do it all himself – at least, not without making the client wait for a long time and perhaps become bored with it all.'

Dr Smalling is hesitating.

'I know this, Dr Smalling,' Julian is smiling, 'because I have had dinner in the shadow of one such painting many times, in my Inn of Court.'

Dr Smalling laughs.

'I know exactly what you are referring to. Van Dyck's portrait of Charles I mounted on a horse, in Middle Temple Hall.'

'Yes. There are one or two others just like it, aren't there?'

'Almost the same. That is true.'

'Thank you,' Julian says. He pauses for a moment or two, eyeing the jury for emphasis. 'Dr Smalling, if I were to put it to you that Exhibit one may be an original painting of the school of Gerrit ter Borch based on "Woman drinking Wine with a Drunken Soldier", would you disagree with me?'

'I would disagree, yes.'

'Why is that?'

I look up. It is dangerous to ask an expert a question

beginning with the word 'why'. It is a licence for the expert to give a lecture, and having asked the question yourself, you can't really stop him. Strangely, I find myself hoping that Julian has thought this through.

'I would classify this as a copy. There are no real differences between this and the original, and the low quality of the brush-work and composition lean against it being a school piece. A bad school piece could tarnish the master's reputation just as much as a bad original. Ter Borch would never have allowed something like this out of his studio.'

I am looking carefully at Exhibits one and two, and I have to think that Dr Smalling has a point. But Julian comes right back at him.

'Except that the wine jug the woman is holding is blue and white, isn't it, where the wine jug in what you term the "original" is white?'

We all look again. Julian is right about that, no doubt about it.

'That's true,' the witness concedes.

'And, if you look at Exhibit three again, the painting from Helsinki, the blue and white wine jug on the table behind the young woman looks very much like the wine jug she is holding in Exhibit one, the painting in our case, doesn't it?'

'Yes. But all that means is that whoever made this copy was aware of the Helsinki painting, and perhaps, therefore, we can date it as being not earlier than 1665.'

'Dr Smalling, isn't it possible for even the most experienced expert to be mistaken in an attribution?' Julian asks. 'That he may quite genuinely believe that a piece should be attributed to a particular artist, only for someone to demonstrate later that his attribution cannot be correct? Does that happen sometimes?'

'Of course,' the witness smiles. 'We are all human.'

'Quite so. Dr Smalling, let's allow for the moment that this was not executed by Gerrit ter Borch himself, and let's allow that it might not have passed his test for being sold under his brand...'

He pauses to make sure the witness is with him.

'Very well, let's allow that.'

'Making those allowances, can you exclude the possibility that this work was created in ter Borch's studio and then perhaps sold to someone with less money to spend – sold as a second, rather like a piece of china that fails the quality test?'

There is a long silence.

'I can't exclude that possibility,' Dr Smalling says, 'but I regard it as unlikely. May I explain...?'

But Julian has already resumed his seat.

'Yes, you may explain,' Susan says, rising quickly to her feet.

'If such a piece existed,' Dr Smalling continues, 'it would have been known and catalogued. Any surviving work which may possibly be attributed to the school of a major artist would be of great importance. Such a work is not going to turn up out of the blue in a studio in London Bridge Road.'

Soon afterwards, Dr Smalling's evidence is concluded. To the relief of everyone in court, I now have to deal with the execution of a bench warrant. A defendant charged with multiple counts of street robbery, who failed to attend court on the last occasion, has been arrested pursuant to the warrant I issued. Now that he is here, I have to begin the process of managing the case – and I have to deny any further bail application he may make so that we don't lose him again when the case is ready for trial. I adjourn Jan van Planck until two o'clock and deal with the bench warrant.

And so to lunch, an oasis of calm in a desert of chaos.

'How is your trial going?' Legless asks. 'Is it still looking bleak for our friend Jan?'

'Yes, I fear so,' I reply, 'though Julian Blanquette did quite well cross-examining the prosecution's art expert. It's probably going to depend on how well Jan does in the witness box, and how well the jury liked the complainant.'

'I heard he was a bit of a pain,' Legless says.

'He was insufferable,' I reply. 'Not only does he know nothing about art, and not only does he have far too much money to throw around buying it, he even tried to tell me how to run the trial.'

'Oh?'

'He wanted me to say "sustained" or "overruled" every time I dealt with an objection.'

'I'm not sure that's such a bad idea,' Marjorie says. 'At least then, everyone knows what you've decided.'

'I've never noticed anyone being in doubt about what I've decided,' I say.

'Careful, Marjorie,' Legless grins. 'Next thing you know, you will have counsel approaching the bench.'

'Counsel are not coming anywhere near my bench,' I say emphatically. 'They can keep that in California. Not that there would be any need for it there. I understood Pratfall to say that they don't have rules of evidence there any more, just something they call the Truth in Evidence Act.'

Legless frowns. 'That sounds a bit Kafkaesque,' he says.

'Oh, I don't know,' Marjorie says. 'We've been doing that in civil cases for years and it doesn't seem to have brought the justice system crashing down about our heads.'

'We don't have to deal with juries in civil cases,' I point out. 'Well, hardly ever. If you let juries loose on some of the stuff witnesses would like to tell them, it would be a disaster.'

'They do that in America,' Marjorie points out. 'They have civil jury trials, I mean.'

'Yes, well that just proves my point,' I reply.

We all take a bite of our sandwiches.

'Where's Hubert?' I ask.

'He popped his head round the door to say that he was working on a ruling he has to give this afternoon, and he's had the dish of the day sent to his chambers,' Marjorie replies.

'Hubert working on a ruling?' I protest. 'What kind of ruling? If he has a point of law, he usually hawks it around the mess to find out what we think. I don't think he's opened *Archbold* for years. In any case, he never misses lunch.'

Marjorie shrugs. 'That's what he said.'

'I hope he's all right,' I say. 'He hasn't been looking quite himself recently, if you ask me.'

* * *

Tuesday afternoon

This afternoon Susan calls the officer in the case, DC Denise Sharp, to deal with the investigation. DC Sharp describes dealing with a distraught Elmer G Pratfall, some weeks after he became aware that the painting he had bought from Jan van Planck wasn't exactly what he thought it was. She contacted Jan to inform him of the allegation. He attended the police station voluntarily with his solicitor, without being arrested, so that DC Sharp could interview him. After being cautioned and told of his right to consult with his solicitor at any time, he handed in a short prepared statement and then spent forty minutes or so answering 'no comment' to every question DC Sharp asked. The prepared statement was as follows:

I have been made aware by DC Sharp that an American gentleman called Elmer G Pratfall has accused me of fraud in selling him a painting, falsely claiming it to be the work of a Dutch artist by the name of Gerrit ter Borch. This is untrue. The painting in question is exactly what I told Mr Pratfall at the time, i.e. a painting of the school of Gerrit ter Borch. The price I charged for this piece was not unreasonable. I had acquired this painting about a year before at an estate sale in the Bristol area. I paid about two hundred and fifty pounds for it. I did have a receipt at the time, but I am now unable to find it. The reason I paid so little was that the estate did not realise what the painting was, and neither did I until much later. I knew it must be seventeenth century, but only on much closer examination did I come to believe that it was from the school of Gerrit ter Borch and was an original work based on an earlier work of ter Borch himself. I stand by this transaction as being fair and reasonable. At no time did I make any false representation to Mr Pratfall, and he seemed very pleased with the bargain we had struck. Since then, he seems to have had a case of buyer's remorse, probably because his wife has given him a hard time about spending so much money.

With that, and a few agreed facts placed before the jury in writing – which include the fact that, perhaps a little fortuitously, Jan van Planck is a man of previous good character – Susan closes her case. Julian asks whether he can begin his case tomorrow morning, to give him a chance for one last conference with the defendant. This is reasonable enough in the circumstances, and we adjourn for the day.

I remove my robes and resume street dress, and prepare to wade through the pile of files on my desk that need some administrative decision or other. But I am interrupted by a knock on the door, and in walk Bob and Stella. Their mood is hard to gauge, but they do seem a bit more upbeat than when they were last here, and I am anxious to hear what they have to say. We all sit down, and Bob leans forward earnestly in his chair.

'How is the investigation going?' I ask. 'Have you found the culprit?'

'Not yet, Judge,' he replies. He looks at Stella who smiles and nods brightly – a gesture quite unlike Stella. I wonder what on earth is coming.

'Have you at least made some progress?' I ask.

'Oh, yes, Judge,' Bob replies immediately. 'We are definitely making progress. I have interviewed several members of the staff. So far, no one seems to know anything about it.' He pauses. 'But… I think we may have caught a bit of a lucky break this morning.'

'Oh?'

'Yes, Judge. I spoke to Annie.'

I must have been looking blank.

'Annie is in charge of the cleaners,' Stella reminds me.

'Right,' Bob continues. 'Well, Annie told me that she was in the dining room just after the reception for Judge McVeigh had finished, and the judges and staff had left. She went in to start clearing everything away and clean up. She says that was about ten past two, certainly not later than two-fifteen. She remembers Judge McVeigh's portrait being on the wall then, because that was the first time she had seen it and she stopped to admire it. She is certain that there was nothing wrong with it then. She was there until about two-thirty, when she left the cleaning partly done because the prison staff needed something cleaned up in the cells. But she returned to the dining room at about a quarter to four, and she saw that someone had added the moustache to Judge McVeigh's portrait.'

I stared at Bob in surprise.

'It was done on Friday afternoon?'

'Even better than that,' he replies. 'Annie narrows it down to just over an hour.'

'Between half past two and a quarter to four,' Stella adds, 'and you know what that means, Judge, don't you?'

Not at first, but it doesn't take me long.

'It means that quite a few of our original suspects have water-tight alibis,' Stella says. 'Three of our courts were sitting all afternoon, from about two-fifteen until four-fifteen; yourself, Judge Jenkins and Judge Dunblane.'

'Are you saying that I was a suspect?' I ask. I feel ever so slightly offended.

'No, not at all, Judge,' Bob reassures me quickly. 'But several suspects we had our eye on were either in court all afternoon with the judges, or were in the general office with Stella and myself.'

'What about Judge Drake's court?' I ask.

'They sat at two-fifteen,' Stella replies, 'but they ran out of witnesses by about three o'clock and adjourned for the weekend.'

'So,' Stella says, 'that leaves us with Joyce, who was the clerk in Judge Drake's court, and Jim, his usher. Bob and I can't remember either of them coming back to the office that afternoon.'

'I can't see Joyce doing something like this,' I say. Joyce is a rather shy lady in her late fifties, who seems to spend most of her time away from court knitting things for her numerous grandchildren.

'Neither can I, Judge,' Bob agrees. 'But Jim… well, he never got on very well with Judge McVeigh.' He hesitates to go on. Stella says it for him.

'It was worse than just not getting on well,' she says. 'They argued all the time. Eventually, Judge McVeigh refused to have Jim as his usher. It got worse and worse, and in the end we had to put Jim in another court.'

'I take it you will be speaking to Jim, then,' I say.

'Absolutely,' Bob confirms. 'Tomorrow morning. Stella and I will see him together. The only thing is…' Again, he seems hesitant.

'What Bob is trying to say,' Stella interjects, 'is that Jim has been with the court for a long time. He goes back almost to when we opened, and he has always been very loyal, always ready to help out if there's a problem.'

'So, this would be out of character?' I suggest.

'Exactly, Judge,' Stella says. 'We were wondering how you would feel about allowing him the chance to pay for the damage and holding off on calling the police.'

I consider for a few moments. Calling the police still seems a very unattractive option, given the virtual certainty of arousing the intcrest of the Grey Smoothies. It may be inevitable, but there would be a lot to be said for avoiding it if we can.

'Well, all right,' I reply. 'But he must admit what he did, and he must agree to pay whatever it costs to restore the portrait – and that may be quite a bit, I imagine. I don't suppose you've...'

'No. We haven't tried to cost it yet,' Bob says. 'Obviously, the best option would be to ask Mr van Planck, but at the moment...'

'We can't,' I say emphatically. 'If he is found not guilty, I will ask him as soon as the words are out of the jury's mouth. If he is found guilty... well, we will have to make inquiries elsewhere. Quietly, you understand.'

'Of course, Judge,' Stella says. She is impeccably discreet, and a loyal ally in the endless struggle against the Grey Smoothies.

'All right,' I say. 'Well, let me know what happens tomorrow.'

'I'm not looking forward to it,' Bob says.

Stella puts a hand on his shoulder.

'He'll be all right, Judge,' she says.

* * *

Wednesday morning

'My name is Jan van Planck.'

'And you are originally from the Netherlands, I think?'

'From Haarlem, yes, that's correct.'

'How long have you been in this country?'

'For more than twenty-five years.'

'Living in London?'

'Yes.'

Julian looks down at his notes briefly.

'Tell the jury in your own words about your career in the art world.'

Jan nods and seems to reflect for some time.

'Well, as a young man I studied art and art history at the Vrije Universiteit Amsterdam – the Amsterdam Free University. I then worked as a docent at the Rijksmuseum for two years. After this, I decided that I must be an artist, do my own work, and I thought it would be better for me to get away from home, to have some new experiences, so I moved to London.'

'And did you set up your studio in London Bridge Road, as the jury has heard?'

'Yes. For some time I tried to make a living just by painting. I received some commissions to produce work, including a number of portraits. In fact –'

'Yes, I'm not sure we need to dwell on that, do we, Mr Blanquette?' I ask quickly. I have suddenly been seized by a fear that Jan may start cataloguing the work he has done for the court, or even worse, demand that the portrait of Terry McVeigh be produced as an exhibit, as an example of his work. Awkward wouldn't begin to describe that situation, quite apart from the fact that he would be trying to use the Court as a character reference, which I have no intention of allowing. Julian looks at me rather pointedly, but mercifully decides to move on.

'Let's not worry about that, Mr van Planck,' he says. 'Would it be fair to say that you had to turn to something else to supplement your income from your own work?'

'Yes, exactly. I began to buy and sell art on my own account.'

'Still working from your studio in London Bridge Road?'

'Yes.'

Julian nods. 'Now, with the usher's assistance, may the witness please be shown Exhibit one?'

At first, the CPS factotum seems reluctant to lend his services to the defendant, as if he doesn't want to be seen to be playing for the other team, and Dawn seems to be faced with carrying it over to the witness box herself. But Dawn is not one to be abandoned in her time of need without a fight. She gives him such a shaming look that the poor man quickly thinks better of it, and lends her a hand.

'Do you recognise this painting, Mr van Planck?'

'Yes, of course.'

'Is this the painting you sold to Mr Pratfall?'

'Yes, it is.'

'Before we come to that, do you remember when and how you acquired this piece?'

'Yes, I remember very well. When you are in my position, and you do not have very much money to buy art, you must look for opportunities to buy pieces without paying too much. I found that, in England, you can often find acceptable pieces at estate sales, garage sales, and so on, and you can acquire them quite cheaply.'

'And then sell them on at a profit?'

'Hopefully, yes. Of course, you often have to do some restoration to the work, or repair a broken frame, but still you may be able to ask a reasonable price.'

'And what was the provenance of this piece?'

'This, I found at an estate sale somewhere near Bristol two or three years ago.'

'What was its condition when you found it?'

'Not too bad, but it did need some cleaning, and the frame needed some patching. Whoever had it had not looked after it very well.'

'How much did you pay for it?'

Jan shrugs. 'I don't recall exactly. I did have a receipt at the time, but I can't find it. As far as I recall, I paid about two hundred and fifty pounds, not more than two-fifty.'

'Did you think that was a fair price?'

He smiles. 'It was a bargain. I didn't know how much of a

good bargain it was when I bought it. I only found that out later. But even then, it was a bargain.'

'Do I take it, then,' Julian asks, 'that the estate didn't realise what they had, and, therefore, under-priced it?'

'Yes. I knew the first moment I saw it that it was Dutch, probably from the mid- to late seventeenth century. Even with all the cleaning it needed, there was no doubt about that.'

'And how did you know that?'

'I gave lectures and tours at the Rijksmuseum for two years,' Jan replies, 'in addition to my studies at the University. Believe me, I know such a piece when I see it. I didn't know exactly what I was dealing with at the time, but I knew I had found something special.'

'When you got the painting back to your studio, did you set about restoring it?'

'Yes. I began the process of cleaning it. It took me about a month to get it to the point where I finally knew what I was dealing with.'

'And what was that?'

'It was undoubtedly a school piece from the Golden Age. I could not find an attribution, but the subject of the piece made that obvious. I was familiar with ter Borch's work, of course, the "Woman drinking Wine", and this was unmistakable. It had to be an original version of that work produced by his school.'

'What did you do when you reached that conclusion?'

'I looked at every catalogue of ter Borch I could find, to see if it might be listed already.'

'Why was that important?'

'Well, you must check the provenance of a piece as far as possible, otherwise obviously, you are at risk of handling stolen goods.'

I find myself thinking about Hubert, and about Harvey Steel, who couldn't have got Fagin convicted of handling stolen goods, and I find myself working hard not to laugh.

'You must at least ask yourself why an original school work from the Golden Age is being offered for sale for two hundred and fifty pounds at an estate sale near Bristol.'

'And did you find an answer to that question?'

He shakes his head vigorously.

'No. I looked everywhere, but there was no reference to this piece at all.'

'What conclusion did you draw from that?'

'I concluded that I had discovered a work which had been in private hands for a very long time, and perhaps not recognised for what it was.'

'Did that surprise you?'

'Not particularly. It was a piece of good fortune, of course, but such things happen from time to time. A huge quantity of art was produced during the Golden Age, and as Dr Smalling said, much of it has not survived. But sometimes a piece will survive. In the case of ter Borch, this would be less of a surprise than in other cases.'

'Why is that?'

'First, not many of his works survive, officially. Only about eighty are catalogued and all these are accounted for. But we know that he was far more prolific, and it is not unreasonable to believe there may be more of his work out there. I just happened to have found one.'

'But Dr Smalling insists that you are wrong.'

'I think Dr Smalling is too attached to the brushwork. He doesn't see beyond that. I agree with him that this is not ter Borch's brushwork. But it could certainly be a school piece. The subject-matter is unmistakable. This kind of domestic scene, with a woman engaged in an everyday act such as drinking wine – this is ter Borch's signature. He produced many such works, and they were very popular. Anyone seeing this piece would associate it with him. In fact, it would have been a very audacious act to produce this piece if you were not associated with ter Borch in some way. Also, we know that a very talented German painter called Gaspar Netscher was working with ter Borch in Deventer in about 1658 and 1659, and it may be that his influence is there, with other students.'

'So, what did you decide to do, once you knew what you were dealing with?'

'I had two options,' Jan replies. 'I could take it to a reputable art house, in which case they would pay me as little as they thought they could get away with. Or I could sell it myself and remain in control of the price. I decided to sell it myself.'

'Turning now to Elmer G Pratfall,' Julian asks, 'do you remember Mr Pratfall coming to your studio?'

'Yes.'

'Did he show an interest in Exhibit one?'

'Immediately. He was captivated by it the moment he saw it.'

'I want to see if you can remember the conversation as precisely as possible,' Julian says. 'Did he ask you what it was?'

'Eventually,' Jan replies. 'After he had told me many times how pretty it was – this was his word, pretty.'

'What did you tell him?'

'I told him the truth: that I believed this piece to be an important piece, that it was an original school piece of the school of Gerrit ter Borch, based on his painting "Woman drinking Wine with a Drunken Soldier," circa 1658–1659.'

'Mr Pratfall claims that you told him it *was* in fact "Woman drinking Wine with a Drunken Soldier". What do you say about that?'

'That is ridiculous. For one thing, I could never get away with such an absurd pretence. The piece is well known. The moment Pratfall had it valued for insurance purposes, I would be exposed.'

'Mr Pratfall also said that the painting was "genuine". What do you say about that?'

'That is not a word we use. I said "original".'

'Why not "genuine"?'

'"Genuine" relates to the question of whether the work is a forgery. There is no question of forgery here. Even Dr Smalling agrees with that. He says it is a copy. I say it is an original school piece. But the word "genuine" is meaningless here, and I would not have said that.'

'Did you say anything to Mr Pratfall that you knew or believed to be false?'

'No. Not at all.'

'Did you intend to act in any way dishonestly?'

'No.'

'How do you account for what Mr Pratfall says?'

Jan shrugs and looks appealingly at the jury.

'You all saw Pratfall,' he almost shouts to the court in general. 'He cares about nothing in art except that it must be old, pretty, and expensive. You can sell him the dogs wearing bow ties playing poker if it will match the curtains in his house. What can be said about such a man?'

'What do you say about the price you charged him, the fifty thousand pounds?'

'It was on the high side for a school piece,' Jan concedes at once. 'But it was not outrageous, and I can take you to some dealers in London where you would pay more. You know, paintings associated with ter Borch don't come on the market every day. If such a piece were to be sold at auction, it might fetch even more. That depends on so many factors. But in a private sale, what I asked was not unreasonable.'

He pauses.

'Besides, he made no complaint. The amount was never discussed. It was irrelevant for Pratfall. To Pratfall, it was enough that it was old and pretty.'

'Which was why you thought you could get away with it, wasn't it?' Susan asks, leaping to her feet as soon as Julian has sat down. Dr Smalling has been sitting behind her throughout Jan's evidence, and handing her notes excitedly. 'You saw a man with money to spend who didn't know much about art, and you saw the chance to make some easy money. That's what happened, isn't it?'

'No,' Jan insists, pulling himself up to his full Dutch height, which as I may have mentioned, is not inconsiderable.

'No? You say that Mr Pratfall might have had to pay even more than fifty thousand at some art houses?'

'Yes, that is true.'

'But there is a difference between buying a piece at an art house, and buying a piece from you in London Bridge Road, isn't there, Mr van Planck? Because if a dealer believed this to be an original school piece, he would have it authenticated before placing it on sale, wouldn't he? He would only charge a price like fifty thousand pounds if an expert attributed it to the school of Gerrit ter Borch.'

'Of course.'

'You agree?'

'Of course.'

'But you didn't have it authenticated by an expert, did you? And that's because you knew, and have always known, that it was a copy, worth at most a few hundred pounds.'

'You are wrong on all counts.'

'Really? Please explain.'

Jan folds his arms defiantly across his chest.

'Firstly, I am myself a dealer. Secondly, the piece has been authenticated. Thirdly, the price was not unreasonable, and was lower than other dealers might have charged. Fourthly, I told no lies about this piece to Pratfall at any time. This is all I can say.'

'I'm sorry,' Susan says after a short pause. 'Did you just tell the jury that the piece was authenticated?'

'Yes.'

'By an expert?'

'Yes.'

'By whom?'

'By myself,' Jan replies with enormous dignity. 'I authenticated this piece. I, Jan van Planck, have authenticated it.'

Susan goes on for some time, but fails utterly to breach the dyke, as it were. She eventually abandons the effort. That is all the evidence the jury will hear. We give them a short break while I discuss my summing-up with Counsel. Everyone agrees about the law, and we are ready for closing speeches.

Susan keeps it short and sweet.

'You may think, members of the jury, that Jan van Planck knows a sucker when he sees one, and in Elmer G Pratfall he saw the perfect victim.'

Pratfall, still haunting the public gallery, does not seem altogether pleased by this image of himself, but Susan is long past caring about that.

'If Jan van Planck were an honest dealer, he would have had the painting independently authenticated, wouldn't he? But the problem with that is that he would have been told in no uncertain terms by someone like Dr Smalling that it was a cheap copy worth no more than a few hundred pounds. So that, you may think, is the last thing he was going to do. It was much easier to wait for someone like Mr Pratfall to come along, and charge whatever price he could get away with, on the pretence that this was a famous work of art. Instead of doing the right thing, the honest thing, Jan van Planck put a grossly inflated price on it and took advantage of Pratfall in a shameless and reprehensible manner.

'And now that the chickens have come to roost, he has told

you a fantastic story about having discovered an important work of Dutch art going for two hundred and fifty pounds at an estate sale near Bristol, for which he conveniently happens to have lost the receipt. That's just nonsense, members of the jury, isn't it? Mr van Planck thought he had got away with selling a cheap copy to a naïve American for a grossly inflated price, and lying through his teeth to do it. The only right verdict is one of guilty.'

Julian is just as short.

'Members of the jury, Elmer G Pratfall may not know much about art, but he certainly understands the concept of fraud, doesn't he? You know that, because you heard him parrot the legal definition of fraud when he told you about his conversation with Mr van Planck. I'm sure you remember. "Mr van Planck is an art dealer. He's the expert. I'm not. He had been recommended to me. I trusted him, and I relied to my detriment on the false representation he made to me." That's what he said, wasn't it? And you remember, I called him on it, and we established that what he was giving you was the textbook definition of fraud – literally, the textbook definition. Elmer G Pratfall a sucker? No, members of the jury, Mr Pratfall is not a sucker. He is not some deluded American tourist wandering helplessly around London being fleeced by unscrupulous art dealers. He didn't get to be the senior partner of a big law firm by buying every story someone like Jan van Planck tells him, did he? He may have bad taste in art – in fact, he may have no taste at all – but a sucker he is not.

'As Jan van Planck told you himself, the suggestion that a fraud could have happened in the way Mr Pratfall described to you is laughable. He could never have got away with trying to sell Exhibit one as a famous ter Borch painting which any dealer would recognise immediately. The moment Mr Pratfall had it valued for insurance purposes the game would be up, wouldn't it? "Ah," the prosecution say, "but what of van Planck's claim to have authenticated the painting himself instead of taking it to an art house?" Well, why shouldn't he, members of the jury? He may not have the same paper qualifications as Dr Smalling, but he is just as much an expert when it comes to this painting. A university graduate, a post-graduate job in art at the Rijksmuseum, years of experience in creating and dealing in works of art. Why shouldn't he authenticate a piece from the Dutch Golden Age?

'But, members of the jury, even if Jan van Planck is wrong about this picture, even if he has got the attribution wrong and it is in fact only a copy, that is surely a mistake anyone could make. Dr Smalling agreed that any expert can sometimes be mistaken in an attribution. Making a mistake is not the same thing as fraud. You can only convict Jan van Planck of fraud if you are sure he was dishonest, if you are sure that he knew that what he said about it was false, or that he did not believe it to be true. Jan van Planck is a man of previous good character, members of the jury, and there is no reason why you cannot accept his word under oath. The prosecution has not come close to making a case of fraud. Your verdict must be one of not guilty.'

Now, all that remains is for me to sum up, which I will do this afternoon.

And so, to lunch, an oasis of calm in a desert of chaos? Perhaps, but not until I have heard about this morning's developments in the investigation.

'Nothing, Judge,' Bob says desolately.

'What?'

'I'm sorry.'

'Nothing?'

'Jim denies it completely, Judge. He says he left the building not long after court ended on Friday afternoon. He cleared a few things away, glasses, carafes and the like, didn't take him long, and that was it. His son and daughter-in-law picked him up outside the building, because he was going to spend the weekend with them, and they will confirm that.'

'At least we didn't upset him by asking,' Stella adds. 'He thinks the whole thing is rather funny, and whoever did it should get a medal.'

'Does he indeed?' I say, rather indignantly.

We are all silent for some time.

'So, where does that leave us?' I ask eventually.

'Back on square one,' Stella replies.

'The only other thing I can think of,' Bob says, 'is a thorough search of the building, inch by inch, to see if whoever did it left any clue behind. I could do that with a security officer this evening.'

'I'd prefer to keep security out of it, if we can,' I say. Security is just another possible leak of information.

'I suppose I could,' Bob concedes, 'but they will be aware that I'm up to something, just from our CCTV.'

'All right, but don't tell them what you're after,' I reply. 'I don't mind them thinking you're up to something. I just don't want them to know what it is.'

'Right you are, Judge,' Bob says.

I don't feel like going into lunch now. I sit at my desk with Jeanie's ham and cheese sandwich and work on my summing-up.

* * *

Wednesday afternoon
The summing-up takes just over an hour. I send the jury out to begin work. They will not have long this afternoon, but it is enough time to allow them to organise themselves. At four-thirty I send them home for the day. I am free to go home

now – but I don't. My mind is not at rest. I sit brooding over the apparent failure of the investigation, and the search of the building which is about to begin. I remember something the Reverend Mrs Walden said yesterday evening over our dinner of tagliatelle primavera and a bottle of Sainsbury's Special Reserve Valpolicella.

'It will be something staring you in the face,' she remarked. 'You can't see it now, but you will, and as soon as you do, you will wonder how you could have missed it.'

Well, I've been thinking about it for quite some time now, and it has certainly not stared me in the face, or anywhere else, yet. But before giving up and going home, I look down at tomorrow's list, just to see what's going on in the other courts. As usual, we have four courts sitting, each with its own court staff and each with its own judge. And in a flash, there it is. I see it. The Reverend Mrs Walden is right, as ever. Excitedly, I pick up the phone to see whether Bob is in the office. He is.

'Meet me in chambers,' I say.

He does. And fifteen minutes later, the mystery is solved.

* * *

Thursday morning

I send the jury back out to resume their deliberations at ten o'clock. To while away the time, I sentence a prolific burglar to the minimum three-year sentence he richly deserves for a long list of domestics. At eleven-thirty, the jury send a note. They are ready to return a verdict. Court is assembled. Elmer G Pratfall has once again appeared in the public gallery, which he has haunted ever since leaving the witness box. Carol asks the defendant and the foreman of the jury to stand. The foreman is a woman in her forties, smartly dressed in a dark business suit.

'Madam foreman, please answer my first question either

yes or no. Has the jury reached a verdict on which they are all agreed?'

'Yes.'

'Do you find the defendant, Jan van Planck, guilty or not guilty of fraud?'

'Not guilty.'

'You find the defendant not guilty, and is that the verdict of you all?'

'It is.'

I see Julian Blanquette and Jan van Planck exchange smiles as I order Jan to be discharged from the dock, and begin to thank the jury for their service. Elmer G Pratfall appears to be muttering to himself, no doubt about how much better things have been done in California since the Gold Rush than they are here. He will be free to take Exhibit one with him, if he wishes. It will be interesting to see whether or not he does.

Now comes the tricky part of the morning. I have asked Stella to loiter at the back of the courtroom and in the event of a not guilty verdict, to stop Jan van Planck leaving court until I have had the chance to talk to him. If possible, I would like her to do this without Julian Blanquette knowing about it, because although it has nothing to do with the case, it does look a bit odd, and he would have every justification for asking what is going on, which I would prefer not to tell him. Mercifully, Julian makes his way to the robing room after congratulating Jan on his acquittal and receiving his thanks, and Stella pounces. She is under instructions to wait with Jan in the courtroom until I am ready to see him. There is something else I have to do first. And I'm not looking forward to it.

There is a knock on the door of my chambers.

'Come in,' I say, quite loudly, hoping to sound authoritative.

Hubert opens the door and gingerly puts his head round it to peer in.

'Ah, Hubert,' I say, 'thank you for coming. I am sorry to have to ask you to rise. I hope it wasn't at a bad moment.'

He hesitates, looking a bit unsure of himself.

'It is a bit awkward, Charlie,' he replies. 'I'm in the middle of hearing a defence witness being cross-examined. Pack of lies, of course, as usual, but I wanted to finish it before lunch.'

'Yes, of course. As I say, I'm sorry it is necessary. I hope it won't take too long.'

I am waiting for him to notice the item I have placed, fairly conspicuously, on my side table, leaning up against the wall. At length, in the silence I have allowed to descend upon us, he does. He walks over to examine it.

'Oh my goodness,' he says. 'So this is the dirty deed, is it?' He appears to inspect it closely. 'My word, someone has made a mess of it, haven't they? Any closer to finding out who?'

He turns to me, almost appealingly.

'Yes, Hubert,' I reply. 'As a matter of fact, I know exactly who did it.'

'Really? What a surprise. That's splendid...'

'Stop it, Hubert, please,' I say. 'I have the evidence.'

I reach down and lift up the incriminating evidence in question, one small tin of black paint. Hubert looks down and says not a word.

'I found this in your chambers yesterday evening, Hubert, and I am sure you are not in the least surprised to hear it. We have both been doing this job long enough to know that there is only one conclusion any jury could reach from evidence that this was found in your possession.'

'That doesn't prove anything,' he blusters. 'Someone could easily have planted it in my chambers to incriminate me.'

I ignore this suggestion.

'Obviously, I don't have an expert comparison, but I think you will agree that the colour of the paint in this tin looks exactly the same as the paint of the moustache on the canvas.

In addition, I can't immediately think of any good reason for a judge to have a tin of black paint in his chambers.'

Hubert tries to bluster again.

'You searched my chambers without my being there, without even telling me? That's outrageous, Charlie. I won't stand for it…'

I wait for him to run out of steam.

'I made the search with Bob, who was in charge of the investigation,' I reply. 'It was either that, or leave Bob to make the search with a security officer. He was already scheduled to conduct a thorough search of the whole building. I thought, on the whole, it would be better for me to do it with him.'

There is a really long silence.

'What do you want from me?' he asks quietly.

'What would you do with someone on a plea of guilty to this?' I ask. 'Previous good character?'

He purports to consider the question.

'Conditional discharge for twelve months, I should think,' he replies, 'provided he agrees to make good the damage.'

'Exactly what I was thinking,' I agree.

'I sincerely hope you were not thinking of going to the police about this, Charlie,' he protests. 'All this talk of a plea of guilty. Surely, that's not necessary.'

'No. I have no intention of going to the police.'

For a moment, when he hears this, a note of defiance rises again.

'So, what would you do if I refused to make good the damage?' I smile.

'Something far worse than going to the police, Hubert. I would report the matter to the Secretary of the Garrick Club.'

He appears horrified.

'The Garrick?' he protests. 'You wouldn't dare!'

I look him straight in the eye.

'Wouldn't I?'

We stare at each other, and to my enormous relief – because I honestly don't know what I would have done if he had called my bluff – Hubert blinks first. He takes a deep breath before raising his hands in surrender.

'How much will it cost?'

'I don't know yet,' I reply. 'But this might be a good moment to find out.'

I pick up the phone and ask Bob to collect Stella and Jan van Planck from the courtroom and bring them to chambers.

'There's no need for any of this to leak out, is there, Charlie? I mean...'

'No,' I reply. 'The only people who know, apart from me, are Bob and Stella, and they are both the soul of discretion, as you well know. I'm certainly not going to say anything. But I must have your word that there will be no more antics like this.'

'You have my word,' he replies. He looks at me curiously. 'How did you know it was me?'

'I didn't until yesterday evening,' I confess. 'We had drawn a complete blank with the staff, and it was only then that I made myself imagine the unimaginable. It had to be one of the four of us. Once I realised that, it was staring me in the face. I knew it wasn't me. Besides, thanks to the cleaner, we knew when the deed was done, and I had a water-tight alibi. So did Marjorie and Legless. We were all in court. You had already risen for the day. Besides, you are the only one of us who dislikes Jan van Planck and Terry McVeigh in equal measure.'

Stella and Bob usher Jan van Planck into chambers, and leave the three of us alone. Jan notices the portrait at once, of course, rushes over to it, and stands with his hands up to his face like a stricken man. He touches it gently, and we see disbelief turn into grief and then into anger. For some time, he stands in silence, breathing heavily. He turns to face us.

'Who has done this thing?' he demands. 'Who has defaced my work in this way?'

I take his arm and lead him away from the portrait.

'I am most terribly sorry,' I say. 'It is an inexcusable crime, quite horrible. We have mounted an investigation, of course, and we have put arrangements in place to make sure that nothing like this happens again.'

'But…'

He is about to say something about the police, I know, but given his recent experience, he is slightly reluctant to bring the subject up. I take advantage of this fortunate circumstance quite shamelessly.

'And, of course, we value your work greatly and we are anxious to have it restored as soon as possible. I know this is scant compensation for the terrible thing done to one of your pieces, but we will pay your fee for the work of restoration, of course. You know Judge Drake, don't you? I have asked him to take charge of raising the funds for the project. He is quite confident that we will be able to raise the money, isn't that right, Judge Drake?'

'What?' Hubert replies. 'Oh, yes. Yes. Quite.'

'And we would like you to start work as soon as possible.'

Jan looks suspiciously at Hubert, then at me. Eventually he walks slowly back to his ravaged work, and begins to examine it in minute detail. Finally, after some minutes, he turns back to us once more.

'Impossible,' he says.

'What?' I ask.

'Impossible. The damage is too great. In trying to restore this portrait I would only damage it further. Look.' He points to the canvas. 'See the length of this black line. Look at the thickness of the paint, and see here, where the vandal has pressed the brush into the canvas so hard that he has caused some indentations.' He pauses. 'This was a very angry man who did this, Judge Walden. I would like to get my hands on him, believe me.'

I am aware of Hubert cringing and taking a step backwards.

'There is nothing you can do?' I ask. I must admit that I am somewhat taken aback. It has never occurred to me that we would be writing Terry McVeigh off like this.

'No, I am sorry. I cannot restore this piece. It is beyond my help. It is beyond anybody's help.'

Again, we are silent for some time.

'The only thing I can do,' Jan says, 'is to start again. I have my drawings, of course. There would be no need for Judge McVeigh to sit for me again. It will take a month, perhaps six weeks. If I can take this canvas with me, this would help also.'

'By all means,' I reply.

But Hubert seems rather anxious about the suggestion of starting again from scratch.

'Mr van Planck,' he says, 'as the fund-raiser for the project, I would need to know how much it would cost to produce another portrait as opposed to restoring this one. It might make a difference to our fund-raising plans.'

'I don't think it will make any difference at all,' I counter.

Jan looks at me, and I see the faintest suggestion of a smile cross his face. He turns to Hubert.

'Yes, of course, Judge Drake,' he replies. 'I understand. I tell you what. I will make you a special deal. Because this is Bermondsey Crown Court, and you have been good to me, I will make you a special deal, a one-time offer. I will make a new portrait for the same price I would have charged if I could have restored the one that has been destroyed.'

'That's very generous of you,' I reply. I smile. 'But will it count as an original portrait?'

'But of course,' Jan replies. He returns the smile. 'Let us say that it will be an original work of the school of Jan van Planck.'

'Excellent,' I say. 'Let me call security and alert them. We don't want them to stop you on the way out, thinking you are nicking the canvas, do we?'

'No, indeed, Judge. I have had quite enough of being suspected of wrongdoing for one lifetime,' Jan replies.

When all the fuss has died down, I sit at my desk and ponder what, with the connivance of Bob and Stella, I am going to tell Marjorie and Legless, and the court staff. Eventually I settle on what seems a plausible enough account, and one which has the additional merit of being partly true. The culprit has approached me voluntarily to offer a full confession and the cost of replacing the portrait of Terry McVeigh, but only on condition that his or her identity is kept absolutely confidential. Naturally, I have only agreed to such a condition with great reluctance, and because there is no other way of ensuring that we have our full complement of RJ portraits. It will cause a storm of gossip in the short run, and I will have Marjorie and Legless all over me for weeks, begging me to make an exception in their case, in total confidence, of course. But in the fullness of time, the gossip will turn to other matters, and the question of our artistic differences will be forgotten.

What I will not tell anyone – except Hubert – is the one circumstance in which the condition of confidentiality will cease to apply. If anything happens to my portrait after I'm gone, I'm spilling the beans.

UNEASY LIES THE HEAD

UNEASY LIES THE HEAD

Lunchtime last Friday

'It's like the Feast of Pentecost, the baptism of the Holy Spirit, you see,' Legless explains, 'the transmission of spiritual gifts by the laying on of hands. Once a chap gets decked out in the red robes and the Lord Chancellor anoints him a High Court judge, the Spirit of the Common Law descends from Heaven, alights on him, and imbues him with the spiritual gift of conducting criminal trials.'

The lunchtime conversation in the judicial mess has turned to one of the most hallowed traditions of English law, namely: that the most serious criminal cases, such as murder, are tried by those judges least qualified to try them. I refer, of course, to their Lordships of the High Court. In any rational world, such trials would be conducted by those of us who had some experience of them while in practice. In the real world, the opposite is true. The type of barrister who becomes a High Court judge wouldn't be seen dead in a criminal court. Not much money in it, for one thing. And crime has always been a bit *infra dig*, actually, old boy, not the kind of thing one wants to be seen doing. No, those destined for the highest preferment learn their advocacy in a more agreeable setting, such as arguing the finer points of a charter party in the Commercial Court, or carving up a fat, juicy estate in the Chancery Division. Yet, as if by magic, once elevated to the dizzying heights of the High Court bench, they acquire the ability to preside effortlessly over the criminal jury trial – an unruly beast whose potential for sudden, total catastrophe occasionally makes fools of the best of us.

How this apparently magical process occurs has never been satisfactorily explained. Personally, I attribute it to the principle that the gods love a true amateur and will always look after him, especially when he is entrusted with some vital task completely beyond his experience. England has always depended on this kind of divine intervention – on the battlefield, on the sports field, and, it seems, in the courtroom.

'Does he assume the form of a dove?' Hubert asks.

'Who, the Lord Chancellor?'

Hubert looks confused.

'No, not the Lord Chancellor; the whatsit, the Spirit of the Common Law.'

'I'm not sure the dove is quite the right image,' I comment.

'An eagle, I would have thought,' Marjorie suggests. 'Clear sight and sharp talons.'

'Bloody vulture, more like,' Legless rejoins. He sounds depressed, as if his theory of the laying on of hands brings him little consolation.

To add insult to injury, High Court judges don't confine themselves to presiding over trials. They also hunt in packs in the Criminal Division of the Court of Appeal, where they can do a lot more damage. In the Court of Appeal they can bugger up not only the case in front of them, but also all future cases of a similar nature unless and until Parliament intervenes to restore order. Arrayed *en banc*, they smugly tell circuit judges like myself off for the errors into which we fall when conducting trials. When they speak of a circuit judge committing error, they usually mean that, lacking a crystal ball, he failed to predict that their Lordships were about to change the law. It's no bloody wonder the criminal law is in such a mess. But you can't tell anyone. If you complain to the Grey Smoothies, they give you the party line about the intellectual superiority of those appointed to the High Court bench, and how they can cope with anything, especially something as simple as crime, given a little time and cooperation from the Bar, blah, blah, blah. Waste of time even raising the issue. They should ask around a bit more. They should ask Legless.

If they asked Legless, he would tell them about the case of the Honourable Mr Justice Gulivant. Now there's a case in point, if ever there was one. Before receiving the Spirit of the Common Law, Stephen Gulivant had spent twenty-five glorious years in the world of urban planning inquiries, helping his corporate clients to demolish listed buildings to provide a grateful nation with another supermarket or underground car park. Just the sort of chap for the High Court bench. He wouldn't have recognised a criminal case if it jumped up and bit him in the arse. It was apparently intended that Gulivant should spend most of his time doing civil cases in the Commercial Court. But the judge he was due to replace hadn't quite retired when he was appointed, so they had to find him something to do for a couple of months, didn't they? Can't waste the taxpayer's money by letting him just sit there with nothing to do. So why not send him to the Old Bailey, let him try his hand at some crime? How can that do any harm? That's the way the Grey Smoothies think, you see. Legless was still at the Bar then. He was prosecuting in Gulivant's first case, he tells us.

'It was your bog standard GBH,' Legless says. 'Chummy's having his usual Saturday night out. Starts off at home with a few cheap vodka concoctions from Tesco's. Then down the pub, where he throws back ten or so pints of Fosters. At which point Chummy convinces himself that the bloke next to him at the bar is staring at his girlfriend. So he tells him to fucking stop it. The bloke tells Chummy to fuck off. Chummy asks who the bloke is telling to fuck off. The bloke clarifies this for him. After a bit more verbal, Chummy breaks a pint glass on the bar and puts the jagged edge into the bloke's face. Blood everywhere. The bloke nearly drowns in it. The ambulance carries him off to the A and E, where they give him lots of stitches and a few pints of replacement blood. Very nasty. In fact, the poor victim is so upset by it all that it's nearly a week before he can even bring himself to go back down the pub. Issue is self-defence; Chummy says the bloke was trying to deck him with a bar stool, you know the kind of thing. Jeffrey Biggers defending. And we come in front of Gulivant.'

'Very competent, Jeffrey Biggers,' Hubert observes. 'He was in my chambers. He's applied to join the Garrick.'

'Nobody tells us it's Gulivant's first case,' Legless continues, 'so we just carry on as usual. I mean, he could have had us into chambers and said, "I'm a planning Silk, I don't know what the hell I'm doing in a criminal case. Would you mind pointing me in the right direction?"'

'That'll be the day,' I observe, a bit sourly.

'No, Archie Halbert did that in his first case,' Hubert interjects. 'Alistair Trimble was prosecuting me down at Winchester. Fraud of some kind. Went down like a lead balloon. But I remember Archie sent the usher for us before we started. "Would counsel be good enough to join his Lordship in chambers?" and so on. He was quite honest about it. "Look, chaps, I haven't got the first bloody idea what I'm doing with this criminal stuff. Where do we start?" So we walked him through it as the case went along, went back to chambers every time he got stuck, and we got through it perfectly well.'

'Well, not Gulivant,' Legless says. 'Not a word. Everything *seems* fine. He seems very nice, very courteous to everyone, doesn't interrupt. Come to think of it, he doesn't say very much at all except, "That may be a convenient moment to break for lunch", or "Ten thirty tomorrow morning", and so on. So we get no warning. Case takes two or three days, perfectly straightforward. I make my closing speech; Jeffrey makes his. I've got the *Times* crossword all ready to keep my mind occupied during the summing-up, when all of a sudden..."

Unsettled by the memory, Legless has to take a draught of his coffee to steady himself.

'...all of a sudden, I hear him say: "So there it is, members of the jury. Please retire and consider your verdict."'

An unbelieving silence engulfs the table.

'You mean, he said that at the end of the summing-up?' Marjorie asks tentatively.

'No', Legless replies grimly. 'I mean that *was* the summing-up. At first I thought I must have dozed off for a few minutes and missed it. But not a bit of it. I could tell from the way Jeffrey was looking at me. Not to mention the usher, who is poised to take the oath to keep the jury in some private and convenient place and so on, but isn't quite sure whether she should. Even the jury are sensing there's something not quite kosher. They're all looking at me, of course, because I'm prosecuting. It's my job to do something. And the bloody fool hasn't summed up at all. Not a bloody word. Just, "There you go, that's your lot, you've heard the evidence, now bugger off and make of it what you will."'

'Monstrous!' Hubert exclaims.

'Absolutely outrageous!' Marjorie agrees. 'What on earth did you do?'

'Well, I was a bit lost for words at first, I don't mind telling you,' Legless admits. 'But after a couple of seconds I recover enough to stand up and ask Gulivant if the jury might retire for a few minutes. He looks puzzled. "Apparently you haven't been following the proceedings, Mr Dunblane," he says, "I've just asked them to retire." "Yes, your Lordship is quite right," I reply. "But what I meant was, not retire to consider their verdict, but retire so that I might address your Lordship on a point of law." So now I've used the magic words, haven't I? I mean, surely, they've told him that much: once you hear the words "point of law", you get the jury out quicker than you can say Court of

Appeal. Not a bit of it. Gulivant considers for a moment or two and says, "I'm not sure that's necessary. If it is a matter which concerns their deliberations, I think they ought to hear it.""

'Oh, for heaven's sake,' Marjorie protests, 'you were trying to bail him out. He was making a complete fool of himself.'

Legless thumps the table.

'Exactly, Marjorie. He's in the water, waves breaking over his head, sharks circling, I'm throwing him a bloody lifeline, and it doesn't even cross the stupid man's mind to grab it. I turn to Jeffrey for inspiration. Nothing. Jeffrey's gone, in a coma, eyes glazed over. So I have to press on alone. "With great respect, my Lord," I say, "it may be better for my learned friend and I to mention this matter in the absence of the jury, just in case we have to go into matters that may not concern them" ("such as your total bloody incompetence," I'm thinking to myself). Long seconds pass, Gulivant eyes the lifeline: will he take it, or won't he, will he, won't he? "We'll cross that bridge if we come to it, Mr Dunblane," he says. By now, of course, the jury are all ears. They know the case is about to get screwed up. No point in buggering around. He's going down for the third time, and there's nothing I can do to stop it.'

'What a prat!' Marjorie exclaims. 'Where do they get these people from?'

'The Planning Bar,' Legless mutters venomously. 'So I say, "As your Lordship pleases. I was simply going to remind your Lordship, respectfully, that it is the usual practice in these courts to offer the jury some direction about the law before they retire to consider their verdict." At last I get a response. Gulivant gives me a look that says, "Oh, God, yes, that rings a distant chord. I'm sure they told me something about that before they sent me here. What the devil was it?" Even now, he could be saved. If he sends the jury out, he can sit there for a few minutes while I tell him the facts of life. He will look stupid in front of the Bar, but at least he can rise until after lunch and give himself the chance to cobble something together for the jury. But no. He still doesn't quite believe me, so he reaches for *Archbold*. What does he think he's going to find in *Archbold*, for God's sake – a passage that says summing up is optional? Of course, ten seconds later he's realised what a total tosser he looks, and he's trying to put *Archbold* back down again without anyone noticing. "Yes," he says slowly, "I take your point, Mr Dunblane. What would you like me to tell them in this particular case?"'

Marjorie gasps. 'Oh no!'

'At this point, for all I care, he could bloody well drown in full view of the jury. Jeffrey has emerged from his coma by now, and is silently mouthing some suggestions. "Well, my Lord," I say, "it's usual to begin by explaining to the jury their function and your Lordship's function in the trial, and then to mention the burden and standard of proof." Finally I've said something he recognises. "Ah yes, you mean, the prosecution must prove its case against the defendant," he says, "that kind of thing?" "Your Lordship puts it perfectly," I say. "Many judges also remind the jury that the prosecution must prove the case so that they are sure of the defendant's guilt. That kind of thing." He nods doubtfully, as though he thinks that might be going a bit far. "Yes, I'm most obliged, Mr Dunblane," he says. And then...'

Legless has to reach for his coffee again.

'...and then, bugger me if the stupid sod doesn't turn to the jury and say, "Well, there you are, members of the jury, you've heard what counsel has said, and of course that's exactly right. Bear that in mind." Whereupon he invites them once more to retire to consider their verdict.'

Around the table we are shaking our heads sadly.

'What on earth did you do?' I ask.

Legless shakes his head dismissively. 'Nothing I could do, short of giving him a summing-up-for-beginners lecture. As soon as he had risen, obviously, I told Jeffrey I wouldn't resist the appeal, so worst case scenario, his client would be out on bail pending appeal within a few days. Mercifully, the jury acquitted. I think they realised what a bloody shambles it all was and decided to pull the plug.'

'You see, that's the problem,' Marjorie says. 'What was needed was for the poor sod to be convicted, for Jeffrey to appeal, and for you to stand up and say you couldn't in all good conscience seek to uphold a conviction obtained following such a monumental judicial cock-up. Then Gulivant gets a bloody good bollocking from the Court of Appeal. They would have moved him out of the criminal courts in double quick time then.'

Legless nods.

'Yes. As you say, Marjorie, that's what it needed.'

All of which may help to explain the look on Stella's face – and mine – when she comes into my chambers just before I am due to go back into court at two o'clock with terrible news. As I may have mentioned before, our list officer has a gloomy disposition at the best of times, but when she has bad news to impart you actually feel the angel of doom hovering above the room.

'Mr Justice Gulivant will be with us next Monday,' she says in a tone of voice she might have used to announce the sinking of the Titanic. 'He's coming to try the Foggin Island case.'

I look at her blankly. I don't know how we ever got the Foggin Island case in the first place. It has no geographical connection with Bermondsey at all. I seem to recall that it had been passed round a number of Crown Courts on the circuit, including Bermondsey, while the Grey Smoothies tried to find one mad enough to take it. It was like pass the parcel, and I had been fairly sure that we were not left holding it when the music stopped.

It had taken some effort. Stella and I tried every Crown

Court on the south coast, because of the maritime connection. We tried Southwark, where they do a lot of fraud cases. At one point I even approached the High Court to suggest that it was really a case for the Admiralty jurisdiction, and so belonged in the Queen's Bench Division. No luck. It was only when I approached the Old Bailey that I was able to move it. I played shamelessly on their sense of their own image. They are always flattered over there when you offer them what seems to be a complicated, sophisticated case with a bit of law in it. They said they would take it. How in God's name has it found its way back to Bermondsey?

'We got rid of that to the Bailey,' I protest. 'Too complicated, we told them, matters of law, possible diplomatic repercussions, should be tried by a High Court judge or at least an Old Bailey judge, that kind of thing.'

'They sent it back,' Stella replies. 'They claim they don't have a courtroom to spare, and it's got to come on this week, so they're sending Mr Justice Gulivant here to try it. I suppose I'll have to put him in court one, won't I?'

That's another annoying thing. Question of rank. I have to vacate my courtroom and chambers and move to a broom cupboard laughably known as court five for the week. In addition, I lose a courtroom for our usual workload, which doesn't go away. And I have to defer to him at lunch, listen patiently to those marvellous old jokes from the world of urban planning. We don't often get a High Court judge visiting at Bermondsey, but when we do it buggers up the whole court for a week.

'I suppose so,' I reply. 'Well, you never know. Perhaps it will plead.'

I know better than that, obviously. They never plead when you want them to. The Foggin Island case is especially unlikely to plead. The defendant is barking mad; he thinks he is about to make history in the sphere of public international law; and he is represented by counsel only marginally less delusional than he is. Plus, they've got Stephen Gulivant trying it. Plead? You could get shorter odds on Tranmere Rovers winning the cup. No, Foggin Island is not going to plead. It's going the distance, and so am I. Oh, and did I mention that it's not a simple matter of guilty or not guilty? The defendant is pleading sovereign immunity. Gulivant will have to sort that one out, first.

* * *

Monday morning

'Stephen,' I exclaim, as Stella shows him in. 'How delightful. Welcome to Bermondsey. And we will have you for at least a week, I understand.'

'It's awfully kind of you to let me use your court and chambers, Charles. Quite uncalled for, but very much appreciated. I'm sure I shall feel quite at home at Bermondsey.'

'It's the least we can do. Please ask your clerk to let me know if you need anything. I'm just along the corridor. Dawn will be your usher. She will bring you your order form for lunch.'

'Marvellous. Look, if you have any odds and ends, sentencing, a dangerous driving perhaps, something like that, I'm only too happy to pitch in and help.'

'Very kind, Stephen,' I reply. 'Very kind indeed. Stella will let you know if there's anything.'

That is not about to happen. High Court judges always make a show of offering to help, in that 'we're all on the same team' sort of way, to show they can get down and dig dirt with the rest of us. But one of the first lessons you learn as an RJ, often the hard way, is that you can't afford to indulge them. Let Stephen Gulivant loose on sentencing a dangerous driving? I feel the ice forming on my spine just thinking about it. He would either disqualify some poor sod for fifty years or give him an absolute discharge, and that would be just for starters. No. Gulivant won't be getting his hands on anything at Bermondsey except Foggin Island. To which he's welcome.

I sit at ten-thirty. Everything is fine until just before eleven o'clock. I'm due to try an offensive weapon case, a day to a day and a half, perfectly straightforward. But first, I am hearing a bail application. Chummy is charged with three counts of fondling his partner's ten-year-old sister, plus an ABH against the partner by pushing her down the stairs and kicking her in the head when she confronts him about it. He has a long record, mostly for petty dishonesty and possessing cannabis. But he also has one for indecent assault on a fourteen-year-old from about five years ago. His counsel calls this an 'historic' conviction, as if to suggest that it belongs to some distant time, so long ago and far away that it would obviously be unfair to hold it against him now.

'The facts of the case are very much in dispute,' she says without elaborating. 'In addition, your Honour, it would be counter-productive to leave him in custody. He's in regular work as a roofer with his brother's company in Bow. He is supporting his elderly mother, who is confined to the house, as well as his seven-year-old son.'

'That would be his son by his present partner, would it?' I ask.

Miss Phipson purports to study her brief carefully. I feel a bit sorry for her. I like Emily Phipson. She's rather short with severe black-rimmed spectacles, and always wears the same conventional black suit. She sometimes comes across as a bit nervous, and she certainly doesn't set the courtroom on fire. But she's good on the law, always well prepared, and she doesn't take too much time, virtues that more than outweigh any faults she may have. The bail application is hopeless. She knows it, and she knows I know it, but she is doing her best, showing some enthusiasm as she goes through the motions.

'Well, actually, Your Honour, no, a previous partner.' She moves on quickly. 'He has strong ties to the community. He can reside at his mother's house. There can be a curfew each evening. He can be ordered not to approach his partner or the alleged victim. He will report every day at his local police station. In my submission, those conditions would be enough to satisfy the prosecution's concerns.'

She looks up at me. I tell her she has said all she could, which she has. I explain to Chummy that despite his counsel's excellent and persuasive arguments, I feel unable to extend him bail at this time because there are substantial grounds for believing that he might commit further offences. By which I mean, though I don't spell it out, having another go at the little sister or bullying her into retracting her story, or, probably, both. Chummy submits to being taken down with ill grace. Next I'm due to sentence a habitual burglar, something I always enjoy. But it's not to be. My clerk, Carol, stands and whispers confidentially.

'Sorry, Judge. Message from Mr Justice Gulivant. Something has come up in court one. Would you mind rising and speaking with him in chambers?'

I glance at the clock.

'But it's only just after eleven,' I whisper in reply. 'He hasn't had time to...'

She looks at me questioningly. I stop myself before I say anything undiplomatic.

'I'm sorry. I have to rise for a short time,' I announce to a mystified courtroom.

I make my way quickly along the corridor to chambers one, removing my wig en route. Gulivant is already there pacing up and down, looking mortified. I'm assuming the worst, though I can't imagine what it could possibly be.

'I can't do it,' he says.

'Can't do what?'

'Foggin Island. I can't do it.'

For a precious moment, I have the illusion that Gulivant has finally confronted his own inadequacy. A High Court judge has finally acknowledged that he is out of his depth in crime. The temptation to agree is almost overwhelming, but this is not the time to indulge myself. I need this bloody case to go away. Gulivant has to do it, whether he thinks he can or not. Only one option: offer encouragement; shore up the judicial ego a bit; talk him through it. If he survives till lunch he will probably be all right. Probably best to try to convince him that it's just like a planning appeal really, except that someone could go to prison. Once he gets into the case he will feel more at home. But my interpretation of 'can't do it' turns out to have been – in words the Court of Appeal once employed when reversing what I fancied as one of my better rulings   fundamentally flawed. Confession of inadequacy is not what he intended at all.

'My wife is an honorary trustee of the Goldbreaker Trust,' he says apologetically. 'I didn't realise the Trust was involved until the case was being opened.'

I'm still trying to work out what in God's name he's on about when, mercifully, he explains.

'The Goldbreaker Trust is one of the bodies defrauded by the defendant – allegedly defrauded I mean, of course. I can't do it, not with my wife involved with one of the Trusts. I have a clear conflict of interest.'

I sit down in something of a daze. He's right, obviously. It is the clearest possible conflict of interest and there is nothing he or I can do about it. It's also really bad news. I see what's coming next in an instant.

'I told the parties, of course, and they agreed. So I said I would talk to you and ask you to take over for me.'

I hold my head in my hands.

'I will be happy to release it to you, Charles. I have every confidence in you.' Gulivant smiles. 'I'm not sure it really needs a High Court judge, anyway. I don't see why an experienced circuit judge such as yourself couldn't manage it.'

'Very kind of you to say so, Stephen,' I mutter weakly. I have no choice, of course. It's the price of high command that you have to take responsibility in a crisis. There is only one consolation, and I grab it with both hands. 'I'll need court one, I'm afraid. Too many papers for court five, no room to put anything.'

'Oh, yes, of course. I'll sit in court five. Let me take over whatever you were going to do. Were you going to start a trial?'

'Possessing an offensive weapon,' I reply, 'silly little case, day and a half at most. But there's really no need. I'm sure you have far more important things to do at the High Court. I'll give it to the first judge who comes free during the week.'

'Nonsense.' Gulivant stands smartly up with the air of a man relieved of a crushing burden. 'Sounds delightful. While I'm off the bench I might as well have a quick cup of coffee, then I'll make a start. What's it about?'

I close my eyes briefly.

'Chummy thinks victim owes him money for cannabis supplied,' I reply. 'He asks victim to pay, politely the first time; but victim says he doesn't have any money until he gets his benefits the following week. Chummy doesn't buy victim's story because he happens to know that he has been seen in the pub, as usual, and he comes back half an hour later with a baseball bat. He's chasing victim through the park when he runs straight into two police officers, who nick him for possessing an offensive weapon. He is arrested and cautioned and replies, "I was just looking for someone to play third base. Can you spare an hour or so?" Open and shut, but he's got form for the same thing, so he won't plead. You can have the jury out tomorrow, Wednesday morning at the latest.'

Gulivant has been scribbling notes.

'Good, so the defendant's name is – how do you spell it C-H-U-M-L-E-Y or C-H-O-L-M-O-N-D-L-E-Y?'

I stare at him for a few seconds.

'No, I'm sorry, I said "Chummy."'

He looks blank.

'It's... just an expression we use. The defendant's name is Martin, Wayne Martin. He's one of our regulars.'

Mercifully, Gulivant leaves without asking anything else. He's got good counsel in front of him, Piers Drayford prosecuting, and Emily Phipson defending. They will explain it all to him.

Reclaiming my seat behind my desk, I turn to Foggin Island. Sovereign immunity? They must be joking. There is nothing useful in *Archbold*, which means I am pretty much up the creek without a paddle unless counsel have done some work on it. There is not much chance that what passes for the library at Bermondsey Crown Court will have a volume dealing with sovereign immunity. A trip to the Inner Temple library threatens – a place I have not visited more than twice since passing my Bar finals, many years ago. As if that's not bad enough, I haven't read the papers since I lobbed the case over to the Old Bailey, fully expecting never to see it again.

The papers are neatly arrayed in front of me in a series of fifteen differently-coloured file folders. Pointless to start before I at least glance at them, so I send word to court one that I will begin Foggin Island again at two o'clock, and I leave Wayne Martin to Gulivant in court five. I begin reading. Fortunately, prosecuting counsel has produced a summary of the case. After about twenty minutes of reading, it seems obvious that they've got Chummy bang to rights on six counts of fraud, and very likely, on two or three counts of money laundering. I briefly feel reassured. Until I get to the section dealing with sovereign immunity. I start to explore this magical world of public international law for the first time. My, how the minutes fly by.

And so to lunch, an oasis of calm in a desert of chaos.

As I enter the dining room, only Legless is seated at the table. He is playing rather unhappily with a mackerel salad.

'How's it going?' he asks. 'I hear you had to take Foggin Island over from Mr Justice Urban Planning.'

'I did indeed. His wife may be one of the victims. I'm starting it at two o'clock. You don't look too happy. How is your list going?'

'My list went very well,' Legless says. 'I had an attempted robbery at knife-point. Chummy pleaded at the last moment and I sent him down for eighteen months. After that, Stella gave me a bit of plea and case management, and I took your plea to burglary, and Bob's your uncle. Then I made the mistake of asking whether I could help any of the other courts.'

'Not Gulivant, I hope,' I smiled nervously.

'No. Marjorie.'

'Where is Marjorie?'

'Gone to the children's school again. Simon or Samantha, don't know which, has been detained on suspicion of having the mumps. I said I would take her list. Bloody long one, too. I'm going to be here all day.'

I make sympathetic noises. I was in a rush this morning and didn't buy my usual lunch *chez* Elsie and Jeanie. I have ordered the cheese omelette, which arrives looking even drier than they usually do. As I'm making a start on it, Gulivant comes in and takes his seat at the window end of the mess, as if by divine right.

'How's the offensive weapon?' I ask. 'Almost finished the prosecution case by now, I expect.'

Gulivant has ordered a prawn sandwich on brown bread from which he is carefully removing the cellophane wrapper. He shakes his head.

'Bloody complicated, these offensive weapons cases,' he replies. 'You might have warned me, Charles. It's got some difficult issues of law.'

'Really?' I ask. 'I didn't notice anything when I read the file. What seems to be the problem?'

'Well, it's not the kind of thing you could really call a weapon, is it?

'What isn't?' Legless inquires.

'A baseball bat.'

Legless raises his eyebrows at me. I close my eyes.

'Why not?' I ask.

'Well, a baseball bat is for playing baseball, isn't it?' Gulivant asks. 'It's not a weapon. I mean, you could do damage to someone with almost anything if you really put your mind to it. When I was at school, a chap caused an injury to another boy using a squash racquet.'

'That's the point,' I explain. 'There are really two kinds of offensive weapon. There are some items, such as a flick knife, which are made or adapted for causing injury to the person. They are called offensive weapons *per se*. A baseball bat is not made or adapted for causing injury to the person, so it's not an offensive weapon *per se*, but it *becomes* an offensive weapon if Chu... if the defendant intends to use it as such. The prosecution say he was going to hit the victim over the head with it, so at that point, it becomes a weapon.'

'Well, I read what it says in...'

'*Archbold?*'

'*Archbold*, yes. But it wasn't at all clear. There seem to be several conflicting decisions of the Court of Appeal. For one thing, I'm not sure whether it is a matter of law for me, or a matter of fact for the jury. I have a nasty feeling this case may go further.'

I feel a sense of rising panic. The case of Wayne Martin shouldn't be going anywhere, except away, by Wednesday at the latest.

'The law shouldn't be an issue in this case, Stephen,' I reply as calmly as I can. 'It's a strictly factual question. Just explain the law to the jury and leave it to them to decide.'

'I'm not so sure,' he says.

'Look, can I suggest that you ask counsel? You've got Piers Drayford and Emily Phipson. Both very good. They will tell you all about it. Piers will set it out in his opening.'

Gulivant shakes his head.

'I don't want to have it opened to the jury until I am satisfied about the law. Anyway, I have asked counsel to address me about it at two o'clock.'

I take a deep breath. I can't allow this to upset me. I have too much to do. I do my best to relax. Piers Drayford and Emily Phipson will explain it all to him. If he gives them the chance.

* * *

Monday afternoon

Despite my reading this morning, my knowledge of the Foggin Island case is still rather vague. So I'm depending on Derek Mapleleaf QC, who is prosecuting, to explain it all to me. I'll have to take copious notes, bluff my way through until four o'clock, and then have another quick scan through the files before I go home.

Mapleleaf is tall, emaciated, and bespectacled. He believes himself to be a High Court judge in waiting. You can tell by the air of superiority. Circuit judges are a bit beneath him, as indeed is the Bermondsey Crown Court. He looks around as if he is perplexed about how he came to be here, and must speak to his clerk to make sure it doesn't happen again. Mapleleaf is thorough and detailed, boring to the point of stupefaction, and had his sense of humour surgically removed before coming to the Bar. But he may be just what I need in this case. My only hope is to pick up as much about the case as I can in the shortest possible time. Behind him are seated two juniors, plus a number of men in dark suits, presumably government lawyers, and a sprinkling of young people with Apple laptops whose reason for being in court is unclear. All a bit intimidating. I'm actually beginning to believe my own propaganda to the Old Bailey about this being a case that should be tried by a High Court judge. But it's too late for that now.

'May it please your Lordship – I'm so sorry, I mean your Honour, of course,' he begins, unable to resist rubbing it in. 'I appear for the Crown, together with my learned friends Mr Stewart and Miss Anderson. My learned friends Mr Warnock and Mr Gatley appear for this defendant, Walter Freedland Orlick.'

Walter Freedland Orlick is sitting in the dock wearing a dark suit and a grey tie with white spots, of the kind that was in vogue for weddings in the early seventies. He has his hands folded across his lap, and is looking up and away to the right, affecting disdain for the proceedings. His counsel, Kenneth Warnock, lunatic of this Parish, sits to Mapleleaf's left. As is his wont, Warnock is smiling up at the bench for no apparent reason. The smile, together with his slightly dishevelled appearance and tattered wig, is actually quite disturbing. We don't see a lot of him at Bermondsey, but when we do, it's always memorable. Warnock inhabits a different plane, from which he returns to earth from time to time to put forward a theory of law so novel and original that it is difficult to respond to. This case was made for him.

'As your Honour knows,' Mapleleaf is saying, 'the defendant is charged with six counts of fraud, three counts of money laundering, and three counts of possession of criminal property. All the counts relate to activities undertaken by the defendant in his capacity as managing director of a company called Foggin Island Enterprises SA, which is incorporated in Luxembourg, and whose directors are the defendant himself, a Miss Suzy Callaghan, described as secretary, and a Mr Eustace O'Toole, described as treasurer. I anticipate that Your Honour may hear from them in the course of these proceedings.

'Essentially, your Honour, the Crown say that over the course of about five years, the defendant obtained almost two million pounds by fraud from a number of trusts, by offering to undertake various accounting and business development services which were never in fact provided. That money was placed in a number of bank accounts in Luxembourg, the accounts being held in the names of companies which appear to have no real existence, and which are no more than alter egos of the defendant, and one of these companies being Foggin Island Enterprises SA.

'But when asked to plead to the indictment, the defendant submitted a written plea disputing the jurisdiction of the English courts, and asserting sovereign immunity. Of course, that issue must be determined before the case can be tried. So, rather than take your Honour's time with the detailed facts now, it may be more appropriate for me to defer to my learned friend Mr Warnock. It is a matter on which my learned friend has the burden of proof.'

Mapleleaf sits down abruptly. Warnock rises without interrupting his smile at all.

'I'm grateful to my learned friend. Has your Honour had the opportunity of reading the papers?'

Warnock and I both know the answer to that question, and we both know the answer I will give.

"I'm sure I must have read them on a previous occasion, Mr Warnock, before the case was sent to the Old Bailey. But I'm afraid my recollection is far from complete. It was only this morning I learned that I would have to take it over from Mr Justice Gulivant, and I have only had a short time.'

In other words, no.

'Then, I will start from the beginning', Warnock beams. 'The defendant enters a plea of lack of jurisdiction based on sovereign immunity. While he is named in the indictment as Walter Freedland Orlick, the defendant is in fact His Majesty King Walter I of the sovereign state of Foggin Island.'

Warnock turns in both directions to glance at those around him, as if expecting a round of applause. Everyone in court knew what was coming, of course, but it is a striking moment nonetheless. I find myself speculating about who might have been the last person to offer a plea of sovereign immunity in an English court. Possibly Charles I, come to think of it, or Queen Charlotte perhaps – not a good omen for the defendant in either case.

'Accordingly I shall refer to him as "His Majesty" or "the King".'

'You will do no such thing, Mr Warnock,' I protest, 'at least until such time as I find that to be his proper title. His title at present is Mr Orlick.'

'As your Honour pleases. To illustrate my submissions,' Warnock continues, 'I must take your Honour to the small but significant plot of land known as Foggin Island. Virtually speaking, of course. I am not applying for the Court to visit the island for a view.'

'I am glad to hear it,' I say.

'No. No need. I have a map.'

Warnock snaps his thumb and middle finger, and before you can say sovereign immunity, his junior, Mr Gatley, leaps energetically to his feet, leaves counsel's row, and seizes an easel which has been leaning against the side wall of the court. The easel has something on it covered by a sheet. Gatley moves it to the front of the court, arranges it so that we can see, and with a final flourish tears the sheet away. The exhibit is a large map entitled 'Foggin Island and Environs', which is a bit of an odd way of putting it, as the environs seem to be confined to the waters of the English Channel. Still, it has nice big letters and an amusing representation of a smiling fish emerging from a wave, just so that we are clear we are dealing with water. Warnock edges out of counsel's row slightly so that he can stand next to the easel. He is armed with a pointer, rather like a conductor's baton but longer.

'Foggin Island, as your Honour can see, is situated in the English Channel, just a few miles from Sark. It is a small island, no more than some two thousand metres from north to south and some sixteen hundred metres east to west. Not that it runs exactly north to south, or east to west for that matter, but I'm sure Your Honour follows me.'

I nod.

'To explain the defendant's position in this matter, I have to take your Honour briefly through certain aspects of the Island's history. Of course, I shall make it as short as possible. The origin of the Island's name is lost in obscurity. Some say it is a reference to the Island's propensity to morning and evening fog at certain times of year. Others, noting its French title, *l'Ile des Fougains*, have speculated that it derives from the French word *fou*, meaning mad, perhaps indicating a French perception that one might have to be mad to live there; though my client would dispute that, of course…'

'Can we get on, Mr Warnock?'

'Yes, of course, your Honour. Foggin Island seems to have come to prominence first in the twelfth century, during the reign of Henry II, a monarch who, as Your Honour will recall, was in the habit of making a circuit between his various possessions in England and France…'

There are times as a judge when, with the best will in the world, you go into a time warp when listening to counsel. It's a form of hypnosis, I think. The monotony of the voice, the efforts to focus on what is being said, a few stray thoughts about the weekend, and suddenly you can come to and not be quite sure where you are or what case you are listening to. It is not necessarily related to how interesting or uninteresting the case is. It's just something that happens sometimes and takes you by surprise. I recall a fairly long passage in Warnock's address about the Armada, and later the Napoleonic Wars, when beacons were lit on Foggin Island. But other than that, the centuries pass by rather vaguely. When I return to my body I realise that some time must have elapsed, because Warnock is saying something about the Second World War, which is some centuries from where he started with Henry II. But I have no idea how much I have missed or whether any of it matters. My judicial instinct says no. I glance up at the clock. Mercifully, it indicates almost four o'clock. Time to rise for the day, and see what I can glean from the papers.

* * *

Tuesday Morning

I creep quietly along the judicial corridor to my chambers in the hope of a few moments alone with Elsie and Jeanie's latte and the *Times* before returning to the saga of Foggin Island. I have been worrying all night about what Gulivant is doing with the case of Wayne Martin, and I am actually trying to convince myself that if I hide away quietly, no one will be able to disturb me with any dreadful news from court five – a silly fallacy if ever there was one. But remarkably, it seems to work; at any rate, I make it into court without any reports of fresh disasters.

Warnock takes a deep breath.

'Your Honour, yesterday I outlined the history of Foggin Island, and the fact that Great Britain has never taken active steps to occupy or assert sovereignty over the Island except for very isolated acts of lighting beacons in times of emergency. We will show that such limited acts are insufficient in law to give rise to an occupation. All of that history is in the documentary evidence which your Honour has, and my learned friend has been good enough to indicate that it is not disputed to any material extent. I now turn to the occupation or conquest of Foggin Island by the defendant, and this is a matter which the Crown does dispute, and about which I must call evidence. I call the Secretary of State of Foggin Island, Mr Eustace O'Toole.'

I feel some sense of disappointment.

'Mr Warnock, I would have thought, given his claim to the title of King, that the defendant himself would have been in charge of any occupation of the Island.'

'He was, your Honour.'

'In that case, I would have expected him to give evidence about it.'

Warnock nods, conceding the logic of my comment. He seems hesitant.

'Your Honour, as the defendant does not recognise the jurisdiction of the court over him, he takes the view that it would be, shall we say, inappropriate for him to give evidence.'

'It might be, shall we say, more persuasive if he did.'

'Yes, your Honour,' Warnock concedes.

But it's not going to happen. Instead, Eustace O'Toole, Secretary of State to His Majesty the King of Foggin Island, continues his slow walk to the witness box, and takes the oath with a pronounced Irish brogue. Warnock recovers himself and proceeds.

'Mr O'Toole, please give the court your full name.'

'Eustace Gerald O'Toole.'

'Where do you reside?'

'Care of the Royal Residence, Kingdom of Foggin Island.'

'What is your occupation?'

'I have the honour to serve as Secretary of State for KFI.'

'I am sorry, Mr O'Toole,' I interrupt. 'What did you call it? KFC?'

'I called it KFI, your Honour, short for the Kingdom of Foggin Island. Many States these days adopt a short acronym for diplomatic purposes, for example USA for the United States of America, RSA for the Republic of South Africa –'

'Yes. I see. Thank you.'

'Not at all, your Honour.'

'When you speak of Foggin Island being a kingdom,'

Warnock asks, 'does that imply that you recognise a person as being the King of Foggin Island?'

'Yes, sir.'

'Will you please identify that person for the court?'

'The defendant, otherwise known as Walter Freedland Orlick. He is the King of Foggin Island.'

'And is it right that, when you refer to Foggin Island, you refer to the territory I identified to his Honour yesterday afternoon using the map?'

'Yes, sir.'

'The island in the English Channel?'

'Yes, sir.'

'The island the defendant, together with yourself and Miss Callaghan, occupied or invaded?'

'Correct, sir.'

'Tell us briefly how the occupation was accomplished.'

To judge by his manner, O'Toole regards the question as one too obvious to require an answer.

'His Majesty had purchased a large power boat during a stay on the Isle of Wight,' he replies. 'We got in the boat with enough supplies and personal effects to keep us going, we took the boat to Foggin Island, disembarked and planted the flag.' He looks around the court, as if to ask those assembled how else you would occupy or invade an island. 'That was it, really.'

'Thank you. Would you please outline for the court your duties as Secretary of State?'

'To deal with various matters of state on His Majesty's behalf, including relations with foreign states and international organisations.'

I think briefly about trying to forbid O'Toole from referring to the defendant as His Majesty, but I soon realise that it would be an exercise in futility and would serve only to increase the temperature in the courtroom. Warnock has carefully positioned a number of files within easy reach.

'Your Honour, there are a number of exhibits I would like to show to the witness. Your Honour has copies. If the usher would be kind enough?'

Dawn carries the files over to the witness box and deposits them in front of the Secretary of State.

'Mr O'Toole, please look at the first file, Exhibit D one. Can you tell his Honour what this is?'

O'Toole carefully dons reading glasses and peruses the file.

'This is a file of correspondence passing between myself and the Secretary-General of the United Nations.'

'Dealing with what subject?'

'My request that KFI be admitted as a member of the United Nations, and that the United Nations should invite its member states to recognise His Majesty as both the *de jure* and *de facto* lawful government of Foggin Island.'

'And does your letter give a detailed account of the occupation or conquest of the Island by the defendant and yourself?'

'And by Miss Suzy Callaghan.'

'Yes, quite so.'

'Yes, it is fully described.'

I skim through the file, all four pages of it.

'What was the Secretary-General's response to this request?' I ask. I see Mapleleaf smirking.

'He acknowledges receipt of my letter and undertakes to look into the matter,' O'Toole replies.

'Has he ever provided any further response?'

'Not yet, your Honour. Our experience is that these things often take some time.'

I nod to Warnock.

'Exhibit D two, please, Mr O'Toole. What is this?'

'Correspondence between myself and the Secretary-General of the North Atlantic Treaty Organization, containing an offer from KFI to participate in certain military exercises, without for the time being seeking full membership.'

Even Warnock seems a bit bemused by this.

'What role would Foggin Island be in a position to play in military exercises?' he asks.

'His Majesty would authorise the lighting of beacons,' he replies. 'They can be very useful in certain situations, as in the cases you mentioned to the court yesterday.'

'Exhibit D three?'

'Correspondence between myself and UNESCO asking that Foggin Island be designated a World Heritage Site.'

Warnock is looking at me.

'I'm not going to ask,' I say.

'Not yet. It takes time, your Honour,' O'Toole volunteers.

Warnock decides it is time to change the subject.

'Mr O'Toole, how many people live on Foggin Island?'

'Three, sir.'

'And those would be …?'

'His Majesty, myself, and Miss Callaghan.'

'Yes. Now, do you and Miss Callaghan recognise any particular person or persons as constituting the *de jure* or *de facto* Government of Foggin Island?'

'Yes, sir. As I said to the Secretary-General of the United Nations in my letter, we recognise the defendant, His Majesty King Walter I, as both the *de jure* and *de facto* Government of the Kingdom.'

'Yes.'

O'Toole turns to me.

'There is something I would like to add, your Honour, if I may?'

'By all means,' I reply.

'His Majesty is not a despot, your Honour. He is a constitutional monarch, in the sense that he knows better than to try and have his own way with Miss Callaghan and myself about everything. He has to listen to our point of view.'

'A remarkable exercise in democracy,' I say.

Soon afterwards, Warnock abandons O'Toole to cross-examination.

Mapleleaf rises to his full height slowly in the hope of looking menacing.

'Mr O'Toole, let me see if I have understood this correctly. The defendant bases his position as a sovereign on the fact that, together with you and Miss Callaghan, he went to the Island by boat and disembarked? Is that right?'

'We occupied the Island, sir, yes.'

'Well, when you say you occupied it, was there anyone there when you arrived?'

'There was not, sir.'

'No sign of habitation?'

'None at all.'

'And you took this to mean that the Island was unclaimed, did you? Virgin territory, waiting to be explored?'

'Exactly, sir.'

'Did it strike you as odd that there should be a piece of virgin territory so close to the coast of Great Britain?'

'Not really. We assumed that people had been to the Island before, but we concluded that the Island was so small that the Government didn't think it worth taking possession of.'

'How do you know the Government has not taken possession of it?'

'We have never been shown any document suggesting that they did.'

O'Toole makes an interesting point. I have been waiting for the prosecution to produce a smoking gun, some kind of deed of title, some evidence that someone in a position of authority took some interest in the place at some time during the past seven hundred years. But so far, there has been nothing except the lighting of beacons. Mapleleaf seems to move on to the next question rather quickly.

'Was there anything else to support your assumption?'

'There was no flag.'

'Flag?'

'It is the usual practice for an occupying country to plant its flag on a territory. We found no evidence of a flag at all.'

'I see,' Mapeleaf says. He seizes his copy of Exhibit D one. 'But you followed the usual practice? You planted a flag, did you?'

'We did, sir.'

'Yes.' He opens the file and removes the final page, which he holds up. 'This is the flag, is it, or at least a drawing of it?'

'It is, sir.'

'With the Royal Coat of Arms on it?'

'Yes, sir.'

'The coat of arms seems to consist of a sword pointing downwards through a shield argent, flanked by two ferrets rampant, and a –'

'They are leopards,' O'Toole insists indignantly.

'Are they?' Mapleleaf holds the drawing up to the light and squints. 'Well... this is not the official document from the College of Arms, I suppose.'

'Can we move on, Mr Mapleleaf?' I suggest.

'Certainly, your Honour. Let me return to the question of the Island's population of three. Where do you all live?'

'In Foggin City, which has been designated the capital city of the Kingdom.'

'Is it also the Kingdom's only city?'

'For the time being.'

'And does it consist, for the time being, of five large tents?'

'That is one way of putting it.'

'Nothing else?'

'Such as what?'

'Oh, I don't know, Mr O'Toole. A bank? A launderette? A club which has a reciprocal arrangement with the Travellers?'

'Mr Mapleleaf...'

'Sorry, your Honour. What was your intent in occupying the Island? Why did you want to live there?'

'We were exercising our right to self-determination under international law.'

'Indeed? The right to self-determination of peoples?'

'Yes.'

'So you, the defendant, and Miss Callaghan constitute a "people", do you?'

'We are not aware of any minimum number required to constitute a "people" under international law.'

'But why does that involve going to Foggin Island? Why couldn't you have exercised your right to self-determination in, say, Liverpool?'

O'Toole is not sure how to answer that one.

'Let me help you,' Mapleleaf offers. 'You exercised a bit of self-determination in Liverpool a few years ago – you, the defendant and Miss Callaghan – didn't you? It ended up in the Crown Court, didn't it? What was the charge? Conspiracy to defraud, wasn't it?'

'That's got nothing to do with it,' O'Toole protests loudly.

'I happen to have a copy of the learned judge's sentencing remarks,' Mapleleaf adds. '"A sophisticated confidence trick planned and executed by professional fraudsters". Ring any bells, Mr O'Toole?'

'That was a misunderstanding.'

'Was it indeed? Well, there has been another mis-understanding, just recently, hasn't there? Isn't it true that your occupation of Foggin Island just happened to coincide with the police taking an interest in your business and financial affairs?'

'Pure coincidence, sir. And we are honest business people. We have nothing to hide.'

'Oh, come off it, Mr O'Toole. The police were hot on your trail again, weren't they? That's why Foggin Island suddenly seemed such a good idea.'

'Certainly not. It was a question of self-determination.'

Mapleleaf pauses for breath.

'Does Miss Callaghan occupy any office of State?'

'She is a Minister without Portfolio.'

'Do her responsibilities as such include the area of fiscal policy?'

O'Toole takes some time to ponder this change of direction.

'No, sir.'

'Do yours?'

'Not as such. His Majesty keeps close control of the country's economy.'

'Yes, I'm sure he does. Where are the funds of the Kingdom kept?'

'Why do you want to know?'

'I thought you said you had nothing to hide.'

'We don't… in the Central Bank of Foggin Island.'

'Thank you. Does the Bank have a governor?'

'His Majesty holds that position on a temporary basis, pending the recruitment of a suitably qualified individual.'

'These things take some time, don't they, Mr O'Toole?' I ask.

He nods emphatically. 'They do, your Honour.'

'And where is the Bank situated?' Mapleleaf asks. 'In one of the tents?'

O'Toole shifts from foot to foot uncomfortably.

'No, pending the construction of a suitable secure building, the bank is housed offshore.'

'I see. Not in Luxembourg, by any chance?'

'Since you ask, yes.'

'In the same building as the offices of Foggin Enterprises SA?'

'I believe so.'

'What is the value of the Kingdom's assets, held by the bank?'

Mapleleaf is smelling blood. Of course, if he could start to prove his case of fraud and money laundering before the trial even starts he would be well pleased, and O'Toole seems a perfect vehicle. But there is a problem. O'Toole is not a defendant, at least not yet, and he is not legally represented. Much as I am cheering Mapleleaf on in my mind, I have to intervene.

'Mr Mapeleaf, if you are going to pursue this line of questioning, I shall have to warn the witness that he is not obliged to answer any question he thinks may incriminate him, and if he so requests, I shall have to give him time to take legal advice.'

Mapleleaf sees the point immediately.

'I will not pursue it. I have nothing further, your Honour.'

And so to lunch. An oasis of calm in a desert of chaos.

I am the last to arrive. At least today I have a nice turkey breast and Emmenthal sandwich from Elsie and Jeanie's, and the memory of the cheese omelette has faded. Gulivant is engaged in some conversation with Legless, which they are both finding amusing, something that happened to a mutual acquaintance at a hunt ball. I wait for a lull in the conversation.

'Everything going well with Wayne Martin, Stephen?'

The smile wanes.

'Oh, there's been another point of law,' he says.

Legless almost chokes on a mouthful of carrot and cumin soup.

'I am probably going to regret asking,' I say, 'but what point would that be?'

'The prosecution want to put in his two previous convictions as evidence of bad character.'

'Yes, I am sure they do,' I reply. 'They are both fairly recent convictions for the same kind of offence.'

I am quite familiar with Wayne Martin's record. I presided over one of his previous trials, and I seem to recall that Marjorie did the other.

'But Miss Phipson is telling me that I shouldn't let them

in because it would affect the fairness of the trial,' Gulivant protests.

'Yes, of course she is,' I reply. 'She is representing the defendant. It is her job to say things like that, and I am sure she said it very well. But I am sure Piers Drayford explained the prosecution's view – that the evidence is admissible because it shows that Martin has a propensity to carry weapons in public.'

'Yes, they both argued the point very well,' Gulivant says, 'so much so, in fact, that I decided that the only safe course was to adjourn the matter for a short time and think about it. I have looked at...'

'Archbold.'

'Archbold. But it doesn't make the law clear at all. So I have sent the jury away until tomorrow, and I have asked for a short skeleton argument from both sides by two o'clock. I shall consider it this afternoon and rule tomorrow morning.'

I am speechless for some time.

'Stephen, I'm really not sure that's going to help you,' I say eventually. 'It's a judgement call. You have to ask how strong the evidence is, and balance that against the prejudicial effect on the defence, bearing in mind that you will be giving the jury a careful direction.'

'Yes, but I have to make sure that we look at all the relevant decisions of the Court of Appeal,' Gulivant insists.

'That's why you have Archbold, and that's why you have counsel,' I reply. 'Trust me, Stephen, they do this kind of thing day in, day out.'

'I am sure they are both very able,' he says. 'But it's not like being at the High Court, Charles. We are a bit out in the sticks here, aren't we? You don't seem to have a full set of law reports.'

I am experiencing a serious rise in temperature now.

'Look, would you be interested in hearing how I would deal with it?'

'No, Charles, I wouldn't want to let your views affect me. It has to be my decision, after all.'

'But that's one reason we all have lunch together. We ask for each other's views on questions like this all the time.'

'Very kind, Charles, but...'

Legless looks as though he is about to choke again. I shake my head helplessly. There is nothing I can do. I am too busy with Foggin Island. There is probably nothing I could do anyway, regardless of Foggin Island.

* * *

Tuesday afternoon

This afternoon we hear from Suzy Callaghan, Minister without Portfolio, who appears in a fetching red dress, rather low cut, with lashings of lipstick and make-up and high-heeled red shoes. Mercifully, her evidence doesn't take long, and it seems superfluous to record it in any great detail.

In summary, she chose to exercise her right of self-determination with the defendant and Mr O'Toole, not out of any political considerations, and certainly not to evade the police, but because she has always fancied living in the Channel Islands on account of the climate being preferable to that of Liverpool. She concedes that she was a bit discouraged when she saw Foggin Island for the first time, and has been frustrated by the slow pace of development of Foggin City. But His Majesty has given her certain assurances about that, and has also committed his Government to constructing a small beach resort on the south side of the Island, where she can work on her tan, and play a modest role in welcoming the inevitable stream of tourists who will arrive from the Continent once the word gets round, and once there is a hotel available. She knows nothing about the financial affairs of the Kingdom, and proves unable to find Luxembourg on a map of Europe when invited to do so by Mr Warnock in re-examination.

All in all, 'without portfolio' sums her up rather well.

By the time we finish with Miss Callaghan it is about three-thirty, and all counsel concur that we should break for the day now in order to prepare for the extensive exploration of customary public international law which must take place tomorrow. Both sides will have their experts available in case their written reports are not clear enough. On my way out, I stop in chambers five to see if I can be of any help to Gulivant on the question of evidence of bad character. He is not there. I call Stella, who tells me that the judge has left for the day to ponder his decision on the bad character evidence.

* * *

Wednesday morning

Elsie and Jeanie seem particularly pleased to see me today, and Jeanie prepares my latte with great verve. Neither complains about life at all. Next door, even George can't find a bad word to say about the Labour Party, and he has my copy of the *Times* ready with a cheerful 'morning, guv, how are we today?' It's all so out of character that it is positively unnerving. I find myself looking around suspiciously. I am not sure whether to regard this showing of collective bonhomie as encouragement for the day ahead or an omen of impending disaster. That's what this job can do to you. Cynicism can become a way of life.

On my desk I find an unfamiliar black file folder with a small white label which reads, 'Foggin Island: Further Legal Materials'. Attached by a paper clip is a note addressed to me, which reads as follows:

> *Charles,*
> *I am really sorry that I had to land you with this case. I'm even sorrier that, in all the excitement of Wayne Martin, I completely forgot to give you this file.*

*Perhaps I can make up for it partially by giving it to you
now. If the author is right, I think it would mean that you need
not consider the acquisition of unclaimed territory by conquest
or occupation at all. It would all be completely irrelevant. I
found it again last night. I knew I had it somewhere. It's a bit
of legal research I had done some time ago, when they first told
me I might have to deal with the case. When I say I had it
done, I mean that I used undue influence to enlist the aid of
my daughter-in-law, an academic at Nottingham who happens
to specialise in public international law. It's useful to have
contacts sometimes. It all seems perfectly comprehensible. I
hope it helps.*
SG

I seat myself behind my desk and start to thumb through the file.
At first, I am discouraged. 'Perfectly comprehensible' is not how
I would choose to describe a paper on customary international
law – replete with the opinions of the most learned jurists
from Grotius onwards; decisions of the International Court of
Justice; reports of various agencies of the United Nations; and
sundry other oddities far removed from the daily practice of
the Bermondsey Crown Court. My thumbing picks up speed
as my eyes gradually glaze over. But then – suddenly – there it
is: paragraph 36, headed 'Conclusion'. I read it carefully. I find
that the conclusion is not only perfectly comprehensible, but
may even be the answer to my prayers. It brings such a palpable
feeling of relief that I briefly feel the urge to cry.

*For the reasons stated above, the defendant cannot make a claim
to have acquired the territory of Foggin Island by conquest.
For this to apply, it would have to be shown that no State had
claimed sovereignty over the Island, or that any such claim
had been abandoned. The defendant appears to rest his case
on the proposition that the United Kingdom has not taken any*

positive steps to exercise sovereignty over the island. He points to the absence of any British activity on the Island, except for the lighting of beacons on certain occasions during the Armada Crisis and the Napoleonic Wars. But this is easily explained by the fact that England expressly ceded Foggin Island to France as part of the Treaty of Calais in 1360, a fact which the defendant appears to have overlooked.

This fact demonstrates that England had already claimed sovereignty over the Island before 1360, because you can't cede sovereignty unless you have first claimed it, and unless the party you are ceding it to recognises your claims. It also demonstrates that France acquired sovereignty over the Island with effect from the date when the treaty was signed. This, of course, would account for the lack of subsequent activity on the part of Great Britain, apart from the lighting of the beacons (which would technically have constituted a violation of French sovereignty). The French gained title to the Island by signing the Treaty of Calais; they did not acquire the territory by conquest; and they were under no obligation to occupy the Island to preserve their claim. I have seen no evidence that they have ever evinced any intention to abandon sovereignty. I conclude that the defendant's claim to be King of the Sovereign Territory of Foggin Island has no merit. For more detail, see paragraph 21, above.

I turn hurriedly to paragraph 21. It explains that the Treaty of Calais, ratified in that city on 24 October 1360 by the Kings of England and France, brought to an end the first phase of the Hundred Years War. Under its provisions, Edward III renounced all claims to the French throne, and ceded a certain amount of territory to France. But he also acquired a good deal of far more useful territory from France, which consolidated his holdings in Aquitaine; not to mention the small matter of three million gold crowns for the ransom of the French King, who had been captured at the Battle of Poitiers. Mentioned as one of the territories ceded by Edward is a certain 'Fogeyne Isle', or in French, '*L'Ile des Fougains*'. There is no ambiguity at all. This is the island I have been hearing about for the last three days. Apparently, Edward's ceding of the Island was widely seen at the time as a cunning act of statesmanship. It allowed the French the satisfying feeling of acquiring land dangerously near to the English coast, while the actual cost to England was a lump of rock of no practical value at all. This no doubt explains the absence of any French attempt to colonise it since 1360.

The author offers an alternative view. She speculates that the inclusion of *L'Ile des Fougains* might have been no more than a bit of late-night treaty-drafting humour. The negotiators on both sides, she says, all knew each other quite well and often got together for a few jars once the day's work was done. She thinks the island may have been written into a draft for a laugh one evening after a few glasses of Malmsey. The intention was to take it out before the final draft was prepared, but it was somehow left in – the opposite of what happened to the city of Berwick-upon-Tweed, which apparently remained at war for several centuries after the rest of the country was at peace, as a result of being left out of a peace treaty. Either way, the result is the same. *L'Ile des Fougains* is as much a part of France as *L'Ile de la Cité*.

I am not sure I can adequately describe the sense of relief this report brings me. The prospect I have been facing is of two days of legal argument in the alien field of public international law, the question being whether international law continues to recognise the right of acquisition of territory by conquest or occupation; and if so, whether a group consisting of Walter Freedland Orlick, Eustace O'Toole and Suzy Callaghan is entitled to exercise that right. There will be a side trip into the area of the right of self-determination of peoples. Not only will

I have to read numerous learned treatises and articles dealing with these subjects, but I will also have to hear from experts, professors of international law, one of whom is being whispered about as a future judge of the International Court of Justice. As if this were not bad enough, at the end of it all I, Charles Walden, Resident Judge at the Bermondsey Crown Court, will have to make a decision about who is right; a decision which will be subject to intense scrutiny by people who know far more about this than I do – including the Court of Appeal and the Supreme Court. But now, suddenly, I sense a reprieve. I feel like a condemned man suddenly pardoned and set at liberty.

I make my way into court and take my seat on the bench with a new spring in my step. Warnock is standing, positively beaming at the prospect of the mouth-watering legal argument he is about to launch. I decide not to intervene immediately. After all there is no hurry now. Best to bide my time, make him commit himself to his propositions of law.

'Your Honour,' he begins, 'we submit that conquest or occupation remains an acceptable way of acquiring territory for the purposes of public international law. My learned friend Mr Mapleleaf concedes that this was once the case, but will seek to argue that it is no longer recognised. He asserts that today, international law does not support wars of conquest, or even peaceful conquest as a method of acquiring territory. Your Honour will have seen the authorities on which we rely, and our expert witnesses on international law are ready to give evidence. I do, however, draw your Honour's attention to one matter which arises in connection with Great Britain, which may differentiate the case from those involving some other countries.'

I look up questioningly.

'What would that be, Mr Warnock?'

'Well, it's a question of the pot calling the kettle black, isn't it?'

Warnock is looking at me with his usual smile, as if his point is an obvious one which requires no further elaboration.'

'Is it?'

'But, of course, your Honour. For this country to complain about conquest and occupation is absolutely outrageous, given the proportion of the earth's surface Great Britain colonised by means of military invasion and occupation over the years. I don't know whether your Honour had the same sort of map as I had as a child, with much of the world coloured pink?'

Mapleleaf is holding his head in his hands.

'I did have such a map,' I concede, 'as I am sure we all did in those days. But I have the impression that they are regarded as a bit politically incorrect these days.'

'Well, they are,' Warnock concedes. 'But the point is that it's a bit much for the Government of this country to criticise someone for doing what the defendant has done in this case, given that it presided over an entire Empire well within living memory. One only has to consider England's annexation of Wales in the time of Edward I. An act of the most blatant military occupation and conquest.'

'I wasn't aware that the pot calling the kettle black had entered the sphere of jurisprudence, Mr Warnock.'

Mapleleaf looks up and actually gives me a thin smile – a rare compliment for him to bestow on a circuit judge.

'I will come to that in due course, if I may?' Warnock replies. 'May I first summarise my arguments? I submit first that the evidence given yesterday by Mr O'Toole and Miss Callaghan makes it quite clear that there was an occupation of Foggin Island by the defendant and the two witnesses. On that basis, my argument will have five main strands.

'First, I maintain that occupation and conquest remain valid ways of gaining sovereignty over territory in appropriate circumstances.

'Second, I will advance the estoppel argument, which I believe to be a new one in international law: that it would be wrong to allow Great Britain to oppose the defendant's claim to sovereignty, given the way in which so much British territory was acquired in the past. It would simply not be right to allow the Government of this country to make the argument that conquest and occupation are no longer recognised.

'Third, I will demonstrate that the defendant, Mr O'Toole and Miss Callaghan are capable in law of constituting a "people" for the purpose of enjoying the right of self-determination of peoples.

'Fourth, I will argue that as a "people", they are entitled to the democratic right of choosing the system of government of Foggin Island.

'Lastly, I will show that, as they have recognised the defendant as King of Foggin Island, and as such the defendant is entitled to advance the plea of sovereign immunity, the courts of this country have no jurisdiction over him and he is entitled to be dealt with on Foggin Island in accordance with Foggin Island Law.'

I resist the temptation to inquire about the sources of Foggin Island Law and the details of the Island's court system. These things take time, after all.

Warnock pauses for breath and turns over a page in his notes. 'I begin with my first point.'

But I'm not sure I can reconcile myself to a day of listening to Warnock's five points and having his experts tell me that Great Britain has forfeited the right to protect its territory against invasion because of Edward I's annexation of Wales. Besides, if the information I have is right, it can't make the slightest difference. The time has come. I abandon my original plan, and jump in without further delay.

'Mr Warnock, I am sorry to interrupt you, but am I right in thinking that your argument, that the defendant acquired the territory of Foggin Island by conquest or occupation, depends on the proposition that there is no evidence to show that Great

Britain has claimed or exercised sovereignty over the Island?'

'Yes, your Honour.'

'The lighting of a few beacons at intervals of a few hundred years being insufficient for that purpose?'

'Yes, your Honour.'

I can tell that Warnock is a bit taken aback. I don't think he had expected me to do my homework.

'And of course, on the proposition that no country other than Great Britain has claimed or exercised sovereignty over the Island?'

This, Warnock regards as self-evident. How could that ever have happened?

'Yes, of course, your Honour.'

'In that case,' I continue, 'I think it advisable to adjourn the matter for a suitable period of time, to allow both parties to remind themselves of the provisions of the Treaty of Calais, 1360.'

There is total silence in court. I see Warnock and Mapleleaf eye each other nervously, as their juniors flick rapidly through their files. I smile. I know they are not about to find anything there. If they knew about the Treaty, I would have heard about it from somebody by now. Both counsel are waiting patiently for me to elaborate. I have no intention of doing so. That would make it far too easy. But to avoid wasting too much time, I provide them with references to the sources referred to by Gulivant's daughter-in-law.

'Once you have had the opportunity to consider the Treaty, you may wish to revise your arguments to some extent.' I pause, deliberately, for effect. 'And if I may make a further suggestion, you may think it advisable to inform someone at the French Embassy of your findings. It occurs to me that the French Government may want to be heard before I make my decision, and it would be quite wrong of me to deny them that opportunity. Shall we say ten-thirty tomorrow morning, for now? If you need further time, let the court know during the afternoon.'

I rise and retire to chambers, to the accompaniment of blank stares from two rows of counsel. I haven't enjoyed myself as much since I don't know when. Stella finds me a sentence to while away my otherwise free morning. The defendant is an unpleasant youth of eighteen, who has committed a street robbery of a mobile phone from a much younger boy, and has form for much the same thing. His counsel has warned him to expect a custodial sentence, which he richly deserves. But I am just in too good a mood to do it. I suspect I may just have discovered how Scrooge felt on Christmas morning. I give him a suspended sentence with a lot of unpaid work and order him to pay compensation to the victim. As I rise, I am aware of counsel looking at me as if concerned that I am not entirely well. I really couldn't care less. It's very likely I'll get a second chance, anyway. If his past record is anything to go by, he will fail to show up for his unpaid work and be back in front of me for re-sentencing before too long.

And so to lunch, an oasis of calm in a desert of chaos.

We have a full house for lunch today. Marjorie is back, and looking distinctly sheepish about what turned out to be the school's mistaken diagnosis of mumps yesterday; she has been falling over herself to be helpful to Stella all morning, volunteering to take two sentences that Legless was supposed to do, and a bail application destined for me. Hubert is sitting quietly, inspecting his chicken dopiaza with basmati rice with an air of suspicion.

'*Ça va bien*?' Gulivant asks confidentially, with a sly smile.

I positively beam. I may have to revise my views about having High Court judges to visit. It occurs to me that they can actually be quite useful once in a while.

'*Ça va très bien, merci*,' I reply. 'Counsel are considering the implications as we speak.'

Legless looks at me inquiringly.

'Stephen has provided me with what may be the key to Foggin Island,' I say.

'Splendid,' Legless replies, with the merest hint of sarcasm. 'And how is the offensive weapon going?'

The smile fades from Gulivant's face.

'These things are not at all easy,' he replies. 'Now there's a question of what amounts to a reasonable excuse for possessing the weapon. I'm not at all sure that what the defendant says is capable of amounting to a reasonable excuse. There is no evidence that there was a baseball game in progress anywhere in the park. But leaving that aside, would it matter if he intended to use the bat as a weapon all along?'

'You can leave that to the jury,' Legless suggests. 'Reasonable means what it says. It's a matter for them.'

'Yes, but is that capable of being a reasonable excuse as a matter of law?' Gulivant asks. 'If so, I surely have to rule on that before deciding whether or not to leave it to the jury.'

Legless looks up at the ceiling.

'There is no legal reason why it can't be a reasonable excuse, Stephen,' I reply as calmly as I can. 'It's a simple factual question for the jury.'

'That's what counsel say. But I don't think I can leave it to the jury unless I am sure I have the law right,' Gulivant objects. 'Again, it's a matter of making sure we have looked at all the authorities. I regret to say, Charles, that many of the cases we reverse in the Court of Appeal seem to be the result of not fully considering all the authorities. Of course, now that I have been to Bermondsey and seen the library, I understand how that can happen. But still, one must do one's best. I've asked counsel to look at it in more depth and address me about it this afternoon.'

The satisfaction I have been feeling about the events of the morning fades rapidly. In fact, I think I may be losing the will to live. Surely to God Wayne Martin is not going to last for four days.

'I'm hoping to get the jury out this afternoon,' Gulivant replies proudly. 'If not, first thing tomorrow morning. I think I can keep my summing-up down to about forty-five minutes.'

I sense Legless about to say something tactless, probably along the lines of forty-five minutes being an improvement over previous performances, and decide to intervene pre-emptively.

'Have you thought about what you will give him if the jury convict?' I ask.

'Two years,' Hubert says, looking up briefly from his curry. 'What is it he is charged with again?'

'Offensive weapon,' Gulivant replies.

'Oh, that's a shame,' Hubert says, sounding disappointed. 'You may not be able to go as high as two years for that.'

'I think, Stephen,' I interpose hurriedly, 'that you will have to order a pre-sentence report before proceeding to sentence.'

'I'm not sure that is necessary,' Gulivant says. 'After all, Chummy did chase the victim through the park with a baseball bat, intending to hit him with it, and he has form for the same thing.'

Gulivant's belated adoption of the jargon makes Marjorie crack up, and she infects Legless. I look at them sternly.

'Yes,' I say. 'But bear in mind his age. You have to consider whether there are alternatives to custody, and you will need a report for that.'

Otherwise, I add in the silence of my mind, you will find yourself getting reversed by three of your mates for not considering all the authorities. And serve you bloody well right, too. But then, Wayne Martin will end up with a conditional discharge or some such nonsense.

'I got reversed the last time I gave someone two years,' Hubert says apparently à propos of nothing. Please don't ask, I pray silently to the room at large.

'On what basis?' Gulivant asks.

'Some technical rubbish,' Hubert mutters non-committally, 'something to do with the maximum for the offence.'

After staring at Hubert for some moments, Gulivant excuses himself to prepare for the afternoon's legal argument. Marjorie and Legless can contain themselves no longer, and laugh uproariously.

'Very funny,' I comment.

'What's the UK and All Comers record for the length of an offensive weapon case?' Marjorie asks. She and Legless are now almost hysterical.

'Three weeks,' Hubert replies.

Somehow, this restores a delicate silence to the room.

'Three weeks?' I ask. 'For an offensive weapon?'

'Oh yes,' Hubert replies. 'Down at Winchester, it was. I was defending, Roger Bertrand prosecuting – first rate prosecutor – it was about a year before he took Silk. We were in front of that awful man Waterstone. Yes, I remember it well. Three weeks.'

'How on earth did it last three weeks?' Legless asks. 'What kind of weapon was it?'

'A number three iron,' Hubert replies. 'No, I tell a lie, it was a wood, a driver. In any case… yes, there were a lot of witnesses, you see.'

'Where was the offence committed?' Marjorie asks. 'On a crowded golf course?'

Hubert shakes his head.

'No, in the city centre. Of course, what took the time were the other charges.'

'Other charges?' Marjorie asks.

'Oh yes. My chap was charged with the offensive weapon, but there were five other defendants charged with affray and GBH and so on, all separately represented, of course. Oh, I'm sorry. Didn't I mention that? Well, anyway, we went down, all of us, needless to say, with Waterstone trying it. He wasn't one to beat about the bush, was he? More or less told the jury to convict when he summed up. Always did. But it did take three weeks.'

With Marjorie's repentant appetite for work coming to the rescue of the day's list, Stella has nothing for me to do for the afternoon. I am about to head for home when I remember that the Reverend Mrs Walden has invited the good ladies of the parish to tea for the purpose of planning the annual service for children and pets, a ghastly event which has unspeakable consequences for the church lasting for weeks afterwards. I can't face it. Instead, I head into town to the Oxford and Cambridge Club for tea – and, come to think of it, quite possibly dinner as well.

* * *

Thursday Morning

Elsie and Jeanie have reverted to type today. Elsie's grandson has been caught smoking a substance other than tobacco in the toilets at school and a community support officer has been round for a little chat. Jeanie's Frank has been spending too much time, and too much of his benefits, at the betting shop again. George looks as though he has had a heavy night and almost hands me the *Mail* by mistake. But nothing can disturb my equanimity this morning. Last night, buoyed by the memory of a splendid dinner at the Club, I was able to listen with apparent enthusiasm for almost an hour before falling into a contented sleep as the Reverend Mrs Walden related the plans for the children and pets service. And this morning I am looking forward to court.

When I take my seat on the bench, I see that we have an additional presence, as I thought we very well might.

'Your Honour,' Mapleleaf begins, 'the representation for the prosecution and the defence is as it was yesterday. But in addition, my learned friend Miss Sinclair appears today on behalf of the Government of France.'

'Yes,' I say with a nod to our newest participant. Well, well, we are moving in distinguished circles now. Abigail Sinclair QC, prospective leader of the Circuit Bar, is what is called a heavy hitter. It's nothing new to her to represent foreign governments, and even with such short notice, she is likely to be well prepared.

'This arises from the invitation your Honour extended to counsel yesterday to examine the Treaty of Calais,' Mapleleaf continues. He is smiling in such a way as to indicate that he has taken full advantage of the invitation, and rather likes the results. 'As your Honour foresaw, the prosecution thought it proper to notify the French Government, through proper diplomatic channels, that its national interests might potentially be affected by the present proceedings. Having considered the matter, the Government of France asked to be heard today, and it may be best if I defer to my learned friend Miss Sinclair without delay.'

'Yes,' I reply.

Miss Sinclair stands. She is almost as tall as Mapleleaf and has the same High Court demeanour. She looks every bit the distinguished Silk she is.

'I am obliged to your Honour for hearing me on behalf of the French Government in this matter,' she begins. 'The Government is concerned that any finding your Honour may make may be interpreted as one affecting the Government's title to *L'Ile des Fougains*.'

'That is a proper concern, Miss Sinclair, of course,' I reply. I can't resist it – 'though I must say that before today, the French Government seems not to have taken very much interest in *L'Ile des Fougains* since 1360.'

'Perhaps not, your Honour. But having been alerted to the possibility of a challenge to its sovereignty over the Island by someone calling himself the King of the Territory of Foggin

Island, France is taking a definite interest in it now, as I believe is the British Government. With some reluctance, I must ask your Honour to take one of two courses.'

Understandably, Miss Sinclair is trying to soften what she assumes is the blow of my having this case removed from my jurisdiction. She starts, of course, with the presumption that a humble circuit judge such as myself would be most reluctant to give up such a sensational case as Foggin Island. Little does she know that, on the contrary, I cannot *wait* for it to go away. All I have to do now is avoid betraying my true feelings.

'The first possibility, your Honour, is to adjourn these proceedings pending an application by France to the International Court of Justice in The Hague to determine the question of sovereignty over the island under the Treaty of Calais. The ICJ is the proper venue for territorial disputes between sovereign States, and of course, the British Government would be a party to those proceedings. That may take some time.'

'How much time?' I ask.

'Certainly not less than five years. Probably more like ten. The wheels tend to grind rather slowly over there.'

'What is the second possibility?' I ask.

'The second possibility is that your Honour finds, in the light of the clear and unambiguous wording of the Treaty of Calais 1360, that France has sovereignty over *L'Ile des Fougains* as a result of the Island being ceded to France by Edward III. That finding would mean that the defendant's actions, and the actions of his accomplices, would be a violation of French sovereignty, and would make them amenable to the jurisdiction of the French courts. In that case, we would apply for international arrest warrants and commence extradition proceedings to transfer them to France and prosecute them there. There could be no prejudice to the defendant. He would be free to renew his plea of sovereign immunity before a French court, if he wishes to do so.'

I smile. I hadn't thought of that one. This is even better than I had imagined.

'Tell me, Miss Sinclair,' I ask, 'if you know: on average, how long would a defendant have to wait on remand in custody for trial in France, on charges of this kind?'

She shakes her head.

'It can be a long time, your Honour, sometimes as long as two years.'

'I see.'

I look around the courtroom. The King of Foggin Island seems to have turned rather pale, as have his accomplices and his counsel. Warnock forces himself to his feet. Abigail graciously gives way.

'Your Honour,' Warnock says, 'if you would allow me some time, it may be that a third possible way forward may be found, a way which would save everyone a good deal of time and trouble.'

'Certainly, Mr Warnock,' I reply. 'Let me know when you are ready.'

We reassemble in court about an hour later. Warnock stands. He does not look well.

'Your Honour,' he says, 'the defendant asks to be allowed to withdraw his plea of sovereign immunity and to be arraigned on the indictment.'

There seem to be no objections to this course. And there it is. The charges are put and he is invited to plead. The King of Foggin Island duly pleads guilty to six counts of fraud and three counts of money-laundering. I remand him in custody for a pre-sentence report, and to allow the prosecution to prepare a timetable for confiscation proceedings, with a view to recovering as much of the Foggin Island loot as can be recovered. Whether or not this result will remove the necessity for proceedings in the International Court of Justice remains to be seen. One suspects that there may be some quiet diplomatic activity taking place between France and Great Britain before too long, hopefully without recourse to the Malmsey. But none of that will involve the Bermondsey Crown Court, and for today the prosecution and the Government of France seem quite satisfied with the outcome. The same cannot be said of Eustace O'Toole and Suzy Callaghan, who try to creep quietly out of court without being noticed. But it seems that the officer in charge of the case wants a word with them, and they don't quite make it.

Poor Warnock. I feel a bit sorry for him. He really did think he was going to make his mark on the world of public international law. He gazes sadly after his client as he is taken down to the cells. But now it is time for him to return to the Mother Ship.

'Well, your Honour,' he says as a parting gesture, 'it seems that Shakespeare was right. "Uneasy lies the head that wears a crown."'

I reflect briefly on my week, and indeed on my whole tenure as RJ at Bermondsey in general.

'Never was a truer word written, Mr Warnock,' I reply.

And so to lunch, an oasis of calm in a desert of chaos.

On my way to the mess for lunch, I make a diversion to chambers five, where I find Stephen Gulivant sitting at his desk, jacket off, sleeves rolled up, writing busily in his red judicial notebook. Not only that, he has *Archbold* open in front of him. Since I cannot conceive of any possible point of law in his case which has not been beaten to death already, it seems possible that he may actually be preparing a summing-up. In the light of the experience Legless had with him, I take this as an encouraging sign in itself. But I am a bit concerned about its content, and I am determined to find a diplomatic way of offering my help. Drawing on my experience at lunchtime this week, I feel fairly confident that he will bombard me with questions. But to my astonishment, he seems to be forging confidently ahead on his own. His handwriting is not the clearest, but I can make out the words 'burden of proof' and 'evidence of bad character', both underlined several times, followed by a whole screed, hopefully copied word for word from *Archbold*.

'Ah, hello, Charles,' he greets me cheerfully, 'just putting the finishing touches to my summing-up.'

'So I see. Anything I can help with?'

'No, I don't think so,' he replies. 'You know, this offensive weapon stuff isn't as difficult as I first thought, really. Once you tackle the question of why a baseball bat is a weapon, and what is meant by "reasonable excuse", it all falls into place, doesn't it?'

'It does,' I agreed.

'Well, I am glad I took my time to make sure I got the law right. This is what I'm going to tell them, Charles. Stop me if you think I'm going down the wrong track.'

'Of course,' I said, sitting down in front of the desk.

'I will start with the fact that it's my job to deal with the law, their job to deal with the facts. Then I will tell them about the burden of proof, and the prosecution's duty to prove the case so that they are sure – except for the question of reasonable excuse, which the defendant has to prove on the balance of probabilities.'

He looks up. I nod encouragingly.

'Good.'

'Then I will take them through the elements of the offence in a bit more detail. I will explain the relevance of the evidence of his previous convictions, the question of his propensity to commit this kind of offence. I remind them of the evidence, and Bob's your uncle. What do you think?'

'Absolutely spot on, Stephen,' I reply. 'The only other thing I might suggest is to deal with the lies he told during his police interview...'

He picks up *Archbold* triumphantly.

'The *Lucas* direction,' he says. 'I was just reading about that. They have to consider why he lied before holding it against him, and they can't convict for that reason alone.'

I spread my hands out before me.

'Perfect,' I say.

He smiles as if greatly gratified.

'I am very grateful for your help,' he says.

I look at him carefully. I don't think he is having me on. I think he means it.

* * *

Thursday afternoon

Late in the afternoon, as I am about to go home, I decide to look in on chambers five to find out how the summing-up went. But, to my surprise, I find it empty. I make my way back to chambers one to collect my things. Stella comes to see me, and I ask about the whereabouts of Mr Justice Gulivant.

'He's gone,' she says. 'His jury came back with a verdict of guilty just after four o'clock. They were only out for about half an hour. Mr Justice Gulivant adjourned it for a pre-sentence report and says he will be back to do the sentence.'

I nod, very relieved.

'There's more,' Stella says.

I look at her inquiringly.

'The foreman of the jury left a note saying that the summing-up was very clear and made the jury's job much easier than they thought it was going to be.'

I laugh. 'Did he indeed?'

'I'll keep it in the file,' Stella says.

'Yes,' I reply, 'but there is one other thing I would like you to do.'

'What's that, Judge?'

'I want you to make a copy of the note and leave it on Judge Dunblane's desk.'

Stella nods cheerfully and makes for the door.

'What do you think it would be like, being king of somewhere?' I ask as she is leaving. 'Perhaps I ought to declare myself to be the King of Bermondsey. What do you think?'

She turns away.

'Good night, Judge,' she replies soothingly. 'See you tomorrow.'

FOR WHOM THE BELLES TROLL

FOR WHOM THE BELLES TROLL

Sunday morning

On Sunday mornings I have a regular date for morning worship – what we used to call Matins in the old days – at the parish church of St Aethelburg and All Angels in the Diocese of Southwark. To be honest, left to my own devices, I would not necessarily be in attendance every Sunday, but when your wife is priest-in-charge, you do feel a certain obligation to spend some time in the pews. The Reverend Mrs Walden does like to see me in the third or fourth row cheering her on – figuratively speaking, that is – when she mounts the pulpit to deliver her sermon or leads the congregation in belting out 'Praise my Soul, the King of Heaven', and if I am absent without leave, it is the subject of comment at home for some time thereafter. Besides, you can learn some interesting stuff at church, and it is surprising how often I pick up information from a sermon which later comes in useful in connection with a case. So here I am again. I have picked up some dark hints from the Reverend Mrs Walden during the week about the subject of this morning's public admonition to the citizens of Bermondsey, and I know it's going to be interesting.

I've been through the weekly process of sermon preparation with her so many times now that I have learned to read the signs. She will often throw out ideas during dinner, sketch out where she is going, sometimes even ask what I think of something she wants to say. I used to bounce ideas off her for my closing speeches when I was in practice at the Bar, so I see this as returning the favour and I am glad to contribute in whatever way I can. Once she has the basic idea, it builds steadily from Monday to Saturday, when it is left to marinate for a day, and by Sunday the sermon is ready to be delivered. There are weeks when it is all a bit routine, nothing to set the world on fire, a reassuring homily about the Disciples, for example. And then, there are weeks when she has *something to say*, weeks when the moral fibre of the nation is to be questioned and challenged, and the public is to have something to think about over Sunday lunch. During weeks of the latter kind, the atmosphere at home is noticeably different, more intense in every way. The Reverend Mrs Walden broods over cups of coffee and, when cooking, brings the large kitchen knife down on some hapless bell pepper with a particular vengeance. This is a week of the latter kind.

She rattles off the parish notices in no time at all, which is always a sign that she has something particularly important to impress on the congregation, and can't wait to get on with it. Sure enough, she begins with a reminder of the kind of bad things that can happen to a wicked and adulterous generation, which, it seems, go far beyond an appearance in the Crown Court. Then, she really gets started.

'Some years ago, my husband Charles and I visited Pompeii together. I found it fascinating that in this ancient city, perfectly preserved in a macabre way by the ash which erupted from Mount Vesuvius, a city which has so many points of interest, the first place the guide takes you to is the city brothel. Not the pizza restaurant, not the famous house with the guard dog mosaic, not even the public bath house. The brothel. I'm not denying that it is interesting. Let's be honest about it. I suppose that on one level we all think it is fun to imagine the various things which went on behind closed doors – or actually, not necessarily behind closed doors, because the brothel does seem to have been quite open to the elements. And perhaps the guides feel that the brothel had a particular importance in ancient Pompeii. Perhaps it was a social centre in some sense, as well as being a place where sexual services were offered. Perhaps we don't understand today exactly what part the local brothel played in the lives of the people in those remote times. Or perhaps it is just that the guides like to kick the tour off with something sensational, no more than that. Whatever the reason, when you go to Pompeii, you can't avoid it. The brothel is going to be the centre of attention for the tourists just as much as it was for the residents before the eruption.'

I allow myself to look around quietly. The congregation, scattered rather thinly and unevenly throughout the massive church, seem politely interested, though one or two mothers with children in tow are fidgeting a bit. I have seen that before, and it will not deter the Reverend Mrs Walden in the slightest.

'But today I want to ask you this question: have we not travelled any distance, morally speaking, from Pompeii? Because I don't think I'm alone in thinking that I can't pick up a newspaper or turn on my TV without reading about prostitution. I read about the control of prostitutes by organised crime families. I see documentaries about the trafficking of young women from Eastern Europe and South America, whose passports are taken away, and who are kept in slavery. And perhaps most disturbing of all – because all worthwhile news is local – I hear about the resurgence of the community brothel. Yes, my friends, just as in ancient Pompeii, the local brothel is alive and well in South London as we speak. And I want you to think with me today about what this means for us as a Society, and what it means for us as Christians...'

It's not that I switch off, but I have learned to anticipate, and I anticipate that the Reverend Mrs Walden will now embark on a thorough examination of the evils of prostitution and trafficking from every angle. It is good stuff, and I would be paying closer attention if she hadn't caused a degree of anxiety in my mind with the observation that the local brothel is alive and well in South London. As it happens, that very matter is on the agenda at the Bermondsey Crown Court for the coming week, and without any real reason, I find myself worrying about whether she is going to infect the jury pool with a hot sermon about the business of brothel keeping. We tell jurors to ignore press reports all the time, but I've never had to tell a jury to ignore their vicar before. In a moment or two I calm down, and realise that the odds on that happening are fairly slim. I take a deep breath and focus on the flower arrangement on the main altar. I allow my mind to wander to the case I will be starting tomorrow.

It's a local issue, all right – no doubt about that. Judges have to be careful about local embarrassments, and I don't mean just brothels, obviously. There are places – pubs, clubs, betting shops, the odd restaurant – which feature regularly in cases in Crown Courts, and which all of us who work in the court soon come to recognise the moment someone mentions them. A number of such places within easy reach of the Bermondsey Crown Court spring readily to mind. The George and Dragon, a dingy pub celebrated for the availability of drugs, stolen goods, and occasional wads of counterfeit bank notes, is one such. The more upmarket Blue Lagoon Night Club is a venue of choice for alcohol-fuelled violence and sexual malfeasance. No judge wants to be seen at a venue which has been mentioned in dispatches a bit too often as the scene of affrays, drug deals, the fencing of stolen goods, and so on. You never know when the press may get hold of the story, and woe betide any judge then. The Grey Smoothies will want to know why you weren't aware of the venue's reputation and why you have risked bringing the reputation of the judiciary into disrepute, to which there is really no very good answer.

Most judges wouldn't be seen dead in the kind of establishment we are talking about anyway. They tend not to be our kind of place. But none of us would have included Jordan's on that list – not, that is, until one Saturday night about four months ago. Jordan's was one of those places where the young, smart set like to go to be seen – which obviously excludes the Reverend Mrs Walden and myself, but wouldn't exclude certain colleagues such as Legless and Marjorie. The décor, I am told, was sophisticated, with subdued lighting and understated murals. The service was highly praised, and most importantly, the food was favourably reported on by the critics. The chef, the eponymous Robert Jordan, had been a contestant in one of those television cooking competitions, called 'Britain's Got the Best Chefs!'. He didn't win, but neither was he booted out at an early stage as being completely useless, and the general opinion seems to have been that the food at Jordan's was very acceptable. Jordan's had everything going for it, and was well on its way to being a recognised venue in London. Then, as I say, about four months ago, Saturday night happened.

As this reflection comes to an end, I hear the Reverend Mrs Walden drawing to a close also. She smiles for the first time, but in a slightly sinister way. Even I find myself slightly unnerved.

'Well, you all know what happened to the inhabitants of Pompeii,' she says. 'They were buried in several feet of volcanic ash. You can still see some of their preserved bodies. That's what happened to them and their brothel. As most of you know, the God I worship is loving and forgiving. I'm not a fan of theories of divine vengeance. I don't see the world in Old Testament terms, with an irritable, bad-tempered Deity throwing His toys out of the pram and striking people down in their thousands every time He doesn't get His own way. I don't see such things as earthquakes or outbreaks of Ebola as evidence of God's judgement on people for their sins, and it's certainly not my intention to scare anyone or to predict any dire happenings in London.'

She pauses, and seems all set to do the 'in the name of the

Father...' bit, followed by her exit from the pulpit. But at the last moment she draws back and points her hymnal menacingly at the congregation.

'On the other hand,' she concludes, 'you never know, do you? I could be wrong.'

After which we all join in a lusty rendering of 'Guide me, O Thou Great Jehovah', while trying to look around unobtrusively, just to make sure there is no immediate sign of volcanic ash.

So, you must be anxious to know: what *did* happen at Jordan's on Saturday night, about four months ago? I will let Piers Drayford tell you.

* * *

Monday morning

'May it please your Honour, members of the jury, my name is Piers Drayford, and I appear to prosecute this case. My learned friend Miss Emily Phipson represents the first defendant, Dimitri Valkov. My learned friend Miss Susan Worthington represents the second defendant, Robert Jordan. My learned friend Mr Aubrey Brooks represents the third defendant, Lucy Trask.'

All counsel nod politely to the jury, twelve good citizens of Bermondsey who have been carefully vetted to ensure that they have never darkened the door of Jordan's. Piers is tall and thin, with a certain understated elegance, and actually looks very much like the kind of man about town who might have given Jordan's a try, though he has assured us all that he never did.

'This is a case about a restaurant and bar in Bermondsey called Jordan's. It opened just over two years ago, and rapidly gained a good reputation for its food and ambience, which built up a cadre of loyal customers. The owner of the restaurant, and its head chef, is the defendant Robert Jordan. His girlfriend, the defendant Lucy Trask, was the front of house manager, which seems to have meant that she would take bookings, welcome customers as they arrived, and generally act as what you and I, in the kind of restaurant we might go to, would call the *Maitre d'*.'

Some members of the jury are looking at Piers in such a way as to suggest that the term *Maitre d'* might not be in quite such common usage as Piers may imagine.

'The defendant Dimitri Valkov is Russian, but he has resided in this country quite legally for several years now. You will hear that he was employed as the bar manager for the restaurant, dealing with any issues relating to the maintenance and upkeep of the bar, and that he also acted as an additional barman when things were busy.'

Piers pauses to hand some copies to the usher, Dawn, who whisks them over to the jury with her customary breezy glide.

'Members of the jury, I am giving you copies of the indictment and of a floor plan showing the layout of Jordan's, which we will be referring to during the trial. If you would look at the floor plan with me now, you will see that we have the ground floor on one side of the sheet, and the first floor, the upstairs floor, on the other side. For reasons which will become clear in a moment, few people even realised that Jordan's had any interest in the upstairs floor at all. On the face of it, everything happens on the ground floor. As you enter, you come to the reception area, where you are welcomed and you can leave your coat and so on. There is a desk there, and behind the desk a small office and storage area. To your right is the bar, and to your left is the restaurant itself. It is quite a large area, as you can see. If you look again at the entrance to the restaurant, just to the left – and I have marked this with the letter A in a circle on the plan – there is a door. You will hear that this door had a notice on it, saying "Private".

'It was indeed private. You will hear that there were only two keys to that door. One was found in the possession of Dimitri Valkov, and the second was found hanging on a hook under the desk in the reception area, where all three defendants would have had access to it. The door leads to a staircase, which leads upstairs to the first floor. The first floor consists of four rooms, each quite small. At Jordan's, everyone called the first floor simply "upstairs", and that is what we shall call it in this case. This case is about "upstairs".

'Members of the jury, you will hear that upstairs, things were happening which were a world away from the fine dining, the carefully selected wines, the cultured ambience and the discreet service to which customers were treated in the restaurant. Upstairs, members of the jury, was a fully equipped brothel, where young women provided sexual services to men who were prepared to pay for those services. The prosecution say that the brothel was managed and operated by all three defendants in this case, although the main responsibility and day-to-day management was in the hands of the man whose brainchild it was, Dimitri Valkov. You will hear that it was a very profitable business, from which each of these defendants made a good deal of money. You will hear evidence of regular payments into the defendants' bank accounts of substantial sums of money which cannot be explained as legitimate income from the restaurant.

'The activities going on upstairs came to light in this way, members of the jury. A police officer based at Bermondsey police station, PC Crane, was off duty one evening in October of last year, when he received a rather strange piece of information, which aroused his suspicions. He reported his suspicions to his sergeant, who in turned passed them on to a branch of the Metropolitan Police called the Serious and Organised Crime Unit. As a result DC Mitchell, an officer assigned to that Unit, attended Jordan's one afternoon during the following week.

'He was welcomed by Lucy Trask. The officer was working undercover, and so did not, of course, identify himself as a police officer. The officer asked to speak to "Dimitri", and in response, Miss Trask showed him in to the bar. There, the officer spoke to Dimitri Valkov, and asked him whether a massage was available upstairs. Valkov asked him to wait, and left the bar, returning a few minutes later. On his return, he asked DC Mitchell to follow him, which the officer did. The officer noticed that Valkov appeared to take a key from under the desk in the reception area. Valkov then led the way through the door marked "Private", and escorted the officer upstairs. He opened the door of the second room along the corridor from the staircase – you will see on the plan that I have numbered the rooms one to four – and invited the officer to enter, which he did.

'DC Mitchell will describe to you what he found. The room was decorated with what seems to have been intended as a Chinese motif, with items of pottery, and prints with Chinese characters on the walls. In fact, members of the jury, you will hear that each of the four upstairs rooms had a different motif. Room one was decorated in a French style invoking the time of *Le Siècle du Roi Soleil* – the age of Louis XIV. Room two is the Chinese room. Room three has a Swiss theme, with murals of the Alps and bucolic scenes of goatherds and the like. Room four is an American room with the feel of a 1950s diner in Chicago. One particular detail of interest was a very fine –'

'Can we get on with it, please, Mr Drayford?' I ask. 'I assume the jury will see photographs of all this in due course.'

Drayford smiles ingratiatingly.

'Yes, of course, your Honour. Members of the jury, what engaged DC Mitchell's attention more than the décor of the room was the scantily clad young woman who greeted him with a warm smile and the offer of a massage. DC Mitchell accepted the offer, undressed, and lay down on the massage table, covered by a sheet. The massage proceeded, and for some time nothing was amiss. But you will hear that, after a certain time, the young woman concerned offered the officer a certain sexual service. He declined the offer, paid for the massage and left the premises.

'Three days later, another undercover officer, DC Mostyn, repeated the procedure. Having spoken to Valkov, he too was led upstairs – the American room, room four, on this occasion – and a very similar scene unfolded. After this, the police concluded that the upstairs area of Jordan's was being used as a brothel. They applied for a search warrant, which was executed by a number of uniformed police officers on the following Saturday evening at about eleven o'clock. You will hear a number of officers give evidence about what they found in the four upstairs rooms.

'To take it shortly, sexual activity was taking place in each of the four rooms. It is right to say that none of these three defendants was upstairs at that time. In fact, all three were working in the restaurant or the bar at the time. But six young women who had been providing sexual services were detained, and their clients, four men, had their particulars recorded, and were told that they would be reported with a view to possible prosecution.

'Members of the jury, I have been asked to make it clear, and I do so willingly, that none of the six young women reported any kind of mistreatment. When the police discover a situation such as this, they are obliged to inquire whether any of the women has been trafficked or mistreated in any way. They were questioned about this, and their answers were recorded. Without exception, they said that they were not trafficked; they had possession of their passports; they were free to come and go as they wished; they received all the money due to them; and they were satisfied with their conditions of work. I am glad to make that clear, but of course I must also make it clear that a well-run brothel is still a brothel.

'Finally, if you will look at the indictment, members of the jury, you will see that Dimitri Valkov and Robert Jordan are charged with being concerned in the management of the brothel, and Lucy Trask is charged with assisting in the management of the brothel. The prosecution say that Jordan, as the owner of the restaurant, leased the upstairs rooms and knowingly made them available for the purposes of prostitution. We say that Dimitri Valkov was the creator and day-to-day manager of the brothel. He was responsible for supplying the furnishing and equipment, for employing the women who worked there, receiving the money paid by the customers, paying the women what was due after deductions, and generally making sure that the brothel operated efficiently day to day. We say that Lucy Trask knew what was going on upstairs, that she took appointments for the upstairs rooms, welcomed customers when they arrived, and assisted Valkov in running the brothel.'

'Duncan Crane, Police Constable 768, attached to Bermondsey police station, your Honour.'

'Yes, thank you, officer,' Piers begins. 'I want to ask you about an evening in October of last year, when you were off duty, and you had occasion to go somewhere in a taxi, is that right?'

'Yes, sir.'

'About what time of day was it?'

'It was between eleven o'clock and midnight, sir.'

'And tell the jury where you were when you hailed the taxi, and where you were going.'

'Yes, sir. I had been out for a few drinks and an Indian meal in Kennington with some of the lads from the nick – sorry, your Honour, some of my colleagues from the police station. I didn't want to drive obviously, because I had been drinking, so I took a taxi home.'

'I see. Did the driver draw your attention to anything during the journey?'

'Yes, sir. As we were passing Jordan's – Jordan's restaurant here in Bermondsey – the driver said to me, "I don't suppose you'd like to call in at Jordan's this evening, guv, would you?"'

Piers raises an eyebrow in the direction of the jury.

'Officer, was that said in response to anything you had said or…?'

'No, sir, it came out of the blue.'

'How did you respond?'

'I was a bit taken aback, obviously. I mean, Jordan's is a bit out of my league, sir, if you take my meaning. It had never crossed my mind to go there. So I just said I'd already had a curry and I was going straight home.'

'And how did the driver react to that?'

'He laughed and said, "That's a shame, guv. I'm on fifty quid every time I take a punter to Jordan's. Not a bad night's work, is it?"'

'Officer, at that time, did the driver know that you were a police officer?'

'No, sir. I wasn't in uniform, obviously, and I hadn't said anything to him.'

'Did you say anything further to the driver?'

'Yes, sir, I said something like, "Blimey, that's not bad. What kind of people do you take to Jordan's?" He said, "All kinds. It could be your foreign tourists I pick up at Heathrow, or off the Eurostar at St Pancras. It could be your well-heeled gents you would usually find in the West End. I drop the name Jordan's and if I deliver them, I get fifty quid in my hand, no questions asked."'

'I see,' Piers says. He pauses. He knows he's going to have a bit of a problem going very much further. 'Did the driver say why it would be worth giving him as much as fifty pounds to bring a customer to Jordan's?'

Emily Phipson is on her feet immediately.

'Whether he did or not,' she objects, 'the answer would be hearsay, and it is inadmissible.'

'That must be right, Mr Drayford, mustn't it?' I ask.

'Yes, your Honour. Did the driver say who at Jordan's gave him the fifty pounds?'

I look at defence counsel, but apparently no one is bothered by this question, whether the answer would be hearsay or not.

'Yes, sir. He said it would be either the barman, Dimitri, or the receptionist, Lucy, depending on who was in the reception area when he came in with the customer he was introducing.'

'So, the driver was saying this had happened more than once.'

'Indeed, sir, yes.'

'Officer, what did you do as a result of this conversation with the taxi driver?'

'Well, sir, it seemed pretty obvious to me...'

Piers interrupts him before Emily can intervene again.

'No, officer, please listen to the question. I'm not asking you about what you may have thought. I am asking you what you did.'

'Sorry, sir. I told my desk sergeant, Sergeant Jenny Cullen, about what the driver had said.'

'Yes, thank you, officer. There may be further questions. Wait there, please.'

At first, no one seems interested in asking further questions, which is probably wise, given that the witness would clearly love to give the jury a few more titillating details. But eventually, Emily decides it is just about worth taking a limited risk.

'Officer, do I gather from what you have said that the taxi driver was given the fifty pounds in the reception area of the restaurant?'

'Yes, I believe so.'

'Where there would be the customer he had brought, and perhaps other customers, waiters, and so on milling around?'

'Yes, I presume so, Miss.

'Yes. Thank you, officer.'

We now turn to what happened when Sergeant Jenny Cullen had digested the information she had received from PC Crane. Her witness statement, a very anodyne document which no one wants to challenge, is read to the jury. It doesn't enlighten them very much. All she tells them is that she passed the information on to the Serious and Organised Crime Unit. Officially, therefore, we still don't know what the police thought worth pursuing about the fifty pound payments to taxi drivers, though I am sure the jury has got the message by now. There is something suspicious afoot upstairs, and they are agog to hear about it. The next witness is DC Mitchell.

'Officer, were you assigned to go to Jordan's restaurant in an undercover capacity?'

'I was.'

'What time was it when you arrived at the restaurant?'

'It was about two-fifteen, two-thirty in the afternoon.'

'When you entered, how did the restaurant appear? Were there many people?'

'There were quite a few. The lunch hour was drawing to a close, but I could see a number of people sitting in the bar and in the restaurant itself, and there were members of the staff walking around.'

'Now, you were there as a result of information received by the police, is that right?'

'Yes, sir.'

'And as a result of that information, what did you do on entering the restaurant?'

'I approached a woman I now know to be Lucy Trask, who appeared to be acting as receptionist, and told her that I wished to speak to Dimitri.'

'Is that the same Lucy Trask you see in the dock today?'

'It is, sir.'

Piers pauses. 'All right, officer, thank you. Would you look please at the floor plan of Jordan's. Your Honour, may this be Exhibit one, please? Can you tell the jury where you were when your conversation with Ms Trask took place?'

The officer holds the floor plan up with his right hand,

indicating the spot with the forefinger of his left hand, and does a sweep around the courtroom.

'Just here, by the desk in the reception area.'

'Did Ms Trask tell you where you might find Dimitri?'

'Yes, sir. She directed me to the bar, where I did in fact find Dimitri.'

'I don't think there is any dispute about it. Is "Dimitri" in fact the defendant Dimitri Valkov?'

'Yes, that is correct.'

'What did you say to Dimitri?'

'I said I was interested in a massage, and asked him if he could arrange one for me.'

'I see.' Piers pauses for a surreptitious glance at the jury. 'Officer, Jordan's is known as a restaurant and bar. Was there any material that you saw, either inside or outside Jordan's, advertising the fact that massages were available?'

'Not that I saw, sir, no.'

'Did you see any indication of a massage room, or changing room of any kind?'

'No, sir.'

'How did Dimitri respond to your request?'

'He asked me if I had been in before. I said no. He took me to one side and asked me to wait for a moment. He left the bar. He was gone no more than a minute or two. When he came back, he said that a young lady was available upstairs, that the cost of the massage was one hundred pounds for half an hour, and that it was expected that I would add a tip if the massage was to my satisfaction.'

'What did you say?'

'I told Dimitri I wished to go ahead with the massage. He asked me to follow him. We went back into the reception area. He ducked in behind the desk for a moment and retrieved a key. His movement suggested to me that the key had been hanging on a hook behind the desk. He proceeded to the door shown on the plan here' – again the officer does a helpful sweep – 'and opened it with the key.'

'Where did the door lead?'

'Immediately inside the door was a staircase, which led upstairs to a corridor with four rooms. This is shown on the second side of the floor plan. I followed Dimitri, and he took me to the second room along from the top of the staircase. He knocked and opened the door, and invited me to enter, which I did.'

'When you entered, what did you see?'

'I saw that I was in a room decorated in what appeared to be an oriental style. On the far side of the room, about two feet from the wall, was a thin table, with a sheet partially covering it, which I took to be a massage table. There was another, smaller table up against the wall, on which there appeared to be plastic bottles containing massage oil, some tissues, an incense burner, and two small red candles in glass candle holders.'

'Was anyone else in the room?'

'Yes, sir. As I walked in, I saw a white female, I would estimate in her early or mid-twenties. She was scantily clad.'

'I suppose people might have different ideas about what "scantily clad" means,' Piers comments. 'Could you tell the jury what she was wearing?'

'Yes, sir. She was wearing a very short black top, not much more than a bra, really, and black shorts. Dimitri introduced her to me as Laura.'

'What did Dimitri do then?'

'He left the room.'

'Then what happened?'

'Laura asked me my name and confirmed that I wanted a massage. She said the charge would be one hundred pounds for half an hour, just as Dimitri had said. I had a sufficient sum with me, the expenditure of which had been approved by the DI in charge of the investigation. I handed Laura five twenty pound notes. She then instructed me to take my clothes off and lie on the massage table on my front under the sheet.'

'Did you understand that you were to take all your clothes off?'

'Yes, and that is what I did.'

Piers pauses. 'Officer, it may be that the jury think this is all a bit unusual, but is this something you have had occasion to do before?'

The officer smiles. 'It is, sir, yes. It is a form of undercover work that some of us have to undertake occasionally, so it wasn't my first time.'

'What happened once you had taken up your position on the table?'

'Laura began the massage. She had lit the candles and put on a CD of classical guitar music, and she began by applying massage oil to my back and shoulders.'

'And did the massage proceed in a conventional way for some time?'

'Yes, it did. For some time it appeared to be a standard, conventional massage, at which Laura appeared to be quite skilful.'

'But did something happen to change that?'

'It did indeed. After she had massaged my back and shoulders and the backs of my legs, Laura asked me to turn over and lie on my back.'

'Did you do that?'

'Yes, sir.'

'Then what happened?'

'As she was massaging my legs and thighs, Laura asked me a question.'

'What did she ask? Please use her exact words, if you remember them.'

'I do remember, sir. She said, "Would you like to try a special, more intimate massage?"'

'How did you respond to that?'

'I asked her what the intimate massage consisted of.'

'I assume,' Piers said, 'that you had some understanding of that without asking her?'

'Yes, of course, sir,' Mitchell replies. 'But if an offence may be committed, my evidence must be as clear as possible.'

'You have to ask her to be precise?'

'Exactly, sir. A response like that is standard practice.'

'Did she reply?'

'In a manner of speaking, yes. She ran her hand up my leg in a very suggestive way, and said, "I'm talking about a full body massage". She emphasised the word "full."'

'What conclusion did you draw from that? The term "full body massage" does have a legitimate use, doesn't it?'

'It does, yes. But it wasn't just what she said. It was what she said combined with the movements of her hand up my leg, and in the immediate vicinity of my private parts.'

One or two of the jurors snigger. It is all fairly obvious now, but Piers is right to be thorough.

'So you concluded...'

'I concluded that she was offering me a hand job.'

'A hand job. Quite so,' Piers says. His tone, I think, is intended to suggest some distaste for the very idea, but it doesn't really work and sounds more squeamish than anything else. I've noticed this kind of reaction in some counsel over the years. It's almost as if there is something not quite right about using explicit sexual language while wearing a wig and gown. With some barristers, the more seedy, older variety, it can even come across as positively indecent. It doesn't come across that way with Piers at all. But even he seems anxious to gloss over the sordid details.

'I then followed the protocol again,' Mitchell says, without being asked, 'by asking her how much an intimate massage would cost.'

'Did she reply to that?'

'She did. She told me that it was up to me, it was in the way of being a tip, but that fifty pounds would be about right, and that was what her clients generally paid.'

'And what does the protocol call for you to do at that point?' Piers asks.

'I have to find a way to decline, hopefully without arousing her suspicions that I may be a police officer. I have a variety of ways of doing that.' He looks across at me. 'Your Honour, I would prefer not to divulge operational details.'

'No. Quite right,' I say. 'It is not relevant.'

'Did you decline?' Piers asks.

'I did.'

'Was there any further suggestion of anything sexual?'

'No, sir. I got dressed, gave her a tip of twenty pounds, went downstairs, and left the premises.'

'Did you see Dimitri again?'

'No, sir. I saw Ms Trask on the way out and wished her a good afternoon. I didn't have any further conversation with anyone. I then returned to the station, reported to DI Price, and wrote my witness statement. That was the extent of my involvement in this case.'

There seems to be an agreement among defence counsel to leave things to Emily for the time being, which makes sense since her client is the only person directly implicated in any of this, thus far.

'When you spoke to Dimitri, officer,' she begins, 'the conversation took place in the bar, did it?'

'It did, yes.'

'In plain view of anyone who happened to be in the bar at the time?'

'I suppose so, yes.'

'He didn't take you into the broom closet, to whisper in your ear conspiratorially, out of sight of anyone else, did he?'

'No, he did not.'

'Didn't tell you to keep your voice down?'

'No.'

'And you were the one who raised the subject of massage, is that right? He didn't offer a massage until you had inquired about it?'

'That is true.'

'As you have said, there was nothing downstairs to suggest that massages were available at Jordan's, was there?'

'Correct.'

'No mention of upstairs rooms at all?'

'Correct.'

'You had to ask about massage?'

'Yes.'

'Officer, Dimitri Valkov didn't say anything about a hand job, did he?'

'No. He did not.'

'Or about any kind of sexual activity?'

'That is quite true.'

'The only person who raised that matter was Laura?'

'Yes.'

DC Mostyn is next, and he tells us that his experience was almost exactly the same as DC Mitchell's, with the exception that it took place in the American room, and the name of the young woman who made the offer of the full body massage was Crystal. And with that, we adjourn until two o'clock.

This would normally mean lunch, my oasis of calm. But I'm not expecting much calm this lunchtime. I'm not sure I will even make it in to lunch, and if I do, it will only be for a few minutes. A new war with the Grey Smoothies seems imminent, and Stella and I have a meeting scheduled, a last-ditch diplomatic effort to avert hostilities. The stakes are high. In their latest effort to make 'improvements and efficiencies' – Grey Smoothie-speak for taking away even more of our few remaining resources – they are proposing to close down the kitchen facilities at Bermondsey Crown Court. I am determined to resist this if I possibly can.

It's not that I have any great affection for the kitchen or for the fare it serves up, but it does serve an important function at court. Quite apart from the four of us judges, there are the jurors, counsel and solicitors, defendants, and assorted members of the public, all of whom have to be back at court after lunch, and don't have time to go very far. There are places they could go to for lunch within reasonable distance of the court, but it's not easy to do it in the hour we allow them. In the case of those involved in the case, particularly the jurors, there are one or two places you would definitely not want them straying into. The George and Dragon comes to mind. And that's before you consider the risk that the jurors, witnesses, and defendants or some combination thereof may all end up in the same place. But the Grey Smoothies seem unable to grasp the importance of jurors and other court users having a decent, and more importantly, safe place for lunch while they are performing a vital public service. To the Grey Smoothies, as usual, it's all a matter of money.

The Grey Smoothies are represented by our cluster manager, Meredith, accompanied by her minion, Jack. Jack will take the notes today. Taking notes is a big thing with the Grey Smoothies. Notes of meetings are sacrosanct. They are preserved for an indefinite period with the same loving care as genealogical records in Salt Lake City, and they can be retrieved from storage, not only years, but decades later, to prove some damning remark a judge may have made in an unguarded moment. 'Ah,' I have had it pointed out to me in the past, when complaining about some item of equipment malfunctioning and causing havoc in court one, 'but the Resident Judge seven years ago said it was working very well.' You can point out until you are blue in the face: first, that no RJ worth his salt would ever admit that anything works very well – that would scupper any chance of it being replaced or updated, ever; and second, even if he did, that doesn't mean that the equipment is working very well now, seven years on. 'Ah, but it's in the notes,' comes the reply. And there it is: the notes – conclusive proof of the state of the world according to the Grey Smoothies.

Today, Meredith is wearing a light grey two-piece suit with a white blouse, a long string of imitation pearls, and black shoes with fairly high heels. Jack, who still looks about fourteen, is wearing his usual grey suit from off the peg at Burton's which looks as though he outgrew it a couple of years ago, and a thin pink tie scrunched into a small tight knot.

'We just don't have the budget for it,' Meredith is saying. 'We have to consider what kinds of expenditure on the courts are good value for money for the taxpayer. We have other areas we have to spend money in. We can't see a business case for keeping the kitchens open.'

'Look, I'm not pressing this on behalf of the judges,' I reply. This is substantially, though not entirely, true. Marjorie, Legless and I have been bringing our own lunch in for some time now, and it wouldn't matter to us very much either way, but Hubert relies on the dish of the day to keep him going until it's time for dinner at the Garrick Club. Closing the kitchen would be quite a blow to him.

'It's the jurors and witnesses I'm concerned about. They have very limited time for lunch, and when they have to go out there is a risk of running into defendants and their supporters. Counsel and solicitors are in the same position. It's not as though they give the food away. Surely the kitchen pays for itself?'

Meredith shakes her head. 'The Ministry subsidises it,' she replies, 'and with so many competing demands we just can't do it anymore. The court kitchen is a drain on resources.'

It is genuinely hard for me to believe this. The quality of the food is, to put it politely, indifferent, and it's not exactly cheap. Not only that, they must have a regular captive clientele, even assuming that some are now following our lead, and bringing in their own lunches. I'm sure the caterers must pay something to the Ministry for the rent of the kitchen space. Why is there any need for a subsidy, and how much can it amount to? But I know, without asking, that the answer to all this is in the notes of some meeting or other, and therefore unassailable.

'We do recognise that some provision must be made for jurors,' Meredith continues. 'We were thinking of installing a vending machine in the jury area.'

'A vending machine?' I exclaim. 'Vending what, may I ask?'

Meredith pretends to flick through whatever she has in her file, in an apparent search for an answer to this question. Before she can find anything, Jack supplies one for her.

'Crisps,' he replies, 'Coke Zero, that kind of stuff.'

'That's not lunch,' I protest. 'That's just a collection of unhealthy snack foods.'

Jack sniffs. 'That's what I have, usually,' he replies.

Meredith coughs. 'Yes, well, I think they can sell other things too. I'm sure they can do sandwiches, fruit cake, chocolate chip cookies and so on. Perhaps even those wraps, you know, Jamaican chicken and so on.'

'They would need some way of heating those up, though, wouldn't they?' Stella points out.

'Microwave?' Jack asks.

'Perhaps,' Meredith replies, apparently doing some quick mental arithmetic to see how much that might cost. She writes herself a note.

'And that's just the jury area,' Stella adds. 'Then you've still got the advocates, witnesses, police officers, and members of the public to provide for. That's without mentioning the judges. They shouldn't be going out for lunch, not with defendants and witnesses wandering around the streets. You never know what might happen.'

'It just confirms our view that people have to get used to bringing their own lunches,' Meredith says. 'That's the most cost-effective way of doing it. After all, people don't expect lunch to be available if they go to the post office, or the driving test centre, do they? Why should they expect it when they come to court?'

Stella and I look at each other blankly.

'Do you really think that's a fair comparison?' I ask.

'I don't see why not,' Meredith replies.

'It was Mr Bagnall who came up with that, wasn't it?' Jack says, with a mysterious smile in Meredith's direction.

She gives him a look which means, 'For God's sake, shut up.' But it's too late. The cat is out of the bag. Now it's all starting to make sense. Jeremy Bagnall CBE is a high-ranking member of the Grey Smoothie *Abwehr*, the High Priest of improvements and efficiencies. *Herr Reichsmarschall* Bagnall would install a vending machine in his grandmother's kitchen, let alone ours, and take away her cooker and fridge to boot, if it would save him five quid. God help us if this is coming from him.

'Mr Bagnall said he was at the post office during lunch and there was nowhere to get a sandwich there,' Jack adds nervously. 'But actually, I know the post office he went to and it was in a WH Smiths and they sell chocolate bars and stuff at the checkout. So…'

'The point,' Meredith resumes after we have waited some time to see whether Jack will complete the sentence, 'is that Mr Bagnall is responsible for administering the budget for an entire cluster of courts, not just Bermondsey, and he has to set priorities. He thinks we can't afford the kitchen any longer.'

'Does that mean Mr Bagnall is closing down kitchens everywhere?' I ask.

'I'm not allowed to discuss the position at other courts,'

Meredith replies primly, almost as if she is unaware that I am in phone and email contact with RJ's at other courts and can find out what is going on without difficulty – one resource they can't take away. 'Mr Bagnall did make one other suggestion,' she adds.

'We are all ears,' I reply.

'The other suggestion he made is that perhaps the judges themselves could reach an agreement with an outside supplier to cater lunch at court.'

'Really?' I reply. 'So that we can subsidise lunch instead of the Ministry?'

'You might be able to find people who do better food,' Jack suggests.

'That wouldn't be hard,' I reply. I have a momentary vision of La Bella Napoli turning up with their wonderful Italian delicacies for the judicial mess every day, but a reality check extinguishes it as quickly as it came. 'But we have enough to do as it is without turning ourselves into catering managers.'

'Well, that's up to you, of course,' Meredith says. 'We will make sure you have some time to make other arrangements if you wish. We have to give the caterers a couple of months' notice. After that we will contact you about installing the vending machines.'

With which the meeting ends, and Meredith and Jack depart, no doubt in search of a vending machine where they get themselves some crisps and Coke Zero. I decide not to go to the judicial mess today. I can't face it. I eat Jeanie's ham and cheese bap at my desk in chambers, feeling that it is a harbinger of things to come.

* * *

Monday afternoon
'I now call Inspector Jarvis,' Piers Drayford begins, once court is assembled.

The Inspector, a tall, thin man wearing an immaculately pressed uniform sporting a couple of service medals, makes his way to the witness box with a measured stride. He introduces himself to the court and takes the oath in a brisk tone.

'Inspector, I want to ask you about the raid on Jordan's on the Saturday evening. Do you wish to refresh your memory from a note you made at or near the time?'

'Actually, sir,' he replies, 'my note was incorporated into the police log of the raid, which is available for all the officers to use to refresh their memories. If I might be allowed to use the log?'

Piers looks along the line of counsel. No one has any objection and the log is duly placed before the Inspector.

'Inspector, were you the officer responsible for coordinating and leading a police raid on the upstairs rooms at Jordan's which commenced at about eleven o'clock in the evening?'

'I was, sir.'

'What was the purpose of the raid?'

'I was asked to assemble a team of male and female uniformed officers to conduct a raid on behalf of the Serious and Organised Crime Unit, in order to investigate suspected activities in the upstairs rooms at Jordan's.'

Piers looks down the line again, and receives shakes of the head.

'I see there is no dispute about it, Inspector. Were you told that the Serious and Organised Crime Unit had reason to believe that acts of prostitution were occurring there, and that they had obtained a search warrant for the premises?'

'Yes, sir.'

'And was it your role to investigate that belief?'

'Yes. Our mission was to visit the premises to investigate the claims. If there was any substance in them, we would then arrest anyone who appeared to be committing an offence, we would seize any evidence at the scene, and we would make sure that any vulnerable persons at the scene were properly safeguarded.'

'By "vulnerable persons", you mean...?'

'It's not uncommon in such a situation to find young women who are minors, or who have been trafficked, or have been abused in some way. We are obliged, for their protection, to ask certain questions of them and to complete a protocol to reflect the results of the questioning. If any such circumstances exist, we must then report the matter to other agencies.'

'No doubt that is why you had a number of female officers present?'

'Yes, sir.'

'And is it right to say, Inspector, and I want to deal with this immediately, that none of the women you found there were minors, none had been trafficked, and none made any claim of abuse?'

'That is correct, sir. In fact, several made a point of saying it was the best place they had ever worked.'

This produces a chuckle from the jury, so Piers seizes the chance to score a couple of points. In the circumstances, the defendants can't really object to being praised as enlightened employers, so Piers can be seen to be scrupulously fair while, of course, twisting the knife somewhat at the same time. He is not going to step out of bounds by asking who should get the credit for the establishment's exemplary employment practices, but he doesn't need to. If he is patient, that should emerge naturally in due course.

'Did you understand by that, that the young women said they had been treated fairly in relation to money and the conditions of their employment?'

'They all said that they had been treated very well.'

'They had been paid what was due to them?'

'Yes.'

'They were free to come and go as they wish, and were in possession of their passports?'

'Yes.'

'Very well. Let's move on. What did you do on arriving at Jordan's at about eleven o'clock that evening?'

'The first thing I did was to secure the premises as far as I could, so that the raid could take place without interference.'

'How did you do that?'

'I stationed an officer at the door leading to the staircase, with instructions to allow no one to enter or leave the upstairs area. I then spoke to the receptionist, a woman I now know to be Lucy Trask. I introduced myself, showed her the search warrant, and instructed her to make the key to upstairs available to me, which she did without any objection. I then instructed Ms Trask to sit down behind the reception desk, and not to attempt to communicate with anyone. I assigned a female officer to keep her under observation. I then asked Ms Trask where I could find Dimitri Valkov, and she told me he was in the bar. I instructed two officers to detain Mr Valkov and have him sit behind the reception desk with Ms Trask, which was done.'

'Thank you, Inspector. Did you then go upstairs?'

'I did, sir. I led a number of uniformed officers upstairs. The only officer not in uniform was DS Hayward of the Serious and Organised Crime Unit, who was present as an observer. When we arrived upstairs, I directed a team of uniformed officers to enter each of four rooms on the corridor at the same moment. In each case, one officer was designated as exhibits officer, whose job it was to take photographs of the scene and to record and seize any items which might potentially be evidence. I myself entered the first room together with two female officers, PC Walsh and PC Hargreaves, and a male officer, PC Davis. PC Davis was my exhibits officer.'

'Was the door locked?'

'No, sir. We were able to enter without difficulty.'

'What did you see on entering the room?'

'I saw that the room was decorated in a style which I later

learned was associated with his late Majesty King Louis XIV of France, sir. It had elaborately carved chairs, a number of gilt-framed portraits, and an elaborate clock, its top depicting a hunting scene, on a dresser...'

'Yes, thank you,' Piers interrupts, anxious not to be drawn into another lengthy cultural detour. 'Was there one particular piece of furniture which caught your eye?'

'Yes, sir.'

'What was that?'

'In the centre of the room was a chaise longue, which appeared to be covered in a rich, deep red cloth fastened with brass fittings. The kind of thing ladies used to lie on, if they were feeling faint, once upon a time.'

'Yes,' Piers says. 'Let's not worry so much about what it was used for once upon a time. I am more concerned with what it was being used for on the night you were there. Was it being used by a lady who was feeling faint?'

'No, sir.'

'Please tell the jury what it *was* being used for.'

The Inspector looks down at the police log, just to make sure that he is going to get the details right. For some reason, it is a bit like pulling teeth. I can't imagine why. Surely, this man has not risen to the rank of Inspector in the Metropolitan Police without having seen this kind of thing once or twice before.

'Sir, I saw a white male, I would say between forty and fifty years of age, lying on his back on the couch.'

'Did you notice anything else about this male?'

'I did, sir.'

'What did you notice?'

'I noticed that the male was naked.'

'Anything else?'

'I noticed that his penis appeared to be erect, sir.'

'Thank you, Inspector,' Piers says. 'Did you see anyone else in the room?'

'Yes, sir. I saw two white females, both of whom appeared to be in their early twenties.'

'And what, if anything, did you notice about the white females?'

The Inspector consults the police log once again.

'They were also both naked, sir.'

'I see. And what, if anything, were the females doing?'

A long pause.

'They were kneeling one each side of the couch, sir, and I noticed that they appeared to be touching the male's penis with their fingers.'

Piers is visibly relieved that he has succeeded in coaxing this evidence from his witness. He pauses for a moment to recover himself.

'What did you do on seeing this?'

'I immediately instructed the two females to stop what they were doing, sir, and I instructed PC Walsh and PC Hargreaves to get them dressed and detain them. PC Davis and I then spoke to the male, and asked him to get dressed. Our protocol was that any males found to be the recipients of sexual services would be required to provide their names and addresses, and would then be free to go, but would be told that a decision would be made in due course about whether to take proceedings against them. When told this, the male replied spontaneously, "But I only came for a massage." I recorded his answer in my notebook. I gave him a slip to present to the officer guarding the door at the bottom of the stairs, who would then allow him to leave the premises, and he left.'

'Then what happened?'

'PC Walsh and PC Hargreaves were going through the protocol with the two females, and as I said before, their answers were satisfactory, and they were allowed to leave once we had their names and contact information. PC Davis took a number of photographs of the room and seized three pieces of evidence.'

'Are those pieces of evidence shown in the photographs?'

'Yes, sir, they are.'

Piers turns towards me. 'Your Honour, with the agreement of my learned friends, I will read the statement of PC Davis later. There is no objection to the jury having the photographs of the Louis XIV room now. With the usher's assistance, there are copies for your Honour and the jury, and may this be Exhibit two, please?'

'Yes, Mr Drayford,' I reply. I scrutinise the exhibit carefully. There are twelve photographs depicting the Louis XIV room from various viewpoints, and giving due prominence to the clock with the carved hunting scene. Judging by the jury's reaction, they would prefer some shots of the action the Inspector found going on in the room, or at least of the participants. If so, they are out of luck. But they do get a good shot of the chaise longue, and with a little imagination they will be able to recreate the scene in their minds. There are also photographs of the three pieces of evidence seized by PC Davis, which appear to be: a large box of condoms, opened; a feather duster; and what looks like a thin, phallic-shaped, white plastic item.

There are occasions in court when judges have to ask stupid questions, or at any rate, questions which suggest that the judge is a century or two behind the times, or must have been hiding away in a cave somewhere while contemporary life developed all around him. The classic case, of course, was the judge who in an earlier era asked the question, 'Who are the Beatles?' and as a result was instantly derided in the press as the typically remote, out-of-touch and pathetically outdated male all too commonly found on the bench. Now, it is possible that the judge genuinely did not know who the Beatles were, in which case the press obviously had a point. But it is much more likely that he thought it necessary to ask the question on the record so that he would get an answer on the record. We shall probably never know. But judges sometimes have to ask questions when no one else will, simply because an answer is required.

This appears to be such a case, because Piers seems to have no intention of asking the Inspector to explain the third piece of evidence. So even though everyone in court, including the jury, are quite well aware of what it is, yours truly has to pretend that he is the only person in court who doesn't. What's worse is that the press are represented in court, and if it's a slow news day, they may quite fancy a picture of me in wig and gown with a paragraph about my sexual naïveté. Well, at least the Reverend Mrs Walden will be amused. I can avoid all this if I can only get Piers to ask before I have to.

'Mr Drayford,' I say, 'would you care to establish from the Inspector the nature of the item shown in photograph fifteen?'

Piers smiles, and you can see him thinking, 'This is going to be a good one to tell in chambers later.'

'Certainly, your Honour. Inspector, what is the item in photograph fifteen, please?'

The Inspector makes a pretence of studying it closely.

'It appears to be a vibrator, your Honour,' he replies.

He is not going to elaborate without being pushed, so the moment arrives.

'What is a vibrator?' I ask.

Two women on the jury now have a fit of the giggles. As do Emily Phipson, Susan Worthington, and Aubrey Brooks, though they are doing a better job of hiding it.

'Your Honour, a vibrator is an electrical device sometimes used to provide sexual stimulation.'

'Yes, quite so, thank you,' I say, trying my best to give the impression that I knew that all along – which, of course, I did.

'I hope that's clear, members of the jury,' Piers says.

I am sure it is, I say to myself, but no bloody thanks to you.

'Now, Inspector, did you receive reports from the officers who entered the other three rooms?'

'I did, sir.'

'The jury will hear from those officers in due course, but is it your understanding that sexual activity was taking place in each room between one or more young women and a male client?'

'Yes, sir.'

'And in each case, were the young women and the male clients treated in the same way as you treated those in the Louis XIV room?'

'They were, sir.'

Piers pauses to consult his notes. 'And when all that had been completed, the rooms photographed and the evidence seized, what time was it?'

'It was after one o'clock in the morning, sir.'

'Did you then go downstairs?'

'Yes, sir.'

'What did you see?'

'The premises were virtually empty, sir. It was already late when we arrived, and I believe our presence had probably caused the restaurant to empty quite soon after we arrived. I saw Dimitri Valkov and Lucy Trask still sitting behind the reception desk. There was also another man sitting with them, who I now know to be Robert Jordan, the owner of the restaurant, whom I had not seen when we arrived.

'I told Mr Valkov that he was under arrest on suspicion of being concerned in the management of a brothel, and cautioned him, to which he replied, "It is legitimate massage; traditional Swedish massage. For the rest, I don't know." He was then taken to Bermondsey police station, where the custody sergeant authorised his detention.'

'Inspector, was anyone else arrested on that evening?'

'Not on that evening, sir. Subsequently, after Mr Valkov had been interviewed and further inquiries had been made, Robert Jordan and Lucy Trask were arrested by officers of the Serious and Organised Crime Unit, but I was not involved with that.'

'Thank you very much, Inspector,' Piers says. 'Wait there, please.'

Emily rises to her feet with the air of a woman who has a disagreeable task to perform which she has put off for as long as possible, but can no longer avoid.

'Your Honour,' she says ponderously, 'may I make it clear that Mr Valkov accepts that he was responsible for the administration of the massage parlour in the upstairs rooms at Jordan's. I do not intend to go into detail about that with this witness. I am sure that the details will become known to the jury quite soon.'

'Yes, very well, Miss Phipson,' I reply.

'Inspector, you did not see Mr Valkov upstairs on that evening, did you?' she asks. 'Because, as you say, you had an officer watching him from the moment he was escorted from the bar to sit behind the reception desk.'

'That is quite correct, Miss.'

'All the young women said they dealt with Mr Valkov, as far as their employment was concerned, did they not?'

'Yes.'

'And so Mr Valkov was the man running what they all agreed to be a fair and well-run place of work, yes?'

'Yes.'

'For the purposes of the protocol, were all the young women asked what kind of work they were doing at Jordan's?'

'Yes, Miss.'

'That's a standard question, for obvious reasons?'

"Yes, Miss.'

'How did they answer that question?'

'They said they were practising massage therapy, Miss.'

'In each case?'

'Yes, Miss.'

'Did any of them say that she had performed sexual services of any kind at Jordan's?'

'From memory, several quite candidly said that they had accepted money from clients for sexual services.'

'Did any of those women make any complaint of having been compelled to provide sexual services?'

'No, they did not...'

'Or of having been asked to do so?'

'No.'

'Thank you, Inspector.'

'But –'

'You have answered my question, Inspector, thank you. One other thing. Did your officers search a small rest area provided for the women working there?'

'Yes, Miss.'

'Did they find notices on the wall of that room, warning the women that they must not engage in any sexual activity or conversation with clients?'

'They did, Miss, yes.'

'The jury will see the notice in due course, but is it right that it was in six different languages?'

'I believe so, yes.'

'English, Russian, Spanish, Japanese, German and Italian?'

'From memory, yes.'

Emily sits down abruptly.

'Inspector,' Susan Worthington begins, popping up brightly out of her seat, 'you didn't see Robert Jordan downstairs when you arrived, did you?'

'That is correct.'

'And you didn't see him upstairs at any time, did you?'

'No, I did not.'

'In fact, do you now know that Mr Jordan is the chef of the restaurant and is to be found in the kitchen whenever the restaurant is open?'

'That is my understanding, Miss, yes.'

'Are you also aware that when the young women found in the rooms were asked, for the purposes of the protocol, who was responsible for employing and paying them and for their conditions of work, not one named Robert Jordan?'

'That is quite correct.'

'In fact, they appeared to have no idea who Robert Jordan was, did they?'

'None of them claimed to have met Mr Jordan, certainly,' the Inspector replies.

'Thank you, Inspector,' Susan says, resuming her seat. That's not going to get Jordan off the hook by a long chalk, but it's a start.

Interestingly, Aubrey Brooks does not pursue any similar inquiries on behalf of Lucy Trask; for whatever reason, he prefers to keep his powder dry for now.

I wait for Piers to explore the question of who did what in re-examination. He thinks about it for a while before asking whether I have any questions. I most certainly do not. If Piers isn't going there, I'm certainly not. I thank the Inspector for his evidence and release him.

That's as far as we will take it today. I am scheduled to sentence a youth who, being short of funds to report to Bermondsey police station to answer his police bail, called in a non-existent robbery at knife-point, in the hope of getting a lift. His call brought a number of officers, including two armed officers, rushing to the scene. When the officers discovered the truth, by the simple device of matching his mobile to the number of the phone from which the 999 call was made, they did indeed give him a lift to the police station, thereby rendering his strategy a complete success in that sense. However, it came at the price of a charge of wasting police time to add to the original tally of two charges of selling cannabis to his mates after school in the company of an adult supplier, whom Marjorie has already sent down for two years.

I sometimes wish Parliament would create an offence of aggravated stupidity, with a minimum penalty of being transported for ten years to some otherwise uninhabited Scottish island patrolled by great white sharks. But I have no power to pass such a sentence, and in reality there is not a lot I can do with him. In the end, given the surprising fact that he is of previous good character and has had a pretty dodgy upbringing, I dispatch him back to the Youth Court for a referral order to be made. We will probably get another shot at him later in his career.

* * *

Tuesday morning
Jordan's has, of course, been all over the *Standard* and the London local radio stations last night, and has even made the dailies this morning, and when I call in on Jeanie and Elsie for my latte and my ham and cheese bap, they have the *Mail* open at the right page for my inspection.

'You're going to be famous, aren't you, sir?' Elsie says. 'I mean, doing a scandalous case like this, And, to think, it's right on our doorstep, isn't it?'

I am quickly scanning the *Mail's* article about the trial. Mercifully, it doesn't seem to include my question about the vibrator.

'I've walked past it lots of times,' Jeanie replies. 'It always looks so respectable, doesn't it? It just goes to show: you never know, do you? You never know what's going on behind closed doors.'

'That's the truth, and no mistake,' Elsie says. 'My uncle Albert was getting up to all kinds of things for years, and nobody ever knew. He lived in a nice quiet street in Chigwell, with lace curtains, and everything, did my Uncle Albert, but in the end it turned out that he was –'

'Yes,' I interrupt quickly. I'm not sure I am ready to hear about Uncle Albert before drinking my latte, and quite possibly, not even then. 'But you must remember that the trial is only just beginning. We don't really know what was going on at Jordan's yet. We have to wait until the jury reach a verdict.'

'Well, yes,' Jeanie concedes. 'But the *Mail* says a police officer actually caught them at it, in flagrante whatsit.'

'Yes,' I agree. 'But the question is going to be what each of the defendants knew about it.'

'It's such a shame,' Jeanie muses, as if she hasn't really taken in the point about the defendants' knowledge. 'He was on that TV show, wasn't he, Elsie, that Robert Jordan?'

'"Britain's Got the Best Chefs!"' Elsie replies. 'I remember watching him the night he lost. I think it was in the semi-finals and they had to cook dinner for a bunch of rugby players. Well, you knew Robert wasn't going to win, didn't you? Not with that continental style of cooking he has. Not with a bunch of rugby players. It was that bloke from Newcastle with the tattoos who won, wasn't it? But the judges said Robert was a very talented chef, and the restaurant is supposed to be very good. I don't suppose you've been there, sir?'

'No, never,' I reply quickly.

'Oh no, well, you wouldn't, would you, sir?' Elsie replies immediately, apparently as an apology for having made such a terrible suggestion. 'Not with your wife being a vicar and everything.'

'I don't think we'd have room for a massage parlour in here, Elsie, would we?' Jeanie asks, turning to survey their business domain, a cosy and often noisy arch under a railway bridge leading to London Bridge station.

'Not blooming likely,' Elsie agrees. 'Not even if we put a curtain up somewhere. We would have to look for bigger premises, wouldn't we? Perhaps we should. What do you reckon, Jeanie? We could probably make a few bob, couldn't we?'

This reduces them both to gales of laughter.

'And he lived in *Chigwell*,' I hear Elsie say from a distance, as I walk over to George's news stand for my copy of the *Times*, 'of all places. You just never know, do you?'

'He's Russian, then, is he, guv?' George asks. 'That bloke Valkov?'

'He is,' I agree.

'Yeah. That's what the papers are saying. Bloody typical, innit?'

'What is?' I ask.

'They come over here and all they do is commit crimes. Why can't they stay in their own country if they're going to commit crimes, that's what I want to know.'

'Not all Russians commit crimes, George,' I point out.

'Or, if it's not that, they have billions of pounds and they buy up all those really expensive houses in Kensington and Chelsea, so they can take cocaine and not pay any taxes.'

I look at George for a moment.

'They're not all like that,' I insist. 'Why do you have such a poor opinion of them?'

'My old man met a lot of them during the War, guv,' George says, 'when he was stationed in Germany and they had to go into the Russian zone for one reason or another. He could tell you some stories about the Russians, could my old man, and no mistake.'

I really must get George and Hubert together one of these days, I think. They could keep each other entertained for hours.

The morning begins with the evidence of the officers who invaded the remaining three upstairs rooms. The activities going on in those rooms were essentially the same as the activity going on in the Louis XIV room. None bears very much resemblance to what I understand to be traditional Swedish massage. The defence have already established that none of the three defendants was seen upstairs at any time during the evening, so there is no cross-examination, and mercifully none of the pieces of evidence seized by the officers requires explanation beyond what is obvious from the photographs.

Next comes the financial evidence. Not long after the raid, the prosecution took the precaution of applying to me for an order for inspection of the Jordan's bank account and the personal bank accounts of each of the three defendants. They also applied to freeze the defendants' assets, subject to provision for living expenses, because if they are convicted, the next thing that will happen is that the prosecution will begin confiscation proceedings to claw back their ill-gotten gains, and they don't want the defendants disposing of them before this can be done.

The financial investigator tells us that there is nothing suspicious about the Jordan's business account, but the personal accounts are a different story. She has laid it out for us in a series of charts, which tell a compelling story. Starting about a year before the police raid, there is a pattern of cash deposits into the accounts of Robert Jordan and Lucy Trask, modest and occasional at first, but quickly escalating to larger and more regular, until both are receiving somewhere between five hundred and a thousand pounds per month just before the raid. These deposits are exactly mirrored by cash withdrawals from Dimitri Valkov's account.

Valkov's account is a mess. It is easy enough to identify deposits of his salary from Jordan's and his regular personal payments for rent, utilities and the rest of it. But beyond that, there is a morass of cash deposits, cash transfers and payments to various suppliers, as well as some which clearly refer to the young women working upstairs. It tells the story, the investigator says at Piers Drayford's invitation, of Valkov running a business on the side, keeping it off the books of the restaurant, and making sure that Robert Jordan and Lucy Trask were getting their cut for the use of the premises and whatever services they rendered. Wisely, the defence allow all this to pass without much comment. All Piers has left now is the police interviews, which we will get to this afternoon.

And so to lunch, an oasis of calm in a desert of chaos.

I break the news to my colleagues as gently as I can.

'Vending machines?' Marjorie exclaims, after we have all observed a shocked silence for some time. 'That's outrageous. I mean, it's not that I eat the food here myself, as you know. I wouldn't dream of it. But we have to provide something reasonable for jurors and witnesses.'

'Not to mention the Bar and solicitors,' Legless adds. 'They only have an hour for lunch, so they can't really go anywhere. They can't be expected to survive on a bar of chocolate and a fizzy drink.'

'I have tried to explain it to them until I am blue in the face,' I reply. 'But it's always the same answer. It's costing too much to subsidise the kitchen and they need the money for other things.'

'They always need the money for other things,' Legless complains. 'It's that bloody woman Meredith, isn't it? She didn't want to give us the secure dock for court three, and she wouldn't have if I hadn't been assaulted by a defendant escaping from the dock. I had a broken arm and concussion. That's what it took to make them listen. What will it take this time? One of their bloody vending machines toppling over and killing a juror?'

'It's not just Meredith this time,' I say gloomily. 'This is coming from on high, Mr Jeremy Bagnall CBE, no less.'

'Never heard of him,' Legless replies dismissively.

'You would have if you were RJ,' I point out. 'I have heard his name breathed reverentially a number of times. Mr Bagnall operates at a very senior level. It is rumoured that he has the ear of both the Minister and the Lord Chief Justice. Once Mr Bagnall decides something, it remains decided, it is said.'

'So, there is nothing we can do?' Legless asks. 'What about Health and Safety?'

'I think Health and Safety might actually be rather pleased to see the kitchen closed down,' I reply, 'for a variety of reasons.'

'Isn't it a violation of our Human Rights?' Legless insists.

'What is?' Marjorie replies. 'Closing the kitchen down or allowing it to stay open?'

'Meredith did make one suggestion,' I say, 'which she led me to believe would have Mr Bagnall's blessing.'

'What, apart from the vending machines?' Marjorie asks.

'Yes. She suggested that we might try to reach some agreement with caterers ourselves to provide a service for lunch, so that they don't have to subsidise it.'

'Of course,' Legless says. 'They've privatised everything else, haven't they – the prison service, the probation service, the court reporters? Why not farm the kitchen out to the private sector too? Makes perfect sense. Of course, it will go straight down the tubes, as everything does when it's privatised, but if the Ministry doesn't have to pick up the bill, they won't worry about that, will they?'

I shake my head. 'I wouldn't mind doing that just for the mess, for the four of us and the occasional guest, if we all wanted it. I don't suppose that would be too difficult, and it could only improve the quality of the food. But I can't take on the administration of a kitchen for the entire court.'

'I suppose what the Grey Smoothies would say, Charlie,' Legless replies, 'is that you wouldn't have to take it on. You just put it out to tender, invite bids, and hold a competition. Let them all take turns doing lunch for a day to show what they can do. Then you choose whichever lot is the cheapest – as long as the food is not too awful, obviously. You wouldn't have to worry about it once it was up and running. You hand over the kitchen to them, and let them carry the can when it goes south. When they go belly up, you throw them out and start again with somebody else.'

'My friend Budgie might want to give it a go,' Marjorie says suddenly, 'if you do put it out to tender.'

'Budgie?' I ask.

'It's not her real name, Charlie, obviously. Her real name is Bernadette, but we all call her Budgie. She does some catering, for parties, weddings, Bar Mitzvahs, that kind of thing. I've been to several of her events, and she does a very good job. The only thing is, I'm not sure she would want to do it every day. She does have a bit of an active social life. But I could ask her if you like.'

'Let me think about it,' I reply wearily.

'I think I could manage,' Hubert says, looking up from his Portobello mushroom risotto dish of the day, 'as long as I could rise for lunch for two hours, say, between twelve-thirty and two-thirty.'

'Two hours?'

'Yes. I think about two hours should be enough.'

'Enough for what?'

'To go for a quick lunch at the Garrick,' he replies. 'Jump in a cab outside court, over to Covent Garden, do the daily lunch buffet, jump in a cab and come back. I might be able to do it in less than two hours, actually.'

'I'm not sure that's on, Hubert' I reply. 'It's the equivalent of losing more than half a day's sitting time per week.'

'But I have to have lunch,' Hubert insists. 'If I can't have my dish of the day, I've got to have something to keep me going in the afternoon.'

'I understand that, Hubert. But let me try to come up with some other solution before you resort to that,' I plead. 'I must admit, I'm not sure there is a solution to come up with, but give me some time to think about it.'

* * *

Tuesday afternoon

The afternoon goes slowly. Piers Drayford and the officer in the case, DS Barraclough of the Serious and Organised Crime Unit, read the police interviews out one by one, in the time-honoured manner – rather like a play-reading session, question and answer, question and answer, page after page, page after page. Fortunately, the story is not too tangled.

We begin with Valkov. His account is as follows. Very early in the Jordan's project, Jordan hires Valkov as his bar manager. Valkov is an experienced bar manager, but as it turns out, he has other professional experience also. After a short time in the job, Valkov approaches Jordan one day with an idea. Instead of having those rooms sitting empty and neglected upstairs, when you are paying rent for them, he says, why not turn them into a paying concern? Jordan already has the idea of turning them into a paying concern, but his idea is more along the lines of private dining areas. He can't do that immediately, because it would be a significant expansion and the funds are not available, not to mention it would require extra staff to cope with the demands on the kitchen. Valkov understands this, but his point is that his proposal would be a temporary expedient which would make money, and thereby make the redevelopment of the dining area affordable within a shorter time frame.

This interests Jordan, but he is initially resistant to the idea of a massage parlour. He is running a serious restaurant, and the last thing he needs is advertising for massage, much less half naked girls wandering through the bar harassing the customers. That's not how it will be, Valkov assures him. Upstairs will be quite separate from downstairs. There is only one door, and it will remain locked except for the girls and their clients coming and going. They will come and go quietly and there will be a dress code consistent with the restaurant's standards whenever they do come and go. There will be no advertising at the restaurant.

Jordan has questions, of course. How will all this work?
How will you furnish the rooms, attract clients? Valkov says
Jordan should trust him. He has run massage parlours before,
in other bars in which he has worked. There will be some initial
capital outlay, for furnishings and so on, but massage rooms
are simple settings, and the cost will not be exorbitant. Valkov
will hire the girls, interviewing them carefully and insisting on
a good level of experience. He will take care of the financial
arrangements, receiving all the money paid, and paying the
girls an agreed rate. The arrangement is guaranteed to make a
substantial profit. In addition, the clients may decide to order
drinks from the bar, which Valkov will deal with personally,
increasing the level of profit even more. There are a couple of
slight technical difficulties about licensing and insurance that
have to be overcome, but Valkov has dealt with this kind of
arrangement before and knows exactly how to handle it.

At first, everything works beautifully. The rooms are nicely
decorated and furnished. Clients begin to arrive. Money begins
to flow in. The girls are excellent, and the customers always
seem happy. Word is getting round, and soon the rooms, and
particular young women, are being booked in advance. He is
paying an agreed share of the proceeds into Robert Jordan's
bank account. He is also paying an agreed share to Lucy Trask,
whose cooperation as receptionist is essential. And then, one
evening, the roof caves in.

The girls – his girls – are caught doing the one thing he
has always expressly forbidden, performing sexual services.
Valkov has no idea this was going on. If he had, he would have
put a stop to it immediately, and he would have fired any girl
involved. He has notices in six languages in the women's rest
area, making this clear. When the police raid takes place, he
is shocked, utterly devastated. He is fully aware of the law, and
respects it, and he is distressed beyond measure that this has
happened to his dear friend Robert Jordan.

Robert Jordan's interview confirms this general history of the matter. Naturally, Jordan, being entirely inexperienced in such matters, has to trust Valkov, but he has no reason not to trust him. Valkov is a competent and honest bar manager, popular with staff and customers alike, and despite his initial reservations, Jordan finds that the massage parlour is indeed completely discreet, and does not impinge on the restaurant at all. Robert Jordan has not been upstairs since Valkov started decorating and furnishing it. He sees the accounts, which all seem in order, and he appreciates the extra money, on which he fully intends to pay tax.

He is a bit less self-assured when confronted with the reality that massage parlours have their own licensing requirements, which are monitored by the local authority; and that his licence to sell alcohol does not actually apply to the upstairs rooms. He was blissfully unaware of all of this at the time, and now recognises that it was a serious error of judgement on his part to allow it to happen. But you must understand, he is a chef, not a manager, and he is ignorant of such things. He relies on people to do such things for him. He is in the kitchen from the moment Jordan's opens to the moment it closes, and he has never had any reason to believe that any sexual activity was going on upstairs while he was labouring over a hot stove. If he had had any inkling of any such thing, he would have instructed Valkov to close it down immediately.

Lucy Trask also has no idea anything is amiss until the police storm in on the fateful evening. She assists with the massage parlour by taking bookings and welcoming clients, and is the custodian of one of the sets of keys to upstairs, which she needs in order to make sure that the girls and the clients can come and go with complete discretion, and without attracting suspicion in the restaurant. She also, at her discretion, bungs fifty pounds in cash to taxi drivers who deliver a new client, or even a valued returning client. She questions this practice at first, but Valkov explains that it is necessary because of the ban on advertising at the premises. She is just as shocked, horrified, distraught, and generally mortified as everyone else when the police storm in. Never in her wildest dreams, and so on.

And there it rests. Piers Drayford will close his case quite early tomorrow morning after sorting out a few things about the exhibits and finalising some agreed facts to be placed before the jury. And then it will be the turn of the defence.

* * *

Wednesday morning

Emily announces that she will call Dimitri Valkov to give evidence. Valkov is about forty, with long black hair tied back in a ponytail. Throughout the trial he has worn a black leather jacket, white shirt and blue jeans, and today is no exception. He has quite a spring in his step, and runs ahead of the prison officer by some distance while making his way from the dock to the witness box. Emily begins with a few introductory questions, establishing his full name, his age, the fact that he is unmarried, and the fact that he has lived and worked in England for a little over ten years.

'Mr Valkov, before working at Jordan's, what was your experience in bar management?'

'I am managing many bars, for many years,' he replies. 'I manage bars in big hotels in Moscow. Then, when I come to this country, I work in three or four bars in London, always do good job.'

'Tell the jury what is involved in good bar management.'

Valkov turns to the jury with a flourish, and enters lecture mode, voice slightly raised, arms waving around, much as I imagine him doing when talking to Robert Jordan about the benefits of Swedish massage.

'To be bar manager is not to pour drinks,' he begins with emphasis. 'You must know how to pour every drink, of course. But this is not for manager. This is for bartenders. So the first thing is, you must have good assistants, good bartenders. You must be able to depend on them. As manager you must be responsible for the money. You must know how much is coming in through the till, and how much is going out, what you need to order and when. You must look out for any sign of dishonesty in your staff and put an end to it immediately.'

'When Mr Jordan hired you to manage the bar at his restaurant, what did you understand he wanted of you?'

Valkov pauses for a moment to look up at the ceiling before resuming the lecture.

'You must understand,' he replies. 'Robert Jordan, he is the artist. He is the great chef. This is not a diner of which we are speaking. This will be one of the great restaurants of London. It will be world famous. There will be Michelin stars. With a man like Robert Jordan –'

Emily intervenes without waiting for me to ask.

'Mr Valkov, the question is, what did he want of you?'

'This is what I am answering,' Valkov protests. 'This man is the great chef, this man, he is not the man to manage the bar. He has no time, and he should not be distracted from his art by such things. So when he hires bar manager, he hires man who keeps good accounts, who makes sure the restaurant is well supplied, man who can talk to the sommelier, to make sure that he understands the wines that will be ordered. I hire good bartenders. I make good atmosphere for customers. I make sure the bar is without problems, so Robert does not have to worry himself about it. He is free to make his creations in the kitchen. This is what he wants of me, and this is what I do.'

'Mr Valkov, were you familiar with the upstairs rooms at Jordan's?'

'Yes, when I first come to restaurant, I see these rooms. They are being used for storage only. Robert tells me that in future they will be private dining rooms, but this he cannot do until restaurant is better known.'

'And until there was more money to decorate and furnish the rooms?'

'Yes.'

'And did there come a time when you made a suggestion to Robert Jordan about those rooms?'

'Yes. To me, it was bad plan to leave the rooms unused. He is paying rent for them, but also, you can have problems with damp when they are empty for long time. I suggest to him that they can be used now already, and make money for him also until he is ready for the private dining.'

'And what did you suggest their use might be?'

'I suggest we have massage parlour.'

'What led you to make that suggestion?'

'Before I come to Jordan's I work for two years at bar in Fulham called Benny G's. I am not manager. I am assistant manager. Manager is Vic. This place is closed now. But then it was bar. And behind the bar was massage parlour.'

'Was the massage parlour something you started?'

'No, no. Massage parlour was there before I came. Vic ran it at the time, but even before Vic, I think it was there. It was well known. So I ask Vic many questions: how this is organised; where he finds the girls; what is the going rate, and so on; what precautions must be taken?'

'When you say, "what precautions must be taken?" precautions against what?'

'Precautions to make sure that it is massage only, and not anything else.'

'By anything else, do you mean sexual activity?'

'Yes, because Vic explains to me that there is law against brothels, and he says you must not make a brothel, this is very important.'

'And was Vic successful in taking such precautions at Benny G's?'

'Completely successful.'

'Because you said that bar had closed…?'

'Yes, but not because of this. It was too much mortgaged. It did not make enough money, and even with massage parlour they could not save it. It was shame. It was a nice place. I make proposal to Vic that we should buy it after it closed, and we went to bank but we could not get the financing. So…' He lifts his hands sadly above his head and back down.

'As a result of this, did you feel that you were qualified to run a massage parlour at Jordan's, if Mr Jordan agreed to it?'

'Yes. Why not? I kept in touch with the girls from Benny G's, and I knew they still had some of the furniture in storage, so I could even decorate without spending too much money. So I say to Robert, "Look, Robert, there will be some expenditure, yes. Painting, decorating, furnishing, heating and cooling. Perhaps we have to spend seven thousand pounds, ten thousand, even. Then there is regular cleaning and other expenses every week. This is not nothing. But I know that at Benny G's you can make five thousand in a week for each room, sometimes even in a night, if you have good clients."'

'And was that how you decorated the rooms, from the furnishings in storage at Benny G's?'

'Yes, and other things I find in open air markets. You have to look around. I know places. I know painter who used to work at Benny G's also, and he gives me reasonable price.'

'And the girls? How many young women did you hire?'

'We have twelve on the books at any one time. This is perhaps not quite enough, but they wanted to work hard, and so they all had their shifts.'

'They were young women you had worked with at Benny G's?'

'Yes, most of them. Some had returned to their countries when Benny G's closed, but most of them were still in London.'

'And as everyone agrees, you were very fair to them?'

Valkov draws himself up to his full height and places his hands on the sides of the witness box for emphasis.

'Yes, of course. Never will I exploit any woman. The women must not be abused. They must be well paid and looked after. This cannot be compromised. Also, by now, they are my friends, not just workers.'

Emily pauses for effect. 'Mr Valkov, please tell the jury what service you asked these young women, your friends, to provide.'

Valkov turns slightly to face the jury full-on.

'They provide the traditional Swedish massage.'

'Anything else?'

He shrugs. 'Some of the girls know other massage techniques, sports massage, head massage, aromatherapy, you know. If they want to offer this, of course there is no objection. But it is massage service.'

'Did you ever require, ask, or even permit any young woman to offer sexual services to a client?'

Valkov brings his fist down hard on the witness box.

'No, no, a thousand times, no. I tell all the girls this is out of order. I put up notice in six languages. They all know, if this happens, it is the end for them. They all know this even if I do not tell them, but I tell them anyway.'

'Did you know that massage parlours, however legitimate, have to be licensed by the local authority?'

Valkov allows his head to sink down on to his chest. He does not reply immediately.

'Of this I am very ashamed,' he admits. 'I know this, of course.'

'Then why did you not...?'

'I could do nothing about this,' he explains. 'Robert was insisting that there must be no connection to the restaurant. This was the condition under which we could go ahead. There could be no advertising, nothing to make any connection between the massage parlour and the restaurant. Certainly, I could not have local authority inspectors coming to the building. That would have been the end, as far as Robert was concerned.'

'But if it was discovered…?'

'Yes, it was stupid thing to do, and I feel badly for Robert now. But I think, you know, this is short term venture, and we have very high class of customer. We will have to be unlucky to be discovered.'

'But you were discovered, weren't you?'

'Yes, we were.'

'Mr Valkov, if there was to be no advertising, how did you attract customers to the massage service?'

He smiles. 'I kept good records at Benny G's. I know many of the customers there. I pay a fee to the same taxi drivers, to bring customers who are looking for this kind of establishment. Word spreads. It takes time. This is not overnight. But it does not take too long if you have a good service, and we did.'

Emily then takes him at some length through his bank account, a process which, to my mind, does more to add to the confusion than to shed light on the subject of Valkov's financial affairs and the administration of upstairs. What does seem clear is that these were in reality one and the same. The massage business was Valkov's personal bailiwick, and he ran it without interference from anyone else. The young women were self-employed. Valkov collected from them all the fees and tips paid by the clients, returned the tips and a substantial percentage of the fees to the young women, and kept the rest to cover the expenses of the house. Nothing went through the Jordan's business account. Valkov took all the receipts and paid all the outgoings, after which he divided the profits between Robert Jordan, Lucy Trask and himself. Finally, Emily offers him one more chance to protest his innocence.

'Mr Valkov, what was your reaction when the police raided

Jordan's and you learned that sexual activity was going on upstairs?'

He closes his eyes and shakes his head.

'I could not believe it, you know. These were my friends. How they could do this to me, and to Robert Jordan? It is not to be believed. I was utterly shocked. Today, still, I am utterly shocked.'

'Did you have any knowledge at all that this was happening?'

'Not at all. Not at all.'

'Were you knowingly engaging in the management of a brothel?'

'Not at all. Not at all.'

Valkov has done no real damage to his co-defendants, and their cross-examination is accordingly short and restrained. Susan and Aubrey ask the more or less obligatory questions to show how easily Robert Jordan and Lucy Trask could have been operating in the dark as far as any hint of prostitution was concerned, and leave it at that. Valkov is not the most convincing of witnesses to use to suggest that idea to the jury, and to a large extent their strategy is to distance their clients from him as far as possible.

'So, Mr Valkov,' Piers Drayford begins, having pushed himself up slowly and menacingly to his feet in an apparent attempt to mimic a screen version of the angel of death, 'have I got this right? On the night when the police visited, sexual services were being provided by your friends in each of the four rooms occupied by your legitimate Swedish massage service, and you knew nothing about it. Is that correct?'

Valkov senses that the atmosphere has changed, and you can see the defensive barriers go up.

'That is correct.'

'That's nonsense, isn't it?'

'No...'

'You weren't paying taxi drivers fifty pounds a time to bring rich clients for a traditional Swedish massage which they could get elsewhere for a fraction of the price, were you?'

'They get good massage from my girls.'

'You don't decorate rooms to look like a Louis XIV salon, or an American diner, to give legitimate massages, do you?'

'Why not? Many rooms people use for massage are so sterile. Why we should not create interesting ambience?'

Piers ignores the question, and asks Dawn, our usher, to hand the witness PC Davis's photographs from the Louis XIV room, Exhibit two.

'Mr Valkov, please turn to photograph thirteen in this exhibit. Do you have it?'

'Yes.'

'It shows a box of condoms which has been opened, would you agree?'

'Yes, that is obvious.'

'Yes. And you understand that this was found by PC Davis in the upstairs room nearest to the door, what we have been calling the Louis XIV room?'

'Yes.'

'Let's pass over photograph fourteen, the feather duster, and come to photograph fifteen. This has been described to the jury as a vibrator. Would you agree?'

'Again, this is obvious.'

'Also found in the same room?'

'Yes. Would you please explain to the jury, based on your experience of Swedish massage parlours, why these items would be found in a room dedicated to legitimate massage?'

'Obviously, I can't explain that. You know, the girls must have been providing other services.'

'Without your knowledge?'

'Of course.'

'Of course. Mr Valkov, do you remember telling the jury,

when you were answering questions from my learned friend Miss Phipson, that your job was to ensure that it was well managed, so that Mr Jordan did not have to worry about it?'

Silence, for some seconds.

'This is true.'

'That was your job as a good bar manager, wasn't it?'

'Yes.'

'How often did you go upstairs yourself to check on what was going on?'

'Myself?'

'Yes, yourself.'

Valkov shakes his head. 'No, no. I would never do so. I must not intrude on the privacy of the clients. You understand, the doors are not locked, but I can't just walk in. I would be sure to lose a client if I walk in and interrupt his massage.'

'But you took clients upstairs sometimes, didn't you? As you did with the two undercover officers who visited Jordan's before the raid?'

'Sometimes, yes, if they were new clients. Once they had been with us once, they knew the way. They could not get lost in such a small space.'

'And when you brought a new client, it must have been obvious if objects like this were lying around, yes?'

'I never saw such things. Never.'

'Did you ever see any of the young women naked in any of the rooms?'

Which is when it happens. Lunchtime is fast approaching, and part of my mind has already turned to the conversation I am likely to have in the mess about the question of replacements for the kitchen, and to the question of how I can dissuade Hubert from rising for two hours to go to the Garrick Club. The jury seem to be enjoying the show, but I am sure their minds also are turning to the pleasant prospect of a break and the chance to eat something for lunch (while they still can, I reflect). When suddenly –

'I can prove I am innocent!' Valkov virtually screams.

He is loud enough to have every eye in the courtroom fixed on him instantly.

'That's not what I asked,' Piers insists. 'My question was –'

'I am innocent!' Valkov screams again. 'I can prove it. I have black book. I have black book with names. Names of important men, who would not come to brothel, who would not be seen in brothel. I will say such names if I must because I am innocent!'

A deathly hush falls over the courtroom – except, that is, for the press seats, where there is suddenly a renewed outburst of whispering and scribbling. My mind returns abruptly from the kitchen to the courtroom.

'I'm sorry, Mr Valkov,' I say, 'did you say that you have a black book containing the names of customers?'

He looks at me as if puzzled at first, and then breaks out in a smile.

'Yes, your Honour,' he replies. 'I apologise. It is cliché. I admit it. Much better I buy red or blue book, something different. I am sure you have all the time black books. For this I am sorry.'

'I am not interested in the colour of the book, Mr Valkov,' I say. 'What I am interested in is…'

I break off, because I am not entirely sure exactly what I *am* interested in, and it might be better if I think about it first. I look at counsel to see if they have any guidance to offer. Emily is looking as though someone has just tasered her, but Piers has recovered, and interrupts me.

'Your Honour, forgive me, but I submit that it would be preferable for the court to go into chambers while this matter is discussed further.'

It does not take me long to see the logic of that suggestion. But there is also a piece of evidence to bring under control.

'Yes, Mr Drayford,' I reply. 'But just before we do, I need to ask the witness one more thing. Mr Valkov, where is this black book? Do you have it with you?'

'Yes, your Honour, of course.' He gestures towards his back-pack which is lying on the floor of the dock. A dock officer retrieves it and opens the door of the dock just enough to hand it to Dawn, who gives it to Valkov. In an instant, he opens it and extracts a thin black volume which looks rather like a desk diary. He holds it up for my inspection. I ask Dawn to bring it to me. I resist the temptation to open it.

'I am going to rise for lunch now,' I announce abruptly. 'I shall take this book with me and peruse it over lunch. I will see counsel in chambers at two o'clock.'

I see Piers poised to suggest some other course, but I am not going to give him the chance. I rise quickly. Valkov may be playing a silly game, in which case the black book will be exposed for the nonsense it is, and Piers will tear him limb from limb and leave him for dead in cross-examination after lunch. Or he may be serious, in which case the press will soon be able to report a scandal that goes a lot farther than they thought when the case began. Before I decide what to do next, I need to know what I'm dealing with.

I sit down with Elsie's cheddar and pickle sandwich and a cup of instant coffee and open the black book. It does indeed contain names, male, sixty-five in all, the vast majority of which mean nothing to me. But I do recognise the names of three members of Parliament, one of whom is currently a minister for something relatively unimportant; of one High Court judge; and of one well-known reporter for BBC Television; and there are one or two others which, for one reason or another, ring a bell with me. One in particular, in fact, which rings a very loud bell indeed.

Whether or not the names mean anything to me, each one undoubtedly means something to somebody, if only the man concerned and his family. One or two of the names I do not recognise have phone numbers with them, but almost all have no further details at all, and there is no clue about when the names were added to the book, much less when they may have visited Jordan's. There is nothing except the word of Dimitri Valkov to establish any connection between any of these men and Jordan's, much less to establish that they received sexual services there, and at this point I'm not sure that Dimitri Valkov's word is a particularly gilt-edged commodity.

Nonetheless, this must be handled delicately. Whether or not you have done anything dodgy, merely having your name in a book like this is liable to expose you to some pretty uncomfortable questioning on the home front, and in many cases, in the workplace also. The names themselves are likely to start feeling a bit panicky as soon as the *Standard* hits the streets this afternoon, but so will many others whose names are not in the book, but very well might be. Valkov's strategy seems pretty clear. His reference to the book is a threat. We are meant to believe that he will not hesitate to reveal names if he has to. If he goes down, he is saying, he will take a few highly placed people with him. The only possible legitimate relevance of the names is the one he gave us in court: to show that such prominent men would not have come to Jordan's if they had known there was any hanky-panky going on. This is hardly convincing. In fact, one might think it more likely that they were tempted to Jordan's precisely because it offered a discreet haven for hanky-panky, and their names in a black book – cliché as Valkov rightly concedes it to be – rather supports that view.

No, this is an attempt to blackmail either the court or the prosecution. It's not going to work, but I have to do my best to prevent unnecessary collateral damage. The first priority is to guard the book itself. Of course, Valkov may well have copies, and he may know the names off by heart. I can threaten him with dire consequences, such as holding him in contempt of court or withdrawing his bail, to try to shut him up. But I can't stop him naming names, if he is really determined to shout them from the rooftops. On the other hand, perhaps I don't need to.

He could have gone to the press with the black book at any time, but he hasn't raised it until now. And if he simply starts blurting out names now, hopefully he won't be taken too seriously.

As the lunch hour ends, I am given my first indication of how fast news like this travels. Legless knocks and puts his head tentatively around my door.

'Charlie, do you have a moment?'

'Yes, of course, come in.'

He makes his way forward with a rather deliberate air, and sits in front of my desk.

'Charlie, I heard that one of the defendants in your case says he has a black book with names of men who used the massage parlour. Is that right?'

I pick the book up and hold it aloft.

'Really?' he says slowly. 'I don't suppose you've...'

I shake my head.

'Look, I can't tell you who is in it,' I say, 'but I can tell you that there are no names associated with the court in any way. Does that help?'

He sighs and relaxes.

'Yes, thank you. Of course, there is no reason why my name would be in the book.'

'Of course not,' I reply soothingly.

'I may have been to Jordan's for dinner. Once. Well, twice at the most. I'm not entirely sure. But I have certainly never been upstairs. Indeed, I didn't know there was an upstairs until your trial started and I read about it in the *Standard*. Or if I did know, I certainly didn't know anything of that kind was going on up there...'

'Of course, Legless,' I say, 'I know that. I would never have imagined otherwise.'

'But that doesn't stop people using your name, does it, if they think they can gain some advantage from it?'

'No, indeed.'

'I mean, I could write the name of the Archbishop of Canterbury in a black book for reasons of my own. Doesn't mean he's been upstairs at Jordan's, does it?'

'Certainly not.'

He stands. 'No. Well, in any case, thank you for letting me know. It's put my mind at rest.'

'You're welcome,' I reply. 'How was lunch? Hubert didn't go off to the Garrick, did he?'

'No. He won't go anywhere as long as the kitchen stays open. After that – well, it's anyone's guess. Have you come up with any ideas yet?'

'Not yet,' I admit.

* * *

Wednesday afternoon

Counsel troop sombrely into chambers just after two o'clock. I have Stella with me with a hand-held recording device, because this definitely has to be on the record. She inserts a tape, pushes record, and puts the date and time and the names of those present on the tape before handing it over to me.

'Judge, I had no idea whatsoever about this book,' Emily says. She seems to have recovered from the appearance of being tasered, but she is still looking distinctly chagrined. She is not allowed to talk to Valkov while he is giving evidence, which may be just as well in the circumstances, but I am sure she has favoured a few people with her opinion about her client over lunch. 'Valkov never said anything to me about it, and I certainly didn't know that he was going to say something like that.'

'We all accept that, of course,' Piers says at once, 'and of course, it came out while I was cross-examining, not as a result of any question Emily asked him.'

I nod. 'That's true,' I say. 'No possible criticism of you, Emily, of course. But the jury and the press heard it, and we now have to decide how to deal with it. By my count, the book contains sixty-five names, including those of a few fairly prominent men, and of course, any publication of names would be embarrassing to somebody.'

'Of course,' Susan says, 'Aubrey and I are worried about the fall-out for our clients. My man says he knew nothing about a black book at all.'

'My girl says the same,' Aubrey adds.

'None of us thinks there is any basis for allowing Valkov to name names,' Piers replies. 'It seems to us that he is perfectly entitled to say that he was running a respectable house, and that he had the kind of clientele that would have run a mile if they thought it was anything other than respectable. But anything beyond that is irrelevant, and it would be the court's duty to prevent any mention of the names of third parties in court if it might cause unnecessary damage.'

'I agree,' I say. 'The book stays with me until further order, and I will leave Mr Valkov in no doubt about what is likely to happen to him if he tries to out anyone.'

'No argument from me, Judge,' Emily says.

'What we would like to do, Judge,' Piers says, 'is to get together and work out a form of words we can give the jury as an agreement between the prosecution and the defence. It will be something along the lines that certain men, including men prominent in public life, may have visited Jordan's, and the jury may consider that point when they come to ask themselves whether they are sure that these defendants were running a brothel upstairs. I will also make it clear that there is no evidence to connect Susan's or Aubrey's clients with the book.'

'That sounds perfectly reasonable,' I reply.

'Yes,' Piers says. 'Of course, your Honour has seen inside the book, while we have not. So we are not sure whether our proposed statement about the names would be accurate or not.

I don't know whether your Honour would be prepared to…'

No,' I reply immediately. 'But I can indicate that, if you were to make the statement that men prominent in public life are mentioned in the book, that statement would be an accurate one.'

'Much obliged, Judge,' Piers says. 'Could we have until tomorrow morning, please? We want to make sure we get it right, and there are some inquiries I want the officer in the case to make about the men who were found in the premises, and some other intelligence the police may have about Jordan's.'

'Yes, very well,' I reply. I was actually thinking of adjourning anyway. If there is one thing we don't need now, it is to rush things, and there is a lot to be said for allowing Valkov – and the press – to pause and take a deep breath. Piers reads my mind.

'The only other question,' he says, 'is what to do about the press?'

'There's nothing I can do about that,' I point out. 'The book was mentioned in open court, and it's a legitimate story. I'm sure they are going to be running around like chickens with their heads cut off, trying to get a lead on men who may have been spotted at Jordan's. That's up to them. All I can do is tell the jury to keep away from the reporting and focus on the evidence. And the defendants are not to talk to the press, about anything at all.'

Susan and Aubrey nod.

'Understood,' Emily says. 'Judge, since I can't speak to Valkov at present, and I'm not sure I would trust myself even if I could, perhaps you wouldn't mind making that clear to him?'

'With pleasure,' I reply.

And when I go back into court, I do indeed spend several minutes reading the Riot Act to Dimitri Valkov, telling him exactly what is going to happen if he mentions any names, speaks to the press, or, for that matter, misbehaves in any way at all. I remind the press of their responsibilities. Finally, I tell the jury to stay away from the press coverage, and remind them that anything the press reports about the black book or its contents can be no more than speculation. I think everyone gets the idea.

It is not until I am back in chambers that I ask myself whether I actually have any power to keep a book which is not an exhibit without the consent of the owner, and to keep it without allowing anyone, including counsel, to look at it. I decide to postpone that question until someone asks me. There is also the question of how exactly I am going to take care of it. All I can do is have Stella lock it in our secure safe. That's as much protection as I can give it, though it occurs to me that I wouldn't fancy its chances against any determined burglar on the trail of a book for which the press might pay a considerable sum.

It is beginning to feel like a long day, and I contemplate cutting out early and making my way home. But when I come to check my email for the final time before shutting down my computer, I get a bit of a shock. There are eight emails marked urgent, asking me to contact the sender as soon as possible. Three are from High Court judges, only one of whom I remember meeting. Two are from Silks I have known for any number of years. The remaining three are from people I have never heard of. None of the emails reveals what it is the sender wishes to discuss, but I have a pretty shrewd idea.

Legless knew about the black book within minutes, no doubt courtesy of the court staff. By now, solicitors, barristers and others will have been spreading the word, and it may even be that the early edition of the *Standard* is on the stands. The word is out, and I have the feeling that I have suddenly assumed a role of some importance in the lives of other people, of having something they very much want. In fact, I confess to my shame a certain unfamiliar feeling of power. I decide to call one of the High Court judges I have never met, who indicates that he will be working in chambers during the afternoon, and that I can call at any time.

'Charles,' he begins cordially. 'How kind of you to call back.'

'Not at all,' I reply. I could, I suppose, put him out of his misery by letting him know without further ado that his name does not feature in the black book. Indeed, the one High Court judge who is mentioned in the book is not one of the three who have emailed. But I am curious to know how he will approach it. After all, this call may be a blueprint for any number of others. There is a silence.

'Charles, look, I will come straight to the point. I've heard about this so-called black book in this case of yours. Complete nonsense, of course, I assume. Isn't it?'

'Well, I'm not sure at this stage, er...'

'Giles.'

'Giles, yes, of course. Well, I'm not sure at this stage, Giles. We only found out about it today.'

Another silence.

'Yes. I understand that, of course. But... I take it, you have been able to look through the book?'

'Yes.'

'And is it right that it does in fact contain some names?'

'Yes.'

'Well...'

'But you must understand, Giles, that I can't divulge any of the names. The information in the book has to be kept confidential. If information were to leak out, it might create all kinds of problems for those concerned. I am sure you have the same problems in the High Court as we do here.'

'Yes, of course.' Pause. 'The thing is, Charles, that I have never been to this place... what's it called?'

'Jordan's.'

'Jordan's. That's it. I've never set foot in the place.'

'Of course.'

'As a matter of fact, I can go farther than that. I'm not sure I've ever been to Bermondsey. I'm not sure I would even know how to get there. South of the River, isn't it?'

'Giles, if you've never been to Jordan's, you have nothing to worry about.'

'Ah, but that's the problem, Charles. I *shouldn't* have anything to worry about, of course, as you say. But you never know when some malicious person might take your name in vain. I've had two or three very high profile cases recently, had my name in the papers every day. People latch on to that, you see. The name sticks. Then, when they need someone's name, someone in the public eye, they use any name that comes to mind for their own purposes. I'm sure you understand that, Charles. I'm sure you have had cases of that kind yourself.'

'We have cases of identity fraud, certainly. But I can't…'

'Look, Charles, I tell you what. I'm not asking you to tell me who is in the book. But surely, there couldn't be any objection if you confirmed to me that my name *isn't* there. Would that be all right?'

I consider this for a moment. I can't see any harm in it, and I've enjoyed having him on the hook for some time. It's time to let him go.

'Well, Giles, yes. I suppose there can't be any harm in that. Let me just look through it again. I've only had time to skim it briefly. Give me a moment.'

'Yes, of course. Thank you.'

I take my time, and eventually assure my new friend Giles that his name does not appear in the book. His gratitude is almost overwhelming, and it is some time before I can get him off the phone. I try another number, then another, and in each case I have the almost identical conversation, so that by the end of the afternoon I am also on first name terms with two important players in the City and a Member of Parliament for a northern constituency. It is quite fun in a way. But I am only too aware that the real problem is going to arise when someone contacts me who *is* in the book. I am not yet at all sure how I will deal with that one, and when I am ready finally to close down my computer, I see there are another seven emails awaiting my attention. It may be just a matter of time.

* * *

Wednesday evening

I know something is up. The Reverend Mrs Walden is being especially solicitous this evening. She has prepared a delicious home-made lasagne and is plying me with large glasses of Sainsbury's Special Reserve Valpolicella. I panic for a moment, thinking that I may have overlooked some special occasion. But none comes to mind. I conclude that she is just being extra-nice to me because of the hard day I have obviously had in court, dealing with a case which could bring volcanic ash raining down on Bermondsey, come Friday. But then I see the headline in the *Standard*, and it dawns on me that she has an ulterior motive.

Eventually she poses the question: what's in the black book? At first, she proceeds on the basis that she is entitled to know: because she is the local Vicar, after all; because there should be no secrets between husband and wife; and because I can trust her not to tell. I explain that I'm not being deliberately secretive; the information is just not mine to share. And indeed, it's not that I don't trust her. I am not worried that she's going to read a list of names from the pulpit this coming Sunday, just to emphasise the point she made last Sunday. But as I already know from the quantity of emails on my computer, once information of this kind gets loose it spreads like wildfire.

She changes her tack.

'Charlie, I just want to know whether there is anyone in the book I should be aware of,' she pleads. 'Everyone knows we are married, and that you're doing the Jordan case. I'm worried about someone asking me questions: who's in the book; who's not in the book? You know how people are, Church people especially. They love a bit of gossip and scandal.' She pauses. 'Besides, you never know who might have ended up in a place like Jordan's. What if I know somebody?'

'Tell them you don't know,' I suggest. 'It is the truth, after all. Blame it on me, if you want to. I'm a mean old spoilsport who won't lift the lid on a juicy bit of scandal.'

This does not appear to satisfy her entirely.

'Your bishop isn't there,' I offer eventually. 'Does that help?'

She breathes a sigh of relief.

'It does. Thank you.'

'Nor are any of the vicars you have introduced me to, as far as I remember their names.'

'Thank you.'

'Try some more names on me,' I suggest. 'If I can, I will tell you they are not in the book.'

'But what if I mention a name and you don't say anything?' she asks. 'That would mean they are in the book.'

'Not necessarily,' I reply. 'It may mean that I can't remember. I've only skimmed through the thing once or twice. I don't have all the names in my head.'

'Well, couldn't you tell me if you don't remember?'

'Yes.'

She mentions a handful of names, none of which rings any bells at all, and we finish the Valpolicella happily talking of other things. But I am wondering how much of this kind of soothing talk is in my future, and what the long term future of Dimitri's black book may be. Perhaps it will become clear tomorrow.

* * *

Thursday morning

We resume Piers's cross-examination of Valkov. After the drama of yesterday, there is a buzz of expectation in the courtroom. The jury are on the edge of their chairs, and the press are poised, pencils in hand. Judging by the expression on his face, Piers is not in the mood to take prisoners.

'Mr Valkov, yesterday you described the black book to his Honour as a "cliché". What did you mean by that?'

Valkov shrugs. 'It is common to have black book, that is what I mean. It is become almost joke. Why not have some other colour book?'

'Yes, but why is the black book a cliché?'

'I don't know.'

'It was your word, Mr Valkov.'

'I don't know.'

'Don't you? Is it because a black book usually contains information that certain people would prefer not to make public?'

'It could be, yes.'

'Yes. There would be no need to have a black book for clients of a legitimate Swedish massage parlour, would there?'

Valkov shrugs.

'Because Swedish massage is a legitimate therapy, isn't it? Nothing illegal about it?'

'That's right.'

'Nothing for anyone to be ashamed about, going for a massage, is there?'

'No.'

'So there's no reason to have your clients' names written in a cliché like a black book, is there?'

'No reason, no.'

'You could keep a client list on your computer, or have Miss Trask keep it on hers, if she was taking appointments. That would be the logical way to run things, wouldn't it?'

Volkov shrugs again.

'The reason you kept a black book, Mr Valkov,' Piers says, 'is exactly because it is a cliché. It's a cliché because like every other book of its kind, it contains the names of men who came to Jordan's for much more than a therapeutic massage. Isn't that right?'

'No.'

'It's because these men came to Jordan's for the purposes of prostitution. That's why you have a black book, isn't it?'

'No.'

'Because you were running a brothel upstairs at Jordan's, weren't you?'

'No.'

'And the men whose names are in your black book would have a great deal to lose if their names were made public, wouldn't they?'

He shrugs. 'I don't know what they think. That's up to them.'

'Is it, Mr Valkov? Or is it that this black book was your insurance policy?'

'I don't understand.'

'You understand perfectly. You were prepared to threaten to expose these men if you were prosecuted, which was what you attempted to do yesterday.'

'No. I only say, look who these men are. Such men would not come to Jordan's if there is brothel. These men have legitimate massage only.'

'Legitimate massages using feather dusters and vibrators, Mr Valkov?'

No reply.

'Done by two naked young women?'

Emily begins to stand, halfheartedly, to object, but Piers has already sat down.

Robert Jordan gives evidence next. Predictably, he tells the jury exactly what he told the police in interview. He agreed to allow

Valkov to open a massage business in the upstairs rooms, partly to avoid having them lying empty, and partly to make some money to convert them into private dining rooms. He insisted that the massage business should be kept entirely separate from the restaurant, and that there should be no advertising on or near the premises. As far as he knew, Valkov was running the business exactly as agreed. He had no idea that sexual services were being provided, though he now accepts that they were, and when he found out he was devastated. If he had known, he would have put a stop to it immediately.

He has to admit to being, at least, grossly incompetent on the matter of massage and alcohol licensing. He seems anxious to assume the mantle Valkov has created for him – the somewhat unworldly culinary genius, leading a lonely life in the kitchen and somewhat out of touch with the realities of life outside the kitchen. Despite Susan's expert use of questions, it doesn't come across as entirely convincing. His history, including his stint on 'Britain's Got the Best Chefs!' doesn't suggest a lack of worldliness, and neither does the money flowing into his bank account.

Wisely, rather than try to dismantle the defence of his enforced isolation in the kitchen, Piers takes him on about the money, and within a short time, Jordan is having some trouble reconciling the amounts he was actually receiving with the amounts he might reasonably have expected from a business offering no more than legitimate Swedish massage. The protestations about his preoccupation with his culinary creations begin to wear a bit thin.

Piers takes exactly the same tack with Lucy Trask, and after some probing, she is also hard pressed to justify her sudden boost in income in terms of conventional massage therapy. As a final touch Piers gently raises the question of the fifty pound bungs to the taxi drivers, and the precautions taken to enforce a dress code for the girls. All of this takes us until one o'clock.

When I check my computer on arriving back in chambers, the number of emails has risen to twenty-six. I do a quick check: still no one actually named in the book. How all these people have got my judicial email address is something of a mystery, but there they are. Fun as it was the first time, I have a summing-up to prepare and other work to do, and I simply don't have time to call all these people one by one, just to reassure them that Dimitri Valkov hasn't entered their names in his black book.

An idea comes to me. On impulse, I reply to the first email – from the Chief Executive Officer of a City investment bank – with an email of my own, which consists simply of the word 'no'. That should be clear enough, I think, but if anyone doesn't get the message he can write again and say so. It is, of course, possible that one or more of these correspondents wants to discuss some other subject entirely, but in that unlikely event they will let me know. Emboldened by the first experiment, I deal with all the other emails in the same way.

And so to lunch, an oasis of calm in a desert of chaos.

Legless is rather subdued today, despite the relief I was able to provide to him yesterday. But Hubert is in fine form.

'Charlie, I do hope you don't have any members of the Garrick in that black book of yours,' he says. 'That wouldn't do at all. The Secretary would have something to say about that.'

'First of all, Hubert,' I reply, 'it's not *my* black book. And secondly, I'm afraid Valkov seems to have omitted to record his clients' club memberships in his list. Rather careless of him, I would agree, as it's such an essential detail, but as a result I have no idea whether any of them are members of the Garrick or not.'

'Oh, I could tell you,' Hubert says. 'If I run my eye down the list, I could tell you straight away.'

'I daresay you could, Hubert,' I reply, 'but that would get us both into a lot of trouble.'

'What are you going to do with the book?' Legless asks.

'I'm not sure,' I admit. 'I think it may rather depend on what verdict the jury returns in Valkov's case.'

'I think you should order it to be forfeited and destroyed,' Legless says.

'I'm not sure I have power to do that unless he is convicted,' I say.

'I would assume the power, if I were you,' Legless suggests, 'and ask questions afterwards.'

'I'm not sure that would look very good,' I reply. 'What do you think, Marjorie? You've been awfully quiet about it all.'

Marjorie looks up from her lunch for the first time.

'If it were up to me, Charlie,' she replies with a certain suggestion of venom, 'I would leak the whole bloody list to the *Sun* and have done with it.'

'Marjorie doesn't approve of Jordan's,' Legless grins.

* * *

Thursday afternoon

Checking my computer before going back into court, I see that I have a number of emails which say 'thank you' in response to my 'no', from which I conclude, to my relief, that I have made my point without having long and awkward telephone conversations with them all.

After a short discussion of the law, we are ready for closing speeches. By now, the issues the jury has to decide are clear, and Piers lays them out for the jury. There is no doubt, he tells them, that a brothel was in operation in the upstairs rooms at Jordan's; there is no doubt that it was a very profitable concern; and there is no doubt that all three defendants shared in the profits. The question is who knew what. The offences of managing a brothel and assisting in the management of a brothel require proof of knowledge on the part of a defendant that the premises were in fact being used as a brothel.

While there is no direct evidence that the defendants were spending time upstairs to witness the goings-on themselves, the circumstantial evidence is compelling. In Valkov's case, Piers says, it is particularly compelling. It is clear from his own evidence, as well as his bank account, that upstairs was his project. He decorated and furnished the rooms. He hired the masseuses. He paid them and regulated their conditions of work. The notice in six languages, Piers suggests, is a deliberate smoke screen to make it appear that he was alive to the dangers, and did everything in his power to keep it all above board. The evidence, Piers insists, contradicts that. It is not to be believed that, when the police show up with a warrant at a random time, they find each of the four rooms being used for the provision of sexual services at the same time, the doors unlocked, and yet none of those downstairs has a clue what is going on. The mere presence of condoms and vibrators in the rooms speaks for itself.

If there were any doubt, Piers concludes, it is removed by the black book, which Valkov himself describes as a cliché – a feeble attempt at humour, which has backfired on him. You don't keep a black book, in the cliché sense, to keep records of the clients of a legitimate massage parlour. You keep a black book to record names of men who are compromised, men who would be damaged if their names were to be revealed. That points inescapably to a brothel.

As to Robert Jordan and Lucy Trask, Piers takes a more restrained approach. Jordan's management, he concedes, is limited to providing the space, allowing clients to access upstairs from the restaurant with some discretion, allowing Valkov to operate the brothel upstairs without proper licensing, and allowing alcohol to be supplied from the bar as required. The most telling point, Piers says, is the money. No one with Jordan's sophistication could have imagined for a moment that the money he was receiving on a regular basis was the profit from a legitimate massage enterprise. At the very least, he knew enough to make him ask questions, and if he had asked questions he would undoubtedly have found out the truth about upstairs.

The case against Lucy Trask is very similar. But in her case, she also had direct dealings with the clients and with the taxi drivers who brought them, to whom she paid a fee for that service on behalf of the house. It is a nicely judged speech, and at the end of it, it is difficult to see an obvious way out for the defendants.

Emily Phipson has a difficult task. Not only must she try to create an aura of doubt around the prosecution's case against Valkov; she also has to overcome what must be her natural desire to drag Valkov personally to the nearest lake and hold his head under water for as long as it takes. Valkov ambushed Emily, as he did everyone else, by his *deus ex machina* stunt with the black book, and in the barrister's list of offences by clients, there are few, if any, as grievous as that. Clients may lie to you and make life difficult with their instructions, but to pull a stunt like that in the witness box during his evidence may be unforgivable. Forget that it does the client nothing but harm, as is the case here; it also puts counsel in an impossible position, because unless and until it clearly appears otherwise, counsel is deemed to know and approve of the evidence given by her client and the manner in which it is given. It is bad enough that the evidence is fairly strong against Valkov. But Emily also has to find some semblance of an enthusiasm which she almost certainly does not feel.

She does, I must admit, a pretty good job. She doesn't pretend that the evidence is not at least very suspicious. It shows that, if not actually aware of what was going on, Valkov must have been the most incompetent, negligent manager in the long annals of that profession. But is it not possible, she asks, that he was cruelly deceived by those he trusted? Is it not possible that his limited exposure to them at Benny G's led him to be too trusting, and that they shamelessly took advantage? Would Valkov have risked doing such damage to a man whom he regards as a creative genius, and for whom he has such obvious respect? Is it not more likely that it was a venture which started out innocently and with perfectly good motives, but which got out of hand because of Valkov's failure to discharge his responsibilities? There is a difference, Emily concludes, between active wrongdoing and incompetence, and the jury cannot be sure that it is not a simple question of incompetence. Not once does she mention the black book.

Susan and Aubrey are competing to see who can distance their client the most from Valkov. If it were not for the money, one suspects that it might not be too difficult to do. Susan's depiction of Robert Jordan as the obsessed and distracted chef who rarely emerges from his artistic studio in the kitchen is actually very believable. One can imagine that, having employed someone like Valkov – and, for that matter, Lucy Trask – he would feel free to do what he does best, and leave the day-to-day running of the restaurant to those he is paying to do it. But the money will just not go away. Nor will the fact of two obvious and gross licensing violations for which Jordan is personally responsible, and which would very likely have resulted in his restaurant being closed down, even if there were no brothel upstairs.

Aubrey paints Lucy Trask as an innocent abroad, out of her depth in the murky world of late night restaurants and bars, a young woman who was given responsibilities beyond her maturity and experience; who naïvely believed that booking clients in for massages and making cash payments of fifty pounds to taxi drivers was all in a day's work for a restaurant receptionist. The trouble is that Lucy didn't come across as particularly naïve when she gave evidence; in fact, she seemed distinctly wise in the ways of the world.

They are both valiant efforts, but one feels that the defence ship has been holed below the water line.

I will sum up tomorrow morning. I return to chambers to find that I have some further words of undying gratitude in reply to my monosyllabic messages of relief. I also have several new emails to deal with. Having now got the hang of it, I begin to work my way through them, one by one, with my cheery 'no', when I suddenly come face to face with the case I had dreaded. In my in-box is an email from a man whose name is recorded prominently in the black book. Not only that, it is the name particularly well known to me, the name that rang the loudest bell.

I swivel my chair around and stare at the wall for some time. I had been dreading this situation in the abstract because I had been unable to see any palatable way of dealing with it. But now that I am actually confronted with it, I see all too clearly that there is in fact only one course of action open to me. I call the number he has left, and invite him to visit me in chambers tomorrow at lunchtime, by which time I shall have sent the jury out. He accepts immediately.

* * *

Friday lunchtime
The summing-up is not one of the most difficult of its kind. I sail through it and get the jury out just before eleven-thirty. Returning to chambers, I answer 'no' to the remaining inquirers whose names do not appear in the black book. There are no new emails in my in-box, and I suspect that the initial panic caused by the revelation of the black book may have subsided. I then sit back and meditate at length about how to conduct the meeting which is about to take place. It will require delicate handling, but I feel strangely optimistic about it.

My visitor arrives on time. Stella has escorted him to

chambers, and has brought her hand-held recording device with her. I understand why, but at the door, I tell her that neither she nor the device will be required. She looks puzzled and is poised to protest. But I insist gently, and she retreats. I escort Mr Jeremy Bagnall CBE to his seat in front of my desk. His grey suit is immaculately pressed, but he seems tense and subdued.

'Charles,' he begins tentatively, 'thank you for seeing me at such short notice.'

'Not at all, Jeremy. What can I do for you?'

Silence, then a deep breath.

'It's about this black book that's come to light during your trial.'

'Yes?'

Pause.

'Well, it's obvious that this Valkov fellow is a bit of a villain, and you never know what they can get up to...'

'Very true, Jeremy,' I concede, 'though as a matter of fact, the jury is out on Valkov just now – literally, I mean, not just figuratively.'

I rather enjoy that one. The jury being out on something is classic Grey Smoothie-speak.

'Yes, of course. But even so... well, anyway, one can't exclude the possibility that one's name might be used by someone who's up to no good. I may be a mere civil servant, but one's name does get bandied about here and there sometimes. Especially with getting the CBE and everything, you know... one is something of a public figure, inevitably. When I heard about the black book, I thought back and tried my best to remember, and I do seem to remember having dinner at Jordan's once or twice, you see. I can't be absolutely sure, but I think so. No more than once or twice, certainly. Probably with my wife, though I can't remember exactly. We had heard that the food was good, and... but I had no idea of what was going on upstairs, naturally.'

I nod. 'Naturally.'

He is showing no sign of adding to what he has said.

'Jeremy, are you asking me whether your name is in Valkov's black book?'

Pause.

'Yes, I suppose I am. If you are allowed to tell me.'

I consider for a few moments.

'Jeremy, there's no easy way to say this. I'm sorry to have to tell you, but I'm afraid your name is in the book.'

He more or less collapses back down into the chair and loosens his tie. He is breathing heavily, and for a moment I am afraid he may be having a heart attack. Not, I think, the reaction of a man who has been caught out having a Swedish massage. But as the minutes go by, his breathing returns to normal and all I see is a man who has had the stuffing knocked out of him, and doesn't know where to turn.

'Oh, God,' he whispers, finally. He repeats it several times.

I pour him a glass of water from the carafe on my desk, which he acknowledges with a nod of the head. He drinks, just a sip at first, then the whole glass. I refill it.

'What am I going to do?' he asks. I'm not entirely sure whether he is speaking to me or himself, so I do not reply immediately.

'Think of my job, my career,' he continues in a similar vein. 'If this becomes known to the Minister, the Lord Chief Justice… I may be ruined…'

Again, I wait.

'And then, there's my wife. We have our thirtieth wedding anniversary coming up in two months. What am I going to tell her? There are our children to consider…'

He seems to be losing himself in his thoughts now. I decide to bring him back to earth.

'Jeremy, let's think about this for a minute or two,' I say. 'At the moment, no one has any idea whose names are in the book except for myself and Dimitri Valkov. I don't imagine he has shown it to anyone else. No one else has looked at it during the trial, and no names have been mentioned during the trial. So at the moment, there is no reason for anyone to find out.'

'But what about after the trial?'

I sit back in my chair. That's a good question. I have been searching my mind for an answer to it ever since Legless made his suggestion about destroying the book, and I'm not sure I am much further forward.

'To be honest, I'm not entirely sure,' I admit. 'In certain circumstances, I may have the power to order it to be forfeited and destroyed.'

For a moment, I see hope reborn in his eyes.

'Really?'

'Well, if Valkov is convicted, it could be argued that it is an article used in connection with the crime. I'm not sure of that. He might oppose it, and I would have to consider whatever he has to say, and in any case, I might not be able to make the order until any appeal has been heard. On the other hand, if he is found not guilty, it would be very tricky. I suppose I could hold him in contempt of court for producing it in court, if I took the view that he was trying to blackmail his way out of the prosecution, and then I suppose the book could be seen as an article used in a contempt of court. But it's a bit of a stretch, to be honest.'

I see the hope begin to recede again.

'Is there nothing you could do beyond that?'

I turn my chair away for several seconds. The crucial moment has arrived.

'Judges have a certain amount of discretion in such matters,' I reply eventually. This is a slightly optimistic representation of the law, but you do tend to get a lot of latitude from the higher courts when you make an order so obviously in the public interest as the destruction of the black book would be. My instinct is that I could get away with it if I want to.

'There is so much at stake,' he reminds me. 'Family, career, everything really. And not only for me, but for other innocent men as well.'

'Yes,' I agree. 'I do understand that.'

There is a long silence.

'If there were anything you could do,' he says eventually, 'I would be eternally grateful, very much in your debt.'

I nod. I thought it would come to this in some form or other. And now I have to make a moral choice. Fate has offered me a rare opportunity. It's not an opportunity for personal advantage. Obviously, I am not going to ask for a hundred grand in used unmarked notes, or to be proposed for membership of the Travellers Club. But if I could achieve something for the general good...?

'All right, Jeremy, give me some time. Let me take a closer look at the problem, and see if I can't come up with a solution. Perhaps I can find some way within the law of ensuring that the book is destroyed.'

He sighs loudly.

'Thank you, Charles.'

'Not at all.'

Pause.

'Jeremy, while you are here, may I mention another matter?'

'Of course, Charles.'

'Well, as you know, we had a meeting with Meredith and Jack recently on the subject of the catering facilities here in Bermondsey.'

He looks at me rather strangely, before sitting back in his chair and folding his arms in front of him.

'Yes, I was discussing that with Meredith again just yesterday,' he replies slowly.

'It's just that I'm not sure that I was able to make my argument to Meredith as clearly as I had hoped. I hold no brief for court kitchens in general. I am talking about Bermondsey Crown Court in particular. I was trying to explain to Meredith that we rely on it to make sure that our jurors and witnesses have somewhere safe to spend their limited lunchtime.'

He nods.

'No, actually, Meredith understood the point perfectly, Charles. Very bright girl, Meredith...'

'Oh, yes,' I reply. 'First rate. It shows. No doubt about it.'

He is thinking very carefully now, weighing every word.

'Yes. It may be my fault, Charles, really. I may not have given what she told me quite the weight it deserved. What you are saying is this, isn't it? Bermondsey has specific problems which may not be shared by all courts. For example, the difficulty of getting a quick lunch without stumbling into some den of crime, and the fact that you are a bit far away from areas which have a decent choice of eating establishments, which could result in chance meetings between jurors and defendants, and could result in delays in the courts sitting in the afternoons.'

'Exactly,' I confirm. 'You have put it perfectly, Jeremy.'

'Yes,' he says. 'Well, that's exactly what Meredith told me. What probably distracted me is the problem we always have in such matters. Of course, we do have to make sure we get value for money for the taxpayer, and we have to make sure that there is a business case for each of the services provided in our courts. The Minister expects that of us.'

'Of course,' I agree. 'Quite rightly.'

'Yes, but on the other hand, we have to look at each situation separately. There can sometimes be false economies. And perhaps I didn't give that as much consideration as I should have.'

He stares up at the ceiling for some time, in contemplation.

'Looking at it again, Charles, I think you may have made your case. I think I have come round to the view that the kitchen at Bermondsey needs to be kept open. Whatever we are paying by way of subsidy might easily be overshadowed by the consequences of taking the facility away.'

'I am very glad to hear that, Jeremy,' I say. 'I must say, I would be very grateful if that were the case. In fact, I would be eternally in your debt.'

He pauses.

'Indeed?'

'Certainly.'

He pauses again.

'Just so that there is no misunderstanding, Charles,' he says, 'are we now in the position that we are mutually in each other's eternal debt?'

'I believe we are,' I reply.

'In that case,' he says, 'I believe we have an understanding.'

He stands and offers his hand. I stand and take it. I escort him to the door.

'Would you like to stay for lunch?' I ask. 'The kitchen should still be open. I am sure we can still place an order. You could sample the kind of fare we can offer our jurors, with your kind support.'

He raises a hand. 'Oh, no, thank you. Very kind, but I have to get back to the office for a meeting. Another time, perhaps.'

'I do hope so, Jeremy,' I reply. 'You are always welcome.'

Stella is still lurking just down the corridor with the hand-held, incredulous that I have entertained a senior Grey Smoothie without making a record of the meeting. I understand completely. It would usually be a recipe for disaster not to record such a meeting, but what I know, and Stella does not, is that not even the Grey Smoothies want a record of *this* meeting. I ask her to escort Mr Bagnall to the staff entrance, from which he can make his escape without being seen.

'I'll explain later,' I whisper in her ear while his back is turned, though of course it will have to be a somewhat general explanation.

I arrive in the mess with Elsie's sandwich at one fifty-five, just as the others are about to leave to get ready for court. But I detain them for a minute or two, just long enough to impart the glad news that the Grey Smoothies have had a sudden change of heart, and our beloved kitchen is safe, at least for now. To my pleasure, though tinged with some feeling of guilt, I am hailed as a hero, and glowing tributes are paid to my skill as a negotiator and diplomat. I am pressed for the details of this notable victory. I fob them off with talk of specific cases, false economies, business plans, and value for money. The only one who seems less than wholly enthusiastic is Hubert.

'Pity,' he comments. 'I was looking forward to having a couple of hours off for lunch at the Garrick.'

* * *

Friday afternoon
At three-thirty, the jury send a note to let us know that they have reached verdicts, and court is duly assembled. Carol orders the defendants and the foreman to stand. The foreman is a woman in her fifties wearing a quite loud red blouse and scarf. Disconcertingly, she conjures up an image of an older version of Meredith.

'Members of the jury, please answer my first question either yes or no. Has the jury reached verdicts as to each defendant on which you are all agreed?'

'Yes, we have.'

'Do you find the defendant Dimitri Valkov guilty or not guilty of being concerned in the management of a brothel?'

'We find the defendant guilty.'

'You find the defendant Dimitri Valkov guilty, and is that the verdict of you all?'

'It is.'

'Do you find the defendant Robert Jordan guilty or not guilty of being concerned in the management of a brothel?'

'We find the defendant guilty.'

'You find the defendant Robert Jordan guilty, and is that the verdict of you all?'

'It is.'

'Do you find the defendant Lucy Trask guilty or not guilty of assisting in the management of a brothel?'

'We find the defendant guilty.'

'You find the defendant Lucy Trask guilty, and is that the verdict of you all?'

'It is.'

'Thank you, madam foreman. You may sit down.'

I thank the jury for their service, and order pre-sentence reports in the case of each defendant. I am not asked to make any orders for forfeiture and destruction of the items seized today, as the prosecution will now begin confiscation proceedings to recover as much of the ill-gotten gains as they can. This means that I can defer action on the black book until a later time, when interest in it will, with any luck, have died away and I can have it finally disposed of without attracting attention. In the meanwhile, it will remain in the secure safe, far from the prying eyes of the press.

I am thinking an immediate custodial sentence for Valkov, perhaps just long enough to interest the Home Office in the idea of deporting him back to Russia. For Robert Jordan and Lucy Trask, a suspended sentence or a community order, probably. Given that none of the girls were harmed, and given that the prosecution will seize what assets they have, it seems enough. I find myself hoping that Jordan will find a way to resume his career in the kitchen before too long, hopefully with a little more wisdom about choosing his friends and employees.

* * *

Friday evening

The news of the verdicts is well received at the vicarage of the parish church of St Aethelburg and All Angels in the Diocese of Southwark. Not only do they apparently avert the immediate threat of the disappearance of Bermondsey under a deluge of volcanic ash, but discreet inquiries by the trial judge have established that neither the bishop of our diocese nor any of the priests of our acquaintance are suspected of participation in the corruption and degradation at Jordan's. I also sense that the verdicts and impending sentences have provided the priest-in-charge with a fitting beginning to her sermon for the coming Sunday, as a kind of update from the world of brothels – hopefully before moving on to a more cheerful subject.

The Reverend Mrs Walden proposes to take me for dinner at La Bella Napoli to celebrate, to which proposal I offer no resistance. We enjoy a fine dinner, starting with spaghetti aglio e olio, going on to an excellent escalope Milanese, and ending with a tiramisu, all accompanied by quantities of a rather good reserve Chianti. She has a lot of questions about the trial, which I answer as best I can, given that some of what I say may be given in evidence from the pulpit on Sunday.

'What about the girls they found in those rooms?' she asks. 'What happens to them?'

'Some of them may be sent home to wherever they came from,' I reply. 'But at least they will be looked after properly as long as they are here. Most will probably just move on to the next place of work. I hate to say it, but the bad part of closing down Jordan's is that they may not find such a good employer next time.'

'That's hardly an excuse for not closing down a brothel, Charlie.'

'I'm not saying it is. All I'm saying is that if prostitution has to go on, it's better that the women shouldn't be abused.'

'Prostitution is an abuse in itself,' she insists.

'That doesn't mean it's wrong to hope that further abuse can be avoided.'

'If you follow that logic,' she says, 'you would do what they did in Hamburg and Amsterdam and license prostitution in the hope of keeping the women out of the clutches of criminals.'

'There are worse ideas, Clara,' I reply.

She looks at me, and I see the wheels turning in the mind of the creator of sermons. I know her well enough to know that part of her is tempted to agree with me. This is, after all, a woman who would legalise cannabis tomorrow for all purposes, and who believes passionately in women's rights, and even if she is a vicar, those qualities always shine through. But there is the bishop to think of, even if he is not in the book, and I still doubt that Hamburg or Amsterdam will be praised openly from the pulpit on Sunday. I am momentarily tempted to up the ante by pointing out that neither of those cities has been deluged with volcanic ash thus far, but I think better of it.

She smiles. 'And what about the men they caught there? What happens to them?'

'They could be prosecuted,' I reply.

'Do you think they will be?'

'No.'

'Why not?'

I shrug. 'Because, in the greater scheme of things, the police and the CPS have bigger fish to fry. But if it's any consolation, just being caught in a place like that should be enough to deter most men. They will have had months to lie awake at night waiting for the Old Bill to come knocking at the door when the wife and kids are home, or for some villain to turn up at the office demanding money in return for not sending the black book to the *Sun* or the *Mirror*.'

She smiles again. 'Would that deter you, Charlie?' she asks.

'Me? I'm a judge, and I have a wife who is a vicar. I don't need any more than that to deter me, believe me.'

She nods.

'So, is that the only reason?' she asks, 'just the fear of the consequences?'

'Isn't that enough?'

'Well, perhaps. I was expecting to hear something along the lines of, "I don't need to go to places like Jordan's." But you know, I'm rather glad you didn't say that.'

'Oh? Why?'

'Because – and don't quote me on this – even if you would never actually do it, I wouldn't be offended by the idea that you might fancy a massage with a happy ending.'

I feign outrage.

'My dear Reverend Mrs Walden,' I protest, 'I can't believe that you would even suspect such a thing. One *is* a judge of the Crown Court.'

She laughs.

'So what? Are you so different from other men? '

She picks up a bread stick wrapped in paper and waves it at me.

'Remember John Donne?'

'John Donne?'

'"No man is an island."'

'"Ah, yes," I reply. "Any man getting nicked in an upstairs room at Jordan's diminishes me."'

She reaches over and pokes me playfully in the chest with the breadstick.

'"And therefore, never send to know for whom the Belles troll."'

Another poke with the bread stick.

'"They troll for thee."'

About Us

In addition to No Exit Press, Oldcastle Books has a number of other imprints, including Kamera Books, Creative Essentials, Pulp! The Classics, Pocket Essentials and High Stakes Publishing > oldcastlebooks.co.uk

For more information about Crime Books > crimetime.co.uk

Check out the kamera film salon for independent, arthouse and world cinema > kamera.co.uk

For more information, media enquiries and review copies please contact marketing > marketing@oldcastlebooks.co.uk